PEPE RIOS

Daniel Cano

Arte Publico Press
Houston
Texas
1991

This volume is made possible through a grant from the National Endowment for the Arts, a federal agency.

Arte Publico Press
University of Houston
Houston, Texas 7204-2090

Cover by Mark Piñón

Cano Daniel, 1947–
    Pepe Rios / Daniel Cano.
        p.   cm.
    ISBN 1-55885-023-6
    1.   Mexico—History—Revolution,   1910–1920
—Fiction.   I. Title.
PS3553.A535p47 1990
813'.54—dc20   90-38829
                                                CIP

The paper used in this publication meets the minimum requirements of the American National Standard for Permanence of Paper for Printed Library Materials Z39.48-1984. ∞

FLORIDA GULF COAST UNIVERSITY

For Maximiano Cano, Santos Ríos Cano, Nicolás González, Eusebia Villalobos González, and all the other abuelos y abuelas whose stories are rarely told. This story is theirs.

CHAPTER ONE

Juchipila, Zacatecas
Mexico
1910

Dark, grey clouds crept over the mountains swallowing the last patches of blue sky. In the distance a thin screen of fog fell and touched the earth. The pointed leaves of the manzanita and mesquite bushes fluttered as the rain released a warm breeze. The rugged needle leaves of the cactus and long armed maguey, like solitary centurians, stood rigid against the mountainside.

At the foot of the tallest mountain in the range, sat the home of the Rios family. On one side of the adobe house a long rolling plateau stretched to the base of the mountain. To the opposite side tiny leaves of corn sprouted on a large parcel of land. When the stocks grew sturdy, beans would be planted, and the vines would climb, clinging to the thick, green stocks.

A dirt footpath ran from the house through the cornfield to an aging rock wall. Through a break in the wall the trail continued down the mountainside where cattle grazed on weeds and tall grass. Looking out over the cattle and into the horizon a beautiful vision appeared as mountains tumbled into canyons, canyons slipped into valleys, and far below like a long piece of dark twine, a river wound its way through the countryside.

Toribio Rios slid his legs from the bed and sat up along the edge. He gazed over the bodies of his sleeping children lying like fallen dominoes scattered throughout the room. He slipped his feet into his huaraches and stepped outside. His sons, Miranda, Jaime, Chavo and Pepe, sat on log stumps in front of the house.

"I'm going now," said Toribio, as he grabbed his sombrero from a peg sticking out of the adobe wall.

"Papa, it looks like a big storm is coming," warned Miranda, Toribio's oldest son.

"Ah, it's nothing. It will take a few minutes to reach Conejo's." He looked at the angry sky. "I can make it before the rains come."

Jaime ran off to the corral and and saddled his father's horse.

"Be careful, Papa," called out Pepe with deep concern.

"Hijos, don't worry," Toribio laughed, "I'm not yet such an old man."

His wife Susana watched as he mounted his horse and rode into the cornfield and down the mountainside. The trail was wet from the rain that had already fallen.

It took Toribio an hour to reach Conejo's ranch. Many times the horse slipped in the sludge as she made her way down the steep path. He passed in front of four straw huts. They were the homes of Conejo's peones. Since the fighting between the federales and the rebels had begun to flare up, many of the men had gone off to join the action, leaving their wives and children behind to work the land. Conejo was content with the arrangement. Now he had all the women he wanted, and if the work became too heavy he could always find help among the poor.

Toribio banged hard on the heavy wood ranch-house door. A minute passed and finally the door opened.

"Hola, Toribio," cried Conejo. "Enter, enter. I have been waiting days to see you. Where have you been, hombre?"

Toribio stared casually at the short, dark skinned man whose hair shot up around the crown like dry weeds. The two men shook hands.

"We have been herding in the cattle. I received some new medicine to inject the animals," Toribio announced, proudly. "Now we will see if they remain healthy through the dry months."

"You remember Rosa, from next door?" Conejo interrupted, extending his hand towards a young woman who stood near the hearth warming water. Toribio smiled at her and nodded as he removed his hat. Her dark eyes met his. Quickly, as if embarrassed, she dropped her glance and returned to work.

"Rosa's husband never returned," Conejo said. "Some rumors have it that he died in a battle somewhere up north. Poor boy. I helped get him into the army. He was a good worker that boy. He died courageously, fighting bandits, you know."

Toribio said nothing, but only listened.

"Anyway," Conejo continued, "Rosa has become an excellent housekeeper and cook. Her two children and mother are of little help. Is it not like that, Rosita?"

"Yes. It's true," she responded dryly.

"Now, bring us a bottle of tequila and two glasses," Conejo ordered. He was proud of his set of American-made glasses. Few people in the mountains owned such luxurious possessions.

Rosa reached up to a high shelf. The men watched as the dress pressed against her.

"No, no, daughter. Not that old stuff. Bring me the good tequila from down below."

Rosa pulled her long, brown hair over her shoulders to keep it from falling in her face. She set the bottle of tequila and two glasses down on the table. Conejo saw the look in Toribio's blue eyes.

"Drink up, my friend," said Conejo, raising his glass in a toast, "We have much time ahead of us."

"Salud," Toribio said, as he also raised his glass.

It took four swallows to finish the drink without a single pause. Conejo refilled the glasses. A warmth began to flow through Toribio's body.

"Toribio," Conejo spoke as he wiped his lips with his shirt-sleeve, "the mayor says that he wants ten of your best cows. One of the generals is bringing an American to look at some land. I understand that the American is a very important man, and he is interested in buying some land. The mayor wants to throw a big fiesta for the gringo's arrival."

"When?" Toribio asked, calmly picking up his glass and twirling the tequila around in circles.

"Oh, not until next week. But he insists you send your best animals."

Toribio did not like the mayor. He did not like Conejo, but he knew that he must deal with them to get the best prices for his cattle.

"Very well," Toribio answered, as a buzzing sensation pricked his nerve endings like a million tiny needles.

"Ah, and Toribio," Conejo added as if suddenly remembering something. "The mayor says that your cattle will be first on the market."

Conejo's nose twitched in quick involuntary movements, a sign of nervousness.

"And did the mayor say how much he wants?" Toribio said, bluntly.

"Well, yes ... yes, he mentioned a number." Conejo hesitated, "I think he said thirty percent, yes, that's it, thirty percent."

"Impossible!" Toribio screamed.

Conejo placed both hands on his glass, calculating, thinking. "All year long the man asks favors, cows for this or cows for the other, land for his nephew to graze sheep. And now that it is I who will profit, he demands nearly half of my earnings ... impossible!"

A silence filled the room. Toribio did not hear the sound of Rosa's bare feet moving over the rock floor.

"I'll take my animals to Guadalajara. My sons, we can make the trip in a week," Toribio said, breaking the silence.

"Many cattle will die. Remember, there are also theives on the roads. Besides, I don't think the mayor will like your decision," Conejo warned in a threatening tone.

"Fuck the mayor. If not for my money and that of the other ranchers, the mayor would still be a captain riding through the mountains with a pack of snotty-nosed federales."

"Listen, Toribio."

"No, you listen," Toribio grew angrier. "Last year I gave the son of a whore fifteen percent. Now he wants double. Does he think I'm an idiot? I'll take my animals to Guadalajara and get a good price."

"Very well, my friend," said Conejo, sounding happy. "You are absolutely right. You've been a loyal supporter of the mayor. Let me talk to him. I'll see what I can do." Conejo filled the glasses again.

"I'll give him twenty percent and the cows he needs for his fiesta. If that isn't enough," Toribio fumed, "he can go fuck himself."

"I'll see what I can do. The mayor is a reasonable man," Conejo repeated, and quickly changed the subject.

The two men talked for a long time. They talked about ranches. They talked about the fighting between the federales and the bandits. Toribio used the word revolution; Conejo laughed at the absurdity of such a thing. He predicted that the bandits would fade away, but Toribio wasn't so sure.

Toribio tried to talk about Diaz's shaky presidency. Conejo's feeling was that the government was solid.

As they talked, Rosa walked about the kitchen performing her duties and making certain that the men had everything they needed.

Conejo noticed that Toribio stared more at Rosa.

Rosa sat on a small bench. She placed her dress over her knees as she mended the hem. Toribio looked at her small feet, her thin ankles and strong, round calves. Conejo rose from his seat, excused himself and left the room.

She pulled the dress above her thighs, making the movement seem like an accident. Then she took the hem of her dress and nudged it back down over her knees. She stood and walked to the table.

Toribio felt as if he were in a trance. Picking up Conejo's half-filled glass, she poured the harsh liquid down her throat and stared at Toribio.

He looked at the smoothness of her neck, the curve of her breasts and the firm, thin body. She placed the glass back on the table, walked to the door and secured the lock. From a shelf on the wall she reached up and pulled down a quilt. She spread the heavy blanket near the hearth. Reaching over her shoulder, she unclasped one button and the dress fell to her feet. Slowly, she sat down on the quilt. The glow from the hearth reflected on her skin.

Toribio emptied his glass. He got up and walked to her. Standing over her, he could do nothing but stare. She reached up, placed her hand in his and brought him down next to her.

CHAPTER TWO

As Toribio reached the stream at the foot of two mountains, he saw what appeared to be a woman stooped down on the trail. A long, blinding streak of lightning shot through the dark night. He shook his head trying to chase the vision from his brain. When he looked again the woman was still there.

"Woman?" he screamed. "It is dangerous to be out here alone at night. Are you with someone?" She did not answer.

His mare nervously stomped her front hooves and slowly backed away as if perceiving danger. He whipped his horse, forcing it closer to the stream. Whinnying loudly and kicking its front legs, the animal reluctantly moved forward.

"What is it? What is wrong?" he asked. The woman said nothing and did not move.

"All right then, get out of my way. I am coming through," he cried angrily. She remained hunched over, solid as a boulder. He yelled again but it did no good.

With the next enormous crack of thunder, the mare reared up on her hind legs. Toribio, unsteady from the tequila, struggled to stay in the saddle. He saw the woman rise. She began laughing, her face a deathly white color. Toribio thought he saw a gun in her hand. As he reached for his rifle, trying to keep his legs about the horse he lost his balance and felt himself falling. He tried to pull himself free, but the stirrup gripped his right foot. The horse bolted and Toribio felt the cold mud smash into his face and the prickly limb of a bush he tried to grab rush through his palm tearing the skin away. He felt his head bouncing until it struck a rock in the stream and then he felt nothing more.

CHAPTER THREE

Susana Esteban de Rios said nothing as her husband's horse trotted away from the ranch. She knew he would not return until very late. It was like that whenever he went to Conejo's. Although Toribio always told her not to worry, she worried nyway. Oh yes, he was still very strong, she thought, and very smart, but old age was slowing him down, something she knew he would never admit.

She sat on the bed and looked over the large room. The youngest children were just waking from their afternoon nap. The bin in the corner was filled with a two month supply of corn. The beds on which her children slept were made of wooden frames; this made her feel proud and lucky. She knew that the poor were forced to sleep on straw mats. Two oil lamps hung on the walls. A round table was placed in a corner. A bench and four chairs lined the far wall. A picture of the Virgin sat on top of the dresser.

Susana walked outside and greeted her older sons. She looked at the stormy sky. It was a welcome sight after so many months of sun. She hoped for a good rain which would bring a fruitful harvest and security to the families in the mountains.

She walked into the kitchen and opened the heavy wooden shutters to let in some light. The girls had done a good job cleaning. Susana stuffed a bundle of twigs into the earthen stove. Within minutes a hot fire warmed the room. The flames played with the dark walls. A half hour later hot chocolate steamed in a large, clay pot. The children drank happily.

By the time darkness fell the children had grown completely restless from remaining indoors. Susana would not allow them to go outside and tramp mud through the house. The rain began to dribble steadily off the roof and onto the earth. Susana's eldest daughter Bougainvillea's jaws ached from telling story after story, but still the younger children's thirsty minds wanted more.

"Is Fernando going to marry you?" one of the eight-year old twins asked.

"Oh, and what business is that of yours?" scolded Bougainvillea.

"Miranda said that all women should marry by the time they're eighteen. He said you should have been married already," answered the other twin, who wished she had remained silent after she saw the hard look cross her older sister's face.

Bougainvillea turned to Miranda, who tried to hide his face when he heard what had been said.

"And who are you to talk about people getting married?" she shouted at her brother. "Here you are twenty-two years old and still living at home."

Miranda laughed at his sister, who was second to him in age. "I'm a man. I can marry whenever I please. But you, you must wait until some crazy fool comes asking," he said, laughing.

"Is that what you think?" she said. "Well then, it seems to me that Josefina and Gamboa have some plans that you know nothing about," Bougainvillea taunted.

The smile disappeared from Miranda's face. Everyone knew that Josefina was his girlfriend. Before he could answer, Susana ordered, "Both of you behave before you start fighting. That's no way to talk in front of the children."

Bougainvillea gave Miranda one last smile before turning away. She knew how far she could go before his temper raged. She did not want to make him too angry. Her boyfriend was Miranda's best friend, and it was Miranda who took her to see him.

The twins jumped wildly on the beds, pretending that with the next leap they could touch the ceiling. The youngest of the children–Rojita they called her because of her red hair–slyly reached into the corn bin, which was nothing more than three planks of wood fencing off a corner of the room. She grabbed a handful of kernels and threw the little pellets at her ten-year-old brother, Ramon, who sat against a wall trying to repair a set of reins. He screamed and looked around the room, accusingly. No one paid any attention. He returned to his work.

Jaime and Chavo, sixteen and fourteen years of age, argued over who had won the most games of dominoes within the past two hours. When Jaime realized that his younger brother had beaten him more times, he grew angry.

"So what. I don't care about these stupid games." He leaned

close to his brother and said, "Who has kissed the most girls, little brother, you or me? You probably can't even remember the last time you kissed a girl," he whispered.

Chavo's face reddened. All of the boys from the other ranches knew that Chavo was deathly shy of girls and had not yet been kissed, while Jaime had been known to kiss the lips of both girls and women alike. Pretending that he did not care, Chavo began stacking the dominoes on top of each other. He wanted to see how high he could stack them without knocking them over. His mind whirled in action and he felt disappointed with his brother.

Rojita, encouraged by her first victorious act against her brother, raised her head from behind the bed. She looked over carefully to see that her brother continued mending the leather strands. When she saw that his head was down and he was busily working away on the reins, she reached into the bin one more time. Afraid to throw too many kernels of corn, she released the pressure on her hand and let most of the corn fall back into the bin. She kept a tight grip on the dozen or so that she would use in her attack. Giggling to herself, she cocked her arm back like a tiny catapult. She took careful aim and just as she was about to release her barrage of ammunition, her target vanished in a dizzying blackness and a sharp pain pressed against her face.

Bougainvillea's slap echoed across the room. The twins fell to their knees, fearfully listening to Rojita's cry. At the domino table, the two brothers looked up to see what had happened. Ramon was not interested, he continued his repairs. Another sister stopped brushing her hair. She wanted to tell Bougainvillea that slapping the younger children was no way to make them behave. Mama could take no more. She ordered Miranda to blow out the lamps and sent the children to bed. After extinguishing the lamps, he struck a match and lit the candles on the dresser; they brightened the picture of the Virgin.

Outside, seventeen year old Pepe stood under the thatched veranda on the patio. He watched as the shadowy clouds passed through the dark sky. Sometimes he could see the moon fighting to break through. He spotted a star but it quickly disappeared behind the wall of clouds. Pepe loved to see the moon and stars shimmer over the mountains. But he also knew that the clouds meant rain, and the people of the mountains could not make it through another year without water to irrigate their lands, so he welcomed the clouds.

Pepe thought of himself as a strange contradiction. Much of

the time he felt so contented with life. There was a deep peace inside him whenever he imagined himself roaming the mountains and valleys for the rest of his life. But when he listened to his friends and they talked about leaving the mountains and going off to Guadalajara or Mexico City to make money and own businesses, he too felt an excitement. It was easy for him to imagine himself living in a large house with a wife and children. He grew fascinated whenever anyone talked of the land to the north where the gringos lived. Whenever his father would take him into town, which was usually twice a month, Pepe would go to the plaza and listen to those who had traveled. They described their journeys through Coahuila, Sonora, Chihuahua and on into Texas.

The stories would include visions of pine trees, pine trees so thick that they looked like fields of grass ... and oceans where large ships arrived from around the world daily. He heard about the great cities like El Paso, Tucson and Los Angeles where everyone went about dressed in suits, leading important lives, and where there were books, paintings and music, but most importantly schools, many different types of schools where everyone could study. Someday he would go. He would wander through the world tasting his dreams and touching his thoughts.

But as Pepe searched deeper into the sky and saw the confusion among the moon, stars and clouds, a sadness came over him. He loved this ranch, the mountains and the people. And there lay his contradiction. How could he ever leave the land and family that were a part of him? Were dreams stronger than blood? Generations of Rios had given their lives to this land. Their ghosts had made permanent homes in the depths of his heart. Would the ghosts hold or release him? Was the longing in his heart so great that he could go against all tradition? Could he bring himself to destroy his father and mother?

"Pepe!"

He jerked as his mother's voice forcefully shot through the patio disrupting his thoughts.

"I'm here, Mama," he answered.

"Come and read to the children; they're driving me crazy in here."

"I'll be right there," he replied.

He looked into the silhouetted branches of the large oak tree that stood in the center of the patio. He knew exactly where the thickest limbs grew. He had given names to the disfigured branches that grew as though they could not decide whether to go up or down. He was proud of the huge trunk that stood massive and powerful. As a young child he had learned that the oak tree knew everything about the family. It was a story he had also passed on to his younger brothers and sisters. He struggled to see the highest limbs, but his vision blurred in the darkness, and his sight dissolved somewhere above the middle of the tree. He laughed, shook his head and walked into the house.

Miranda sat in a chair next to the dresser fiddling with an unlit cigarette between his lips. Bougainvillea sat at the foot of her bed brushing her hair and feeling sorry that she had struck her younger sister. Jaime and Chavo played a game with their fingers trying to see who had the fastest reflexes. Mama and the other children were already in bed. Ramon pulled on the reins he had just repaired. He felt happy with his accomplishment. Pepe sat in a chair and moved one of the candles to where it would light the pages of his Bible. He opened the wrinkled black book and began to read.

His voice was soft yet clear and loud enough for everyone to hear. Pepe had the type of voice that made people want to listen to the words he spoke. It was nothing that he practiced or did consciously. It was more that the listener could feel Pepe's intense nature and commitment to the subject, and through this, know that Pepe held high respect for those he was reading to.

Pepe knew the Bible so well that he had already outlined many parables from both the Old and New Testaments. Depending on his audience, he would choose his readings carefully. Usually he would read a parable and then ask questions, but tonight he knew that the children were tiring, so he selected some of the beautiful passages from the Book of Wisdom and just let them listen. The children fell off into a deep and penetrating sleep as Pepe read late into the night.

Mama felt proud of Pepe as she listened. She remembered the first time that the people from a nearby village asked if Pepe could read for them. It had been many days since a priest had come, they told her, and no one else in the village knew how to read. When he had finished, the people were stunned by the beauty and depth of Pepe's delivery.

She remembered how neighbors from other villages asked for Pepe to visit their homes and ranches. After a day's work, in the early evening, Pepe would ride Macho, the family mule, and make his rounds to the different ranches. He tried to understand the feeling of power that gripped his body during his readings to the people. Whether his audience was one person or thirty, a strange energy flowed through him. Sometimes its wholeness and strength frightened him, but at the same time it offered him complete control over the world around him. Mama did not understand this part of it when he had once tried to explain it; she only knew that her son was becoming very loved.

Mama also remembered that not everyone was enthusiastic about Pepe's role. One day a priest stopped Pepe as he was leaving a ranch. The priest became angry and accused Pepe of stealing his parishioners. Pepe tried to explain that he was only reading the Bible to the people during the priest's long absences. But the priest would not listen. He gave Pepe a good thrashing with words and told him to stop playing priest.

Pepe told his father what had happened. Furious, Toribio raced from the house looking for the priest. When he found him surrounded by a group of people at one of the ranches, he accused the priest of entering the mountain ranches only when he could not take enough money and food from the townspeople in the valleys. Days later, Conejo was sent to tell Toribio that he should not have been so rough on the priest; after all, he was the sheriff's brother-in-law. If it had not been for his need to sell his cattle, Toribio would also have run Conejo off his land.

Mama smiled as she thought of these things, and she knew that Pepe could not stop reading to the people. He was more in demand now than ever before; yet he also enjoyed reading to his own family, as he did this night. When it seemed that the children were asleep, Pepe closed the book and sat back in his chair.

Miranda leaned over towards Pepe and whispered into his ear so that no one could hear. "I go to church only to see the girls. I make love to them in my mind, right there as I kneel in the pew."

"Well, nobody is perfect," Pepe replied, knowing his older brother was trying to shock him.

"You don't think so?"

"No."

"Well then, what about the saints? If they were not perfect, how could they become saints?"

"Who ever said a saint had to be perfect?" Pepe responded.

"Do you think the saints thought about sex?"

"Sure. I remember a story father Salazar told me. I think it was about St. Benedict," Pepe said to his brother quietly. "St. Benedict was in the desert fasting and praying. And even during this he kept having thoughts about sex."

"What kinds of thoughts about sex?" smiled Miranda.

"I don't know. Use your imagination ... anyway, the thoughts were very strong and he couldn't get rid of them. He felt unclean and very unworthy to be a monk."

"Those thoughts make me happy to be alive," said Miranda.

"You're an imbecile, big brother. Are you going to let me finish?"

"Continue," Miranda instructed.

"Well, the thoughts were getting the best of St. Benedict. He could not take them anymore; he had to do something to relieve himself." Pepe hesitated a long time.

"So what did he do?" Miranda asked, impatiently.

"St. Benedict got up from where he was, and he ran out into the desert. The first cactus plant he saw he ran up to and jumped into the middle of it."

Miranda looked at Pepe suspiciously. "Horseshit," he said.

Pepe smiled, "No, I swear, that's what father Salazar told me. He said he read it when he was studying to become a monk."

"So that makes St. Benedict perfect?" Miranda questioned.

"No," Pepe thought for a moment, "it just makes him a saint."

Miranda stood up and stretched. "That is all craziness. I'm going to bed. You can have your cactus and I'll take Josefina." Miranda smiled, walked over to the bed where his brother Ramon slept and crawled in next to him. Pepe placed the Bible on top of the dresser. He leaned back against the chair, closed his eyes and fell into a dream-like state. The world he created inside his mind seemed so real and the rain that tapped at the roof became a part of that reality. Pepe attempted to find answers in his surroundings but found only more and more questions.

A banging noise from outside startled Pepe. He sat up straight and realized it was the gate leading into the patio. Toribio always let out a shout whenever he entered at night. Pepe heard no shout. Miranda, Jaime and Chavo were now sitting up also.

Miranda darted from the bed and took the carbine from the wall. He was taking no chances. There had been many robberies the past few months. Pepe, his heart thumping, rose from his chair and lighted the oil lamp. Jaime reached into the closet and pulled out a long .44. Chavo, shaking the sleep from his head, looked to Miranda for directions. Miranda motioned with his head for Chavo to stand near the door. Mama and the girls were now also sitting up staring at the large wooden door. They all waited for a knock.

Miranda placed his finger to his lips signaling for silence. They could hear a horse's hooves moving about the rock porch right outside the door. Still there was no knock. Miranda motioned for his brothers to position themselves around the door. He took the carbine, placed it to his shoulder and aimed at the door. Jaime held the pistol firmly, his arms outstretched. Pepe kept the oil lamp down low so that the light shone against the ground. Miranda gave Chavo a nod to open the door.

Chavo lifted the heavy metal bolt and quickly threw open the door. Miranda rushed forward with the carbine, but the horse on the porch stood so close that it blocked the entrance.

"Pepe, hold up the lamp so we can see," Miranda ordered.

Pepe raised the lamp, lighting up the darkness outside. Everyone immediately recognized their father's horse. Miranda slapped the rump, pushing the animal from the door. When the horse turned, the entire family, from the youngest child to the mother, saw the crumpled body of Toribio Rios sprawled on the patio slab. The back of his head had been torn away, his clothes were in shreds and his right foot, crudely jammed in the stirrup, was twisted like a jagged branch. He had been dragged a long way.

CHAPTER FOUR

The sun bore a hole in the sky. The last clouds, enormous boughs of cotton, moved westward. Already the ground began to harden. The nopales, mesquite and sheer rock barrancas shimmered on the surrounding mountainsides. Susana prayed silently for the hand of God to touch her; she felt nothing but sadness.

Miranda shoveled the last pile of dirt over the grave. He felt the sun burn his neck but thought nothing of it. The girls cried. They called out to their father even though they knew he could not hear them. Susana remained strong. She did not cry.

The boys knew they must stand valiant and dry eyed. Men did not cry nor did they show their feelings. There was neither room nor time for such petty emotional outbursts. But Ramon felt his eyes watering. He struggled to keep the tears inside. He stiffened his body, clenching hands and feet. One tear managed to free itself and run down his cheek. He bent over and rubbed his knee, at the same time brushing his shirt sleeve secretly against his cheek.

Pepe did not read his Bible as he did at other burials. He knew the right passages, but today, now that death placed her fingers on his own family, a bitterness gripped at him and he turned away from God.

No one said a word. Bougainvillea tried to muffle her sobs but could not. A stillness settled over the mountains. Miranda looked at Pepe to see if his younger brother would speak. Finally Pepe moved forward.

"I can't think of anything to say," he began. He bit his lower lip and looked at the sky, not really seeing anything.

"Maybe sometimes words mean nothing. Can anything be said to make us feel better? Our father is gone and he will not return. We won't ever see him laugh. We won't ever hear him sing out to the cattle. We will miss his anger, even the time he chased Jaime down the mountain for setting fire to a cow's tail, those things we will see no more."

Pepe dropped his head and placed his hands into his pockets. Bougainvillea placed her hands over her eyes.

"I remember when my father walked all night through the mountains to get a doctor when Miranda broke his arm. And the time he threatened to kill Artemio Montez for calling my mother a chismosa," Pepe smiled. "Remember, poor Artemio pleaded forgiveness a thousand times."

Pepe hesitated for a few seconds, then continued. "Do you remember the blue of my father's eyes? They were a very light blue like the sky when a mist hangs in the air. He said he got them from his great grandfather, a true Mexican tainted by the blood of an Andalusian adventurer sent from Mexico City to fight the Chichimecas.

"My father told me that he did not remember who first bought our land, it was just handed down from generation to generation. He loved this land. He loved it like he loved us. We must always remember our father. Our children and grandchildren must be told of Toribio Rios. His memory must not die. He ... "

Pepe could not continue. He tried to speak again, but the words choked him.

Cristina, who was sixteen years old and looked more like Toribio than any of other the other children in the family, fell to her knees and wept. Her cries sailed over the fields and echoed off of the canyon walls. The younger girls moved close to her and placed their arms on her shoulders as they also wept. Bougainvillea fought back the tears. She was only two years older than Cristina, but always saw herself as the family's second mother. Ramon walked to his mother and took her hand. They all left the gravesite together but walked in different directions. The girls walked back to the house; Jaime and Chavo walked towards the corrals. Miranda saddled a horse and rode off. Pepe walked over to the rock wall next to the cornfield and looked down into the massive canyons below. He worried that without a strong leader the family would not survive.

CHAPTER FIVE

After dinner the older brothers gathered near the corrals. Miranda stood with his hands in his pockets. He looked at each of his brothers and spoke. "This was no accident. My father was too good a horseman. Nobody could ride like him. What do you think, Pepe?" Although he was the oldest, Miranda always looked to Pepe for the answers.

"We know that he went to see Conejo about business," Pepe said slowly, carefully picking through the ideas in his brain. "I know for sure that my father was concerned about not getting cheated."

"Why didn't he say anything to me?" Miranda responded, irritated.

"Miranda, with your temper ... " Pepe paused, "my father wanted you to run the ranch and me run the business."

"Ay, it's all the same," answered Miranda, becoming angry.

"No it's not, brother. Taking care of the cows and taking care of the money are two completely different worlds. My father did not even begin to teach me what he wanted me to learn. But he did say that there were men who would sell their own children to get our land."

Jaime, with a look of arrogance on his face and a twig in his mouth, asked, "Pepe, do you think Conejo was one of these men?"

"I don't know. Right now nothing is certain."

"It's strange," said Jaime, "How the sheriff asked so few questions. Almost like he wanted to get away from us quick."

"That's right," Miranda responded, "that man's usually more suspicious than a priest in a confessional. Yet he seemed satisfied with the little we told him."

"Bueno, then what do we do?" asked Chavo. The others turned

21

to him surprised, since Chavo normally said little. As the youngest of the senior brothers, Chavo always felt insecure; quickly, he turned to Pepe.

Pepe picked up a small stone and turned it over in his hands. Finally, Pepe said, "Nothing. We won't do a thing except attend to business. We will wait."

"Wait! Wait for What?" screamed Miranda, unable to control himself. "Let's go to Conejo's ranch and confront him."

"Confront him with what?" Pepe asked, firmly. He threw the stone across the corrals. "What proof have we that Conejo was involved? For all we know our father's death was an accident."

"No!" cried Miranda, angrily. "Chavo said it. Our father could master any horse. It's impossible for him to get dragged to death, especially by Viento."

Pepe knew his brothers were right. His father could control any horse. "So what is your plan? Shall we go grab the man by the throat and accuse him of murdering our fath ... ?"

Miranda cut Pepe off. "We can tell him that we want to know exactly what happened the night our father went to visit him. We can tell him that we don't believe our father's death was an accident. We can tell him we want to know exactly what they spoke about that night."

"Fine. And let's suppose this man actually was involved in our father's death ... ," Pepe was very careful in arguing with his older brother, especially in front of the younger boys; Pepe would never humble his older brother in their presence. "Do you think Conejo would ever tell you the truth? You know him. You know his reputation. He's a shrewd businessman who has dealt with mayors and governors."

"I will go alone. I will tell him that I am there to finish my father's business. I'll ask respectfully and tell him we are still interested in making a deal."

"Miranda, we don't know the business. We don't know how much my father made last year," Pepe said, concerned.

"Well, did my father say anything to you about the business, anything at all?"

Pepe thought carefully. He tried to remember the most recent conversations he had with Toribio. "All I remember my father say was that if the fighting gets any worse, the price of cattle will drop, since the soldiers will simply take whatever they want."

Miranda looked pensive. He sat down on a boulder and leaned back against the corral's rock wall. "I'll go see Conejo tomorrow," he announced.

"Miranda, let's go together," Pepe advised.

"No. It is my place to go. My father would have wanted it that way."

"And what will you find out from Conejo?" Pepe pushed.

Miranda looked sternly at all his brothers. "If the man played any part in my father's death we will know tomorrow."

Pepe would not argue. His father's death weighed heavily over the ranch. But as he looked at Miranda he remembered something else his father had said. It was after watching a bullfight in town. The torero had been knocked down by the bull. Angrily, the torero got up and ran wildly at the animal. The bull hooked and sent his right horn ripping through the man's stomach. Toribio shook his head slowly, turned to Pepe and said, "Never let anger control your actions." Pepe would say nothing more to Miranda today.

CHAPTER SIX

The pounding at his door did not surprise Conejo. He pulled open the door and offered Miranda his home.

"You don't know how your father's death has affected me," said Conejo, moving his glass so Rosa could fill it with tequila. He also signaled her to fill Miranda's glass.

"I felt ashamed and embarrassed," continued Conejo, "that I could not even bring myself to visit your ranch and offer my apologies."

Miranda had prepared to tell Conejo what he figured was the truth. Conejo had somehow been involved with Toribio's death. But here was Conejo, crying and confessing his guilt. "What do you mean?" Miranda inquired, looking directly at Conejo.

"I feel as guilty about don Toribio's death as though I myself had killed him."

"What are you saying?" exclaimed Miranda.

"Your father was a fine man. I, who have known your father for many years, would have given my right arm for him."

Miranda began to soften. "Then what is this about your shame and embarrassment?" he said.

Conejo looked at Miranda with eyes which radiated the honesty of an old nun. "My boy," Conejo began, "your father came to me to talk business. We have done business together for years, he and I. Ah, but you know all that," he said, swishing the air with the back of his hand. "We worked out a deal and celebrated over a bottle of tequila. Before the night was over, your father and I drank more liquor than the devil himself could take." He sighed, stopped talking for a moment then continued, "I have repeated that night in my head many times. I should not have let him drink so much," Conejo sounded angry. "Ay, pero, who, you tell me, who tells Toribio Rios how to act?" To do so would have been disrespectful on my part." Conejo pointed a finger a Miranda as if in warning, "Your father was a man of great pride. Was that not so?" Conejo's eyes filled with tears. He let out a loud, raspy cough and quickly regained his composure.

Miranda felt sorry for Conejo. He believed the old man was truly suffering over Toribio's death. "And what happened next?"

"I had business to take care of," Conejo went on, "I left your father here to finish his drink. Rosa ... that is Rosa over there ... " The young woman turned and offered a humble smile. "Yes, well, Rosa said that when don Toribio departed he had trouble mounting his horse." Conejo threw his hands up in the air, "The next thing I know the sheriff comes to tell us that my good friend Toribio has been dragged to death by his own horse." Conejo got up, took a couple of steps away from the table and grabbed the back of his chair. Miranda watched his bony fingers tremble under the pressure with which he held the chair. "If I had not offered him so much to drink, he might be alive today."

All of the questions Miranda had planned to ask were washed away. He looked at the pathetic little man and sympathized with him. Rosa continued working as if never hearing a word.

"And the business ... what kind of arrangement did you and my father make?"

"The usual," Conejo said, sitting back down and sipping at his tequila, "forty percent if I sell all his stock within a week."

"But that is nearly half," Miranda answered, surprised.

"Your father's words exactly." Conejo reached for the bottle of tequila and refilled Miranda's glass.

"But you see, as I told your father, it is not so much. The buyers will come to the ranch and drive the cattle to the market themselves. Otherwise you and your family would have to drive the animals to Guadalajara, a five day journey. And if the bandits did not steal the cattle from you, the outlaw federales surely would. Besides, many cattle would die on the road. You would lose more than half of your profits just trying to reach the city."

Miranda tried to clear his thoughts. The tequila made him feel peaceful and lazy.

"I don't know," he answered with a note of uncertainty, "forty percent still seems so much."

"Hijo, your father told me you are the best vaquero in these parts. I agree. I have seen you work." Miranda beamed at the compliment. "Now, you have made the trip to Guadalajara before, no? Think what it was like," Conejo told him.

Miranda remembered. He remembered the horrid journey. It had been an arduous trek through dry mountain ranges and washed-out roads. A scorpion had stung Pepe and he nearly died. Jaime had gotten himself lost along the way. Yes, maybe Conejo did speak the truth. Forty percent suddenly did not seem so unreasonable. "And you say my father agreed to the price, and he also agreed to donate fifteen cows to General Mendoza's fiesta?"

"Since you, Miranda, are now the patron, you must come to the fiesta; many people will want to meet you. After all, you are now the boss of a famous ranch.

"You say my father already agreed to this deal?" Miranda asked, seeking assurance as he raised his glass to salute. Conejo already held his glass out to him.

"Like you, Miranda, your father also was a clever businessman. Yes, of course, he accepted the offer. It was he who had made it."

Conejo did not realize that this one would be so easy for him.

"Come now, let us drink. A token of our friendship and respect for one another and for the memory of don Toribio Rios." Conejo threw back his head and emptied his glass of tequila, and as if a second thought had occurred to him he said, "Listen, Miranda. Think about it. Take your time. You still have a couple of days to decide. Do what you think is right for your family. Now, I have work to do." Conejo rose from his chair and walked towards the door.

Miranda also began to get up, "No, no," insisted Conejo, "stay a while, finish your cup." He walked outside and closed the door behind him.

For the first time Miranda looked closely at Rosa. She stood to one side of the room smiling at him. Her eyes were large, deep brown and shining. Her hair fell onto her shoulders. She had dark Indian skin, but her features were very European.

"Can I pour you another glass of tequila?" she asked.

Miranda searched for words. How was it that he had never seen this woman before? How did he miss such loveliness among the cactus and rock of the land?

"No-n-no, I-I don't think so," he stuttered, "I must return to the ranch."

"Couldn't you stay just a little while, to talk. Hardly ever do I get to talk with anyone my own age," she said, in a voice that was a near whisper. She moved closer to Miranda.

"You are so beautiful." The words escaped from his mouth. He felt embarrassed. He had never said such a thing to any woman. Rosa smiled.

"Please, sit down," he invited. "Do you drink?"

"Only when I must," her answer puzzled him, but he did not pursue it.

They both sat quietly as if they were young children meeting for the first time. Miranda felt awkward. Never did he feel awkward around women. He had loved many times with his body but never with his heart.

"I am sorry about your father."

The sudden reminder sent a sharp pain through Miranda. He acted as though the death bothered him little. "Thank you, but it is done, finished. One cannot live in the past," he answered.

Frowning, she asked, "But how can you forget so easily? Did you dislike your father?"

"Dislike ... God, no, he was a good man," Miranda answered, trying not to show too much emotion.

"Then why would you want to forget him so easily?"

"There is no place for sadness in my life. I have too much work ahead of me to allow the past to slow me down."

"Miranda. Are you saying you feel no sadness?"

"No, I am not saying that. I am saying that I do not allow sadness to enter my thoughts or slow me down."

"But that is impossible," Rosa insisted, "how can you choose whether to allow an emotion to enter your life or not. If you choose to feel no sadness, then is that to say you feel no fear, pain, courage, sorrow," she paused, "love."

Miranda held the glass to his lips, looked at Rosa's face and placed the glass back onto the table without taking a drink.

"I do believe you feel sadness, Miranda Rios. One must face the night alone. One must walk these mountains alone. I cannot believe you do not cry alone," she spoke, almost as if the words were meant as much for herself as for him.

Anyone else speaking such words would have been halted with either a flurry of angry words or with a fist. But Miranda felt such deep passion for Rosa. Her beauty and the sincerity of her voice stunned him. "Why do you speak to me this way?" he asked.

She heard his question but responded with one of her own, "Can you love, Miranda?"

"I have never loved before."

"Could you love me now?"

Miranda swallowed hard. She looked more beautiful than he had ever seen a woman look before. His heart pounded and his chest burned. He wanted to touch her, but he couldn't move.

As if dreaming, he watched her hand move towards him. He felt the soft fingertips slide over his forehead, touch his eyebrows, slide down his cheek and press against his lips. Still touching him, she walked over and stood beside him.

Slowly she pulled back her hand. He looked up at her. She bent down and placed her lips to his. They did not kiss but simply allowed their lips to touch. Gently she moved her lips over his. He felt her tongue moisten his lips. He opened his mouth and the tips of their tongues touched, lightly, like two feathers meeting. Without parting he stood up, wrapped his arms around her and kissed deeply, letting his tongue explore the moist and tender corners of her mouth.

Rosa breathed deeply, releasing small breaths. She placed kisses over his entire face. She took him by the arm and led him to a bed. Undoing his buttons she removed his clothes. She kissed his chest, his stomach and his sides. Each kiss sent sparks through his body. He felt sensations that forced him to hold his breath, let out gasps of air, utter sighs and cry out her name. Her mouth was everywhere, kissing, rubbing, licking, touching and feeling. When it seemed that he could take no more, she removed her dress and pressed her body against his. She guided his hands and his mouth. Never had a woman completely controlled him. His gentleness also captured her.

CHAPTER SEVEN

Conejo walked across the room to where he kept the tequila. He took a glass, poured himself a drink and sipped slowly. "Well, how did it go?" he asked.

Rosa did not answer. She had done what Conejo had ordered. She always did what he asked. But this time for the very first time something beautiful had happened. "Everything went fine," she finally answered.

"Can I count on him?"

"Miguel," she said, using Conejo's real name, "I think I like Miranda very much."

Conejo looked at the tequila moving in his glass. "Do you love him?"

Rosa never knew whether to answer Conejo truthfully or not; there was much evil in him, yet at times, if not for him, her mother and small daughter might have already starved. "Yes, I think I love him."

His fist caught her by surpise. She felt the hard knuckles dig into the side of her head just above the ear. She fell back against the bed.

"You do not love anyone," he commanded. His face grew hard. He reached down and grabbed her by the hair. "Do you understand," he whispered through clenched teeth.

Afraid, Rosa nodded in agreement as her head throbbed.

"Good."

He tore the clothes from her body, threw her into the center of the room, pulled her legs apart and mounted her. As he neared his climax he screamed at her to bite his shoulder. Rosa bit hard. She wanted to bite through the skin right down to the bone, tearing his shoulder to shreds.

"Harder! Harder!" he screamed. She bit until she felt her teeth draw blood. He cried out like an animal. The other women and the girls who heard understood.

CHAPTER EIGHT

The wind whipped through the canyons, howling as it moved. The sun cast a warm coat over the land. Tiny blades of grass sprouted over the mountains. A certain calm captured Las Amapolas, the name given to the Rios' ranch, the kind of calm that acts as a warning. Pepe, Jaime, Chavo and Ramon rode down a steep trail that led to a well which provided the cattle with fresh drinking water.

Pepe looked at the sky. He worried that he saw no clouds. He did not want another rainless year. The family did not need another tragedy.

"When do you think Miranda will return?" asked Ramon, bouncing along on the family burro. He pulled hard on the reins, proud of his repair work.

"How in the fuck are we supposed to know that," snapped Jaime, picking at a painful boil on his neck.

"I was only asking," answered Ramon, embarrassed by his brother's outburst.

"Well, don't ask, pendejo. How are we going to know when we are here and he is there?"

"Calm down, Jaime." Pepe's words angered Jaime more.

Ramon slapped the burro on the rear with a short piece of rope. The animal moved forward quickly, slipping on the soil and rocks as he neared Pepe's horse.

"Pepe," Ramon spoke softly so that his other brothers would not hear.

"What is it?"

"Pepe, I miss my father a lot."

"I know, hermanito, I miss him too."

Chavo began singing loudly. His voice carried through the mountains. He sang beautifully and with tremendous feeling.

"How long will it hurt like this, Pepe? I don't know if I can take it."

"You can take it," Pepe answered firmly, "don't think that you are the only one who hurts."

"Pepe. I cried," Ramon said, shamefully.

Pepe turned and looked at his little brother sympathetically, "You did not cry alone."

"You cried?" Ramon asked, surprised.

"We all cried."

"Miranda too?"

"Miranda too."

"Did you see him cry, Pepe?"

"No, I didn't need to see him cry."

"Then, how do you know? Miranda says a man must never cry."

"Believe me, he cried."

Ramon let the reins loose and grabbed the wooden saddlehorn. "Then it's all right to cry?" he asked.

"Of course, it is all right to cry."

"But Miranda says that if he sees me cry he will beat me."

"Then don't let him see you cry, unless you are willing to take a beating for your tears."

"What does that mean, Pepe."

"It means that one day when the pain is too great you will cry regardless of who is present."

Ramon scratched the side of his head, as if confused. "Pepe."

"Yes."

"Do you think my mother hurts more than we?"

Pepe looked at his little brother and smiled. "I think you are beginning to understand," he said. "You see, my father was our father, but he was my mother's husband and the father of her children. Yes, I know my mother hurts much more than we."

Jaime squeezed the inflamed red sore. He had been trying to break it, but each time he squeezed he found the pain unbearable. He decided to end the discomfort. He would make one last gallant effort. He gripped the horse's reins tightly with his left hand. He placed the fingers of his right hand on each side of the swollen lump. He closed his eyes tightly, clenched his hands around the reins and gritted his teeth. He took a deep breath and pinched the boil with all his strength. The pain shot from his toes through his

legs and into his chest like a sizzling metal blade. The day turned
black. When Jaime opened his eyes, Pepe was picking him up from
the trail.

"What happened?" Pepe asked.

"Nothing. I lost my fucking balance," answered Jaime, angrily.

"Nothing, you screamed like someone cut off your balls,"
laughed Chavo.

"Shut your mouth or I'll drag you from that horse and beat the
fuck out of you."

"Jaime! Take it easy," Pepe said, "get back on your horse, we
have much work to do."

Jaime got up trying to ignore the throbbing in his neck. He
wiped the dirt from his trousers and mounted his horse. As they
again started down the mountainside, Chavo began singing. Jaime,
nervously lifted his fingers to his burning neck. Softly, he touched
the sensitive skin. The swelling rose. A soft cap of skin still covered
the boil. It had not popped.

"Fuck!" Jaime yelled.

"What's wrong now?" Pepe called back, irritated.

"Nothing," Jaime answered. "I was thinking about a girl,"

Chavo's voice filled the air, "Vamos cantando y volandooo," he
sang as though he lived in a problem free world.

"How can you sing after all that has happened?" cried Jaime.

"I'll sing until I run out of song," came Chavo's reply.

"Crazy bastard," said Jaime. He did not understand that music
built a wall around Chavo to help keep the sadness away.

CHAPTER NINE

Little rain had fallen throughout the year. Toribio Rios had been determined to conserve this year's water supply and keep it clean. Except for the river, which was located at the base of the mountains, there was only one watering hole for the cattle. The pond was surrounded on three sides by ten foot mountain walls, and the only access for the cattle consisted of an entrance just large enough to permit one cow through at a time. Tree branches were chopped and placed across the entrance as barriers to keep the animals out. Somehow the cattle always managed to pull down the barrier and make their way into the water. This created a problem, since many of the cows would not just drink, but they would urinate, drop their waste and bring much filth into the pond.

During the rainy months the water overflowed and the filth would wash down the mountainside. But during the dry months the water in the hold became black, and a thick residue, white and gray, floated on the surface.

Each year many cattle died of diseases contracted from the contaminated water. Infuriated at what seemed like such a minor problem, Toribio had discussed a plan with Miranda and Pepe to keep the pond clean. Pepe was convinced he could complete the plan.

Pepe dismounted, tied his horse to a tree and began issuing orders. "Jaime, you and Chavo bring the bamboo. Ramon, push the animals away from the hole. They will try to get in when I remove the branches." Pepe always gave good instructions. He never became angry, and he was always explicit in details, not like Miranda who issued half orders and could not see how everyone could be so stupid as to not understand him.

Pepe lifted the heavy branches and threw them to one side.

A couple of cows and a heifer pushed their way to the entrance. Ramon kicked one cow on the snout, grabbed the other by the tail and screamed menacingly at the heifer. The animals backed away, swaying their large heads from side to side. One cow reached Ramon's chin. He shoved the animal until it walked off.

Jaime began to complain. He could understand none of this. As far as he was concerned, there would be dead cows every year and whatever they tried would not work. Pepe told him that the plan had been his father's idea. This quieted Jaime down. His throbbing neck bothered him. "I didn't know it was my father's plan," Jaime said to Pepe.

"There is much you don't know."

"Still, I would rather be with Miranda, finding out who killed my father."

"Miranda needs no one holding his hand. Now put down the bamboo and grab a shovel. We will dig a trench where I have marked a line."

The trench which they dug started at the pond. It stretched across the trail and dropped down the mountainside about fifty yards where it ended at a big, rectangular trough that Toribio and Miranda had built with brick and mortar. The sun grew hotter as they worked. Although the dirt was soft, it was filled with rock. It seemed to Pepe that with each strike of the hoe the sun burned even more. After five hours of battling with dirt and rock the trench was complete.

The boys sat down under the shade of a tall guaje tree. They did not speak. Each was lost in his own world of thought. The wind had stopped blowing and the immense silence of the mountains penetrated deeply into each of them, except for Jaime, who continued to battle the boil.

Pepe heard his father laugh. He knew the sound existed only in his imagination, but he sat up and looked around anyway. The laughter seemed real.

He looked at a spot on the mountain behind him, just next to a large cactus. He peered hard, hoping that maybe God would allow him one last glimpse of his father. Pepe believed in visions and miracles. Surely God could grant him this small wish, just a quick appearance of his father standing beside the cactus. Pepe closed his eyes tightly and believed that when he opened them his father would be standing there on the mountain. But when he opened his eyes, Pepe saw only the cactus and an empty dirt spot. A lizard scurried across the dirt and disappeared into the trunk of the cactus. Pepe watched carefully. The lizard ran back into the open, moved its head in a quick mechanical motion and rushed back into the cactus.

"It's time to get back to work," Pepe announced quietly, almost dejected. The brothers rose without a complaint.

"What should we do?" asked Chavo.

"Take the bamboo and lay it in the trench so that it goes all the way from the pond down to the trough," Pepe ordered, picking up one of the smaller pieces of bamboo and looking through it. A metal rod had been driven through each shoot to hollow the inside.

Pepe showed the boys how to connect each piece to make one continuous line. Since the pieces did not fit into place, he took a sharp knife to slice the female ends, making them large enough for the male ends to enter. Once the ends connected, he wound them tightly with thick twine and brushed sap over the joints to keep them from leaking.

The sun had passed the center of the sky and leaned towards the west. Pepe wiped his brow. He walked down the trench to make sure that all the bamboo was connected correctly.

"Bueno, let's eat," he finally said.

Chavo started a small fire. He placed the twigs in such a way that their ashes were used to warm the tortillas. Ramon handed Chavo a pot of beans, and Chavo put them where they would warm quickly. None of the boys sat too close to the fire, but all stared hypnotically into the flames.

"Jaime," said Ramon, "do you miss my father?"

Jaime looked at his little brother with a blank expression. No one spoke. Then came the explosion. "Why do you ask me that?" screamed Jaime. "It is none of your business how I feel. What do you care how I feel anyway. Just keep your mouth shut!"

Pepe was quick to respond. "Is that how you feel, Chavo?"

Chavo pushed the flames with a long stick. He didn't answer right away. He continued pushing the flames as if playing a game. He looked at Pepe, opened his mouth and closed it again. He looked at Jaime and back at Ramon. "I don't know how I feel," he finally answered. "Ever since I was a child I have been told not to cry and not to feel bad when bad things happen." Chavo looked at Jaime again, "I know how Jaime feels," he continued, "because we all grew up with the same rules. I remember I cried when our dog coyote got crushed by the stampede of cattle. I was only seven. Miranda beat the shit out of me. He said that if he ever caught me crying again he would kill me. Well, I know he didn't mean it, but the words scared me, anyway."

"What is all this crap about?" screamed Jaime, "let's forget it."

"No Jaime," Pepe said, "all we ever do is forget it. We never talk about how we feel." Pepe's new position as the second in command gave him a new confidence.

"Shit, I wish Miranda were here, then we wouldn't be wasting time on any of this."

"What are you afraid of, Jaime, that we might find out you are scared and hurt like us," Pepe said.

"Man, you're a bastard," came Jaime's gritted reply, "just because my father or Miranda are not here, you try giving us all this Bible shit."

Ramon jumped up, his arms and legs quivering. "I want my father back," he cried.

Jaime also jumped up and yelled, "Stop crying, you gutless little shit." But Ramon did not stop, he cried even more.

Jaime grew furious, "I said to stop!"

When Jaime saw that Ramon would not stop, he rushed at him closed-handed. Pepe leaped to protect Ramon. Jaime stood directly in front of Pepe.

"Leave him alone," Pepe warned.

"He cries like a girl! Send him back to our sisters," Jaime shouted.

Pepe could see the rage in Jaime's eyes.

"Your Bible has turned you into a woman, Pepe."

"Go sit down and eat your food," Pepe ordered.

But Jaime would not sit down. He had challenged Pepe. He would wait to see Pepe's actions. "You are not a saint," Jaime said to Pepe.

"You are an idiot, Jaime."

Pepe did not think Jaime would hit him. They had not fought in many years. They stared at each other like two angry lions. Jaime sprung, wrapped his arms around Pepe's neck and wrestled him to the ground.

Pepe tried to throw him off, but Jaime was the heavier of the two. Jaime tried to pin Pepe's arms to his sides, but even though he was tall and slim, Pepe was very strong. They wrestled and rolled, grunting and snorting. Both were tiring. Jaime grabbed Pepe's hair and pulled hard. Pepe felt as though his hair would be yanked from his scalp. He reached for Jaime's neck and squeezed, trying to cut his brother's air supply. Jaime let out a tremendous scream and let go of Pepe's hair.

Lifting himself from the ground, Pepe watched as Jaime rolled around in agony.

"What, what did I do?" Pepe yelled. Chavo and Ramon also came close, concerned at Jaime's pain.

Jaime sat up, his eyes full of tears. "Look, look," he cried, showing them the huge red blotch on his neck. "You popped my fucking pimple. I've been trying to pop the son-of-a-bitch all day long."

Chavo began laughing. Jaime looked like a bewildered, lost child kneeling there on the dirt, rubbing his neck. Ramon grinned. Pepe scratched the back of his head. He didn't know if Jaime was crying tears of happiness or of pain.

"Shit, let's eat and get back to work," Pepe commanded, picking up his straw hat and putting it back on his head.

Pepe stood near the pond. Ramon kept chasing the thirsty cattle away from the entrance.

"Good, put your hand over the end," Pepe called down to Jaime, who stood at the other end of the bamboo line. Jaime placed his palm over the end of the bamboo so no water could get out.

"Pour in the water," Pepe said to Chavo.

Chavo filled a pail with water and began pouring the water into the bamboo which Pepe held up.

It took about five minutes to fill the entire line with water. Excitedly, Pepe took the bamboo shoot and quickly pushed it into the pond before any air could get into the line.

"Bueno, let the water out," Pepe called down to Jaime who held the end of the line over the brick tank. Pepe ran down the hill to see if any water came out. He watched as a small trickle leaked from the end. A steadier stream of water suddenly emerged. Chavo, Jaime and Pepe smiled at each other. But their smiles faded as the water turned back into a trickle and stopped.

"Let's do it again. Too much air must have gotten in," Pepe told them as he ran up the mountain. Again they went through the same process. Toribio had guaranteed that the thing would work. Pepe took his time. When he saw that the line was full, he pushed his end back into the pond and ran down to the trough to watch. This time the water rushed out and did not stop until the trough was filled. Pepe jammed the tip of the bamboo with an old rag to stop the flow of water. The boys, all of them, jumped around in celebration. They splashed water at each other. Jaime jumped into the tank to show his pleasure.

"Ho! Ho! Ho!" Jaime called to the cattle. Slowly, one at a time, the animals made their way down the mountainside towards Pepe. Immediately they smelled the water as surely as if it had given off the aroma of cooked food. Seven animals drank at one time. The water remained clear and free of filth.

"It's good," Chavo said proudly, as he watched the animals drink.

"Our father was a smart man," Jaime replied.

Pepe smiled. He felt happy and excited. He looked over the mountains and down the canyons below. He loved this land. He thought, maybe God had given him the miracle that he had asked for. The presence of his father permeated the ranch as if he were standing right there with them. A chill ran through Pepe, and he shuddered. "Vamonos, let's block off the well securely. The animals will never need to go into the drinking water again," Pepe said to his brothers.

They worked the rest of the day filling the trench and building the strongest barracade they had ever constructed. They laughed and joked as they worked. The sun slid behind the mountains as they rode their horses back up the trail to the house. Chavo's voice sounded pure; his song echoed across the mountains. Susana Rios could not understand how her sons returned in such a good mood. She did not question them. She too felt the strong presence of her husband. It was enough.

CHAPTER TEN

The sun parched the land. The earth turned hard like stone. The tiny sheaths of corn that took hold after the first rains wilted and lay dying against the dry dirt. Movement became slow. Even the birds did not sing with enthusiasm. Townspeople filled the churches and prayed for rain. Some said the drought was a sign and that suffering and death would soon befall their lands.

CHAPTER ELEVEN

Pepe could not understand the change in Miranda. His older brother talked like he was employed by Conejo. Pepe flew into a rage. Never would his father have agreed to such an outrageous price. Susana Rios was not sure about the forty percent, but she figured it was better than no profit at all. Miranda refused to talk about the subject any further; and Susana, watching the suffering caused by the drought, was content with any money they could receive.

The family saw little of Miranda. He spent most afternoons at Conejo's ranch. Pepe tried to speak to him, but he insisted that nothing needed to be said. Miranda made it clear to the family that he was taking his father's place and that he would handle the business. Even Jaime, who respected Miranda more than anyone, could see the change in him. He claimed that taking care of the business was a full time affair. And while Miranda spent more and more time with Rosa, Conejo started to come over and visit Susana.

Conejo told Susana how he loved Toribio like his own brother. He felt a responsibility to the Rios family, and if he could be of any help, she should call upon him any time. Susana thanked Conejo, but she could see that he was not as virtuous as he appeared. Still, she would not dismiss his offer completely.

The sun continued its relentless war. Susana felt terrified when she saw the seedlings of corn wither and die. She purchased beans and corn with the money from the sale of the cattle. The prices had increased throughout the valley, since many vendors knew there would be no harvest this year.

Susana went into Juchipila and bought each of her girls a dress and shoes. She bought her sons new shirts. Pepe tried telling her that the money would not last if she spent it foolishly. She did not think that spending money on clothes for her children was foolish.

As the months passed and the rains failed to appear, the supply of food dwindled. Miranda practically lived at Conejo's. And as for Conejo, he moved to Guadalajara. It was said that there he enjoyed life with the generals and staff of President Porfirio Diaz.

Pepe felt lost. Each day he would come across the carcass of another cow. He was certain that at least ten animals, young, healthy calves, had been stolen. Desperation was everywhere. He saw it in the eyes of his fellow ranchers, their wives and children. He understood the drought and knew the damage it could cause. He could even see how the crisis could force friends to steal from one another. He thanked the drought for one thing: the fear of starvation and loss of property caused him to think less of his father's death.

He and Jaime discussed ways to make money without selling what remained of their livestock. When Miranda found out that they had sold many of their best animals, he became enraged. He and Pepe argued until neither made any sense. Susana stopped them. Miranda stormed off to Conejo's ranch.

Pepe, Jaime, Chavo and Ramon worked hard to round up the cows that roamed the steep mountains. After five continuous days in the saddle, they herded three calves, five cows and a bull. It was all that remained of a herd of seventy-eight.

Corraled, the animals appeared agitated. They struck their horns against the rock walls of the corral. They cried out, deep, dry rasping moans. The boys called out to them by name, trying to calm them down. There was little feed, and the water from the pond was nearly gone.

Pepe saw his mother sweeping dirt from the porch. He walked over to her. "Are the children here?" he asked.

She shook her head, "Only Margarita. The rest have gone to bring water." Margarita was the other eight-year-old twin.

"How does she feel?"

"Not too well."

"Mama. I will be the first to die before I let anyone here starve," he said, brushing at his pants.

"No one will starve," she said.

"But everything seems so bad."

"I know, hijo. When your father died, he took everything with him. All of us are ignorant of the business," she said, looking up as the girls walked into the patio through the gate.

"I can learn," Pepe said, excitedly. I'll go to Juchipila for a month or so. My friend Romulo, his father owns a grocery store. I am sure he can teach me something about business."

Bougainvillea heard Pepe as she walked up to the house. "Maybe we can sell the ranch and buy a grocery store in town," she said.

"No!" Pepe screamed, "how can you even think of that? I would rather die than sell the land."

"You are talking crazy, Pepe. If we lived in town, Ramon and the girls could go to school with other children. We could buy a nice house. My mother could have a garden. We would no longer battle the dust and the smell of cattle."

"Bougainvillea, you do not understand what land means. Generations have died so that we can own this land."

"Ay, Pepito. You are so sentimental."

"That's enough talk about selling the land. We won't speak of it any more," Susana said. She did not let on that the thought had also crept into her mind. Out of respect for her husband she would struggle to keep the land, as long as possible.

"Cristina," Susana called out, "go warm up the beans."

Susana tried feeding the children once a day. They cried and begged her to give them more. Usually she gave in and served them a small plate of beans in the morning.

She explained that one good meal each day was plenty. They should be thankful that they were not poor like other children who had no food to eat at all.

Pepe told them stories about hermits who lived in the mountains, dedicating their lives to God and practically eating nothing at all. "Imagine," he said, "in the monastaries, big, cold cement buildings, the monks get up early in the morning when it's still dark and the air is cold from the blowing wind. In freezing little rooms they read their Bibles by candlelight. After reading and praying they go out into the cold and work in the gardens or milk the cows."

"Do they ride horses like you and Ramon and Jaime and Chavo?" asked Rojita.

"Horses! No, they don't ride horses," Pepe said, sounding dramatic. "The good monks must walk every place they go. And do you know how they get food?"

Celia and Rojita, and even Ramon, wide-eyed, shook their heads.

"They go through the town knocking on doors and begging for a little bread. If no one gives them bread, then," he said shrugging his shoulders, "they don't eat. And sometimes they go for days and days without eating anything at all. They just drink water."

"Pepe, why do men want to become monks?" Celia asked.

"They dedicate their lives to God. They believe that by always praying and thinking about God they will become closer to him. They also say that since many of us do not pray, well then, they are also praying for us. Do you know, some say they have even seen Jesus and the Virgin and the saints."

"Do you think they have seen Juan Diego?" Rojita asked.

"Oh, I imagine they have. Don't you think it would be a beautiful thing to see Jesus or the Virgin? Then all the prayer and suffering would be worth the wait, no?"

Ramon, sitting on his usual stool by the door, said, "But what about the ones who pray and pray and suffer and do not see anything?"

"Bueno, I remember one story about a monk who was praying. He knelt down and his eyes were closed in deep prayer, see; then an angel comes down from heaven and stands right beside him. 'I am an angel sent from heaven,' the angel says. And the monk does not even look up. You know what the monk says to the angel?"

"What?" replied the three children.

"The monk, he says," Pepe bowed his head as if in prayer, "he says, 'Angel, I do believe you are from the Lord, but I think that you have made a mistake and are visiting the wrong monk. There are others here much worthier than I.'"

"Why would he say that? After praying and praying and suffering, you mean he doesn't want to see a real angel?"

"No. You don't understand, Ramon. By praying and being alone for so many years, a monk learns that he is no better than a tree, a rock or even a piece of dirt. He becomes humble. And the things that are so important to us mean nothing to him."

"That sounds dumb, Pepe," Celia giggled.

"Si, hija, you are probably right. But what I am trying to say is this, you should be thankful even for one plate of beans every day. There are others who have much less. When your stomach hurts, just remember the monks."

"Then you think we will see Jesus, Pepe?" Rojita asked, seriously.

Pepe raised one finger in the air and said, "Only once and no more," not even understanding why he said such a thing.

Margarita, shivering with fever, sat straight up in bed, "There, look!" she screamed, "do you see him? He has no clothes, only a cloth around his waist."

"Shh, hija," Susana placed her arms around Margarita, trying to comfort her, "No hay nadie. Try to sleep, no one is there."

"No! No! He's big and dark," she insisted, pulling herself back against her mother's breast. She screamed, "Mama, he is coming to get me. Please, please don't let him take me away," she cried.

"You see," Bougainvillea said, looking angrily at Jaime and Chavo, "you come back from the mountains telling stories of Indians and silver and lost temples and murders. Snakes don't scare the girls as badly as you two."

"It's true, there is a temple ... "

Susana cut Chavo off, "Enough. I do not need you to start arguing now."

Worried that her twin sister might die, Rojita started to cry. "Mama, what's wrong with Margarita?"

"Stop crying and go sit over with Ramon," Bougainvillea said, sternly.

Pepe soaked a rag in the water jug. He gave it to his mother who placed the wet cloth on Magarita's forehead. The heat from the fever quickly warmed the cloth. Margarita's face turned from a bright red to a pale white color. Susana began to worry.

"Pepe, you must go for help. She needs medicine. Go to Conejo's and see if Miranda can help," Susana ordered.

Pepe hesitated. He had not spoken to Miranda in weeks. He swore he would never ask Miranda for anything again. Pepe looked at his little sister, she lay shivering in bed. This is different, he thought to himself. I must go.

Pepe ran to the corral. He felt the air press against his chest. There was no relief from the night's heat. He opened the door to the rock hut where the tools and riding equipment hanged on the walls. He pulled a saddle from the wall, a bridle from the table and quickly saddled a horse.

As he rode through the gate, he heard the sounds of riders coming towards the ranch. Dismounting, Pepe made his way along the rock wall which separated the house from the open fields. He stood close to the wall where he could not be seen. He watched as two riders approached. They opened the gate and rode into the patio.

Few people traveled through the mountains at night; and a strict rule among the people was to call out for an invitation before entering a man's property. Pepe's stomach turned as a frigidness crept into him. Tying his horse to a rock, he leaped over the wall and ran around the house. Sneaking to the opposite side of the patio, Pepe situated himself so he could get a better view of the two men. The moon was shaped into a smile and many stars lighted the night. Pepe stayed in the shadows.

"You knock first," he heard one of the riders say. "Let's see what we have here."

"Maybe the rancher has a daughter to help us forget about this heat," said the other rider as he dismounted, keeping his voice low.

Pepe felt his heart begin to pump faster. He watched as the man walked to the door and pounded hard. Moving quickly and quietly, Pepe positioned himself behind the tree in the center of the patio.

One man remained on his horse, a large pistol holstered at his waist. He appeared to wear a light colored uniform. His boots were leather and nearly reached his knees.

"Who is there?" came a weak voice from inside the house. Pepe knew it was Jaime.

"We are two riders in need of directions, and a little food if there is any to spare."

After a moment of silence the voice from inside replied, "There is sickness here. Tell me where you are going, and I will try to help."

"Señor, we have been traveling two weeks. We ask only a little rest and a chance to cool off. If you have little food we understand. Food is scarce. We can do without that. But if you are children of Christ, please allow us a little water and rest."

The man on the horse, placing his hands at the corners of his mouth to keep his voice low, whispered, "Ay, Lalo, that was very good, muy bonito, hombre."

"Señor, we have but two days to reach our families," the man pleaded. Pepe stepped quietly away from the tree to the rock hut some twenty yards behind him.

"My wife is with child and my family has little food," the grand actor continued, "I am on my way from Guadalajara where I have made some money. My brother and I must travel all the way to Zacatecas. I have debts to pay and the collectors will be waiting. If I do not arrive, I hate to think what they'll do to my wife and children."

Pepe unlocked the clasp on the door of the rock hut and entered. Slowly, he opened the shutters to let in a little evening light so he could see. Desperately staring into the darkness he tried to think what he could use as a weapon.

The pick was too heavy and awkward. The shovel would not do. A rope would be useless against guns. He saw his father's machete. He took the heavy blade down from the wall. Gripping the instrument firmly, he felt himself very strong.

As he made his way out the door, Pepe accidentaly kicked the plow. The man on the horse heard the sharp clank and turned. He saw only the shadow of the huge oak tree and the outline of the hut in the distance.

"Who's there? Speak ... I heard you," he called out.

In panic, Pepe creeped along the outside wall of the hut, keeping himself in the shadows.

"Who is there, I say?"

Instinctively, Pepe screamed, "Move, cabron, and I'll blow your head off."

Pepe saw the man freeze in the saddle.

"You, by the door, move back or I'll kill you where you stand," Pepe threatened, continuing the pretense.

"We only want a little food," the rider explained.

"Shut your mouth!" Both men tried to see from where the voice came, but Pepe hid himself well.

"Jaime," Pepe screamed.

"What?" came Jaime's voice from within.

"There are two them of out here, thieves, madmen, maybe both. Get the carbine ... "

"Now listen to me," said the man on foot, "we meant no harm. Let us ride away."

The blood raced through Pepe's veins. He could not back down, and he felt that if he let them go, they would soon return.

"You think I'm stupid, you horse's ass. You're going to wish you never saw this ranch.

"Jaime! Point the carbine directly at the front door. Chavo. Do you hear me?"

"Yes, Pepe."

"Grab the pistol. Have Ramon open the door; we are going to butcher two pigs." Pepe let out a devilish laugh, trying to sound as wicked as possible. Maybe if he could scare them badly enough, they would not return.

An explosion shattered the night. Pepe heard a bullet tear into the rock wall above his head. The rider had drawn his pistol, fired and fallen to the ground. The other man threw himself up against a wall and drew his pistol.

"All right," screamed the man nearest the porch, "let's see now who will do the butchering, kid."

"Pepe, what is it? What happened?" called Jaime.

"Don't open the door," Pepe yelled out, "keep it locked."

Both men crawled towards the rock hut. Terrified, Pepe leaped over the rock wall behind the hut and ran through the dry grass, making his way to the back of the house.

"Jaime, let me in," he cried, banging on the thick wooden shutters.

The shutters flew open, and Pepe jumped into the house. Jaime and Chavo closed the shutters and placed a metal bar across them.

"Mama, quickly, take the children to the corner. Make them sit down on the floor."

"Ay, Pepe, let's give them what they want and let them go away," said Susana.

"I heard them talking, Mama. They are criminals. They want to rob us," he looked at Bougainvillea and Cristina, "and do much more."

"Let's go out and get them," said Jaime, excited.

"No!" cried Susana. "Stay inside, it is safer."

"We must do something," Chavo said to Pepe, "we can't stay locked in here."

The younger girls began crying. Everything seemed confusing. Pepe reached down and picked up the machete from the floor.

"All right, listen. I'm sure they have enough guns to fight a war. There are two them and three of us," he tried to reason.

"There are four of us," announced Ramon, bravely, as he stepped forward.

"Five," said Bougainvillea, also moving closer to the boys.

As if an earthquake had struck, the back shutters and front door trembled on the heavy metal hinges.

"Ah ha, you fooled us one time, but not two times. Now let us in or we will burn this place down," came a raspy voice from the front of the house.

"There's nothing here for you. Leave us alone," Ramon yelled.

"Shh," Pepe warned, whispering, "don't say anything. The less they know, the better."

"What if we kill a horse or two. Will that bring you out?" laughed the man at the back window.

"We have done nothing to you. What is it you want?" Pepe said, trying to salvage some time to think.

"Open the door and we'll tell you."

Pepe looked around the room. He walked over to a bed, grabbed a wool blanket and handed it to Jaime.

"When I give the signal, roll the blanket into a ball and set it on fire," Pepe whispered.

"Come on, you are wasting time. Open the door." The voice demanded. Both men continued banging at the doors and shutters.

"Ramon, when I give the word you open the door. Chavo, take the blanket. Jaime will light it and you throw it into the man's face. Jaime, take the pistol and fire to the right of the porch. I will fire to the left side with the rifle. Bougainvillea, if they get in, you use the machete."

"Light the blanket." Pepe ordered.

Jaime lit the match and placed it at one end of the coarse blanket. Chavo blew the flames to make them rise higher.

"Mama, blow out the lamp." The lamp went out, leaving the room completely dark except for the erratic flame of the burning blanket.

"Señor, we are opening the door. There is only me and my brothers and sisters. Please do not harm us," Pepe called to the men outside.

The banging stopped. Pepe waited about thirty seconds and nodded at Ramon to open the door. Ramon lifted the metal latch and pulled back the door. Chavo stepped up and threw the blazing ball into the night. A rifle blast lit the porch. The bullet caught Ramon in the forehead and threw him back against a bed. Pepe and Jaime both fired their weapons into the man who crouched down at one corner of the porch. The force of the bullets lifted him to his feet, spun him around and pushed him into the dirt.

The other man appeared from the darkness and ran into the house. He pressed his rifle to Pepe's throat, but before he could get off a round, Bougainvillea struck with the machete, slicing through half of the man's neck. He collapsed with a moan as the children and Susana screamed.

Pepe tried to calm everyone down. The smell of smoke and death filled the little room. A small flame lit the porch as the blanket continued to burn.

"Chavo, light the lamp," Pepe yelled above the screaming voices. Chavo, after a moment of searching through the darkness, found the lamp. Quickly, the light filled the room.

Dark stains splattered the walls. The head had been nearly severed off the man hit by Bougainvillea's machete. Chavo dragged him outside.

"Is everyone all right?" Pepe said, trying to speak above the cries.

Jaime saw Ramon's body first. It was crumpled and shoved against a bedpost. Jaime screamed, covered his eyes and backed away.

Susana ran from where she had been standing. She said nothing but walked over to her youngest son, knelt down and brought him to her breast. She held him tightly, then began rocking as if putting him to sleep. Still, she did not cry. Calmly, she asked for a wet rag to wash the blood from his face. The bullet had torn away much of his head. Susana wrapped his head in the cloth so that the others would not see him.

Pepe noticed that one of Ramon's huaraches was missing. He moved around the room, numbly, until he found it. Chavo cried along with the rest of the girls. Jaime stood in a corner unable to hear, see or talk.

Pepe moved close to Ramon. Gently, he removed his little brother's other sandle. He took a cloth and wiped the mud from Ramon's feet. As he wiped the mud his tears fell onto the toes. He rubbed the tears into the warm skin. When both feet were clean, Pepe bent down and placed a kiss on each foot, then he slipped the huaraches back onto his young brother's feet.

CHAPTER TWELVE

Pepe and Chavo dragged the two bodies across the patio to the side of the rock hut where Toribio and their grandfather had excavated the land many years earlier. Toribio had once told his sons that he and his father had unearthed the remains of four people. The bones had been the thickness of grown men. The heads had appeared larger than normal, but the bodies were no more than four feet in height. They also said that they had found stone tools that were buried with each body. No one was ever told of the discovery, since they feared losing their land to the government.

"Leave them here, tomorrow we will bury them," Pepe said.

Chavo coughed. He began spitting mucous. He tried not to vomit, but he could hold it no longer. Running to the side of the corral, he threw up violently for a long time. Pepe brought him a cup of water. Chavo rinsed his mouth. Neither of them wanted to go back to the house. They listened as the girls continued to cry. Pepe blamed himself for Ramon's death.

Susana and Cristina lifted Ramon's body and placed it on one of the beds. They covered him with a blanket. A scream pierced the air. It came from the kitchen. Susana and Cristina arrived first, followed by Pepe and Chavo. Jaime wandered around the patio.

Bougainvillea had placed Margarita on a straw mat in the kitchen. Margarita's body shook as if a demon had entered. Her eyes flew back into her head and her mouth closed tightly.

Pepe pushed through the screaming children and grabbed his little sister. He could feel the heat from her body warm his hands.

"Quick, get me some water," he commanded.

Bougainvillea reached for a rag and began to wet it.

"No, bring the whole jug."

Chavo grabbed the heavy, red earthen jug and poured water into a cup. Pepe took the cup and poured the water over Margarita's head. He took off her dress and soaked her body. Susana massaged her daughter's legs and feet, hoping to keep the circulation going.

"Chavo, pour the whole jug over her, slowly."

Chavo tilted the jug and slowly poured the water over Margarita's body, trying to bring down the temperature. The convulsions stopped. Her eyes closed and she lay motionless.

No one spoke. Susana held her breath. Pepe placed his ear over Margarita's mouth. He felt no sign of breathing.

"Margarita!" Celia, her twin sister, finally called out.

"No. No, por favor, no." It was the first time the children had seen their mother express pain. Susana looked towards the ceiling with the fierceness of an Indian priestess preparing to battle the heavens. Suddenly, Margarita opened her eyes. The fever had broken. She took deep, shaky breaths. Although exhausted, she managed a smile as she recognized her mother.

"Quickly, get a blanket," Pepe ordered.

Susana looked down at her daughter. Tears came to her eyes. She felt ashamed before God. She made the sign of the cross and silently begged forgiveness.

CHAPTER THIRTEEN

Pepe and Chavo buried Ramon next to their father's grave. A number of wooden crosses marked the sites where other family members had been buried. Toribio told the children that he could never remember which was his father's grave or his grandfather's grave, but this made little difference, he made his children understand that the family, generations past, were buried in this plot, and that was all that mattered.

Jaime had not spoken since Ramon's death. His eyes appeared blank and lifeless. Cristina took his arm and led him from one place to another. Susana worried about him but did not know what to do.

Rojita and Celia stood close to Susana as Pepe placed the last shovels of dirt over Ramon's grave. Miranda and Conejo remained off to one side.

Chavo cried silently. Miranda shot him an angry look. Chavo stared back at his older brother without fear. Angrily, Miranda turned away.

Pepe spoke, "What does one say to a child who died for his family. Ramoncito was a man. He stood by his family. He cried and shared his pain, making the rest of us realize that we cannot hide from pain. Ramon will not be forgotten. He will live within each of us. He will add strength to our lives and help us through hard times."

Pepe hesitated. He looked at the adobe house in the distance. A shimmer of sunlight sparkled, perhaps a reflection from a stone or glass. Pepe watched as the bright ray expanded and quickly vanished.

"Ramon is in heaven. He will see the Virgin. He will see angels and speak to the saints since he is now one of them."

Pepe looked at Miranda as he continued speaking, "Milagro, how the youngest brother grew to be the bravest and the most responsible."

Miranda felt the rage inside him. He hated Pepe for these words. Pepe tried to say more but was too close to tears to speak. The girls cried softly. Susana felt numb. She could not think clearly. She performed on instinct and habit. Turning, she took the girls by the hands and led them back to the house. Cristina took Jaime's arm and led him like one of the animals. They walked up the hill to the house.

Miranda walked over to Pepe and Chavo. Both boys turned their backs to him and walked off. They made their way toward the corral. Neither of them said anything.

Pepe saw that the animals needed water. Later he and Chavo would take them to drink. He then saw Conejo enter the house. Automatically he clenched his hands. He felt the heat rise to his chest.

"The bastard has no business in there with my mother," Pepe said to Chavo.

Before Chavo could answer, they both saw Miranda approaching. They began to walk away.

"Wait!" Miranda called, "don't act like two idiots."

They turned and waited to hear what he had to say.

"How was I to know anything like this would happen. If I thought any of you was in danger, I would never have left."

Miranda waited for one of them to respond, but neither spoke.

"Why didn't you tell me you needed help. I didn't know you were having such a bad time." He paused, trying to decipher their expressions.

"Conejo has been like a father to ... " Immediately he knew that he had said the wrong thing. Pepe looked down at the ground. Miranda continued speaking, trying to cover his mistake, "If I knew you were in any trouble, I would have come right away."

Chavo looked at him calmly, spit on the dry earth and said, "Why don't you go back to your whore."

Miranda's fist caught Chavo high on the cheek. The blow snapped his head back and sent him stumbling against the corral wall. Miranda moved forward to hit Chavo again. Pepe pushed Miranda, catching him off balance.

"If that is as hard as you can hit," said Chavo, "it's better that you were not here with us; you might have gotten hurt."

Again Miranda started towards Chavo. Pepe jumped in front of him. "You can beat us one at a time, but together we'll destroy you," Pepe warned, looking straight into Miranda's eyes. Miranda controlled the urge to slap Pepe across the face.

"Listen to me," Miranda said, "Conejo and I have returned to help. You cannot handle the ranch. Most of the cattle have died or been sold."

"Or stolen," Pepe said, accusingly. Miranda did not respond to the remark.

"I have learned much from Conejo. In a short time I will be able to run the ranch."

"We can manage the ranch ourselves," Pepe replied.

"You'll starve and so will my mother and the children."

"What concern is that of yours?" Chavo said.

"We are still a family."

"Family. Ha, you weren't much of our family when Ramon was killed," Pepe told him.

"Goddamn it," screamed Miranda, "I couldn't do anything about that. I would do anything to bring Ramon back. I loved him too. How was I to know someone would try to rob the house?"

"How do you know they were thieves?" Pepe asked.

"My mother told me." Pepe looked at Chavo as if asking him to explain something.

"The two men wore soldiers' uniforms. They had money, weapons and food, probably they were better off than we."

Miranda appeared confused, "Then what did they want?"

"We think someone sent them. Maybe the same person who killed my father," said Pepe.

"No one killed our father. I told you before, his death was an accident."

"Well, something is going on. First our father is killed, then our cattle is sold at a ridiculous price, other animals have been stolen from us, and two murderers attack the ranch. Are you going to tell me it is all coincidence?" Pepe asked, his voice angry.

Miranda spoke as if he had not heard a word that Pepe had said. "Now listen. Conejo and I have been talking. He knows many people, important people. He has made money while everyone else is losing theirs. Nothing stops him. He knows business."

"So what?" Pepe responded quickly.

"So what? Don't be stupid. Conejo can make us all very wealthy. But first we must join forces with him."

"What the fuck is this idiot talking about?" Pepe said to Chavo. Chavo shrugged his shoulders.

"With our land and Conejo's land joined together, we will have more than any other landowner in the region," Miranda explained, excitedly.

Pepe looked at his older brother closely. It seemed as though he were under some spell. Miranda had never gotten excited over anything before. Other than herding cattle, he tried to stay clear of ranch work or business.

"You mean you want us to sell out to Conejo?" Pepe asked, curiously.

"No, nothing like that." Miranda paused before uttering his next words. He wanted no misunderstanding. Closely, he looked at his younger brothers and said, "Conejo will ask my mother to marry him."

No one spoke for a long time. Without warning, Pepe burst out laughing, "My mother was married to a man. Do you think she will settle for a rabbit? She will spit in his face," Pepe said.

When Susana Rios heard Conejo's proposition she did not spit. She listened very carefully. He made the entire offer of marriage come across like a business deal, which he explained it really was. No such thing as romance was involved, he told her. He knew how she felt about Toribio, and he knew that no one could take Toribio's place. It would be a marriage of convenience and prosperity, he told her, nothing more.

Conejo promised that the children would lack nothing. He would buy a house for them in town so the children could attend school. Miranda and the boys could manage the ranch, and Conejo would handle the business. Everyone would inherit a piece of land. The family would never lack money or food.

Later that night Susana told the family that she had decided to accept Conejo's offer. She explained that there was no other way. She did not want to lose the ranch, and she did not want to lose any more of her family.

Pepe argued and pleaded, trying to make her understand that everything would work out. A little time to learn the business was all that he and Chavo needed. Susana countered that there was no time left.

Angrily, Pepe turned and walked from the house. He saddled his horse and rode through the gate, into the cornfield and across a long mesa that led to the tallest mountains.

Pepe could not get a grip of his senses. The anger within

him sizzled. He dug his spurs into the horse's sides and galloped through the darkness. He tried to put everthing into perspective, but nothing made sense. Pepe could not get the idea out of his head that all the events of the past months had somehow been an ingenious plan. But the loose ends he encountered seemed to flounder in all directions. He could tie nothing together.

He thought of riding to Conejo's ranch and talking to Miranda. But Miranda had already been carried away on the same emotional flood as his mother. He tried to think of someone who could give him some answers. Rosa's name entered his mind.

Of course, he thought, Rosa. Pepe knew of her relationship with his brother. He also knew that Conejo had kept her on the ranch many years. Pepe had once met her at a Bible reading. He knew that she must have answers. Women always had answers.

In Mexico the women were always kept in the positions of listening but not of speaking. They went about their daily tasks as if they were mute. After so many years of this, the men unconsciously programmed themselves into believing that women knew nothing. Pepe had learned this well. In his travel through the mountains, he realized it was always the women who knew everything.

But what if he did talk to Rosa, he began to think, was he any better off knowing the truth? Would his mother or Miranda believe any different? And the truth, he laughed, once he discovered one truth, perhaps there would exist another to uncover behind that one, and possibly even another, until all truths became distorted and reverted back to lies.

Pepe jumped from his horse, walked to the edge of a cliff and looked over the sea of darkness that lay before him. He could barely see the outline of his L-shaped adobe home in the distance.

How could his mother make such an incredible decision as to marry Conejo? he wondered. As far as Pepe was concerned, the idea was blasphemous to his father's memory. Such a thing was inconceiveable, and he grew angry at his mother. In a near rage he vowed that on the day of the marriage, if it should take place, he would leave home forever.

Forever? Where would he go? The ranch was all he knew. His father had nurtured a love within each of his children, teaching them that the land was the family lifeline. The land chained each of them together. It was the foundation of their basic beliefs. Without the land they were nothing. And now, sadly enough, Pepe found himself questioning even that belief.

Why was the land so important? Other men had left the ranches and made new lives in the cities and towns. Even some of his childhood friends had moved to Guadalajara and were attending school. Why could a person not travel far away and begin over again?

Pepe thought about the land to the north. It was a land covered with trees and snow and large rivers and lakes. Men had built cities where motor cars roared through the streets. On Sundays, Pepe had been told, orchestras performed in the parks; and the people, dressed in nice clothes, listened all day to the music. There were schools and stores and homes and hotels. There were never droughts, and everyone had plenty of food.

Pepe grew excited as he thought about such a place. He could go to school and read all of the books he wanted. He could even become a teacher, a real teacher, and stand before a group of students and discuss ideas.

"Without land you are like an uprooted plant." Pepe heard the words as though his father had just spoken them. His heart fell and confusion split his mind. Would a curse follow him if he left the land? Perhaps God might punish him for deserting the family. He did not want to hurt his mother or his brothers or sisters. Each member of his family was also a part of himself. Even Miranda, after all of his cruelty, was still his brother and nothing would destroy that bond.

After all, was it not Miranda who jumped into the flooded river to save Pepe when he was a child? And Miranda again who carried Pepe over his shoulders for half a day, when a scorpion had stung him? Miranda had borne the burden of caring for the family in the days when his mother and father had been forced to journey for three weeks to Guadalajara.

The family and the land were one. The river, the canyons and the mesas, the valley and the mountains had all educated him. He had played in every cave, walked every inch of the land chasing cattle from one ranch to another. He had seen part of his family die here. He had helped wipe his father's blood from the stone porch. He had learned here how to work, how to cry, how to laugh, how to fight, how to kill and how to die.

It was one thing to say that he would leave this ranch if his mother married Conejo; it was another to do it.

Pepe knelt down on one knee. He picked up a handful of dirt and ground the granules in his palm. He closed and opened his hand. The dirt slipped through his fingers and fell from the corners of his hand. Mexico was this one handful of earth. Mexico was way out beyond the mesa. Mexico lived in each breath that he took.

CHAPTER FOURTEEN

Susana Rios sat on a chair inside her house. She could hear her children outside. She knew that Conejo and the Justice of the Peace were among them. She felt calm, curiously calm, but had told everyone she needed a few minutes to herself. So she came inside and sat down.

Pepe would forgive her. He would understand the severity of the problem once he grew older. He was still young, she told herself. Someday he would even thank her for the sacrifice she was making. She needed Pepe and would do nothing to hurt him, but sometimes adults are forced to make decisions their children can't understand.

Bougainvillea and Cristina offered their support. Somehow they understood. A few nights before, they had spoken of love.

"It is rare that men and women marry because of love," Susana had said, frankly.

"Then for what other reason do people marry?" Cristina asked.

"Security, companionship, for fear of being alone," answered Susana.

"I'm eighteen years old," said Bougainvillea, "already three men have wanted to marry me, since I was fourteen. But Mama," she said, looking at Susana, "I do believe in love, and I don't think I could marry a man for any other reason."

"Yes, hija, you are growing older, and you have hopes that Fernando will marry you, isn't that true?"

Bougainvillea nodded yes to her mother.

"And if he does not ask, what then? Will you wait around and wrinkle, wake every morning by yourself with no one to share your life. People become desperate, daughter. They reach for whatever salvation is available. Love exists, and how lucky are they who recognize it and take hold before it gets away. It's not a thing that comes often."

"And you, Mama, you and my father loved each other?" Cristina had never asked her mother such a personal question. Susana had never spoken of it, nor did she ever feel comfortable talking about such things to her children. But this was different. Her daughters could enter marriage at any time, and they had to know.

"I was fourteen," Susana began. "My mother, two sisters and I knelt alongside the river washing clothes. I had heard that there was a certain Toribio Rios, the son of a wealthy rancher, who liked me. One day, a girlfriend pointed him out. I didn't like his looks, especially after he whistled at me in front of a crowd of people.

"As we washed our clothes, we became tired. We finished and it was time to return to the house. When we turned we saw the three men on horses a short distance from us. I recognized your father immediately.

"I could tell they had been drinking by the way they laughed and slapped each other on the back. Their horses blocked the trail. My mother asked them what they wanted. Your father was very polite towards her and said that he had come to take his future wife.

"With that he rode forward. I backed away, frightened of this man I didn't know. My sisters began to cry, and my mother pleaded with your father to leave us alone. I dropped the clothes that I carried and ran into the river. I heard the hooves of the horses behind me. The next thing I knew I was being lifted from the water and placed on a horse. I struggled, pounding my fists against your father's chest and trying to scratch his eyes. He just laughed and held me around the waist as he rode off to his father's ranch. Then he turned me over to his mother."

"But did your brothers do nothing?" asked Cristina.

"My brothers were drunk most of the time. Besides, we were poor, your father rich. When your father kidnapped me, he also took away food from my mother's table, because we made our money washing clothes. But he proved to be a good man, and once I became obedient to him, he saw that my mother and sisters never lacked anything.

"Were you angry with him?" Bougainvillea asked.

Susana smiled, "I did not speak to him for two months. He could not get a word out of me. But finally his mother convinced me that I should marry him."

"Eventually you came to love him, didn't you?"

"Cristina, I don't think that love is a thing that develops; you either love a man or you don't. Let us say that I respected your father."

It hurt the girls to think that their mother probably never experienced love.

"You did not love my father?" asked Cristina, with a note of sadness.

Susana thought before answering. She looked into the anxious faces of her girls. "Yes, I loved him," she finally said. She lied. Susana was shaken from her memories by a hard knock on the door. "Enter," she said, and Pepe walked in.

"How do you know that Conejo did not plan my father's death to gain control of our land?" He looked desperate, and he hadn't slept for days.

Susana nodded her head and looked up at her son.

"Pepe, did Conejo also cause the drought that wiped out our food?"

He felt disappointed. He could not offer a strong argument.

"I don't know, Mama. Right now I understand little. I feel so confused."

"Life is not an easy thing to understand," she said.

"Listen, Mama," Pepe interjected, "I know that my father was killed the same night he visited Conejo's ranch. I know that Ramoncito was killed by two men we have never seen before. They were not only trying to rob us but to terrorize us. Look at Miranda, the one who always saved us in time of trouble; he was lured away when we needed him most. And I know one more thing for certain," Pepe's words rushed from his mouth as if he'd lost control of them. "When you marry Conejo, our land will become his."

Susana could not believe that everything was a conspiracy. Pepe made sense, but he was young and still had much to learn. "Listen to me, Pepe. I know one thing, and that is when I marry Conejo we will all be secure again. You and your brothers will each receive a portion of the land. You don't need to worry about him stealing our land. He promised me that everyone will receive shares. We will put it on paper."

"Ay, Mama," Pepe felt the strain, "it isn't only the land. It is our lives. Is this the man you want to raise your children? How can you expect us to accept a replacement for our father so soon after his death? You don't love this man. Or maybe you never loved my father." Susana's hand struck quickly. Pepe took the blow. He didn't move.

"You are confused, and you don't understand. Please, I would like to be alone before the ceremony."

Pepe realized that it was over. He turned and stepped from the room.

Conejo, Miranda and the Justice of the Peace stood near the oak tree. They laughed loudly. Chavo sat with Jaime near the corrals. Jaime had still not spoken since Ramon's death. Bougainvillea and Cristina cleaned the younger girls and combed their hair.

A little while later people began to arrive. Some brought bar-b-que goat, others brought beans and tortillas; these were the more fortunate, the ones who were surviving the drought. All were happy and ready for the wedding to begin.

Pepe watched his mother emerge from the house. She wore a simple dress. Her hair was a litle neater than usual, pulled tightly back in a bun. She didn't smile, but nodded to those present. The Justice of the Peace motioned for her to stand next to Conejo. Miranda and Rosa stood as witnesses.

Pepe felt the heat in his chest as Conejo took Susana's hand. He heard the marriage words mumbled. Pepe could not believe it. Silently he walked through the back gate, along the rock wall and over to the hill where his father and Ramon were buried. He apologized and asked forgiveness. He cried, loud penetrating sobs. Falling to his knees, his body began to shake. In the background, he heard applause come from the patio. It was done.

Instinctively he turned and ran. He ran through the cornfield and up an incline that led to the main road. Small puffs of dust rose from the earth as if following him. His chest heaved, and he gasped for air, but he ran faster. The sun pounded him. Jumping from the main road, he took a trail that led through the thick brush directly down the steep mountain. He grabbed at the harsh limbs to keep himself from falling. Thorns tore at his hands and ripped his pant legs.

Pepe saw a large jackrabbit dash into a clump of rocks and a black snake slither into the brush. But Pepe had no reason to stop. He continued down the mountain, slipping over loose dirt and tripping on rocks. He moved faster and faster, trying to kill the pain that jabbed his heart. Finally, after reaching the bottom of the first mountain, for there were many more to climb and descend, he found a boulder where he rested. Unable to think, he raised his face to the sky and screamed, "Ay, Ma!"

The cry echoed through the mountains and shot between the trees. No one heard.

CHAPTER FIFTEEN

Pepe knew little about his family's history. In the mountains there are things of much more importance. But stories always live and re-live from grandfather to father, father to son, mother to daughter. The funny stories of drunken uncles chasing donkeys through the church during Sunday mass or the tragic stories of sisters killing each other over a common lover, or the tales of passed-along children, cousins who were really brothers and sisters.

The stories travel from generation to generation. But with each new generation many of the older stories become distorted or lost, which causes no problem, for every generation possesses its own arsenal of heroes and clowns, lovers and enemies, vagabonds and saints...a circle in time, a beautiful circle over many lifetimes in which nothing ever really changes, like the waves of the ocean, so many different shapes but all born from and returning to the same sea.

As he wandered through villages and towns, Pepe tried to remember such stories. He tried to see every face, hear every name that ever meant anything to him. The more he remembered the less frightened and lonely he felt. He played this game continuously, and sometimes he felt downhearted because he knew that there were many things and people he would never recall. But everything must mean something or why else did the forgetable exist? Such thoughts, maybe, he felt, were better left unanswered.

After more than thirty days on the road, Pepe reached Saltillo, a growing town in northern Mexico. He made his way through the dirt streets where the poor lived and where an old woman offered him a dry tortilla. He did not stop but made his way across the middle of town and out the other end.

The sun had already disappeared behind the mountains. The

entire horizon sizzled in an orange blaze. He watched but did not contemplate it, not like he would have when he lived on the ranch.

Making his way along the railroad tracks, he found shelter. He looked cautiously at the ashes where a fire had been built, and inspected the wooden slats that leaned against a crumbling brick wall, finally, allowing his tired legs to collapse. Sliding over the dirt, he propped his back up against the brick wall.

What month was it? He thought it was November but he wasn't sure. He remembered hearing someone talking about Christmas. Could it possibly be December? He placed his head on his knees, closed his eyes and thought about a woman he had talked to when passing through the city of Zacatecas.

"I feel as though I'm fifty and have been traveling for years," he told her.

"Why did you leave home?" she had asked.

Pepe tried to hide the memories, kick them down into the dirt and bury them among the dead, but he found that impossible. He often thought about his family. Sometimes the regret of leaving home overpowered him. He blamed himself for his decision and reevaluated the circumstances, but he could not go back. Besides, the situation with the soldiers kept him moving.

He thought about the thunder caused by the pounding of horses' hooves and how he had dashed through alleyways and streets escaping capture. The federal soldiers searched ruthlessly for new recruits. Pepe once watched from a hiding place as the soldiers dragged boys as young as ten years old from their homes.

Everywhere he traveled he saw signs of war. Small bands of rural deputies, not sure which side to fight for, robbed families who barely survived. Large garrisons of federal troops patrolled the towns and cities, coldly executing anyone suspected of sympathizing with the rebels. Sometimes he slept in the mountains, alone among the emptiness and silence, only to awaken at the sound of long exchanges of rifle fire. He would sit and listen and in his mind see Mexicans falling dead. Pepe wanted no part of this thing the people began to call "La Revolucion."

His father had once told him and his brothers that no matter how many wars Mexico fought, nothing would change. The poor would remain poor, and the rich would see to it that they did.

But for the moment, he found himself relaxed and comfortable. He would let the past take care of itself. He felt safe enough snuggled close to this brick wall.

Pepe closed his eyes, but strangely he could not sleep. Since he had not eaten decently in days, his stomach had become numb. Hunger was no longer a pain but a desire. A few centavos remained in his pockets. He would force himself to endure much before spending them. He thought that maybe someone would find him starved to death. What a disgrace, starved to death with money in his pocket. God might even consider such a thing suicide. It could create a difficult last judgement. Pepe laughed out loud. These sudden outbreaks of humor caused by incredible, ridiculous circumstances, somehow held him together. But then came the visions always before sleep.

First, fragmented pictures, singed along the edges, pictures of the road, sometimes dry, sometimes muddy. He saw pictures of mountains, deserts, red flatlands and the sky, never blue, always purple and dissolving like a candle in a fire. In his reverie, he watched as adobe houses crumbled, seeing inside the distorted faces of people struggling to escape. At last came the flood, a wall of water wiping everything clean. But the purification failed to make him feel any better. Often he would wake trembling. The visions entered the same way a flock of sparrows flies solidly clumped together and just as quickly separates and disappears. The visions became a burden, for afterwards came the memories, vivid and real. They touched him deeply and brought smiles and tears. They made him want to rush home, but they also gave him the urgency to move on, farther and farther away.

As he twisted in his slumber, he saw his mother, brothers and sisters. Like a stranger peering in from the outside, the scene within the kitchen came alive.

Susana twirled tiny pieces of diced nopales around the walls of a ceramic pot. Bits of sizzling grease jumped into the air, sometimes landing and burning her dark, wrinkled arms like wood ticks burowing themselves into a branch. As the fire quickly burned, she would reach down under the hearth and pull out another long twig, break it in two and slip it into the low flame. In a minute, as if treated in gunpowder, the stick would erupt into a bright flame.

Over the same grill, next to the nopales, his mother would remove the cover from another dirt colored pot. Steam poured forth into the slightly lit room, filling every corner with the aroma of freshly cooked beans. Tina mashed the chiles, vegetables and spices into salsa that she poured into the frying pork meat.

Pepe's weariness would leave his body. He would forget the pains. Some nights the nightmares of the final months on his father's ranch would come, and some nights he would be soothed with visions of his mother, as he was this night. He never knew at what point the memories turned into dreams. But he curled himself up like a puppy, laid his head into his arms, wrapped his poncho around himself and fell asleep.

CHAPTER SIXTEEN

It was still dark when Pepe opened his eyes. In his weary, sleepy mind, a strange glow penetrated the darkness. He felt the heat warm his sandled feet. Realizing that a fire burned close to him, crackling and hot, he sat up and pulled his poncho around his shoulders to keep off the morning chill.

Pepe watched as a man with heavy Indian features poked at the fire with a stick, moving small twigs into the center of the flames where they quickly ignited.

"Who are you?" The words slipped from Pepe's mouth involuntarily, like a muscle spasm or a cramp.

"Good morning," the man said, turning his head toward Pepe, his dark skin shining against the burning coals. "My name is Rafael. This is my hacienda where you have decided to spend the night."

Pepe looked around at the splintered planks leaning against the brick wall. Rafael laughed and said, "Don't be so critical of my hacienda ... my tastes are quite humble."

"I hope I haven't intruded," said Pepe.

"Of course not. My hacienda is open to everyone. In fact, you have been very considerate, other travelers often crawl into my bed to sleep." Again Rafael laughed, pointing to the blanket beneath the planks.

"I would have slept there too," answered Pepe, "but I couldn't make it the extra few feet."

"That bad, eh?"

Pepe nodded.

"Where are you from?" asked Rafael casually.

"Los Cañones de Juchipila, in the state of Zacatecas."

68

Rafael looked closer at Pepe. He could not see too clearly in the dark, but he could recognize a tough one easily enough.

"You have traveled a long way. Isn't Juchipila near Guadalajara?"

"Yes, maybe a day's ride on horse. Have you been there?"

"Just passed through. It's beautiful country."

"Yes it is."

"Where are you going?"

"North," answered Pepe, proudly. "To the northern border."

Rafael poked his long stick into the fire. From the ashes he pulled a hot tortilla and handed it to Pepe.

"I haven't eaten in two days," Pepe confessed.

"Then take it and eat slowly. It should satisfy the worm for awhile."

The two men chewed silently. A soft breeze blew off the sierras from the north, played with the quivering flames and then moved on. They felt it come, and they felt it go. To country people these things are as alive as a heartbeat. Pepe pulled his poncho tighter. He jerked his head to get the long strands of hair out of his eyes.

"Have you lived here long," Pepe asked.

Rafael tore off a piece of tortilla, placed it on the tip of his tongue, reverently. He did not chew but let it melt slowly, savoring every particle of corn.

"I don't know," answered Rafael. "I've been here long enough to watch a man plant his corn and harvest it, and now the land is being prepared again for planting. Is that long?"

"It seems long to me," said Pepe.

"Ha, then, my friend, you have an eternity ahead of you." Both men remained silent for a long time. At last Rafael spoke. "Why did you leave home?"

Pepe didn't want to answer. He would spare himself the details, he thought. "We owned a large ranch, maybe over a thousand acres. My father died. To provide for the family, my mother began to sell the land. I wasn't needed anymore."

"Was your father murdered?"

Pepe looked at the Indian. He saw confidence and truth in the dark face.

"Maybe, but we never found out. My father was wealthy in cattle and land. Many men envied him. Some of the most envious acted like his best friends."

Rafael knew people. He understood the art of conversation and used it wisely. He could make people unfurl themselves as if they were flowers in springtime. But he knew that if a flower blossomed before its time it was susceptible to sudden frost and death. So he was careful not to let a person reveal their innermost thoughts before they were ready, unless of course, he despised the person. Then he could cripple them.

Pepe wanted to say no more about his family, not yet anyway. If the Indian persisted, Pepe decided that he would simply lie. Maybe it would be better to come straight out and tell the Indian that he cared no more for such talk. Yes, that's what he would do. Pepe opened his mouth to speak, but the Indian's words arrived first.

"Why do you go to the northern border?"

The question caught Pepe by surprise. For an instant, he felt as though the Indian had read his mind. Pepe was thankful for the change of subject. But now he was aware that he had no answer. After a long pause, Pepe said, "I've heard there is much work and no fighting. Maybe I can buy some land."

"There are many different kinds of fighting," Rafael answered. "When men fight with weapons, men can see the enemy and take aim, or even run and hide. But when men wage war with words in a foreign language and care nothing about breaking promises, one stands little chance of survival."

Pepe sat still. He understood Rafael's words but could not grasp the idea. Rafael saw Pepe's bewilderment.

"Mexico has a thief for a president, a henchman for a vice-president and outlaws for politicians and policemen. Isn't that right?" Rafael asked.

"Yes. So?"

"Diaz is a crook. He knows it, and so does everyone else. He doesn't try to hide it. But in the north, men smile and welcome you until they have used every bit of your strength. Then they toss you to one side or send you back to Mexico, unless you are willing to become like them."

Pepe looked curiously at the old man. "How do you know all this?" Pepe asked.

"You don't believe me?"

"It's not that. I'm just curious how you, an old Indian, knows so much about a country like the north."

"Ah, it means nothing whether my words are true or not. The important thing is that now you have heard something different. What you do with it doesn't concern me."

"Well, I don't have any reason not to believe you. But the north still has to be better than Mexico. What kind of life do I have now?" Pepe said, thoughtfully.

"You have the life you have made for yourself."

"I've done nothing. I believe that my life has already been planned out. I'm simply following my path, and if that path leads me north, then that's where I'll go."

"You mean to say that you have no choice in the matter? Are you saying that you have ended up here by my fire because of fate and through no actions of your own?"

"Yes, that's what I believe."

"Humm, that is very convenient," uttered Rafael, nodding his head, as if hearing a joke.

"What do you mean?"

Rafael scratched his stubbled chin. "You accept responsibility for nothing. Somehow, by some miraculous plan you have followed the tracks, just as a train follows its tracks, and you have ended up here. Whatever you do wrong, whoever you hurt along the way, well, it's not your fault, you're simply acting out your role. Right?"

"Yes," answered Pepe, weakly, "that's the way it is."

Rafael let out a roar of laughter.

"I think it is time for me to leave," said Pepe, anxiously.

"You think!" blurted Rafael. "You mean you don't know."

"Of course I know," Pepe answered, angrily. "Haven't I come all this way on my own. I can take care of myself, make my own decisions."

"Yes, I suppose you have, and maybe you can. But Mexico will suffocate you. Your children and their children after them will long for a true home. And after they have been raised in another man's country, with his ways, they will be forever confused. No matter how Americano they become, they will never be satisfied. They will remain a people without a home."

"If you're trying to frighten me, indio, it won't work. Home is wherever a man wishes to remain."

"Boy," Rafael said, as he stood up, "take care. You are not all that you think," he warned.

"I don't understand you," said Pepe, noticeably concerned.

"No, perhaps you don't, not now anyway. But you will, believe me, you will."

As Rafael spoke he wrapped a small pile of tortillas into a soiled white cloth,

"Here, take these. It will keep the worm, if not satisfied, then at least confused."

"Thank you," said Pepe, "I will not forget you," and he turned and headed towards the tall, bare mountains to the north. As he crossed an arroyo he heard the Indian's voice for the last time.

"I know you won't," came the echo.

When Pepe turned for one last look, he saw no fire. The planks were gone and no sign of the Indian remained, only a long, crumbling brick wall. Pepe reached into his sack and felt the tortillas he'd been given. He looked back a second time and everything appeared hazy, as if the world behind him had disintegrated. A painful homesick feeling overcame him. "People without a home," he whispered to himself and then laughed. "Crazy old man. Ha, crazy old Indian." But the feeling in his stomach grew stronger, and he became frightened of himself and the unknown.

CHAPTER SEVENTEEN

A few days later, while preparing to join a group of people heading to El Paso, a small band of rebels surrounded Pepe. His first instinct was to run, but the rifle barrels pointing at him from all angles changed that. Frightened by the bestial reputations of both federales and rebels, he calmly raised his arms in surrender.

He tried to disguise his fear by staring confidently into their faces. A man with a wooden stump strapped to one leg gave the orders. He wore a straw hat, the front brim folded upwards revealing the face of a handsome, hardened rebel of about thirty. His shirt and pants appeared of good quality, although they were ragged and dirty. Heavily armed, he carried a rifle, and strapped to his waist was a pistol and a belt full of ammunition.

Next to him stood an old man with a scraggly white beard, torn sweater and soiled khaki pants. On his feet were ancient huaraches with wood soles, and on his head he wore a black beret. The old man crouched down low and held a club, as if prepared to take off Pepe's head.

Standing alongside the old man was a young boy with knotted blond hair, dirty face and a runny nose. He held a buck knife out in front of him. The next man, who stood at Pepe's side, was tall, thin and about Pepe's age. He held a long rifle. Pepe tried to see the man who stood to the other side, but the faces began to mesh together. Fear gripped him. He felt flushed as if a fever had come upon him. But as quickly as the fear had come, his concentration returned. He saw that each man dressed differently. Their weapons looked old, with chipped stocks and rusted barrels, but deadly. Forcing himself, he looked into their eyes. He saw anger and determination.

Someone yanked Pepe's arms and tied them roughly behind

him. They all marched off into the mountains, some on horseback and some walking. They spoke little and moved swiftly along the cattle trails. When they reached their camp five hours later, the sun had begun its descent. Pepe was thrown into an adobe hut where he remained in darkness for two days, hands tied at his back.

The visions tormented him. At times, he felt himself going insane. He cried and laughed. He talked to himself and answered his own questions. Sometimes the presence of his father and brother, Ramon, overwhelmed him. They rescued him from the brink of madness only to make him examine his life. Pepe developed a system where he could finally remember each year of his life going back to his third birthday. But often the things he remembered became confusing, and he wasn't sure whether he really remembered them or whether someone had told him.

By the third night of captivity, Pepe had experienced every emotion possible. He was riddled with guilt and forgiveness, sadness and happiness, pain and relief, love and hate, good and evil, fantasy and reality. Hunched up in one corner of the hut, he finally felt nothing. He had simply resigned himself to death.

CHAPTER EIGHTEEN

Pepe let out a gasp as the light from the open door rushed in and burned his eyes. He looked to see who had entered. Although it was late evening and the brightness from the day had softened, his sensitive eyes saw only the dark outline of a bulky figure.

"They want you outside," he heard a woman say.

He cringed as she took his arms, cutting away the rope that had torn away much of the skin about his wrists. His eyes began adjusting to the light. The woman was short but very wide. Her hair was a mixture of brown and grey. Pepe did not know why, but the presence of this woman comforted him.

As he followed the woman, he could feel his legs preparing to collapse. His right knee buckled, but he recovered, bringing himself back to an upright position. His muscles and bones began to ache. The dryness in his mouth nearly glued his lips shut. He had never felt so weak or vulnerable.

The men paid no attention as he approached. They sat around a fire, each of them hungrily attacking a plate of beans, using tortillas as utensils.

"Lilia, más café," ordered a big, gruff man, his mouth full of food as he spoke. The woman walked to the fire, picked up the coffee pot and filled each man's cup.

Pepe, a pathetic, sickly figure stood before them. His face was pale and it drooped beneath the eyes. The corners of his mouth hung heavy. His clothes appeared to be made of discarded cloth. It hurt him to bring his arms forward, so he kept them behind his back. He looked at the ground and remained silent.

"What do they call you?"

Pepe heard the words but did not see who had spoken. He raised his eyes. His lips moved to pronounce his name, but no

sound came out. Pepe became frightened. His pale face turned red
as a nervous anxiety released a rush of heat which burned through
his body.

"Pepe Rios," he finally said. The heat dissolved.

"And where do you come from?"

This time Pepe saw the speaker. He was the most neatly dressed.
Maybe twenty years old or so. He wore a beard, closely trimmed.
Pepe noticed that the man wore a pair of expensive looking black
boots.

"I asked where you come from?" the man repeated, showing
no emotion.

"Zacatecas ... I mean, the cañones ... near Guadalajara," Pepe
said, stammering, unable to think clearly.

"What are you doing here?"

Pepe rubbed his eyes with his palms. He did not want to appear
weak. His father had told him that at times of greatest weakness,
he must show greater strength.

"I'm going north."

The woman, Lilia, brought Pepe a plate of beans and a cup of
coffee. She took him by the elbow and sat him on a mound of dirt.
He asked for a little water.

"Have you ever ridden with the federales?" came the next question.

Pepe tore a tortilla in half. He filled one half with a pile of
beans and shoved the little taco into his mouth. Looking at the
man who had spoken, Pepe shook his head.

Lilia brought him a gourd of water. Pepe put down his plate
and savagely drank the water, spilling much of it over his chin.
"I've been lucky enough to hide from the soldiers. But I've seen
others who were caught," Pepe finally answered.

"Can you use a gun?"

Pepe stopped chewing and turned to the speaker. He peered
from the face of one man to another. He swallowed slowly, wiped
his face and answered, "I can use a gun, when needed."

"Very good. Right now we need all the men we can gather
together."

Pepe didn't answer, but continued eating, feeling nervous.

"The federales are weak. Everyday we get stronger," said the
big, gruff man who had asked for more coffee.

"Do not underestimate the pelones, Chispas," the young man
with the beard replied, "Porfirio still has many faithful soldiers."

"They are no match for us," Chispas said, his voice angry. Threateningly, he added, "Before they fought only women and children, now they fight against men."

The bearded man, El Estudiante, turned the conversation back to Pepe. "And what do you think of the fighting, Pepe Rios?"

"Pepe set his plate on the dirt and wiped his hands on his pants,

"I know nothing," he paused, and remembering something else, said, "I watched the soldiers beat many men and take them from their families, I ... I did not understand, none of the people did."

"Are you willing to fight with us?" asked the man with one leg, Mariano, in a humble tone.

Pepe feared that he would say the wrong thing. He knew that there was no way he could say no and live. "I am not much of a soldier," he answered.

The boy, the one about Pepe's age, let out a laugh and said, "Eh Rios, how many of us look like soldiers. El Maestro is past sixty years old. Does he look much like a soldier?"

Pepe looked over at the old man with the black beret. El Maestro smiled, only two teeth in his mouth.

"Guero is thirteen. He's the Maestro's son. Does he look like a soldier?"

Guero sat on a boulder, whittling away on a branch with his knife.

"And look at Lilia, she's ridden all over these mountains with us."

"What he is saying," cut in El Estudiante, "is that we are an army of the people. We fight against the tyrant rulers who think nothing of letting children die of starvation, a government which kills Mexicans and gives their land to gringos."

Still Pepe did not understand. He had seen suffering. In the mountains where he had lived, he saw children die because there were neither doctors nor medicines. But it was what the people had come to expect. They never blamed anyone.

"Is this a war?" Pepe asked, embarrassed by his question.

El Estudiante shrugged, "Who knows?" he said, as if the question had no answer.

"Of course it is a war," Mariano answered in a disturbed voice, standing up and leaning on a staff, since he had removed the wooden stump from his severed leg. "Chispas and I, we have been fighting this war many years," he continued, as the gruff man grunted in agreement. "I tried working. No one can live on the wages they paid."

"Poor men either live in disgrace or become bandits and steal with pride," Chispas blurted.

"We became bandits and have been at war with the army and the rurales ever since," said Mariano.

"But things are so bad that now all the people have become bandits," said El Estudiante. "Besides, what are bandits except people who are tired of being treated like animals by the rich bastards, people who decide that they will no longer obey laws that have been created and enforced to make slaves of them?"

Chispas let out a loud, enthusiastic cry, showing his pleasure at El Estudiante's words.

The excitement and awareness of words and ideas tickled Pepe's curiosity. He wanted to understand everthing. On his journey, he had noticed and felt the turbulance over the land. He had watched as people grouped together for protection. He saw the young men run off into the mountains to form their own bands to fight the federales. He helped people pack their belongings to make the trip to the northern border. He had not understood. It seemed as if no one did. But now, here were men who had chosen to give their lives for a cause. Pepe could actually feel his aching body growing stronger.

Pepe spoke slowly and carefully, "And if you win this war ... I mean, if the people win, what do you expect to gain?"

El Estudiante rubbed his beard, thinking of an answer. The others waited for his response. After some seconds, El Estudiante turned to Pepe and said, "I believe that each of us is here for a different reason. Each of us hopes to gain something different," he said, reaching down for his cup of coffee. "Let's ask. You, Maestro, why are you here? What do you want if we win this war?"

"My land," the old man answered, instantly. "I want the government to give me back the land they took from me and my family. It was not much, just a small piece, but it was mine."

"And you, Buddha?" El Estudiante asked the young man, who was about Pepe's age.

Buddha rubbed his hands together as he thought of an answer. As if shocked by electricity, he quickly raised his head, "Justice. I want to see that the poor are given justice. There should be no reason for even one child to die of hunger. I would want to see food given to the poor. And doctors ... " he cried out, as if preaching. "Doctors should come out to visit the villages and towns regularly." Buddha was quiet for an instant, and said finally, "Must we kill each other for such simple things?"

A silence floated over the camp. Pepe realized that the young Buddha was right. How could any government allow hunger to exist?

"How about you, Mariano?" El Estudiante asked the man with one leg.

"I want the men who own the farms and the factories to pay the workers a decent wage. Men should not be forced to work fourteen hours a day, and women and children should not be forced to work at all."

"And destroy the company stores!" Chispas screamed. "The workers are forced to buy everything at prices even the rich would refuse to pay."

"And Lilia, how about you?"

Lilia had removed the empty coffee pot from the fire. Without turning to look at the men, she answered, "Send all the gringos back to their side of the border. I watched as they brought their guns and shot down the strikers at Cananea. They killed my husband and my son. They just shot them down like animals and then laughed afterwards. Either send them back or kill them as they have killed us."

"And lastly, the little one. How about you, Guero."

Guero simply shrugged his shoulders. "I don't know. I go wherever my father goes. That's all," he said, and continued whittling away.

"Well, as for me," said El Estudiante, "I want to see every government official and every soldier either chased from this country or killed. If the things that all of us have asked for are to take place, we must start over ... a new government is needed."

Chispas opened his mouth to speak, closed it, thought for a moment and said, "Estudiante, you have been to the university in Mexico City. You are educated and understand about governments and such things, but we ... we only understand what we see. When you start your new government, remember not to make the same mistakes as the old one."

El Estudiante turned to Pepe, saying, "Well, Rios, what do you want out of this war?"

Pepe did not want to fight in any war. He wanted to get back on the road and go to El Paso. He pushed the thought from his mind and tried to think of an answer. "I ... I ... am not sure. No one has stolen my land or forced me to work if I didn't want to. I have never seen men strike."

"But you saw the cabrones federales. They kill for no reason," Chispas screamed, rising to his feet in excitement.

"Yes, I have seen how they treat the people," Pepe answered, but silently in his mind the phrase continued, I have also seen how the rebels treat people and many times it hasn't been much better.

"You and I are much the same, Pepe," said Buddha, "My father owned a farm. He had money and never allowed me to leave the farm. Everything I needed was there." Buddha paused, then continued, "One day a friend and I sneaked into town. We went to see one of the girls who worked on the farm. When we arrived the whole barrio was quiet, not loud with laughter or music as we had heard." Buddha's voice went soft, "When we entered the house, we saw an old man laying on a bed. The girl we had come to see, and her family, were crowded around the bed; there was much crying. The old man had been beaten. His teeth were broken, his nose pushed to one side of his face, his eyes swollen shut. When the girl saw me, she jumped at me, trying to scratch my face. Someone pulled her off. I later learned that my father had ordered two of his foremen to teach the old man a lesson. Someone had caught him stealing five potatoes. My father wanted his workers to know that none of them could steal from him and get away with it."

Buddha took a deep breath. Although the others had heard the story before, they remained quiet and let the words seep inside them. "I fight this war against my father and all men who are like him," Buddha announced firmly.

El Estudiante carried the majority of the conversation from that point on. He told them about Emiliano Zapata and about how the army feared entering the land where Zapata's campesino warriors lived. He tried to explain about Francisco Madero, his political ideas and government reforms, and how Madero did not want a war to break out. The men spoke about the man all of Mexico was talking about, Pancho Villa. Some said that he was half man and half god. Others heard that he was Saint James returned to rid Mexico of all political infidels. Mariano and Chispas laughed at the tales and legends, since they knew Villa, and they knew that he was a bandit who had been branded an outlaw by the sheriffs and presidents of many small towns.

Chispas pulled out a bottle of whiskey that he had taken from the last raid and all, except Lilia and Guero, began to drink. El Maestro got so drunk that he began dancing on top of a large boulder. Guero did not want his father to exert too much energy, so he finally took him by the arm and put him to bed. Chispas and

Mariano talked about the two girls they had slept with in the town of Cachucha. Now, two weeks later, they could laugh at how the girls stole their money and their boots. But both men swore over the bottle of whiskey that if they ever caught the girls they would marry them. Any women with so much nerve would make excellent soldaderas.

Pepe and Buddha talked about their families. Pepe asked how Buddha had received such a name. Buddha told him that El Estudiante had named him after some god who lived in India or China or some such place. Something about how they had both lived sheltered childhoods.

"Do you ever miss your home?" Pepe asked, wrapping his poncho around himself.

"Only my mother," Buddha said, quietly, "how I would love to see her one time." He hesitated and added, "just to let her know that I am well. I know she must worry."

The pain quickly entered somewhere into the depths of Pepe's heart. He had not considered such a thing. Always his thoughts focused on his pain at missing his mother and family, but never once did he think about the pain his mother must feel. How many months had it been? Not even a word about him ... She would torture herself wondering whether he was even alive. Guilt struck at him like a burning iron. Buddha saw anxiety in Pepe's face.

"Your mother knows nothing about you?" Buddha asked.

Pepe looked at the ground. He shook his head.

"How long have you been away?"

"Who knows, a month, two, maybe even three?"

"Someday we will have children. Then, then we will know what we have put our mothers through," Buddha said. "But my father," he continued, "the bastard could care less about me. The people say that anytime the soldiers enter the villages they ask if anyone knows Romuldo Jimenez. They even offer a reward for my capture."

Pepe forgot about his own problems. "What have you done?" Pepe asked.

Buddha shook his head and laughed, "After I left my father's house, I found work on a friend's farm. I told him I wanted to work in the fields alongside the campesinos. When my father learned that his son was ploughing and pulling weeds, he became outraged. He sent three of his best men after me.

"They rode into the fields to get me. Naturally, I refused to go. A fight started. I'm not even sure how it happened. Everything seems so clouded. The others in the field came over to help me. When the fighting finished, one of the foremen was dead. Someone hit him in the head with a pick. The foremen had come armed. It was self-defense."

Buddha tired of talking, and he became saddened by his story. His voice lowered. "I told everyone to say that I had killed the man. I ran into the mountains from one village to another. I had few friends and no one knew me, but the people treated me kindly. I met El Maestro and Guero. They too were running from the federales. When we did not know where else to go, we heard about a camp of men who had banded together to protect themselves from the federales. That's where we met Mariano and Chispas."

Pepe could hear Mariano and Chispas carrying on their own conversation, at times breaking into loud laughter.

"Where did you meet El Estudiante?" asked Pepe, anxious to learn more about the men.

"It's getting late. We have many more nights to talk about it," Buddha said, standing up, stretching his arms over his head.

"Who will take first watch tonight?" Buddha called to the others.

Breaking off his laughter, Chispas turned to Buddha, "You go to sleep. We will call you when it is your turn."

All the others, except El Estudiante, had already rolled up in their blankets and gone to sleep. Pepe noticed that El Estudiante sat next to the fire reading some sort of fold-out newspaper.

"Do the federales know where this camp is?" asked Pepe, as Buddha gave him an extra blanket.

"No, but they know that we are not too far ahead of them."

"You mean they are following you?"

"Only when they have nothing better to do," Buddha answered, spreading his blanket on a straw petate.

"Could they attack as we sleep?"

Buddha laughed, "They could, but they won't."

"Why not?"

Buddha moved about, trying to make himself comfortable, "Because no one fights at night. The federales are in the cantinas or with their women. Why would anyone want to fight at night?"

Pepe was confused, "If they are out trying to catch you, wouldn't the night be the best time?"

"Listen, Pepe," Buddha said, pulling his blanket up to his neck, "nobody pays the federales enough money to go riding through the mountains at night. Besides, you think they want to get killed?"

he smiled. "If we had the money to pay the federales, they would join our side tomorrow. Now go to sleep and don't worry. Nobody in Mexico fights at night." As an afterthought he added, "Fighting is hard work ... we work from sunup to sundown, but that's it."

Pepe could not move around. His joints ached, and they were still tight. He thought about the past few days. The fear and misery was still fresh in his mind. He listened as Buddha snored. Mariano and Chispas continued talking. Pepe could not understand their words. His eyes became heavy balls. He looked at the spray of the stars that filled the sky. The air smelled fresh and crisp. For the first time in many nights, he slept peacefully.

CHAPTER NINETEEN

Pepe sprang from his blanket when he heard the first shot echo through the mountains.

"Get down! You want to get your head blown off," Mariano screamed at him.

The second shot whizzed past Pepe's ear. He fell to the ground. Breathing heavily, he placed his cheek against the dirt, feeling gravel dig into his skin.

Mariano hopped on his one good leg, setting up a position behind a large boulder. "Buddha, can you bring my leg, hijo; it is over by the fire?"

Buddha waved to Mariano. He got up quickly and dashed to the fire. Another shot cracked the early morning air. Chispas returned the fire, although he didn't know where the snipers were hidden. Buddha grabbed the wood stump. Running low, crouched over at the waist, he made his way to Mariano. Everone took positions behind rocks and trees. Pepe still lay flat on the ground.

"Oiga, Rios, you like the smell of dirt or what?" Chispas said, as he looked at Pepe who still had his face to the ground.

Pepe lifted his head and felt silly as he saw every one in fighting positions. He crawled on his belly to a large fallen tree stump where El Maestro and Guero prepared to fire back.

"Eh, Rios." Pepe recognized Chispas voice. "Are you going to shoot the federales with your fingers?"

Pepe looked around helplessly as another rifle shot rang out.

"Go see La Lilia. She is in the far hut," El Maestro told Pepe.

He ran from the fallen log to another tree. Again a shot split the air. Chispas and El Estudiante both fired back. Pepe ran quickly to the hut. Once inside, La Lilia gave him an old carbine and a belt of ammunition.

"Don't shoot wildly," she warned, "ammunition is precious."

Throwing the belt over his shoulder and tucking the rifle under his arm, he ran back to his position.

"Who do you think it is?" Pepe asked El Maestro.

Looking carefully across the mountain, the old man responded, "Well, I think it is the federales."

"How do you know?" Pepe asked, keeping his eyes on the bigger mountain across from them.

"Because if it was the rurales," El Maestro answered, "they would have killed some of us already."

"Are they that good?"

El Maestro turned to Pepe and paused, "They are better. Every one of them is an expert with horses and guns. Ex-bandits and bank robbers, cattle thieves that the government hired to protect the country roads, except of course that they are ruthless. Now they go after rebels like us."

Pepe saw a man on the opposite mountain move from one bush to another. Chispas' rifle exploded. The man fell. El Maestro smiled, "Chispas used to be a rural," he said.

The sun began its ascent over the mountains behind them. Pepe felt a chill slide up his spine as a warm ray of light touched him. He kept his eyes searching the nopales and rocks on the opposite side. The new light made everything much brighter. The sounds of horses galloping away sent a relief through all of them.

"Quickly, pack everything. They'll be back soon," said Mariano.

Pepe watched as each man moved with precision, knowing where to place weapons and equipment. La Lilia packed away the food, extra clothing, blankets and ammunition in little packs so each man could help carry a bundle. Mariano had promised to get her a mule. It would make packing easier, but he also knew a mule would slow them down.

Lilia brought Pepe a horse. She handed him the rope which was tied around the horse's neck. "There's a saddle in the hut. You are lucky, boy. It's the last saddle and the last horse," she said to him.

Within minutes, they were packed and ready to go. Mariano never allowed them to bunch up. Separated, they were many small targets. Together, he had warned, they were one big target.

Chispas uncorked a bottle of tequila, raised it to his lips and took a good hard drink. He walked from one man to another and offered them a drink. Guero winced as the harsh liquid burned his stomach. Chispas slapped him heavily on the back, "Eh, Maestro, we'll make a man of him yet, que no?"

El Maestro looked proudly at Guero, his only surviving son. "He is a good boy." El Maestro called to Chispas. "Don't teach him any of your evil ways," he laughed.

Chispas' laugh was more of a happy grunt. "Ah, you are like my own father, and Guero like my own son, would I do such a thing?"

Pepe tugged at the leather cinch which secured the saddle to the horse. Chispas approached. "Looks like you know what you're doing, boy," he said, holding out the bottle of tequila. Pepe didn't feel like drinking, but he knew better than to refuse. He placed the bottle to his lips, leaned his head back and filled his mouth. He swallowed slowly as Chispas watched, carefully measuring Pepe. The tequila sent a quiver through Pepe, straightening him. It felt good. The morning looked fresh. He thanked Chispas and continued to adjust the saddle.

"How does it feel to be a rebel? You're riding with outlaws, you know?" Chispas said, watching Pepe's expression.

"I don't know. I haven't had time to think about it. Besides, do I have any choice?" Pepe wanted the last words back.

Chispas looked at him suspiciously. He had noted a sound of irritation in Pepe's voice. "No, you have no choice," Chispas answered, harshly. "We could have killed you the minute we saw you. You might say you owe us your life." He began to walk away but stopped. "If you want to stay alive, boy, don't make any foolish mistakes." Pepe heard the warning as a near growl. He watched Chispas walk to the next rider.

"How goes it?" Pepe saw El Estudiante coming towards him.

"I'm fine."

"Have you ever killed a man?"

The vision of the two men who had attacked the Rios home came sharply into Pepe's mind,

"Yes. My brothers and I once killed two bandits who tried to enter our house."

"Well, you are going to see much more killing now."

"Where are we going?"

"I can't say. If anyone of us is captured, it is better to know nothing," El Estudiante said, rubbing the mane of Pepe's horse.

"Have you fought many battles?" Pepe asked.

El Estudiante thought for a moment, and answered, "Not many. We're still learning. Ah, Mariano and Chispas are the experts.

They've been fighting all their lives. Only now they fight as soldiers, before they fought as bandits."

"Vámonos!" Mariano yelled, his horse kicking up dirt as he sped across the center of camp.

"Just follow Mariano," said El Estudiante, slapping Pepe's shoulder.

Pepe jumped into the saddle. He reached down and touched the butt of the rifle holstered in front of his right leg. One belt of ammunition was strapped across his chest. Pepe felt for the bedroll tied behind his saddle. He pushed down on the straw somebrero, the brim dropping low on his forehead. A great rush of excitement overcame him. He tugged at the reins, trying to calm down the frisky pinto beneath him. A wave of pride rolled through him. He wasn't sure why he was here or where he was going, but he was anxious to find out.

Mariano started down the mountainside followed by Guero, El Maestro, La Lilia, Buddha, El Estudiante, Pepe and Chispas. They rode for two days, stopping only to get food from friendly villagers and to sleep. The pride and courage that Pepe experienced at the beginning of the trip vanished. The insides of his legs burned from rubbing against the rough saddle. Every hour was filled with dust, sweat and a searing heat that ceased only when darkness fell and a brisk cold took over. The ammunition on his chest seemed like bricks. Whenever he felt that he could no longer go on, he looked at La Lilia and felt embarrassed.

She never complained. Riding her horse side-saddle, she was constantly checking to see that the load of food and supplies assigned to her remained secure. When they stopped at villages, it was La Lilia who would go house to house asking for food or extra clothing. When the little band of rebels stopped for the evening La Lilia's work would begin. Unloading her horse, she would rummage through the food, cook the evening meal and always keep a full pot of coffee brewing. As the men sat for their evening talks, La Lilia cleaned up and loaded the supplies for an early morning start.

Pepe guessed La Lilia was in her mid-forties. She looked older, weather-beaten, with deep wrinkles at the corners of her eyes and mouth. The gray hair was much more noticeable than the brown. A bulky, dominating figure, always standing upright, her presence commanded respect, and each of the men gave it to her. She spoke little, asked few questions and gave few answers. With a fiery temper that in fleeting instances reached passion, had it not been for her femininity, she may very well have been the leader of this group. This woman, this mother-figure, sex illusion, woman warrior, somehow always made Pepe's aches and pains more bearable.

In his new role as revolutionary, Pepe saw the mountains take on a strange, ominous beauty. Always the glare of the sun threw sparkles against the bushes, trees, cactus, rocks and earth. His eyes struggled to pierce the shimmer and haze of a wonderous landscape that could hide an enemy army around any bend. One round from a sniper's rifle would bring the beauty to an end.

Sometimes Pepe would run his hand over the rough ammunition belt across his chest. Stroking the tips of the bullets with his fingers sent him whirling into a frenzied realization. As if waking from a long dream, one question bounced against the walls of his brain. "What am I doing here?" Slowly, like a remorseful hymn the words imbedded themselves stubbornly in his mind. "Rebel ... I am a rebel," he thought, "fighting for what? Against whom?" And in an instant the sight of a thousand-foot granite bluff shooting downward, superior to any wall he had ever seen, sent a shiver of wonder and awe through him, reminding him that only life was important and that nothing else, not even death held significance.

The sky which spread out like a great inverted blue ocean suddenly seemed more exquisite than ever before. In the face of danger, and possible death, life came to him as a finely etched web, subtle and delicate. How would he react in the face of battle? The delicacy turned crude, but still his every feeling, his every nerve sent precisely timed messages to every corner and crevice of his body.

In the mountains, a few kilometers outside a small town called El Remolino, they made camp inside a large cavern. It was spacious enough to conceal twenty men, horses and supplies. The jagged ceiling rose thirty feet at the highest point. It reminded Pepe of Jonah inside the belly of a great fish. The entrance to the cave, which from the distance was not visible, was wide enough to allow two horses to enter side by side. Mariano made sure everyone knew that such a place was not the best hideout, since the federales and rurales knew the land.

"I only hope," Mariano said, "that they have not discovered this cave."

El Maestro shuffled through the entrance carrying three torches he had made of dried branches. "We will need them when darkness falls," he said, smiling proudly.

"If it weren't for you, Maestro," Buddha said warmly, "we

would be lost."

"Sí, sí," giggled the old man, moving around the cave looking for places to set the torches.

Although no one told Pepe anything about plans or strategies, he could feel that the men followed some guided direction. For the past few days they had moved at a steady pace, never stopping unnecessarily. They had not tried to recruit new members, and they stayed clear of enemy contact. Pepe never asked where they were going. He knew that he must do whatever they commanded.

They relaxed for most of the afternoon. La Lilia managed to get some potatoes, a welcome change to the diet of beans and tortillas. Mariano told everyone to clean their weapons, that they may need them soon. As they cleaned their weapons and relaxed, they spent much time talking.

After what seemed like many hours, Chispas stood up from where he lay. He strapped on his pistols. "Rios, get ready. You're going with me and El Estudiante," he said.

Pepe got to his feet dusting himself off. He reached down to pick up his rifle.

"No. Don't take your rifle. Pretend you're a rancher going into town on an errand."

Pepe was confused. He felt the heat of anxiety and fear rise inside him. He had not heard Chispas sound so serious. Everyone else sat up and watched. Pepe hesitated, looked around and tried to give himself time to think.

"How far is the town?" Pepe asked.

"Half hour, more or less," Chispas responded.

"Will we take horses?"

"Yes. I have a pistol for you. Hide it under your saddle."

"And bullets?"

Chispas nodded to Lilia. She walked over to the supplies. Returning, she gave Chispas a pouch. He opened the pouch and moved towards Pepe. "Take a handful," Chispas said, peering into Pepe's eyes. Pepe could not hold the stare and looked quickly at the pouch before him.

"Rios!"

Pepe looked up at Chispas. "Learn to stare a man in the eyes. I want you to look like a rancher and act like a rancher. But you must feel like a soldier ... a warrior ... or you will not survive."

Pepe swallowed hard. Feeling a weakness in his legs, he reached into the pouch and pulled out a handful of bullets. He stared into Chispas' eyes.

"I'll do whatever you say."
Chispas grunted and walked away.

CHAPTER TWENTY

The three men spoke little as they rode into town. Pepe tried to enjoy the sight of the town, but the strain on his nerves would not allow him to relax.

A large concrete gazebo stood in the center of the main plaza. Gardens of roses separated by gravel walkways jetting out in four directions encircled the three-tiered gazebo. Growing along the perimeter, completely surrounding the plaza, great cottonwood trees stretched their tremendous branches over the walkways and formed a natural wall to protect passersby against the summer sun. A colonial administrative building, aged and complete with arches and gargoyles, housed a squad of federal soldiers, a sheriff and a number of rurales who came and went as they pleased. Vendors set their wares on blankets spread out on the street corners. Selling everything from puny watermelons to straw sombreros and leather huaraches, the vendors sat stoically alongside their products as townspeople strolled by, occasionally sneaking a look, but preferring to act indifferently. Few heads turned as Chispas, El Estudiante and Pepe rode through the crowded streets.

"Eh, Rios, you ever had a woman?" Chispas asked.

The question took Pepe's attention from the street scene. "No, I never have," Pepe answered.

"Have you ever thought about it?"

Pepe shrugged.

"Good, today you will fuck."

"I don't know, Chispas. I don't think ... "

Chispas didn't let Pepe finish, "I don't want to hear you ever tell me 'no.' Today you will fuck. I want no excuses."

"What does this," Pepe was embarrassed to even say the word, "have to do with fighting federales?"

"Ha, listen to how he answers me," said Chispas to El Estudiante. "The little fellow gets braver each day."

El Estudiante pulled back on the reins. His horse began stepping backwards. "I will leave you here," he said to Chispas.

"Bueno, don't be late," was all Chispas said.

El Estudiante tipped the brim of his hat as a parting salute. He led his horse down a narrow street and disappeared between the buildings.

Chispas and Pepe followed the cobblestone streets away from the main plaza. Nodding and smiling at every woman he passed, Chispas received no return smiles.

Feeling less tense and more relaxed, Pepe dismounted and walked his horse down a small dirt road. In front of an adobe building, Chispas was already tying his horse to a post. "Follow me, boy, I will show you something worth dying for," Chispas said, as he entered the dimly lit cantina. Two men stood at the bar, and one man sat at a table in the corner. Chispas sensed an air of desperation about the room.

"Oiga, Compadre," he said to the bartender, "What's going on here?"

"Business is slow," the bartender answered, pouring himself a little pulque.

"Sí, but, wha ... what's happened?"

The bartender leaned close to Chispas so no one else could hear. "The federales came everyday for a week. Anybody that looked like he could hold a gun was taken away."

"And the women?" Chispas asked.

"Gone. Took the women too. Said they needed everybody."

Chispas looked the man directly in the eyes, "Eh, how come they didn't take you?"

The man laughed nervously, "I keep them supplied with liquor and a woman whenever they want one."

"Well, we have been riding for a few days, me and my brother here," Chispas said, patting Pepe on the shoulder, "taking some cattle to San Anselmo. Look, are there any women here at all?"

"Ha, I've always got at least one woman around. Her name's Matilde; she's out back with the animals. I'll get her for you."

Chispas spoke much louder, as if he wanted the others in the cantina to hear. "All right, that's why we're here, que no, Pepito?" he said, nudging Pepe against the ribs with his elbow.

It seemed to Pepe that Chispas was playing a game. The others in the cantina appeared to pay no attention. Two more men came through the door and sat at a table in the center of the room. Chispas poured Pepe and himself a glass of tequila. Pepe began to get nervous. He took the tequila and quickly swallowed it. The bartender returned, a large smile on his face. "Matilde is waiting, first door to your right."

"Ha, that's what we came for," Chispas repeated, but before entering the back room, he said to Pepe in a low voice, "Don't drink anymore, and keep an eye on everybody in this place. Just watch who comes and goes."

Chispas stood up straight, pushed out his chest and said to Pepe loudly, "Sure you don't want to go first?"

Pepe didn't answer but only shook his head.

"Muy bien, you can go second. You like second, eh?"

"Sí, mucho," Pepe said, nervously.

Chispas pulled aside a curtain that hung over the doorway leading to the back rooms. Pepe watched as more men entered the cantina. Most spoke in quiet voices. The men stared around the room, eyes jumping from face to face. Pepe did not understand why there was no loud talk or laughter, like in the other cantinas he had entered with his father. No one played dominoes or cards. The men simply huddled about in small groups talking.

Pepe poured himself another glass of tequila. He remembered Chispas' words. He held the glass in his hands, looked at the liquid and drank it. Then he pushed the bottle far from him.

Fifteen minutes passed before Chispas entered the bar again. He placed his arm around Pepe's shoulder and said, "The lady is waiting for you. Just think that you are going in there to conquer the world."

"I don't know, Chispas. I ... I" Pepe could think of nothing to say.

"Go on, don't act like a baby. Shit, when I was your age, I already had kids, and besides that, remember Artemio the grocer, I was fucking his wife on the side." Chispas looked at the bartender. "His first time," he said.

Pepe could feel his heart smashing his chest. The temperature rose. He seemed to struggle for air.

Chispas winked at the bartender, then bent down and whispered in Pepe's ear, "Did you see any soldiers come in."

"No, only these men," Pepe said, softly.

"Bueno. Now go, before I get mad. We don't have much time."

Pepe pushed the curtain aside and walked into the back. He entered a dimly lit hallway that smelled of chicken and pigs. Halfway down, to the right, he tugged at another curtain and entered a darkened room. A lighted candle at one corner threw shadows against the walls.

"Come in, I haven't got all day," Pepe heard a woman's voice say.

He saw the bed and tried to focus his eyes on the woman who lay stretched out on top.

"Come closer," the woman said.

Slowly Pepe walked to the edge of the bed. He could see the woman's face. She had the face of a million women. There was a plain expression, sad eyes, the smell of animal and urine, he thought. She propped up her knees and opened her legs. She wore a dress which was up above her hips.

"It's your first time?"

"Yes," Pepe said.

"I'm sorry."

"Why?" Pepe said, puzzled.

"It is too beautiful a thing to do in such an ugly way."

Matilde sat up on the bed and began removing Pepe's trousers. He stiffened. He could feel her tugging at his buttons. She pushed the trousers down his legs. He stared straight across the room at a plough which leaned against a wall. Her fingers played with him, touching, caressing, stroking, but Pepe felt only the coldness of her skin.

"Maybe it will be better if you get on me," she suggested, lying back on the bed and opening her legs.

Pepe crawled onto the bed. He felt the hard straw scratching his knees. Making his way between her legs, he lowered himself on her body. He lay on her and felt nothing except her lumpy body. Her fingers explored, found him and tried to push him inside. Still, Pepe felt only the cold touching and groping. He closed his eyes wanting to feel the rise of passion, tensing his body to respond to Matilde's touch, clenching his hands and teeth, as if knotting every muscle would help him to harden.

"You don't want to," she said.

"Yes, I do."

"Then your body doesn't want to."

"I don't know what's wrong."

The stench of the building and the animals caused a sick feeling in his stomach. He wanted to puke. He could smell a strong unnatural odor coming from the woman. Pepe wanted to push her away and get out, get out as quickly as possible.

"It's no good. Your time hasn't come," she said, climbing from the bed and straightening her dress.

Relief rushed through Pepe's body. He pulled on his trousers and buttoned himself up.

"You friend has already paid me. I can't give you your money back."

"I don't want it. I ... I'm sorry," he said, feeling as though he had somehow insulted her. She said nothing. He looked at her as she sat on the bed quietly. He wanted to say more but couldn't. He walked through the doorway, back up the hall and entered the cantina.

The wild voice jolted Pepe.

"I don't care who the bastard is," Chispas screamed, belligerently. "If you got a rooster that can beat his and you don't fight, you are a child."

Pepe walked to the bar and stood next to the little man who was listening to Chispas.

"Por favor, señor, you do not understand," the man pleaded.

"Ah, I understand plenty. You got no balls."

"You do not know don Emilio," the little man shouted.

Chispas turned to Pepe. "You know anything about the gallos?" he asked.

"A little," Pepe answered.

"Well, this midget owns a rooster that has won every fight, and he is afraid to enter him in tonight's fights."

The man, who Chispas called Chaparro, grabbed his glass of tequila and gulped it down. "Ay, señor."

"Don't call me señor. My name is Chispas."

"Muy bien, señ ... Chispas. Don Emilio has lost only two fights," he said, "and both of the men who won haven't been heard from again."

"So what," Chispas snarled.

"So what?" the little man cried in desperation, "they disappeared. Some say they were killed. You should have seen the look on don Emilio's face when he realized his roosters were dead. He turned into a madman, a devil. He chased everyone from the courtyard, except the men who had won. No one saw them after that."

"Exaggerations ... superstitions, that is all you country people believe in."

"Who is don Emilio?" Pepe asked.

"He's the chief of the local police, brother-in-law of the governor ... "

"Owner of thousands of acres, a pig and a miser," Chispas interrupted.

Chispas leaned over and said to the little man, in a low voice, "Suppose I fight your rooster. Me and my brother, Pepe; we are not afraid of this don Emilio. Anyway, we will say that we are strangers in these parts."

"No. No. Don Emilio has heard of my bird. He has seen him before."

Chispas thought for a moment, "I know, I will say I bought him from you. If we win, I will give you half of the money."

The little man looked hard at Chispas. "I don't know," he said slowly.

"Come on. You don't even need to go, and I imagine that we are talking about muchos pesos, no?"

Pepe noticed that many of the men in the bar tried listening to the conversation. Although Chispas spoke in a lowered voice, he spoke loudly enough for those closest to hear. It took only minutes for the conversation to pass from the bar to the farthest corners of the cantina. Pepe could not understand Chispas' desire to enter this cockfight.

"You know that anyone who places money on my rooster will win big."

"I told you, I'll give you half," Chispas said to the little man.

Pepe listened as the buzz of conversation moved through the cantina. The mention of much money raised an excitement in the men.

"My bird is good," responded the little man, Chaparro.

"So, you have nothing to lose."

"Don Emilio and his friends bet big."

"More for us, and for those who bet with us when we win," Chispas said.

"I will be taking a big risk."

"That is what life is all about."

"I need another drink."

Chispas poured the little man another glass of tequila. He was aware that everyone in the cantina knew of the fight. He knew that many of the men would be there. The word would soon be in the streets, on the roads and into the countryside.

The little man smiled, "Bueno, you win."

"Okay, let's go see your bird," Chispas said, smiling.

CHAPTER TWENTY-ONE

Don Emilio's house was located at the west end of the town. Unlike most of the homes in town, don Emilio's house, a small rancho, was built far from the main road and covered two acres of land. A wall eight feet high, surrounded the house and stables. In front was a small patio which don Emilio used for parties and dances. In the back, far from the house but still inside the wall, was another patio much larger than the first. In the middle of the patio a tiny arena had been built. Many wooden benches circled the arena; those benches towards the back had been built on higher legs, so that wherever spectators sat they had a clear view. Far to the side of the patio, don Emilio had installed a stage against a wall. No cockfights were held without music. Sometimes he brought mariachis from as far away as Saltillo. Everyone from town, and those from the neighboring villages, knew that don Emilio took his cockfights seriously. When Chispas and Pepe arrived, the third fight of the evening had just finished. The mariachis, a band of local musicians, played a jumpy ranchera that had been written as a tribute to don Emilio's love of the roosters.

Chispas handed the rooster to Pepe. Pepe placed the bird in the crook of his arm as a mother holds an infant. He petted the animal behind the neck, stroking its feathers and messaging the muscles.

"That's it, treat him gently," Chispas said, "I'm going to see who sets up the fights around here."

Pepe stood back from the crowd. He watched as the money went from one man to another. He could hear men arguing about roosters, handlers and owners. Except for the large fiestas back in his home town, Pepe had never seen so many men attend a cockfight.

As he continued cradling the rooster, Pepe looked around with interest. Some of the men wore huaraches and were dressed in old work clothes. Others wore boots and the tight-fitting outfits of the ranchero. He spotted two or three men who wore suits and cloth hats. Pepe figured that anyone with money was allowed to enter. Still, it was a strange sight, after so much time living as a vagabond. He had seen so much poverty and hunger on his journey, it didn't seem right that some had money to throw away on silly games.

Pepe held the warm, white rooster close to his breast. He felt a sense of security as it cuddled in his arms. He wondered if the animal knew that in a few minutes it would be fighting for its life. The bird seemed calm, extra calm. Its eyes were half closed, as if trying to sleep. It wasn't right that this rooster lived only to fight. Pepe could feel the scars on its head. Maybe it would be better to chop off the head once and for all, serve the poor thing in a meal, and save it from this suffering. But it was a fighting cock, bred from a fine line of vicious birds, born for only one reason— to fight. He wondered if it was true what El Estudiante had told him, "Always," he had said, "there were those who benefited from the suffering of others." The bird would fight and either live or die. And regardless of the outcome, someone was going to make money. Pepe thought how glad he was that men were not roosters. How terrible to be born an animal.

Chispas walked quickly towards Pepe, a large smile splitting his face. "It's very good. We got the fight after next," he said, happily.

"Which is don Emilio?" Pepe asked.

Chispas pointed through the crowd. "There, see the tall, light complected man, the thin one. He's got curly hair and he's wearing the norteño cowboy hat."

Pepe saw him. He was surrounded by three other tall men who all wore pistols. Pepe was surprised that don Emilio was so good looking.

Chispas took the rooster from Pepe. He tied a cord to the rooster's leg and threw the bird to the ground. Flapping and crowing, it fell hard to the earth, landing on one side.

"Let it walk around, loosen up. You stay and keep an eye on it. I'm going to see how the betting is going," Chispas said.

Pepe watched the rooster strut around, stretching its neck, lifting its wings and crowing, a loud cry wailing over the screams of the other roosters. Then Pepe understood that the rooster knew why it was there.

After a short time passed, Chispas returned. He seemed anxious.

"Listen carefully. Go to the horses. Get your pistol and hide it somewhere on you."

"Wha...why?" but the instant he asked, Pepe knew that he shouldn't have.

Chispas turned on him savagely, "You do what the fuck you are told! Stay alert and keep your eyes on those with the guns. Now go. Don't let anyone see your gun."

The crowd cheered. The music played and the screams grew wild. Chispas felt the excitement race around inside his belly. It had been months since he had handled a rooster. But he knew that he was still good. Tonight he would show don Emilio. He would humble the arrogant son of a bitch in his own house.

When Pepe returned, Chispas moved close to a wall where a lantern hung. Beneath the bright light he prepared the rooster for battle. Handing the bird to Pepe, he said, "hold him firmly, not too tight."

Nervous, Pepe had trouble gripping the rooster. One wing flew out and struck Pepe in the face.

"Take it easy," Chispas said, "hold him like you would hold a woman's breast. Love it, rub it as if it were gold dust."

Pepe nodded, trying to relax. He knew there was something more about this night that Chispas was not telling him. He loosened his hold on the bird, pretending the animal was a baby. Pepe remembered holding his little sister, Margarita, when she was an infant. A spear of sadness struck him, but Chispas' voice shattered the memory.

"Think about nothing except the rooster," he said, wiping a small knife clean on his trousers.

Carefully and very slowly, Chispas took the knife and scraped away the dry, scaly skin from the rooster's claw, chipping away at the tiny pieces, one scale at a time. He moved closer to the light trying to keep the shadows away. Once he was satisfied with the smoothness of the claw, he poured water from a jug and wiped the claw clean.

Chipas then picked up a box he had placed on the ground. Opening it he pushed the contents around until he found a long, thin red cloth. He took the narrow cloth and wrapped it around the rooster's leg leaving a small nub exposed. The nub, once an upper limb on the claw, had been removed when the rooster was very young.

"But what if..."

"Shh," Chispas cut Pepe off. "Concentrate on the bird. He needs your energy and mine if he is going to win. Treat him as if your life depended on his victory. No more talk."

After wrapping the leg and part of the claw securely, Chispas again reached into the box. This time he came out with two tiny wooden blocks. He held them at arms length up to the lantern, feeling for weight and shape. It took him a minute or so, but finally he chose the one painted black.

A hole had been drilled into the center of the block. Chispas positioned the block on the rooster's leg so that the nub fit perfectly into the hole. He unwound a piece of flat twine. He took the twine and wrapped it around the block and the bird's foot to hold the block into place. Every turn of the twine fell directly into place as carefull and neatly as the threads on a screw. When he finished the delicate job, he wiped the perspiration from his forehead, walked outside to where he had tied his horse and got a bottle of whiskey.

He took a long drink and handed the bottle to Pepe. Pepe refused. Filling his mouth with whiskey, Chispas motioned for Pepe to hold the rooster away from his body. In one quick movement Chispas spat the whiskey out, covering the rooster with the harsh smelling alcohol. Roughly, he began messaging the whiskey into the feathers, under the wings and over the head.

"It helps keep him cool," he said to Pepe.

Once again, he rummaged through the box. This time he came out with two smaller boxes. Opening the two boxes, he held them out for Pepe to see. Inside each box, Pepe saw a sickle shaped blade shining under the glow of the lantern. Smiling, Chispas removed one blade and held it close to the lantern, carefully inspecting the razor sharp edge. He turned the blade from one angle to the next. Satisfied with the inspection, he removed the second blade and did the same thing. After inspecting both blades, he placed them in his palms and felt the weight. Finally he chose one blade and put the other back in the box.

Pepe could not believe how nimble and precise Chispas' fat fingertips had become. The rebel worked with the sensitivity and care of a watch-maker. Continuing with the ceremony of arming the feathered knight, Chispas firmly held the rooster's foot. At one end of the sickle, two long prongs protruded. He slipped the prongs under the strands of twine and against the wood block. Dropping down to one knee, Chispas moved the sickle until he set it into the exact angle he wanted. With the deadly instrument positioned, he took another twine. He wrapped it tightly around the block and

the prongs on the blade. It surprised Pepe to watch this hardened
man work. Chispas made a small loop when he reached the end of
the twine, slid the lead tip through and pulled, making two small
knots, one over each prong.

"Hurry! Bring in the next roosters," a man screamed from the
center of the arena.

Pepe looked up. Chispas paid no attention. Closing one eye and
sighting in on the blade like a jeweler studying a rare gem, Chispas
moved the little sickle the width of a hair. Standing, appearing
happy with his operation, Chispas slipped a metal sheath over the
weapon and relaxed his muscles.

"Bueno. Let's go," he said to Pepe.

Walking to the arena, Chispas took the rooster from Pepe.

"You bring the whiskey and the box," he ordered, "and bring
the horses closer to the patio. We might have to get out of here
fast."

Chispas stepped into the arena. He held the white, golden
rooster up for all to see. Lovingly, he stroked the bird and placed
a kiss behind its head. He spotted don Emilio sitting at ring side.
The man puffed on a cigar and watched Chispas closely.

Another man, much younger than Chispas also stepped into the
arena. In his arms, he cuddled a large, red rooster, don Emilio's
most consistent winner. The two men walked around the arena.
Already the money began to flow.

A third man came into the arena carrying an old, scarred rooster.
He moved close to Chispas. The bird in Chispas' arms went wild
and almost flew from his hold. The two birds pecked furiously at
one another, but because the men held their faces inches apart, they
did not touch. They both placed the roosters on the ground but did
not release the animals. Striking with the speed of rattlesnakes, the
two roosters lunged at each other, ruffling their feathers and pecking their beaks. Chispas felt the rage rising inside his rooster. He
knew that his bird was limber and angry. He took the animal back
in his arms and waved the man off. The man walked over to don
Emilio's handler and went through the same ritual. Some men
murmured, while others screamed across the arena. The combatants had excited the crowd.

"Eh, let us see that gallo again," a man yelled at Chispas from
the crowd.

Chispas held the rooster high for all to see. He knew it was a
strong bird, and it would draw much money. But he wasn't sure
how many men would bet against don Emilio.

Pepe walked over to Chispas. "The man with the brown hat," Pepe said, pointing into the crowd, "he told me to tell you that ten men have joined the family."

"Ah, muy bien. That's all we needed," Chispas responded.

"What does it mean?" Pepe asked, curiously.

"Each man puts up fifty pesos. If we win, everyone in the family gets an equal share of the money we take in. It's simple."

"But what's the family?"

"It's the name given to those who side with a rooster and put up the necessary money."

"So don Emilio has a family also?"

"Yes. But he does not need it. He has enough money to bet on his own rooster," Chispas said, squeezing the rooster's neck, gently.

"I've got the jug of water you wanted."

Chispas seemed calm, a strange calm as if he himself were entering a battle to the death. Pepe thought he saw a glimpse of fear in the man's eyes, but he could not be totally sure.

"Our lives depend on what happens here. Be alert," Chispas said. Then he turned and gave a cocky smile to the audience, which was becoming anxious. The catcalls and the whistling began.

"You take care of the water and the whiskey. When I ask for either, give them to me quickly. Timing is important," Chispas said to Pepe.

"Gallos center ring!" a man called out.

The crowd screamed, and then the voices dwindled to a hum. Chispas slipped off the sheath. The silver blade sparkled. Holding his gallo tightly, he walked to the center of the arena where he stood facing don Emilio's handler. The two men held the animals firmly, moving them closer together. Chispas felt his gallo stiffen. At a foot's distance the roosters bellowed cries of strength and contempt. Chispas gripped firmly. He needed to use much muscle to hold his rooster back. The birds began pecking violently at each other. The men, digging their feet into the ground, placed the animals closer. The beaks struck, the skulls cracked, hard as if two mallets had crashed. Chispas turned quickly. He did not want to chance injury. He walked back to the edge of the arena wall. Both roosters knew the enemy.

Stooping down on his haunches, Chispas held the quivering white bird out in front of him. The crowd was silent. The animals were magnificent. Chispas nodded to don Emilio's handler. The man nodded back. They released the gallos.

Like two feathered knights in a medieval joust, the roosters shot to center ring, flew into the air and collided, their weapons striking out to sink into something solid. They screamed as if demented and sent a gust of feathers flying. The crowd screamed.

Stretching out its wings, don Emilio's red rooster vaulted over the white one, dragging the armed foot as it flew past. Both roosters turned and faced each other, their breasts heaving. Instantly, the white rooster took to the air, rising even higher and whipping the blade about, expertly controlling the weapon.

Once on the ground the roosters again charged. Their bodies crashed, but they quickly separated and attacked again, wings flapping, heads buried in feathers, and for a brief moment, it appeared as if there were only one bird tussling in mass confusion.

Dust rose and the red rooster sank to the ground. The other straightened up, saw the opportunity and quickly pounced on top of the enemy. The red rooster jumped up and struck back.

A trickle of blood ran down the white rooster's neck. Both animals stood back and prepared to charge. They were tiring. Chispas and the other man stepped in, scooped up the roosters and took them to the corners.

"The whiskey, hurry," Chispas called to Pepe.

The crowd stood and cheered, howled and whistled. Seldom had it seen strength, such courage. Don Emilio looked stern. His smile had disappeared.

Chispas filled his mouth with whiskey. Spitting, he sprayed the alcohol over his rooster's breast. He rubbed the whiskey gently into the feathers, hoping to numb the hidden cut. Placing his mouth above the rooster's tail, he blew hard. He did the same thing high on the rooster's head. He blew air into its lungs. Again filling his mouth with whiskey, he spat over the rooster's entire body and quickly massaged the alcohol into the feathers. He turned and walked back to the arena's center. Dropping to one knee, he looked at don Emilio's man, who was already waiting. They nodded and released the combatants. Like enraged devils, the animals tore at each other again, wings flapping, beaks striking, and they lashed out with deadly claws.

The white rooster fell to the ground, hard. It leaned to one side. Blood dripped steadily from its breast. The red rooster stood over it, holding its breast high, ruffling its neck feathers and triumphantly crying out. It rushed at the fallen prey and continued the attack. The crowd wailed happily. Don Emilio smiled.

The sharp spur struck the white rooster, slicing the right eye.

Its head fell and the spur struck again high on the head. A gash
opened up, and a stream of blood flowed down the neck. The white
rooster tried to raise up but fell again, unable to find strength in its
legs. Clinging to the dirt, the wounded rooster struggled to keep
its head high.

Chispas rushed to the rooster. He whispered close to its head.
Taking it into his arms, he softly stroked it behind the neck. Blood
dripped from his hands. He walked back to the corner, took more
whiskey in his mouth and sprayed the rooster. It shuddered with
pain, but it made no sound. He blew into the mouth and above
the tail. The once white feathers turned crimson. Chispas kissed
the animal on the head, marched back, faced the roosters off, and
the slaughter continued.

Blind in one eye, sliced over the head and across the breast, the
white rooster fought courageously. The red bird, strong and filled
with confidence, flew into the air and came crashing down on top
of its adversary. Falling to the ground, the white rooster sat there,
dazed, hurt, looking around with its one good eye. The red rooster
whirled around and attacked furiously. The crowd was a mesh of
distorted, screaming faces.

Pouring out one last surge of energy, the white rooster lifted
himself from the dirt, spread his wings and leaped into the air,
appearing as if he were going to fly away. Stunned, the red bird
looked up. In a twisting, twirling descent, the white rooster spun
its claws and with a hard swipe slit the stretched neck of the red
rooster. As if poisoned, the body twitched with hard jerks; it ran in
a circle, not understanding it was fatally wounded, jerked again and
fell dead. The crowd was silent, and then it erupted into madness.

Chispas ran into the ring, picked up the rooster and jumped
around laughing. He walked around the arena holding the rooster
high for everyone to see, blood dripping on his shirt. The audience
applauded. Pepe kept his eyes on don Emilio.

The man had thrown his cigar to the ground. Pepe saw the
furious look. Don Emilio talked to the three armed men closest
to him. Pepe reached back to touch the pistol sticking out of his
waistband. He tugged at his poncho afraid that the pistol might
show.

The blast from the rifle silenced everyone. People looked around
to see who had been shot. Those who held handfuls of money
stuffed the bills into their pockets. Don Emilio walked to the center of the arena.

"Nothing to worry about, my friends," he said, pulling his hat down low about his eyes, "it was a good fight. The white gallo fought valiantly."

Already a large number of men had left the hacienda. Those who had won money remained to collect.

"My men will collect all the money. Tonight we will count it and tomorrow you can come and receive your shares."

A rumble of voices spread through the crowd. Don Emilio's men, weapons in hand, went straight to the men who held the money. Hesitating at first, but knowing better than to refuse, the men turned over the money.

"We have invested much here," called out a young farmer.

"You have nothing to fear. Tomorrow you will get all that is coming to you," don Emilio assured him.

"I do not like it!" said an old man, angrily.

One of don Emilio's men walked behind the old man and stood so close that the barrel of his rifle almost touched the old man's ear.

"The fights are finished for tonight. Give your names to my men, and they will make a list." Don Emilio's tone, and his armed men, left no room for disagreement.

The men began walking from the patio. Pepe turned to leave but was stopped by one of don Emilio's men.

"No. You will remain. We will have a toast to the winners," don Emilio announced.

"That's good of you," Chispas quipped, "I would love a drink."

"You are strangers in these parts?" don Emilio asked, walking closer to Chispas.

"Yes."

"How is it that you came to the fights tonight?"

"In a cantina I heard a man talking about the fights. You know, señor, I love the gallos. It's been a long time since I handled a rooster. Bueno, I decided to buy a bird and fight."

"You are a liar."

Chispas stared directly into don Emilio's eyes.

"I have seen this bird fight before."

"I told you, I bought it. A man from this town sold it to me."

Don Emilio looked at Chispas suspiciously. He turned and stared at Pepe.

"Search them," he commanded.

It took only a second to find Pepe's pistol. Smiling, Chispas raised his arms. They found a small derringer tucked inside his boot.

"Plan a little target practice?" don Emilio said, sarcastically.

"Señor, do you expect us to ride through the countryside un-armed. The roads are filled with bandits. Everyone needs protection these days."

"What is your destination?"

"Zacatecas. My brother there, Pepe, we own a ranch. The drought killed many animals. We've been traveling, trying to make enough money to buy more cattle."

Chispas looked around, scratched his head, and at the same time saw that five armed men surrounded him and Pepe.

"You see, you are outnumbered," said don Emilio.

Chispas, irritated, answered, "Listen, I have won many cock-fights and I have lost, but no one has ever surrounded me with guns before."

"I do not like to lose."

"Everybody loses."

Don Emilio laughed, "Still, I do not like it."

"Give me the money so we can get out of here," Chispas demanded.

"The money is mine."

Don Emilio drew his pistol, walked to where the white rooster sat cuddling near the wall, pointed and blew the animal's head apart.

"You see," don Emilio said, holstering his pistol, "your rooster is dead. It did not win." He laughed, "My rooster took off his head."

Chispas lunged at him. He rammed his head into don Emilio's chest, slamming him to the ground. But before he could land a blow, three men pulled him off.

"Don't kill him! Don't kill him," don Emilio yelled, lying on his back.

Four men had Chispas by the arms, around the waist and neck. The fifth man pointed his rifle at Pepe's head.

Don Emilio got up and dusted himself. "Take them away. I don't want any mess in my patio. My children must play here," he said.

"I'll get you for this! You won't get away with it!" Chispas screamed, trying to break free.

Pepe stood still. He felt nauseous. A sense of helplessness swept through him as he was ordered to mount his horse. Confusion gripped him.

Chispas and Pepe rode in front. Three of don Emilio's men followed. They were on the road leading out of town. The fear and despair that had caused chaos in Pepe's mind disappeared. His thinking became clear and sharp. His eyes searched the road and the landscape to the side of him. There was a chance he could fall from his horse and dash into the brush. Maybe the men were not such good shots. Besides it was dark. They might miss him.

A loud voice broke the silence just as Pepe prepared to leap.

"Turn and I will kill you instantly."

Pepe's body stiffened.

"Chispas! Pepe! Take their weapons."

"Holy Jesus, it took you long enough," Chispas cried as he dismounted. He quickly grabbed the weapons from don Emilio's men, who sat rigid in their saddles, hands raised in the air.

"Come on, Rios, give me some help here," he called to Pepe.

Shaken, Pepe jumped from his horse and rushed over to help Chispas. He pulled a rifle from a holster and ordered one man at a time to hand over the ammunition strapped to their chests. Laughing, as if touched with insanity, Pepe felt relieved.

In the darkness Pepe could see El Estudiante standing in the middle of the road, holding a rifle to the back of don Emilio's men. To one side, standing on the edge of the road, La Lilia stood also holding a rifle. On the opposite side Guero crouched down pointing a pistol.

Pepe quickly turned towards the town as he heard a volley of gunshots. One of the riders jerked as if to turn around. El Estudiante pointed and fired, blowing the man out of the saddle. The stricken man rolled around, moaning. El Estudiante walked up to him, placed the rifle to his head and pulled the trigger. One of the horses reared back on its hind legs. The two remaining riders pleaded with El Estudiante to spare them. The blast tore a huge chunk from one man's neck. Without hesitating, he turned the rifle on the other. The bullet entered the man's skull, killing him instantly.

"Hurry, take whatever we need and let's get out of here," El Estudiante ordered, calmly, as he pulled money from the dead men's pockets.

About fifteen minutes later, Mariano, El Buddha and El Maestro came riding up quickly.

"We got it! Just like we planned, the monkeys didn't know what happened."

"Did you kill them?" Chispas asked.

"All of them," said Mariano, breathing heavily.

"Good."

"It will take the federales hours to figure out what happened," Mariano said. "Let's go," he commanded and rode into the lead.

Pepe pulled on the reins, forcing his horse to whirl around. He looked at the still shadows lying on the ground. He could still hear their last pleas, an echo in his mind. One minute they were alive, crying, and the next they lay dead on the road.

CHAPTER TWENTY-TWO

They traveled all night and into the next afternoon. Riding down mountainsides, crossing dry arroyos and skirting over grassy knolls, Mariano knew the federales would have a difficult time following their trail. Feeling safe for the moment, he allowed them a short rest at a place where a small stream ran between two mountains. The water was dark and appeared dirty, but no one complained as they all drank.

Pepe walked over to where El Estudiante sat against the trunk of a sycamore tree. Squatting down, Pepe broke a piece of dry grass and placed it between his teeth.

"What is it?" El Estudiante asked.

"Last night, back there on the road," Pepe said, slowly, "did you have to kill those men?"

El Estudiante rubbed his beard. He thought carefully and answered, "We had no choice. They are six less enemy than before."

"I have never seen men die like that."

"We cannot take prisoners. If we had let them go, they would either now be on our trail or fighting our people later in other battles."

"Does it not bother you to kill in such a way?"

"No. They fight to enslave the poor and the helpless. They think nothing of sending old people and children to work the coal mines. They send Indians to work in the jungles hundreds of miles from home while their children and wives remain at home to starve. The gringos and the English own all of our oil. Those men I just killed are the tools that other countries use to keep us from what is ours. I have seen it with my own eyes."

"But they had no chance," Pepe said, thinking that there should be some fairness in battle.

"Yes, that's true."

"Can I ask you something ... something more personal?" Pepe said.

"Sure, but I don't have to answer."

"Did you enjoy killing them?"

El Estudiante wrinkled his brow, puzzled that Pepe would ask such a question. A few seconds passed, and then El Estudiante spoke, "I felt nothing, and even now I feel nothing. As far as I am concerned, you cannot make the supporters of the old government accept the new. I do not want to transform or restructure the old government. It is too corrupt. All of the old rulers, merchants, army officers must either be killed, sent to prison or placed in work camps for the remainder of their lives."

"I don't understand that. I only see death, and it does not seem right. God doesn't want killing," Pepe said.

"God! God! Who do you think has been one of Diaz's biggest supporters? The church, my friend. The church asks us to accept our miserable destinies and suffering as God's will. And what do the rich suffer? Don't you realize that the Americans start wars with countries that can barely feed themselves, steal their land, resources, and then claim that it is God's will. They call it Manifest Destiny. The Spaniards arrived here, wiped out a civilization, slaughtered men, women and children under God's name. The church defended them. Why? For God and gold."

"You know a lot about politics, but little about God," Pepe said, feeling comfortable to talk about religion.

"Why do you say that?" El Estudiante answered, a little surprised at Pepe's courage.

"No one can understand why God allows injustices. But you are wrong about the rich not suffering. Everyone suffers, Estudiante; each of us, rich included, in his own way."

"Are you saying that a man who can buy everything suffers the same as one who must watch his children die of illness?"

"No, I am not saying he suffers the same. He suffers differently, but I believe he suffers just as much. Maybe it is just that some people's suffering is more visible."

"I cannot agree with you," said El Estudiante, standing. "I'm not saying it is right that one owns more than another. But it is reality."

Pepe stood also. "Forever there will be those who have more than others, whether it is money, brains or strength," he said.

"But is it right that those who have more take advantage of those who have nothing?" El Estudiante said.

"No. And that's what I've come to understand the fighting is all about. Not that one has more than another but that because one has more does not give him the right to make others suffer."

Pepe realized that he had come full circle. Both he and El Estudiante had defended different arguments, but strangely, they had once again arrived at the beginning. And still Pepe could not understand how one could kill without remorse.

"Make sure your canteens are full," called out Mariano, "we still have much riding ahead of us."

Mariano sat on his horse. He rubbed his knee, feeling the numbness in his severed leg. He remembered the moment the federal had taken the machete and sliced through the leg. Shaking his head, he smiled at the absurdity of man. It was a bet. While a prisoner, the guards who had been drinking made a bet that a man's leg could not be cut off with one blow. They dragged Mariano from the cell. The four federales stretched him on the ground. The fifth, raising the machete high over his head, laughed as he let the heavy instrument fall, putting all his strength behind it. The metal sliced through half of the bone. Mariano winced as he thought about the instant the machete had struck. A cold chill pulled at his back.

"Andale, let's get going!" he screamed.

El Estudiante said to Pepe, "You will see, killing is not always such a bad thing."

Pepe shook his head. He could never see himself taking the life of a defenseless man, even in war.

El Maestro did not look well. Lilia saw that he was feverish and in great discomfort. She rode her horse alongside his.

"How do you feel, Maestro?"

His head bobbed up and down. He looked at her through half closed eyes. "We showed them, Lilia," he smiled. "Don Emilio, did you see how he begged us not to kill him. God, did we show him. He can never hurt another person again."

"Maestro, how do you feel?" she repeated.

"Strong as a bull on the day of the corrida."

Lilia motioned for Guero to ride closer to his father. El Maestro looked as though he could collapse at any time. She rode to the front to talk to Mariano.

Mariano knew the old man was sick, but he could not slow down or stop. He had to keep moving. He knew that the rurales would take action after discovering the bodies of don Emilio and his men. The town of Maricopa was a two day ride. It was a strong, rebel-occupied town.

After Lilia spoke to him, he stopped his small band and rode back to see El Maestro. "How goes it, Maestro?"

"I think it is the years, Mariano. They are not so kind to an old man."

Mariano saw the frightened look on Guero's face. El Maestro was the only thing the boy had left in the world.

"Can you make it just a little farther? There is a farm about an hour away."

"Seguro, Papá. You can make it," Guero cried out.

The old man smiled at his son, and he felt sad. He did not want to hurt his boy by dying.

"Sí," he answered, "I can make it."

"Buddha!" Mariano called. Buddha rode up quickly, his spurs jangling and his sombrero bouncing on his back,

"Qué pues, patrón?"

"The Maestro doesn't feel well. Ride alongside. Guero will ride on the other side. We'll get him to a farm up ahead."

"Don't worry. Oiga, Maestro, we will get you to a nice comfortable bed where you can sleep all night and day." Buddha smiled at Guero.

It was the longest hour in the old man's life. His body burned and his muscles throbbed with pain. He coughed continuously. Perspiration dripped down his forehead moistening the dust on his face. A few times everything went dark, but he quickly shook himself to consciousness. He tried to keep his mind on Guero. He did not want him to worry.

The boy rode close to his father. He reached out to stop his father from falling, but each time the old man caught himself first. Guero wondered if his father was dying. He loved him very much.

For El Maestro and Guero it had all started when the federales came to their home to confiscate his small parcel of land. If he could not show a deed of ownership, they had told El Maestro, the government would take control of his land. There was no deed. A fight started between El Maestro's oldest son, Guadalupe, and one of the federales. When the fighting finished, Guadalupe had been killed, Sonia and Alicia, the two oldest daughters were taken away, Guero escaped into the chaparral and El Maestro played dead. Luckily, they did not harm Luz; she was barely six. El Maestro had thanked God for taking his wife. It would have been a terrible thing for her to see the destruction of her family.

El Maestro took Luz to live with his nephew, Antonio. It was a sad separation. He knew that he would never see his daughter again.

He and Guero headed into into the sierras moving from one village to another. Once the federales knew that he was alive, they tried to hunt him and Guero down.

In the village of Campana, a settlement of fifteen adobe homes, they met Buddha. He too was running from the federales. On directions from one of the villagers, they made their way to a camp of men who also were running from the federales. There they joined company with Mariano and Chispas.

El Maestro had always been a rugged, hard fighting man. Age was not easy for him to accept. As a rebel his mind knew what had to be done, but his body did not always obey. And now as he rode along, a sick old man endangering the others, he felt as useless as a spent cartridge.

CHAPTER TWENTY-THREE

The man ploughing his land stared at the approaching riders. He called to his youngest son, "Go bring your brothers, quickly."

Mariano saw the young boy run from the farmer, jump onto a mule and ride away.

"Should I get him?" Chispas asked.

"No, we don't want any trouble," Mariano said loudly, making sure everyone heard.

The farmer dropped the reins and released the plough.

"Good afternoon," Mariano greeted him.

The farmer nodded. He eyed the rugged looking men, immediately noticing the weapons and ammunition.

"We are on our way to Juarez. One of our men is very sick," said Mariano. "We have been traveling, it seems, for days, and we are hungry. We have money to pay," he added.

"I have seen men like you before," the farmer said, spitting on the ground and wiping his mouth. "It's better that you continue on your way."

"We only want food and a place to rest," Mariano persisted.

"We have little food," the farmer said.

Pointing to El Maestro, Mariano urged, "He is an old man and very sick. We want no trouble."

"We have little food," the farmer repeated.

"Old man!" Chispas shouted, "do as we ask or we'll take whatever we want."

Apologizing for the outburst, Mariano said, "My men are tired; our patience is limited. We mean no harm."

Again the farmer looked them over carefully. His gaze rested on El Maestro. He could easily see that the man was older than he. El Maestro was slumped over like a race horse rider. It looked as though he would fall from the saddle.

"His fever is very high," Mariano said. "If he doesn't rest, he will die. You can see he's an old man."

Chispas growled in a low voice. He prepared to dismount. He did not like gentlemanly negotiations. As he was about to release a stream of obscenities at the farmer, El Estudiante jammed the butt of his rifle into Chispas' spine.

"Compadre," El Estudiante whispered to Chispas, "let Mariano handle it."

Chispas settle back into his saddle and did as he was told.

"Why don't you ride on? There is nothing for you here," said the farmer.

"There is food and shelter. It's all we need," Mariano told him.

Four men came riding up behind the farmer. He did not bother to turn. He knew exactly how they had positioned themselves. This was not their first challenge.

Mariano studied the men carefully. They were clean cut, well dressed, carried fine weapons, and they appeared very young, probably in their early twenties. He guessed they were the farmer's sons.

"So this it what it must come to?" said Mariano, looking straight into the farmer's eyes. "You would prefer the deaths of such young men rather than allow us rest and food?"

"Once bandits take from the weak, who knows how many times they will return," the farmer said, stepping closer to his sons.

"We are not bandits!" cried Chispas, unable to control himself, "we are revolutionaries. We fight for you and for Mexico."

The farmer laughed,

"Nobody fights for me," he said, "and as for Mexico, she has managed to take care of herself this long, so don't pride yourself on being her savior."

El Estudiante moved his horse up slowly next to Mariano, "Señor," he began, "you are an intelligent man. The way things are going here, one of three things can happen: first, we can simply kill you all and take what we want. In which case much blood will be spilled. Secondly, we can buy the food from you and be on our way, but then there is a good chance our friend, El Maestro here, will die. Third, you can invite us to dinner and allow us to exchange ideas with you instead of bullets. Our companion will have received a much needed rest, and possibly the rest of us can become friends with you."

The farmer's hard expression softened. He studied El Estudi-ante's face, looking at the full beard and brown hair hanging over the ears, the sharp nose and penetrating eyes.

"Your words are interesting, young man," the farmer said, walking toward El Estudiante.

"We not only seek a revolution of guns but also one of minds," said El Estudiante, holding his hand out in friendship.

The farmer took El Estudiante's hand and shook it. He did not feel completely comfortable with the rebels, but neither did he want to see any of his boys killed.

"My name is Panfilo Ortiz," the farmer said.

"They call me El Estudiante. This is Mariano, our jefe, Chispas, Lilia, El Maestro, Buddha, his son, Guero, and Pepe."

The farmer introduced his sons. The youngest was fourteen and the oldest twenty-six. None of them smiled or made gestures when the farmer called their names. Although young, they had much experience with weapons and killings.

Mariano and his men followed the farmer to a well located about 100 yards from a long adobe house. Lilia took El Maestro to the house where he was given a bed. The others washed vigorously until their shirts were soaked with water. Mariano and Chispas shaved. It was their first time with the razor in weeks. Pepe took a pot of water and poured it over his head. He felt the water run down his face, behind his ears and over his chest and back. It amazed him how such a small thing could bring such pleasure.

A long wooden table was placed on the patio. The farmer's wife and young daughter brought out plates of steaming freshly cooked beans and warm tortillas. The farmer had not lied. Although the food was good, there was little of it. Lilia gave the farmer's wife beans, salt and coffee from her supply. Everyone ate. There was small talk about weather and crops.

Pepe sat on a bench that stretched along the outer wall of the house. He sat down and relaxed his legs. All of the others found chairs and sat down, circle-like, in the patio. Pepe tried to listen as the men talked. His eyes grew heavy and his head nodded. Every few seconds he would shake himself and open his eyes wide, but within a little while his eyes closed shut and he slept soundly.

The loud voice shook Pepe from his sleep. Darkness had fallen. An oil lamp, hanging on the post which held up the porch roof, lit up the patio.

"I'm not so sure I deserve any thanks," Pepe heard the farmer bellow. "Didn't you say that if you weren't fed, there would be blood spilled."

"We want to thank you just the same," said Mariano, rolling a cigarette.

"Why are you against a revolution in Mexico?" El Estudiante asked, rising to his feet and placing his hands in his pocket.

"I am not against revolution; I am against stealing and rape."

"Sometimes sacrifices must be made for growth to take place," El Estudiante answered, philosophically.

Pepe rubbed his eyes and face.

"Tell that to the victims," the farmer responded.

"Then, you will not support revolution?" El Estudiante paced back and forth like a professor in front of his class.

Everyone listened as though the discussion were a battle.

"I will never support murder, robbery or rape."

"But a revolution is much more than that," El Estudiante screamed, raising his face to the dark sky, "we are talking about change which will benefit the poor. More food, health care, a decent life ... "

"You children," the farmer said, shaking his head and looking directly at El Estudiante, "you are blinded by ideas and do not see reality."

Angered, El Estudiante leaned over, putting his face inches from the farmer's,

"Ideas? Reality?" he blurted, "ha, men have tried to talk peacefully with government officials. What has it gotten them? Prison time and firing squads. Is it not reality to see injustices?"

The farmer stood up, keeping his face close to El Estudiante's, "What is government? It is those who have much, controlling the lives of those who have little. And whether the government is a king, a cacique, a revolutionary government or what the gringos call a democracy, they are all the same."

"How can you say that?" El Estudiante's arms quivered.

The farmer sat down. He thought, looked up at El Estudiante and said, "Look at the Romans. Did the wealth not manage all power? The feudal landlords and kings of Europe, was it not the same? Our own ancestors, the Mayas and Aztecas, did the strong not rule the weak, the rich slaughter the poor?" The farmer's voice dropped down to a whisper, and as if telling a story to children, he pointed at each of the men and said, "Man is human, too human to ever rule justly. We are animals just like the mountain lion or the wolf. Have you ever seen a mountain lion corner a deer and

tear it into a thousand pieces, devouring and enjoying each piece
of meat?"

Chispas sat with his mouth wide open, astonished at the man's
words. Mariano stroked his mustache, slowly and thoughtfully.
Pepe stared at the farmer. El Estudiante fell back into his chair,.

"Who are you? Where do you get these ideas?" he asked.

"I read and I write," said the farmer, "as a young man I worked
in a government office in the capital. Yes, I learned about rulers
and ruling."

"But if we win the revolution there will be a new government.
There will be land for everyone," said El Estudiante, as if pleading.

"And after all the death and suffering, how much better off will
a man and his family be with a few feet of land ... if, I say ... if
he even receives that much? Do the poor gain? Who really gains?
How about the new revolutionary president and his people? Will
he also be satisfied with a little land? No, young one. He and his
people will receive the best of everything. A new ruling class will
rise. And mark my words, many of the new supporters will be the
wealthy of the last regime."

The old farmer crossed his legs and arms, showing his comfort.
He continued speaking, "After your revolution, a new rich will
rule, and the poor, those who lose sons and husbands and brothers
in the fighting, they will remain just as poor. Look at our friend
Napoleon, such a champion of the people, no? A savior turned
tyrant ... "

"Bueno, so you are saying that there's no hope? We are to
remain in the grasp of tyrants?" El Estudiante exploded.

"Mmm, one tyrant or another, federal or provisional, conserva-
tive or liberal, all keep a tight grasp," the farmer answered, calmly.

"Muy bien. Then tell us what you propose? How does one fight
injustice?"

"For you, Estudiante, I propose nothing."

"But there must be an answer?"

El Estudiante looked around at the faces staring at him. He felt
confused and angry, but before he could answer, the farmer continued his barrage of words, "If you want to make changes and you
want to win the revolution, then kill, rape and steal. It is your only
chance to become somebody. But, son, at least be honest about it.
Don't hide behind fancy words like revolution, movement of the
people, and such. You don't know it, boy, but you're being manip-
ulated by those with larger ideas than your own."

"The people, they need me," El Estudiante cried.

"Ha. I'm people. I don't need you. Isn't it true that you came here looking for food and shelter? You didn't see me going to you."

El Estudiante walked from the patio and made his way into the darkness away from the house.

"Estudiante, wait," called the farmer. El Estudiante stopped, the light from the lamp shining on his back. "I don't like Diaz or his government. But at least he does not pretend to hide his tyranny. He is a vulture and everyone knows it. Some rats would have us believe they were mice. Te chingan, and you don't know whether to moan with pleasure or scream with pain."

"Yours is a comfortable but unfulfilled life, señor." Pepe heard the words slip from his mouth. He remembered thinking them, but was stunned that they had actually been transformed into sound.

Everyone turned. Chispas and Mariano stared at each other in surprise. Ther farmer studied Pepe's face.

"What is that you say?" the farmer responded.

Desperately Pepe searched for words. He felt his mind shiver with excitement as all eyes fell on him. "You understand evil," Pepe said, slowly. "You see the injustices, the pain, the suffering, and you do nothing. You prefer your comfort and say to hell with the rest of the world."

"Who are you to judge me?" answered the farmer. "Only God can judge."

"I hear no judgment passed. What I'm saying is that you own land, you have a home, your sons ride fine horses. So then, as long as no one bothers you, it makes little difference what happens in the rest of Mexico."

"I worked for everything I own," the farmer said in his defense, "no one gave me a thing."

"And what about those who have worked just as hard or harder than you, and still they own nothing. They are those without a voice," Buddha said, from his place on the bench.

"No man can save the world. Let each person look out for himself."

"And that's exactly what the revolution is, those who are looking out for themselves, many for the first time in their life," Buddha cried out, enthusiastically.

"Things in Mexico aren't as bad as you would have us believe," the farmer said, looking to his sons.

La Lilia walked from the house and stood behind the farmer's chair. In a strong voice, she said, "My husband and three sons worked at a textile mill in Saltillo. The owner was an American.

He owned the factory and the land. He made his home in New York. We worked twelve hours a day, seven days a week. And with that we could barely afford to buy our food or pay our rent.

"We started having meetings. It was beautiful, the workers, men, women and children, we came together and sang songs and said prayers. We decided to strike for better wages and lower prices at the store. Yes, the gringo owned the store, also. We wanted to work fewer hours and have more breaks for the women and children.

"One day, I remember it was a hot day," she said, folding her arms, "we all met in front of the main office. We refused to work. Dios, there must have been a thousand of us. We even prayed, right there. We asked the bosses to try to understand our position. They smiled at us and said that they would consider our situation.

"After some hours passed, the soldiers arrived. American bosses gave all the directions. The soldiers began shooting." Lilia stared straight into the darkness, as if she were watching the scene unfold before her.

"People screamed as they tried to dodge the bullets. The soldiers charged and began crushing skulls with the butts of their rifles. My husband was shot through the neck. Two of my sons were beaten to death. The third was taken to prison, and I haven't seen him since." Lilia paused. "The revolution is our only hope."

"Our war is here at home defending what we own against both rebel and government troops. And understand, already we have killed many who would try to rob us." The speaker was the farmer's oldest son. He leaned against the house, a rifle propped on his leg.

Mariano spotted the other sons reaching for their rifles, "You don't need to do that," he told them, "once we are sure that El Maestro will receive care, we will be on our way."

"El Maestro is dead. He died a short time ago," Lilia answered.

Mariano entered the room first. Chispas pushed his way past Pepe and Buddha. El Estudiante was the last to enter. Guero sat in a chair next to the bed where El Maestro lay, looking as though he were asleep. The boy's eyes were filled with tears. He looked up at the men. "Just before he died he said to tell you all to be careful," Guero said in a low, jerky voice. "He said to keep fighting until the revolution is won. He said, he ... " Guero couldn't speak anymore. He sobbed silently and quickly wiped the tears from his face.

CHAPTER TWENTY-FOUR

The men were up and ready to ride by the time the sun broke over the mountains. They made last minute adjustments to their saddles and supplies , tightening straps, pulling cintures and securing ropes. Chispas checked his pistols to make sure they were fully loaded. He strapped two belts of ammunition over his shoulders and across his chest. Pepe tied a red bandana over his head and pulled a large sombrero down tightly. He cocked his rifle and blew inside the trigger mechanism; he wanted no dirt in the chamber. Buddha put on leather leggings he had stolen from federales in an earlier fight. Tucked into the leggings was a ten inch hunting knife. On his hip he carried one pistol holstered in a leather ammunition belt, and alongside his saddle he carried a carbine.

Mariano and El Estudiante wrapped El Maestro's body in a serape. They draped him over his horse, securing him into place with a rope. Guero watched as they stretched the rope and tied it around his father. Somehow it did not seem right that the body of a human being should simply be strapped to a horse and carried into the mountains for disposal.

Guero wore his father's beret. He also carried a large knife, one belt of ammunition and a rifle. La Lilia, her hair pulled back and tied in a bun, strapped two belts of ammunition across her breasts. She wore a long, full dress, men's boots and a pistol belt strapped to her side.

Panfilo Ortiz and his sons watched as the rebels prepared to ride out. There was a certain beauty in the way Mariano and his men went about their preparations. The horses whinnied and raised dust as their hooves pounded the earth. Mariano screamed commands and the others obeyed. Panfilo immediately recognized a rugged discipline in the men. They acted like soldiers, brave and confident. He then realized for the first time that if all Mexico raised in arms against Diaz' army, if there were hundreds, thousands of rebels, men and women, with the same dedication and zeal, the federales, weak and disorganized—hungry only for booty but not battle—would not survive the onslaught of the people.

"Vámonos, muchachos," Mariano screamed, straightening up in his saddle and raising a hand into the air. He wore the same hat, the brim folded upwards in front so that his dark, handsome face was clearly visible. His horse spun in a circle, reared up on its hind legs, perfectly controlled by Mariano. He led the small band away from the ranch in a single column, crossed the main road and headed into the low mountains west along an ancient cattle trail.

The sun was still young when they reached the top of a mountain that overlooked a long valley. The men could see little streams of smoke rising from the homes of campesinos which sprinkled the valley floor. Pepe watched as a man and two children followed by a scrawny mule walked along the main road. No doubt they were off to squeeze a few centavos from an economy which offered many profits to the rich and almost nothing to the poor. Buddha caught sight of an old woman walking along a ditch. He watched as she felt her way with a stick to guide her. What was hidden from him because of the distance was that she made her way among the garbage and trash, turning over papers and discarded rags, bloody cloth, egg shells and potato peels.

"This is a fine place," Mariano announced. "What do you think, Guero?"

Guero stared at the horse which carried his father's body. He tried not to think about the rolled bulk hanging over the saddle. "Sí, it is a fine place," he answered.

Pepe made a cross from two branches. After El Maestro's body was buried, Buddha stacked a number of rocks to hold the cross firmly in place. Lilia knelt down and prayed silently. The others, standing with hands in pockets or pulling loose strands of straw from their sombreros, appeared nervous. They would not allow their emotions to show. El Maestro had been like a grandfather to them. Although they had only ridden together for eight months, his presence had affected them deeply.

"Eh, Estudiante, do you remember the time we sent the Maestro to steal some food for us?"

The hardened expression on El Estudiante's face faded and a smile took its place,

"What, the duck?"

"Yeah. Remember how scared he was because he'd never stolen anything in his life?"

As they continued talking, El Estudiante saw a rider racing up the mountain towards them. He called to the others, "Look who is coming."

"What the devil is he doing here?" Mariano cried out as he watched Panfilo's youngest son, Loza, approaching.

"I'm going with you. I want to join the revolution," he screamed, making his way towards the men.

Chispas took off his sombrero and slapped it against his leg, "Chingao! That's all we need, a spoiled kid riding with us."

"Does your father know what you have done?" Mariano asked.

"I left him a note."

"He'll come looking for you." Chispas spat the words.

The boy's face sagged. He hadn't thought about that. His father and brothers would come after him once they found his note. They would catch him and beat him.

"Please. We have to go fast. If they catch me, they will punish me," the boy said, frightened.

"Punish! Punish!" Chispas bellowed, moving his horse close to the boy. "If the federales or the rurales catch you, they will torture you, cut off your ears, break your knees, slice your nose ... pray that your family comes first."

"Mariano, let him come with us. We need all the men we can get. Even his wild bullets might find their way into a federal's chest," El Estudiante said, looking the boy over.

"Okay, but let's get out of here fast. We don't have much time," Mariano said.

Something about El Maestro's death affected Pepe deeply. A pounding loneliness rammed its way inside him. Riding in the rear of the column, he watched as each man bounced along in his saddle. He began to wonder which of them would die next. For the first time, he started to contemplate his own death. Visions of his bloody body passed through his mind. He saw himself standing against a wall. Before him were a line of federales, faceless, rifles at the ready. The command sounded and the soldiers fired. Pepe's body quivered as each bullet tore into his flesh. Pepe shuddered. The vision seemed real.

Mariano had the men ride at a fast trot. The sun rose higher and a long cloud of dust followed them. Pepe's mind would not rest. He felt tormented. He suddenly wanted to go back home to his family.

He thought about the ranch. He saw Conejo's face. It distorted and dissolved leaving a clear image of his dead father. He thought about the country north of the border. He saw Ramoncito's crumpled body. Pepe shook his head. He wondered how long it would take to get to Juarez and what they would do once they arrived. He knew that something big was waiting, but he didn't know what. Then in an instant, like an explosion, it came to him. He would go home. He would ask his mother to forgive him. He knew too well the story of the prodigal son.

It would not be difficult to escape from Mariano and the others. He could find a job back in Saltillo and make enough money to catch the train to Zacatecas. From there a mule train could get him to Juchipila. He would be back in the canyons that he loved.

The whole idea sent a river of relief through him. No more guns, no more killing. He would support the revolution from his home. He began to plan his escape.

"Go home, boy!" The words shook Pepe from his reverie. For a moment, he thought Mariano was talking to him. "Go, you can't come with us," he said to Loza.

"But I want to go. I can fight."

"No. I shouldn't have let you come."

"Please, señor. Don't make me go back," the boy begged.

"Are you willing to fight your own family? Kill your brothers and maybe even your father?"

"I don't know what you mean," the boy said to Mariano.

"Chispas was right. I've been thinking. Your family is probably on the trail now. We have enough problems fighting federales. We don't need to fight farmers too."

"I coud never kill my father, señor," the boy answered.

"That's exactly why you must go back," Mariano told him,

"A real rebel would shoot even his father if his father was the enemy."

"Could you kill your own father?" Loza asked, wide eyed and nervous.

"And my mother, too."

Chispas interrupted harshly, "Vámonos! We don't have all day to sit here and yap about our parents."

"I'll ride back with him," Pepe offered, "I'll see that he reaches his family safely. I can catch up to you in an hour or so."

Mariano didn't feel comfortable letting Pepe ride alone. Since Pepe was still so new, Mariano still wasn't sure whether he could be trusted.

"Hurry, hombre, let them both go!" Chispas pressed, "we are wasting time already."

"Muy bien, go," Mariano ordered, "we'll stay on this road."

Pepe knew that he was free. He would drop the boy off and ride back to Saltillo.

"I refuse!" Loza cried out.

Pepe lashed out with his arm. His hand caught the boy on top of the nose. A trickle of blood began to drip.

"Get going before you get all of us killed." Pepe sounded angry. He was in control. His action surprised the others, but no one said a word.

Loza turned his horse and started back down the trail. Pepe followed. When they were out of hearing range Pepe said, "I'm sorry I hit you, but you don't know what you're doing."

"Why do you ride with them then?"

"It just happened that way, that's all. I didn't choose it, it just happened," was all he could say.

They rode about five kilometers when they saw a funnel of dust in front of them. "Your father and brothers," Pepe said.

"I don't want to go with them," Loza insisted, frightened.

"Don't be stupid. If you stay with us, you'll be dead in a week," Pepe warned.

"I'm old enough to choose what I want to do."

"Listen, your family cares about you, they love you. Us, we only care about ourselves, and even then," Pepe looked at Loza but saw that the boy wasn't listening, "forget it. You're going back and that's it."

Pepe grabbed the reins of Loza's horse so that the boy couldn't ride off. Both of them were nervous as they watched the riders approach.

"Let him go!" the farmer ordered, guns drawn.

"Señor, no one is holding him. He's free to go," Pepe answered, releasing the reins.

Loza slapped the horse on the rear and the animal moved forward. He could see that his father and brothers were furious.

"You left right on time. The federales came a short time later," the farmer said.

"How? What did they say?" Pepe asked, confused and scared.

"They had two rurales and an indio following your trail. They said you killed a government official and his guards a few days ago."

"Why haven't we seen them on the road?"

"They took the back roads over the mountains. It's much quicker."

"What are their plans?" asked Pepe.

"They didn't say. But an easy guess is that they will set up an ambush; they have many weapons. One of them carried a machine gun."

"Why are you telling me all of this?"

Panfilo smiled, "I told you, I don't like Diaz either. War is not the way to solve our country's problems, but maybe if you rattle enough people something will happen."

The farmer turned to the boy and slapped him hard across the face. Pepe watched as they spoke, but he couldn't hear. They turned and rode back to their farm.

Pepe sat in the saddle without moving. He was free. He let the farmer and his sons gain some distance. And then Pepe started east, back towards Saltillo. He felt sick. There was a rock in his stomach. The bile choked him. He couldn't do it. He couldn't run out.

CHAPTER TWENTY-FIVE

A shot whizzed past Chispas' ear. The rebels leaped from their saddles, grabbed their rifles and crawled into the brush. Echoes tore the silence of the mountains. Hissing bullets passed low overhead, pinning the rebels to the ground.

The federales hid themselves in the low, dense foliage of the mountains across the road. The brush grew in thick, dry clumps. Mariano tried to see how many there were. The mountain seemed filled with them.

Chispas looked for the flash of the muzzles. Twice he saw a bright spark fly from the same bush. Lying on his belly, he pointed his rifle and fired. A body in a grey uniform rose up from the bush, straightened and fell forward.

Mariano, hidden behind a rock, lifted his rifle to fire. Bullets pelted the rock and sent puffs of dirt flying all around him. He ducked down clinging to the boulder.

"Chispas, there are too many of them," Buddha called over the roar.

"Is everyone all right?" screamed Mariano.

El Estudiante and Guero lay hidden behind a mesquite bush. The ground sloped downwards, which allowed them some protection against the federales. One by one they all called back to Mariano that they were okay.

Lilia touched the side of her calf, just below the knee. A bullet had grazed her. She did not yet feel the pain, but felt a furrow of shattered flesh.

The monster sound of a machine gun sent terror through all of them. Each pressed his body tightly to the earth. Guero panicked and started to rise. El Estudiante grabbed him by the collar and pulled him back down.

"Did you see where it came from?" Chispas called.

"I didn't see anything!" Mariano hollered at him.

Buddha got to his knees. Slowly he lifted his head over the boulder which protected him. The machine gun flew into a rage. He could feel each round as it tore away chunks of rock. Buddha fell to the ground. His breath came in deep gasps.

Still on his stomach Mariano crawled to the side of a rock. He was able to bring his rifle to his shoulder and aim. He saw a man rise and run from one bush to another. Mariano focused his sights on the bush. Seconds later the man rose again. Mariano pulled the trigger. His mauser kicked. The bullet struck the man on the shoulder, tearing away part of the arm. Again the machine gun roared. Pieces of sharp rock split the air. Buddha began praying silently.

Pepe yanked at the reins and brought his horse to a jerking stop. The echo from the battle sounded like clashes of thunder. He knew that he could not continue forward or the federales would see him. He forced his horse to climb the steep mountainside. The animal slipped on the loose dirt and rock. Halfway up, Pepe dismounted. He grabbed his rifle, threw an extra belt of ammunition over his shoulder, and climbed to a spot where he could see the battle clearly.

Once reaching the top, he saw the rocks where Mariano and the others were pinned down. Two horses lay dead on the road. The soldiers fired steadily. Pepe jerked each time he heard the machine gun fire. Its spray ripped at the mountain below. If he could knock the big gun out, Mariano and the others would have a chance.

The dry needles tore Pepe's shirt as he hurried through the brush. He ran down the mountain, walked along a narrow ridge and climbed the backside of the mountain where the federales were positioned. He saw that two men operated the machine gun. The rest were spread out to the sides and in front of the gun. Pepe dropped to his stomach. Quietly, carefully, he moved slowly towards the clattering weapon.

At fifteen meters, Pepe sighted down the barrel of his rifle. He aimed at the spot between the machine gunner's shoulders. Pepe breathed deeply. He released half of the air in his lungs, held his breath and squeezed the trigger. The gunner reached down to pick up a belt of ammunition. Pepe's finger froze when he saw the man's face. It was his brother, Miranda.

Pepe released the trigger. He dropped his head and lay perfectly still. The machine gun dominated the battle. Miranda shifted the

big weapon from one side to another, sending out a stream of fire
that forced the rebels to keep their heads buried in the dirt.

Pepe rose to one knee. He saw the federales making their way
down the mountainside behind Miranda's cover. There was little
return fire. Pepe wanted time to think, but there was no time.

He leaped forward, pointing his rifle at the man who kneeled
alongside Miranda.

"Stop firing or you're dead!" Pepe shouted.

The two men turned. "Don't shoot! Don't shoot!" cried Miranda's comrade, his short, fat body trembling.

Miranda stared at Pepe. His eyes grew large, his face taut.
He turned away and continued firing. The fat man pleaded with
Miranda to stop.

Pepe screamed at his brother, "Stop firing. Stop!"

Miranda didn't listen. The bullets from his weapon cut down
the brush and split pieces of rock where the rebels hid.

"Miranda, listen to me." Pepe yelled, desperately. Miranda
would not stop.

Pepe shifted the rifle in his hand, and using it like a club, he
hit Miranda behind the head. Miranda's body crumpled to the
ground. Pepe grabbed him and pulled him to one side. The fat
man fell to his knees, tears streaming. Pepe pointed the rifle at the
man's face.

"Can you use this thing?" Pepe asked, his face as firm as a
brick.

"Yes, yes, anything you say," said the man, rising to his feet
and taking hold of the weapon. Pepe held the belt of ammunition
for him. The man began shooting. The bullets strayed over the
federales' heads.

"Lower, shoot lower," Pepe commanded.

The first pass from the weapon killed three federales and
wounded many others. Confused, the soldiers looked back towards
the machine gun. Some soldiers dropped their rifles and ran. The
more experienced turned and began shooting at the fat man and
Pepe.

Mariano and the others lifted themselves and saw the federales
scrambling in all directions. They pointed their rifles at the easy
targets. The federales were caught in a crossfire.

The shooting lasted a few minutes more. The remaining federales, confused, disoriented and wounded, raised their arms in
surrender. The shooting stopped. The rebels stepped out onto the
road, weapons drawn and ready to kill.

Mariano, who had broken his wooden peg when he leaped from his horse, limped to the base of the mountain where the federales stood scattered about the brush.

"Keep your hands raised. Walk down slowly, one at a time, beginning with you," he called to the federal closest to him.

Chispas and the others spread themselves out on the road. They held their weapons against their shoulders, prepared to shoot anyone who disobeyed.

Pepe ordered the fat soldier to tie Miranda's hands and feet.

"Bueno, now go down and line up with your friends," Pepe said.

"Please, señor," the man begged, tears still running, "I don't want to die. Let me go. I can disappear in the mountains."

"Go down there. Nobody will kill you."

"Honestly, señor?"

"You're a prisoner."

Smiling, the fat man made his way down the mountain. He stumbled over a rock, fell, picked himself up and surrendered to Chispas.

Pepe thought of leaving Miranda where he lay. No one would ever know. And once he gained consciousness, he could free himself.

Miranda opened his eyes. He saw Pepe standing there. Realizing that his hands and feet were bound, he screamed furiously at Pepe.

"Rios," Mariano called to him, "what's going on?"

Pepe looked at Miranda and knew that he could not leave him now. "Just an angry prisoner." Pepe yelled.

Buddha ran up the mountain to help bring Miranda down. Pepe watched as Buddha led him through the bushes. The absurdity of the whole thing caught Pepe. How could this be, he asked himself as he made his way down the mountain, stepping over broken, bloody bodies. He picked up some of the discarded weapons. A voice called to him, weak and child-like. Pepe searched the area. A young boy, an arm severed from his body, tried to talk. Pepe walked over and stooped down.

"Agua, por favor," the child said, in a low, raspy voice.

Dressed in the federal uniform, he could not have been more than twelve. Pepe knelt over him. The boy tried to talk. He cringed with pain. His chest rose and fell heavily. He looked at Pepe and smiled.

"It's good. I'm not thirsty anymore," he said, crying.

Pepe couldn't think of anything to say. Words seemed useless.

"I'm fine. There's no more pain," the voice, barely a whisper, fell into a silence. The boy closed his eyes. The chest stopped moving. Pepe stood and stared.

"Rios," Chispas called, "come on down here."

"God forgive me," Pepe said to himself.

Chispas made the prisoners kneel down on the road and place their hands behind their necks.

"They're just kids," El Buddha said, as he moved from one boy to the next.

"Kids kill just like anyone else," said Chispas, angrily.

"Let the boys go," Mariano said, looking at El Estudiante.

El Estudiante walked down the line. Those who appeared less than teenagers, he slapped on the backs of their heads.

"Go, get out of here," he told them, "we will be around. Don't ever let us see you in a government uniform again." They thanked him and ran down the road, stripping away their uniforms.

Pepe took hold of Mariano's arm, "The one over there," he said, nodding towards Miranda, "he's my brother."

"Be serious, man," Mariano responded.

"I'm telling you, he's my brother," Pepe repeated, irritated.

"You never told us your brother was a federal."

"When I left home, he lived on the ranch. He wasn't a federal."

"What is it? Qué pasa?" El Estudiante asked.

"Rios says that the one over there is his brother."

"What?" El Estudiante cried, disbelieving.

"Hombre, what's going on over there?" Chispas called.

Mariano threw up his arms in disgust, "Pepe says the machine gunner is his brother."

Everyone turned to see Miranda. He got up from his knees and yelled, "He's a liar. I don't have a brother."

"So, that's why you didn't shoot him when you had the chance," said Chispas.

"What do we do with him?" asked Buddha.

"Kill him with the rest," came Chispas' blunt reply.

"Ay, Dios no, no, please do not kill me. They forced me to fight. I did not want to. They made me go. I have a wife, children," it was the fat man, pleading for his life.

Chispas walked up to him. The man's eyes grew wide. Chispas' fist landed flush to the man's chin. The man let out a cry and tumbled to the ground. He sat there, whimpering like a puppy.

"Let my brother go," Pepe said.

"You know better than that, Pepe," Mariano told him.

"Then let him come with us. I'll watch him."

"Hurry. We don't have all day. Let's kill them and get out of here," Chispas said, anxiously.

Five prisoners remained. One rural and four federales. Except for the fat man, the others looked at their captors bravely.

"If your brother steps out of line one time, I will kill him myself," Mariano warned Pepe.

"He'll be my responsibility," Pepe said.

"Later, we will decide what to do with him. Now," Mariano instructed, "take care of the rest. You, Buddha, Guero, go get as many weapons as you can carry. Destroy the machine gun, it's too big for us to carry."

"Do we have to kill them?" Pepe asked Mariano as they walked to bring back the horses.

"They are better off dead," Mariano answered.

"But why?"

Mariano looked at Pepe and shook his head, "You haven't seen what the rurales and federales do to villagers who cannot protect themselves?"

Pepe said no.

"I have seen men killed by the federales. They were pulled apart, limb by limb, tied to horses which split them in half. Once I saw the bodies of victims who the rurales had executed. Their balls had been cut off and shoved down their throats."

"But why? Why would anyone kill in that way?" Pepe asked.

"Their orders come from the richest Mexicans." Pepe turned as El Estudiante approached. He had overheard and given his own answer, "If they can frighten the poor with such brutalities, they think the poor will not fight back. They will behave, work the fields and mines and not complain about the inhumane conditions. These men," El Estudiante pointed to the prisoners, "are animals. They will do anything for money. Our country is ruled by the Americans, the British, French and Germans. The British and French support Diaz because he gives them larger concessions than he does the Americans. And the Americans support the rebels because American oil men feel Diaz has sold them out. Mexico is split, and not by our own doing, but by the meddling of foreigners who want to suck every last resource from our land."

"But," Pepe tried to speak.

"Later," El Estudiante said, "we must attend to business first."

Pepe didn't look but listened as Chispas and El Estudiante executed the prisoners. He heard the blast of the pistols. He heard moaning and crying and strange gurgling sounds coming from those who did not die immediately. He listened to the fat man's pleading until the explosion silenced him. Pepe tried to understand, but somehow the killing still seemed like murder.

He tied his brother's hands to the saddle. Miranda looked away, as if Pepe did not exist. They did not talk, although both had many questions.

CHAPTER TWENTY-SIX

For Pepe the war had become difficult to understand. Sometimes the fighting seemed like nothing more than Mexicans slaughtering Mexicans. Maybe if the enemy was of a different race the killing would have come easier. Something had to be terribly wrong for brothers to fight brothers.

How much loyalty should a person give to a cause? Pepe thought the question through. He even asked himself how far he would go to save Miranda from death. As for a cause, Pepe still did not understand the reasons he was fighting. He tried to grasp the ideology and politics behind the struggle. He understood the plight of the poor, and he believed about the brutal methods the government used to rule. But what if it came down to choosing between the rebels and his brother? He chased the thought from his mind.

They stopped for the night at the bottom of a deep canyon. A tremendous rock wall protected them on one side. A shallow stream which formed many tiny pools in the rocky bottom ran along the base of the wall. The water echoed quietly in the canyon as it tumbled over boulders and splashed downward.

La Lilia passed out pieces of dried beef and hard tortillas. The men pulled lazily at the meat. They were too exhausted to eat.

Buddha walked to the creek. Removing his clothes, he slipped into a pool of water. He lay still and let the cool water seep into his tired body. Nothing he could remember ever felt so good. He slid lower into the pool and put his head under the water. Opening his mouth, he let the water rush in over his tongue and between his teeth. Buddha was careful not to make a sound. He knew that the rurales could always be near.

Closing his eyes he began remembering the night he had made love to señora Villegas, his friend Geronimo's aunt. She had asked

Buddha to go with her into the fields; she said that she had forgotten some potatoes there. It was dark when they reached the spot where the vegetables had been left.

A smile came to Buddha as he continued reminiscing. Señora Villagas had been about 35 years old at the time; Buddha was 15. He remembered how there had been a softness in her voice that he had not heard before. After looking for the potatoes for a few minutes, she asked Buddha if he would scratch her back. He felt a little uncomfortable because of the respect he held for her. Nervously he walked over to her and scratched gently.

"Not there," she said, "a little lower, closer to the side."

Buddha took his hand from her shoulder and scratched a few inches below her right arm. Her breathing grew heavier.

"Let me show you," she told him and placed his fingers on her breast.

He knew that he should pull his hand away, but he couldn't. He too got excited. She began explaining how she felt lonely since her husband had gone off to Chihuahua three weeks before. She needed a man, and she knew that Buddha wouldn't tell anyone. He laid down with her between the potatoes and the alfalfa. He told her it was his first time. He soon found that she was an excellent teacher. She made his body throb. He let out small cries, but she did not make a sound. He moved faster and faster. Perspiration dripped down his forehead. He felt his groin ignite. The sweet burning sensation took away all his strength. Still she made no sound. When he finished, he felt a sadness he had never experienced before.

"What about the potatoes," he asked as she walked away.

"Tomorrow. I'll get them tomorrow," was all she said.

Buddha, now lying in his pool of cool water, smiled. It had been a night he would always remember. How he would like señora Villagas tonight. He crawled from the pool, put on his clothes and walked back to where the men sat.

Pepe untied Miranda's hands. He offered him a piece of meat. Miranda, never the martyr, took the beef, tore a piece with his teeth and chewed hard. He finished the meat without saying a word. Pepe gave him a cup of water. Miranda emptied the cup in one gulp.

"You eat like the government doesn't feed you," Pepe said, trying to sound casual.

"What the fuck are you doing with these bastards?" Miranda said.

They sat near an oak tree about twenty meters from the others. Pepe told his brother to speak quietly.

"Answer me. Why are you here?" Miranda persisted.

"They have given me the chance to help the poor. They are my friends. Besides, they provide food and safety, something I could not get at home."

Miranda gave Pepe an angry look. "Now what the fuck does that mean?" he asked.

Pepe didn't answer.

Miranda said, "You were my mother's favorite. You could have had anything you wanted, you idiot."

Pepe looked down at the ground. He did not feel like arguing.

"How did you get mixed up with these sons of whores?" came Miranda's next question.

"By accident. But that means nothing now. I choose to ride with them."

"Pepe, how can you be so stupid? The government is organizing a huge army. Weapons are pouring in from all over the world. These men will soon all be dead."

"How is my mother?" Pepe asked.

"Why would you want to know? You ran out, didn't even say where you were going."

Pepe felt the anger rising inside him. "Bueno, but I didn't run out because some cabrón offered me land and a whore."

Pepe saw the fire in Miranda's eyes. "You stupid little bastard," was all Miranda could say.

They sat quietly for what seemed like a long time. Pepe finally broke the silence. "Why did you join the army?"

Miranda was still angry. He took a deep breath. "Conejo. He talked to some people. Because I knew horses and guns they let me in as a sergeant. They promised to make me a lieutenant after six months."

Miranda saw Pepe shake his head.

"What is it?" Miranda asked, perturbed.

"Don't you see. As a federal you will probably be killed. I am already out of the way. So who will get all my father's land?" Pepe nodded slowly, "That's right, your friend the rabbit, don Conejo," said Pepe, sarcastically.

Miranda looked at Pepe skeptically. The idea had never occurred to him. "That's crazy. Conejo has treated me like a son," Miranda said.

"Oh yeah. Well think it over carefully. By marrying my mother, Conejo gets all of the land. It won't be long before you are dead. Look at your army ... kids who have never even held guns. The older veterans desert as soon as they get the chance."

Pepe could see the puzzled look on his brother's face. Miranda scratched his forehead slowly.

"I've had time to think it through," Pepe said, "Conejo planned my father's death, and even the men who came to our house—I'm sure they came to kill me. You and I are the oldest; we are the heirs."

"I cannot believe it," Miranda said, "it's crazy."

Pepe thought carefully. "All right then, look at it this way. What has Conejo got today and what have you got?"

The look of arrogance on Miranda's face faded. He spoke as if talking to himself, "Me, signing up, it was Conejo's idea. I did not want to. He said I would become a lieutenant and in no time a captain. I would have a good chance at becoming a mayor or governor. Everything—it was all his idea."

"I don't know how he did it," Pepe said, "but I know he killed our father."

"When I left, Conejo said that he would take care of Rosa," Miranda spoke as if in a daze. "She tried to get me to stay—she begged—and I remember she was afraid of something. She would not tell me."

Miranda turned his face from Pepe. Pepe could see his brother's confusion. Pepe thought it better to leave him alone.

"Do you want more to eat?" Pepe asked, as he rose to his feet.

Miranda did not answer. Pepe walked back to the others.

Mariano watched closely. When Pepe left his brother, Mariano motioned with his head for Chispas to go tie the prisoner.

Chispas had a better idea. "Let's bring him over and talk to him. Maybe he can tell us something."

"All right, bring him over," answered Mariano.

As Chispas went to get Miranda, Mariano turned to Pepe.

"Listen, we are going to question your brother. Maybe it's better if you go for a walk.

Pepe watched as Chispas grabbed Miranda and pulled him up from the ground.

"No. I want to stay," said Pepe.

"Well then, not a word from you. Your brother is a federal, an enemy soldier. We need all of the information we can get."

"I think he's coming around to seeing his mistake," Pepe said.

"Don't be stupid, Pepe," El Estudiante said.

"No, when I spoke to him, I told him about things that ... "

Just then Chispas and Miranda walked up. Mariano held up his hand to silence Pepe. El Estudiante and Buddha moved closer. Chispas rolled a cigarette and handed it to Miranda.

"Who is it you ride for?" asked Mariano.

"Colonel Villaseñor," came Miranda's reply.

"How did you find us?"

"We were ordered to search for you. We ran into a farmer who said you kidnapped his son, and he told us which way you went. We rode around you and set up an ambush. You know the rest."

"No others followed you?" Chispas asked.

"No, but they'll come looking when we don't return. Comandante Figueroa has been after you for weeks. He won't stop until he gets you."

"Maybe. I know Figueroa. He spends more time in the cantinas than anywhere else," said Mariano, "he's a slob and very sloppy."

No one spoke for a while. Chispas pulled out a bottle of whiskey, took a drink and passed it to Miranda. Miranda drank and passed it on. The bottle slid from hand to hand until everyone had drunk.

"You are pretty good with that machine gun," said Buddha.

Miranda didn't answer.

"Why did you join the federales?" El Estudiante asked, passing the bottle to Pepe.

"Somebody told me I would make good money at it."

"Well, how much have you made?"

"Very little."

"We fight for free," Chispas said, "no pay, only what the people give us and what we take from the rich."

"And how much do people give you?" asked Miranda.

"Enough to keep us alive and ready for the next battle."

"The people respect us," said Miranda.

"The people are terrified of you," El Estudiante responded.

"There is no way for you to win. The government has thousands of troops and many, many arms," Miranda warned.

"We will win. The people are with us. Whenever you search for us, the people, even in small villages, hide us. Every day more people take up arms. They are tired of living like pigs," said El Estudiante.

"What do you know about Ciudad Juarez?" Mariano asked.

"Nothing. Why?" said Miranda.

"It will be big. There the government will witness our strength. There the world will see that we are serious."

La Lilia walked quickly towards them.

"Someone is coming," she whispered.

"How many?" asked Mariano, reaching for his carbine.

"Only one."

"Chispas, go get him," commanded Mariano.

Chispas disappeared. The rest of the men reached for their weapons. Mariano told Pepe to tie Miranda's hands. The others hid in the brush.

"Quién vive?" called out Chispas.

"Juan Magaña?" answered the man.

"Qué gente?" came the next challenge from Chispas.

"Hijo de Francisco Madero."

Before the man realized, Chispas stood behind him, holding a knife to his throat. The man understood and said nothing.

Chispas took the man's rifle and searched him. When he was satisfied, Chispas said, "Bueno, vámonos," and followed the man down the hill where the others waited.

They sat in a circle. The late moon came into full view, casting shadows over the ground.

"Where are you from?" asked Mariano.

The man answered in an excited, jumpy voice, "Here, from these mountains. I came to join the revolution."

He was a young man in his early twenties, dark skin, handsome face, thinly built and very short. He wore white cotton trousers and shirt.

"We heard about today's battle," he continued, smiling as he spoke. "The soldiers came into our village saying they had been ambushed by one hundred bandits."

Chispas laughed, and looking at Miranda, he said, "You see with what brave souls you fight. And how truthful they are."

"This is it? This is the size of your army?" Juan Magaña said, looking at El Estudiante.

"Ay hijo," Juan replied, "you scared them so bad, some are burying their uniforms and going back to their home towns." He let out a yell of excitement and triumph,

"Ayyyy!"

"Cállate, hombre," whispered El Estudiante, "you want everyone to know where we are?"

"Forgive me," said Juan, "sometimes I get a little loquito."

Pepe spoke for the first time, "Why do you want to join us?"

"Madero, hombre! Everywhere we hear the name of don Francisco Madero. The people of my village are tired of working the land of others and gaining nothing in return. We want land." Juan became thoughtful for a moment, then continued, "besides, working is too hard; it is much easier to fight, no?"

"And your family?" Buddha asked.

"My father is an old man." Juan's voice softened, "the rancher who he works for beats him down, each year a little more. He has tried his best to give us a good life, but there is little pay and food. I left my wife and child with him and my mother. When he heard the Maderistas fight for land for the poor, he told me to go, it was our only hope."

"The government calls us outlaws," said Buddha.

"So what. The ranchers call us animals," came Juan's reply.

"Can you handle a horse and rifle?" asked Chispas.

"I can learn. I worked the fields for the rancher. I know burros better than horses. I can use a knife better than a rifle."

Chispas handed Juan a knife. Mariano nodded for Juan to use it. Juan looked around. In the darkness he spotted a tree that had been struck by lightning. One jagged branch reached outward about two feet. It was no more than six inches round. Juan threw the knife effortlessly. The knife whizzed through the air, stuck and vibrated an inch from where the branch ended. The men smiled.

They gave Juan the name Loquito, the little crazy one. Loquito liked it. But there were more important things to consider.

Loquito told them that many rurales had been sent to find them. How many he did not know, but they were out for revenge. They would allow no one to escape alive.

"No more games," Mariano warned, after listening to Loquito.

"We knew the federales were after us, and we knew how inexperienced and stupid they were. But now that they have the rurales on our trail, it means that they think we are a serious threat. They no longer think of us as mere bandits."

"We don't have enough men to fight them," Chispas said.

"That's true," answered Mariano, "we can't ride blindly any longer. We must plan our movements carefully. There are eight of us. We must use each man's talents. For example, El Loquito here knows the land better than any of us, since he is from these parts." El Loquito smiled proudly.

"Pepe," Mariano called, "you fought bravely today. You saved our asses, but I know that you are still confused. I want you to leave, now, tonight ... unless you choose to fight for a reason ...

for a cause. I don't want you with us if you are only fighting because
we are friends and there is nothing better to do. You have proved
your loyalty, your friendship to us. But we are nothing. It is to the
cause that you must devote your life."

Pepe's mind whirled. He understood exactly what Mariano
meant. And even after today's battle, Pepe still found many things
about the fighting ambiguous. He needed more time.

"If you ride with us for the sake of your own survival, Pepe,"
said Mariano, "then you make us nothing more than bandits."

Everyone felt the heavy silence as Mariano stopped talking.

"Here it is," Mariano finally said, after a long pause, "El Estudiante will talk to your brother. If he chooses to ride with us and
become a soldier of the people, we welcome him. If not," again
came a pause, and then his next words, "you kill him."

Pepe looked wildly at Mariano ... and then at the others. He
saw the same firm expressions on their faces that he saw when they
first captured him.

"I can't kill my brother," Pepe cried out.

"Then leave us," said Mariano.

"And my brother?"

"He is a prisoner of war."

Pepe became frightened. He felt the heat rush to his head. He
knew that he would not be able to change Mariano's mind.

Mariano told El Estudiante to go talk to the prisoner.

"Go and convince him to see things our way," he said.

El Estudiante walked over to Miranda, sat down next to him
and began talking.

Mariano sent Guero and Buddha out as sentries. He ordered
everyone else to check their weapons, ammunition and supplies.
He wanted a full count of everything.

Loquito told Mariano that the village of Las Murallas was sympathetic to the revolution. Men lived there who were prepared to
join the fight. There they could get food and supplies.

The government had stationed a small group of federales at
Satevo. A swift attack could get the rebels enough weapons and
ammunition to get them to Juarez. Loquito impressed Mariano
with his knowledge of the area.

"No es nada, capitán," said Loquito, "es mi tierra."

Pepe knew Miranda well. Out of spite or stupidity, Miranda
would spit in all of their faces. And the reason had nothing to do
with his patriotism to the state. The rebels had nothing to offer him
financially or socially. Pepe knew that Miranda preferred death to

living a life where he had little chance of gaining money or stature. Miranda was even too damn dumb to lie to save his own life.

After Pepe finished checking his horse, supplies and weapons, he walked back to where Mariano sat. Pepe laid his carbine across his lap. Chispas walked up next and then Buddha. El Estudiante and Miranda continued talking. Nobody could hear them. Mariano told Buddha, angrily, that he wanted him to stay out as sentry until he was called for. Buddha walked back to his post.

Ten more minutes passed before El Estudiante returned.

"Well, what is it?" Mariano asked.

"He wants nothing to do with us," said El Estudiante with a note of finality in his voice.

The men looked at Pepe.

"Do you want to try?" Mariano said.

Pepe nodded his head and went to his brother. He knelt down and said in a low voice, "We must move carefully. When I cut the rope, you take the pistol I give you. We'll hold them up and ride out of here on two horses."

Miranda tried to speak, but Pepe stopped him.

"Don't complicate things with words. Just do what I told you. It's our only chance, otherwise they will kill us both."

In the darkness the men could see neither Pepe nor Miranda clearly. Not one of them had the slightest notion that Pepe could turn on them. Not even to save his brother.

Pepe stepped to the side of Miranda and cut the rope that bound his hands. Miranda felt the hard, heavy metal that Pepe placed in his hand.

"Let's go. Just follow me."

As he approached Mariano and the others, Pepe said, "Don't anybody move. We'll ride out of here quietly, and you'll never hear from us again."

"Traitor! Lousy traitor!" screamed Chispas.

"Do not be an idiot, Pepe," said EL Estudiante, his eyes gleaming.

Chispas moved his arm. Pepe pointed the carbine at his head. Slowly Chispas let his arm fall.

"Go get two horses, hurry," Pepe said to Miranda. "Don't any of you move. I don't want to hurt anybody," he said, in a shaky voice.

"I'll hunt you down until I find you, and I'll tear each finger from your hands," promised Chispas.

No one said another word. They all kept their eyes on Pepe's rifle. Not one of them doubted that Pepe would use it. Miranda came forward with the horses. They both mounted.

"I'm sorry, but I couldn't let anyone kill my brother," Pepe said.

"You are committing a crime against us, Pepe; you are committing a crime against the people of Mexico, and the people will judge you," said Mariano.

"If either of you moves, I'll kill you." Pepe immediately recognized Lilia's voice. He froze. Miranda turned, and as if moving in slow motion, he reeled around on the horse and aimed his gun at Lilia, but before he could fire, she pulled the trigger. The blast shattered the silence of the canyons. The bullet entered Miranda's heart. The force threw him from the horse. His eyes went blank. Pepe knew he was dead. Lilia aimed at Pepe and pulled the trigger again. The weapon misfired. Chispas reached for his pistol. Pepe saw him move. Instinctively Pepe twisted, aimed his carbine and put a bullet under Chispas' left eye. The others dove to the ground. Pepe stared at his brother's body, kicked his horse, leaped over the fallen men and rode towards the road.

"Alto! Alto!" screamed Guero, as Pepe neared. Pepe lifted his rifle. Guero jumped onto the trail. Pepe aimed the rifle at Guero's chest, but he could not pull the trigger.

CHAPTER TWENTY-SEVEN

Pepe rode down the last mountain. He looked out over the Chihuahua desert. It was a vast universe of sand, cactus, rock, rattlesnakes, scorpions and silence. The early rays of sunlight cast a purple glimmer across the sky. Every muscle in his body throbbed. He lifted his head, closed his eyes and massaged the back of his neck where the pain burned. The desert seemed to stretch from everywhere to forever. Exhaustion dominated his fear.

Pepe patted the horse on the neck. He tried to calm the animal down. The horse moved backward as if sensing the desert's brutality. With only one canteen of water and a few strips of dried beef, Pepe dropped down off the last hill and entered the fiery flatlands.

He rode until the sun shone directly over his head, the heat penetrating his flesh. Breathing became difficult. He looked desperately for a house, a tree, a large bush. He saw nothing but cactus and sagebrush.

It was strange, he thought, the earth appeared entirely of desert, yet nothing moved, not a breeze or a sound, not a bird or a snake; it was as though life did not exist.

The blinding brightness reflected off the sand and forced him to hide behind the sparse shade of a tall cactus. He took one swallow of water from his canteen, poured a little into his palm and let the horse lick the water. Because of the sun's position, the cactus offered little shade. Pepe rigged up his poncho so that it spread from his horse to the cactus. He sat beneath the coarse roof and wondered what he would do next.

His thoughts converged on him. He knew he would never be safe from the rebels. They would find him. Should he hide? Maybe he could reach the border before they found him. But Miranda, he thought, how could they have expected him to turn his back on his brother? And the sadness overcame him.

He saw Miranda's face the instant the bullet penetrated his heart. The picture rushed into his mind. He shook his head, trying to make it disappear, but it would not go away.

"Miranda," he whispered. It was the only sound in the desert.

"Miranda," he whispered again. The vision of death vanished and was replaced by a scene which took place long ago.

Pepe had been about eight years old. His father told him not to pick the mangoes that grew near the rapids. But Pepe could not help himself. The beautiful mango hung innocently on the forbidden branch. Miranda, climbing a tree downstream, saw Pepe and hollered for him to get down. Pepe straddled the branch and inched his way to the mango. He reached out and brushed the mango with his fingertips. He reached again but could not grab the fruit. His legs slipped and he fell from the tree. He latched onto a clump of branches, but they were weak; he screamed, the branches broke and for his disobedience, he fell into the swift current.

Pepe tried to scream, but each time he opened his mouth water rushed in. He tried to swim but the current was too strong. Finally he reached a spot where the river slowed. He stretched his legs to grip the sand below, but he felt nothing except rock, rock as slick as wet marble. He could not walk and was too tired to swim. He looked over his shoulder and saw even rougher rapids filled with jagged rocks. He prayed for strength but it did not come. His chest heaved, he could hardly breathe; he gave up and let the current take him. His body went limp, and the water whisked him downriver. He prepared for the collision with the rocks, but the next thing he felt, he was being pulled by the hair and plucked from the water. Miranda had seen everything, run ahead of him down river, climbed out over the rapids on a branch and yanked him from the swirling torrent. Pepe had cried. It was the only time Miranda allowed him to cry. No one else ever found out what happened that day.

And now in this desert, this sea of nothingness, the sadness hit Pepe in waves. He cried. No one would know about Miranda's death. He wanted to pray but was embarrassed. Pepe had turned from God. He had convinced himself that he needed no God. But he was wrong. Always he had turned to God in times of trouble, ever since he was a child. But these last months he looked only to himself. And now he knew that he did not have the strength to survive alone.

"Lord, what have I done?" he began, the words forming slowly

in his mind. "What am I doing in this desert? Please forgive me.
I have sinned. I need you so much."

Pepe rose from where he sat and got to his knees. He closed
his eyes and said the words out loud, "Mary, holy mother of God,
how many times have I asked for your help, and how many times
have you come to me? Pray for me. Help me through this. Help
my brother Miranda wherever he is. I don't know where to go or
what to do." He felt embarrassed but continued to pray, "I know
I am nothing without you. You are my strength. If I survive, it's
because you want me to live. Do whatever you want with me."
The more he prayed, the better he felt. "Jesus, give me another
chance," Pepe whispered. "I will change. I love you. Stay by my
side and help me. Wherever this road leads me, please stay with
me."

He didn't realize it as he prayed, but his face was wet. He
wiped away the tears, made the sign of the cross and slowly kissed
his thumb and index finger, which he shaped to form a cross. He
sat down on the sand and thought about the story of the Indian
Juan Diego and the Virgin of Guadalupe. He saw the bouquet of
roses, red, pink and yellow. He heard the disbelieving words of
the bishop. He imagined Juan Diego's last visit to the bishop, the
pleading, the humiliation of a poor Indian in the presence of the
great church. At that point, Pepe grew drowsy. In the distance he
saw a figure, a woman in a white dress and a shawl covering her
hair. He fought the haze in his mind but was too weak. He could
not move. The woman came towards him and reached her hands
to him. His body shuddered. He looked long and carefully at her,
and he slept.

CHAPTER TWENTY-EIGHT

Pepe awoke as the sun slipped away. It was still light and one small cloud in the north radiated with the last red of the day. The desert looked smaller, more controllable than it had first appeared. He rolled up his poncho and placed the rope back onto the horn of his saddle. He mounted his horse and moved away from the saguaro cactus.

The desert transformed itself into a beautiful mosaic. Pepe breathed freely, and he felt secure as he rode into the landscape. For a moment he found peace. He became one with the magnificence that surrounded him.

He wondered how far he was from the border. Someone had said three days; El Estudiante had said two days. Pepe knew that there had to be a village or hacienda somewhere. He needed food and water. He would not be safe riding a horse and carrying a rifle. If the federales saw him, they would take him for a rebel. If the rebels found him, only God knew what would happen.

Pepe rode for three hours when he saw a tiny light shining in the distance. He continued forward, slowly and carefully. As he neared he could hear the faint sound of music. He stopped about a quarter of a kilometer from what looked like a large hacienda. He was tired and hungry. He wanted water and rest. Since he had been with the rebels, he hadn't slept a full night. Each had been forced to rotate guard duty. He would gladly sleep with the animals.

Dismounting, he buried his rifle in the sand near the base of a cactus where the plants grew in a circle. He slapped his horse on the rear and sent it galloping off into the desert. He knew it wouldn't go too far before someone found it. Pepe wrapped his poncho around him as a cold wind blew across the desert. He pulled his sombrero low over his forehead and walked towards the hacienda.

As he neared the hacienda, Pepe's stomach buzzed with anticipation. He felt his heart bouncing in his chest. He did not know what to expect. Probably the hacienda wasn't much different than his father's ranch. But he didn't want to act or appear to know anything about ranching. Riding with the rebels he learned that those who can use a horse, rope and gun are the first recruited as soldiers. Pepe whispered to himself in slow repetition,

"Soy campesino, I am at your service."

He began to relax as he heard the music become louder. Like the parapets of a medieval castle, large walls surrounded the hacienda. Pepe could hear violins, guitars, trumpets, the shouts of men and the happy cries of women.

There were no guards that Pepe could see. Men and women walked freely through the large entrance. People crowded the courtyard. The music came from the house. From where he stood in the darkness, Pepe could see through the open doors and windows. Couples danced excitedly to the music. Moving along the walls, Pepe entered the courtyard unnoticed. He spotted a well at one corner of the patio. He walked over to pour himself some water, but remembered that pacificos, those peasants neutral to the fighting, were too humble to take anything without asking.

Pepe looked carefully around the courtyard. The main house was low, very long and made of adobe. The roof was covered with red tile and a long wooden porch stretched across the front. In the middle of the courtyard stood a large fountain set on a stone patio. Adobe troughs were built along one end of the courtyard walls, and a number of horses were tied there. At the other end was another wall, about eight feet high. A wooden gate was built into the wall. Pepe walked through the gate and called out to see if anyone was there.

The place smelled of hay and cattle. Lanterns hung on the low thatched roofs. A small man came running out from under one of the roofs. He wore white trousers and was buttoning his shirt.

"A sus órdenes, señor. Hector Casillas, para servirle. I am at your disposal."

Pepe introduced himself, explained his situation and asked if he could have some water and possibly a place to sleep. The man became suspicious and his politeness faded. He studied Pepe.

"Did anyone see you enter?"

"No. I don't think so. Everyone is too interested in the dance.

I thought that I should ask before I took any water," said Pepe, in a quiet, almost shy voice.

"You do not look like a field worker," the older man replied.

"I have traveled from Zacatecas, señor. I have taken clothes and food wherever I could find them."

"How old are you, boy?"

"Eighteen."

"Do you carry any weapons?"

"No, señor, only this canteen I found in the mountains. I'm not familiar with this part of the country. It's been difficult finding water."

"You understand," said Hector Casillas, "I am not the one who can give you permission to stay. If you want water, there is a jarro there in the corner."

"Señor, if you'll allow me to sleep among the animals, I will be grateful."

The man was about to speak, but Pepe cut him off, "I have slept in the mountains and deserts for months. I have been at the mercy of mountain lions, federales and rebels. Just one night to sleep safely is all I ask."

The man rubbed the side of his head. He told Pepe to get some water and showed him a small stack of hay next to a corral. Pepe thanked him. The man warned Pepe that if anyone discovered him there, he must say that he entered on his own.

"These are very bad times. I am probably a fool for trusting you," the man concluded and went back into his hut.

Pepe did not want to sleep. He wanted to go see the dance, but he could not ruin the good fortune that had befallen him. He would be able to sleep comfortably and in peace. The music sounded beautiful. The women's voices excited Pepe. He listened for a while, watched the stars, grew drowsy and finally slept.

CHAPTER TWENTY-NINE

The sound of gunfire jerked Pepe from his sleep. His dreams had carried him back into the mountains with Mariano, Chispas and the others. It took him a few seconds to clear his head and remember these new surroundings. Again he heard the guns.

It was morning. The sun had barely broken through its shell to give light. Pepe got up from the hay and walked over to the edge of the corral.

"What is it? Why are they firing?" Pepe asked Hector, as the man ran towards him.

"It is don Anastacio's soldiers. They found two boys hiding in the brush not far from the hacienda.

"But what are the bullets for?"

"Don Anastacio ordered the boys shot. The soldiers found them with rifles. Only rebels and outlaws carry rifles in these parts."

Pepe saw the fear on Hector's face. Deep wrinkles covered his forehead and pinched at the corners of his eyes.

"What is it? Why are you worried?" Pepe asked.

"You should have been gone by now. Don Anastacio's men will find you."

Pepe could see that Hector was in a panic. Pepe thought for a minute and then said, "Take me to don Anastacio. I can explain. I'm a good worker. I am looking for a job."

"Dios," stammered Hector, "it is suicide."

"Listen, I'm a field worker. In my pueblo in Zacatecas, I had a fight with my cousin. I nearly killed him by accident, but still, I was forced to run. I'm a hard worker. I'll ask the patron for a job."

"I am the patron, but I cannot hire anyone, only don Anastacio can do that," said Hector.

"Well then, let's go talk to him."

"He is a busy man. Besides, no one asks to see don Anastacio."

"Isn't there anyone here with authority?"

"You speak bravely for a farmworker. There are other ranches, why have you chosen this one?"

"I'm sorry that I seem so anxious. I don't mean to be. But I have traveled a long way. I need to eat and sleep to get my strength back. I won't stay long, only a few days. I can work hard. I ask for no pay, only food and a space to sleep."

Hector thought for a moment and them replied,

"Bien, we will go talk to Perico."

Perico sat on a tall stallion. He watched his men drag the bodies across the sand. Many riders, well armed, surrounded him.

"He is a mean one, this Perico," Hector warned Pepe as they waited for him.

Perico began shouting orders. It reminded Pepe of his own family's ranch when Miranda would shout instructions to all the brothers. But Perico ordered his men to prepare for war, not ranching.

"You, Julian," screamed Perico, "take the south end today. Enrique, you and Norberto go with him. At noon I want two of you to ride to Milpitas. Stop anyone entering our land.

"Maximiano!" Perico yelled at another man, "The federales will send patrols out through the north ends. Wait for them at Las Negras. After they have passed through, I want you to pick up Miguel at La Sonorita and ride across Las Chivas."

And so the orders went out. Pepe was impressed with the orderliness and organization of these men that Hector called don Anastacio's soldiers.

Perico did not intimidate or scare Pepe, neither did any of the other soldiers, even though Pepe knew that any one of them could kill him as easily as stepping on a worm. At this point Pepe wanted only peace, a job and a little security. After that, he would be on his way to El Paso and the northern border. He knew that life had to be better there.

Perico pulled hard on the reins. The big stallion lifted its front feet off of the ground and spun around on its hind legs, causing a cloud of dust to rise from the dry dirt. Hector and Pepe walked up to him.

Perico wore a large, straw sombrero, the kind worn by the char-
ros. His coat was the white military coat of a federal officer. His
trousers were the expensive wool trousers worn by rich ranchers.
His boots were brownish red, carefully crafted and decorated with
silver spurs. Two pistols protruded from his custom-made holster.
A large knife was fastened to one boot, and a new carbine, a gift
from Anastacio was holstered in his saddle. Perico was a big man,
strong and handsome. His light brown hair always seemed to be
combed, even after wearing a sombrero all day long. The mustache, which he groomed so carefully, touched his upper lip and
grew down sharply at the corners of his mouth.

"What is it?" said Perico, in a strong voice to Hector, who
stood near the horse.

Hector removed his dirty straw hat and then spoke. "Perico,
this boy came to me asking for food and water," he began, "he asks
if he can work in the fields with us. He wants no pay, only food
and a place to sleep."

Perico shot a long, hard look at Pepe. He stared at the worn
huaraches, the dirty, torn trousers and soiled shirt that was tied at
Pepe's waist.

"What's the matter, Hector, don't you have enough monkeys
working for you?"

"Yes, of course, Perico ... I, I ... "

Pepe spoke up as Hector stuttered, "I arrived last night, señor.
I came out of the mountains from Saltillo and walked through the
desert. I saw the lights here last night. I wanted only water and a
place to sleep."

Perico said nothing. He stared at Hector. Pepe was waiting for
a response, but no one spoke, so Pepe continued talking. "I am a
hard worker, señor. Like this gentleman said, I will work for just
a little food and a place to sleep."

"You are from Saltillo?" Perico asked.

"No, señor. Zacatecas."

Perico dismounted. He stepped closer to Pepe. At five feet ten
inches, Perico stood three inches taller than Pepe.

"You appear as though you have been through much," said
Perico, looking Pepe over carefully.

"Nothing I could not handle, señor."

"You speak strongly for one who comes begging."

"I'm not begging. I work for anything I'm given."

"Then you aren't a beggar?"

"I am the son of a rancher," said Pepe, proudly, forgetting his new campesino identity.

Perico would usually throw beggars out. But Pepe was different and he intrigued Perico.

"Come, I want you to have breakfast with me. You, Hector, get back to your work." Surprised at Perico's reaction towards Pepe, Hector rushed off to take care of his business. Perico handed the reins of his horse to a young boy who stood near.

"Go over to the fountain and wash yourself up. I'll wait inside the dining room for you," said Perico, pointing to a door at the end of the adobe building.

Pepe did not know what to think. He wanted to know what Perico had in mind. Maybe by some intuition Perico figured out that Pepe had ridden with revolutionaries. But if that were the case, Pepe thought, Perico would have killed him as simply as he had killed the other two boys outside the hacienda.

He stopped trying to figure the thing out and washed himself. He stuck his head under the water. It felt fresh and cool. A mirror hung on a wooden post. Pepe looked at himself. He was deeply tanned. He ran his fingers through his hair. He hadn't realized how long it had grown; it was over his ears and down his neck. Reaching into his back pocket, he took out a soiled handkerchief and tied it over his head. A razor laid on top of the post, and Pepe took it and shaved off the thin stubbles from his face. After replacing the razor and rinsing his face, Pepe walked towards the door to which Perico had pointed.

It was a large white room. Long wooden beams supported the roof. The floor was made of red tile. A dark wood table, floral engraving along the legs, stood in the middle of the room. Eight high-backed chairs were neatly tucked under the table.

Perico poured a serving of chile over his food and nodded to Pepe. "Sit down over there," he said, motioning to a chair at the opposite end. As soon as Pepe sat down, an old woman placed a plate in front of him. Pepe stared at the eggs that were mixed with potatoes and beef. The woman walked to the other end of the table and picked up a bowl of steaming beans. She set the bowl in front of Pepe.

"Well, are you hungry or not?" Perico asked, tearing off a corner of his tortilla and picking up a piece of meat with it.

Pepe looked up at Perico, "I have never eaten such a breakfast before," he said.

"Gringo style," answered Perico, "it's how they eat in the north."

"You've been to the north?" Pepe asked, excitedly.

"Yes. I lived there for two years–Los Angeles, that's where I lived. A very beautiful place. Now eat."

The food sent a delightful shiver down Pepe's spine. The taste seemed to affect every nerve in his body. He took a small piece of his tortilla, curved it like a leaf and scooped up the fresh beans. He didn't raise his head again until half of his plate was empty.

"Good, eh?" said Perico.

"It must be a marvelous place where people can eat a breakfast like this," Pepe replied.

"Mmm, some things are good, some things are not so good," Perico told him.

"I'm on my way to the north," said Pepe, sipping his coffee after he spoke.

"Why?"

"I have an uncle who went to live there. He wrote my father a letter. He said he owned his own house and he had a good job."

"Yes, that's probably true, if you like the worst jobs."

"What do you mean?" asked Pepe.

"The Americans give Mexicans the worst jobs; we are the field workers, the ditch diggers, the mule drivers. They don't give Mexicans the good jobs."

"But is that so different than what we have here?"

Perico gave Pepe a curious stare. He sat back in his chair, rolled a cigarette and continued talking. "You see, some of us are born to be leaders, and it makes no difference where we live. It is something that chews away at us, and we will never be satisfied unless we are leading."

"Well, what does that have to do with anything?" Pepe asked.

"In the north," said Perico, "the gringos do not allow Mexicans to hold the type of jobs that make a man feel proud. They try to make us feel stupid, inferior, and because we don't speak their tongue, they succeed by saying we don't understand anything."

"Is that why you didn't remain?"

"Partly." Perico lifted his coffee and took a long drink.

"But the main reason is that I killed a man. I grabbed him by the throat and choked him to death. It gave me a lot of pleasure to watch his eyes plead for mercy as he swallowed his tongue."

Perico looked at Pepe. Pepe didn't speak, but Perico could tell that Pepe was bursting with curiosity.

"I had been in the north two years," Perico began, "working the most degrading jobs. I had started a new job, breaking rock at a place called Fontana. I'll always remember the name of that place. When pay day came, the foreman refused to pay me. The others who worked there said that he had done the same to them when they first started working. The man was a heavy gambler, and when he lost all his money, he took our checks to pay his debts." Perico took a puff of his cigarette, squinting his eyes as the smoke passed his face.

"The other men just accepted it. They were afraid to lose their jobs. He was a big man, fat and ugly. I told him if he didn't give me my money that I would kill him. He asked those who spoke a little English what I had said. He turned and slapped me. A slap–can you believe it–the humiliation of a lifetime. If he had punched me like a man, maybe I wouldn't have reacted as I did. I jumped on him and wrapped my fingers around his neck. I felt every nerve in his pig neck stiffen. I felt the veins fill hard with blood, but I would not let go. I couldn't even feel the others trying to pull me off him. I watched his eyes grow big with fear. He knew he was dying and he panicked. I made sure that he looked me straight in the face. This was one Mexican who was not afraid to be fired. Many people who act brave behind big fronts, in reality, are cowards."

Pepe stopped eating to listen. Perico looked beyond him.

"Many of our people," said Perico, "have sacrificed their pride for a little gringo security. It was pathetic to watch grown men act like servants. The gringos are an ugly race. They smile in your face and spit at your back. They will sell their mothers to guarantee themselves success."

The words struck Pepe powerfully. He couldn't comprehend their full meaning. He couldn't believe that people could be so cruel.

"How does one survive in the north?" Pepe finally asked.

Perico crushed his cigarette in his plate. He thought for a moment, and then answered, "You must be as ruthless as they are and ten times as sneaky. They respect aggression and power. But if you slow up for a minute they will eat you alive. Don't accept a helping hand, for they will carry you only as far as they want to take you. Don't believe in their government shit, they use it effectively to keep people slaves."

The words registered in Pepe's head, and he locked them away. He was swimming in ideas, but he could not make sense out of the chaos. He would have to think about this later on; it was much too important to dismiss.

"But enough about all of that now." Perico could see the bewilderment in Pepe's face. "I can talk to you later about the north. What I want you to do now is to go out into the fields and help Hector and his men. Remember, I am the one giving you this job. I may need you later on. When I call, you be ready. Tell Hector to fix you up with a place to sleep."

Pepe had to shake himself back to reality. "Yes," he heard himself say, "thank you a thousand times."

"No need to thank me. Your labor will be enough," replied Perico.

Perico planned to keep close watch over Pepe. The boy seemed bright and tough. There were many tasks for which Perico could use him, especially now, since the rebels in these parts were becoming so active. Many large haciendas had recently been taken over by rebel bands. It was a thing don Anastacio liked about Perico, his judgment for hiring good men.

CHAPTER THIRTY

Pepe had been working in the fields for three days. Two of the other campesinos, Juan Lara and Ignacio Montero, looked upon him as an intruder. Juan's cousin had been trying to get a job on the hacienda for over a year. He felt bitter towards Pepe when he heard how Pepe had come into the hacienda one night and received a job. Pepe felt the tension but decided to let it alone and see if it would work itself out.

One night after supper, Pepe and Hector sat near one of the corrals. Hector knew that something wasn't right with Pepe. "What is it?" Hector asked.

It seemed to Pepe that everyone had always confided in him. When Pepe was growing up, his brothers and sisters never went to Miranda with their problems; always it was Pepe they approached. But Pepe never shared his problems with anyone, except Miranda, and Miranda was dense, so Pepe never expected much of a response from his older brother.

Hector's probing startled Pepe.

"I'm not sure," Pepe answered, "I feel confused."

Hector smiled. "Are you talking about something that happened, or are you talking about life in general?"

The question split Pepe's confusion into two parts. Pepe found it easier to focus his concentration.

"My life, I guess," Pepe said, "I'm not sure what it is I've done these past months. I haven't had time to weigh my actions, you know, whether I've acted good or bad."

Hector's voice was firm, even if he was being sensitive, his voice carried a rough edge. "And what difference would it make if you did examine your actions? What could you do about the past now?"

"I could stop myself from making the same mistakes."

Hector chuckled. "No, hombre, you do what you feel you should do at the time, and right or wrong, good or bad, that has nothing to do with it."

"I feel empty inside, numb, you know?"

"The only problem you have," answered Hector, "is that you are becoming more aware, and with awareness comes knowledge, and with knowledge comes confusion. In other words, my boy, you are becoming a man."

"Knowledge, ha! That's far from me."

"Ah, maybe not so far. You're a smart boy. I never saw Perico take to anyone the way he took to you. I still don't understand it," said Hector, expressing his own confusion.

Pepe didn't respond to the remark about Perico. It always seemed that people liked him, so he wasn't surprised.

"But, Hector, doesn't peace come with knowledge?" Pepe pressed.

"I thought that you told me the other day that you read the Bible to the villagers around your home," said Hector.

"Yes, it's true, I did."

"Well, what happened to Adam and Eve once they ate from the tree of knowledge? Did they find peace?"

"No." Pepe thought, then answered, "Their knowledge cursed them, and it also cursed the rest of us."

"Bueno. There you have it. A child knows no knowledge, so he is at peace. But each day he grows smarter. He learns about danger, and with this doesn't come peace, no, confusion and anxiety. So there it is, we are confused forever, so what."

"Then there is no such thing as peace?"

"All I can tell you is what I have learned. I haven't seen too much peace, or happiness," said Hector,

"No one can ever be totally at peace, or always happy. And I guess sadness is as important as happiness. How can we know one without the other? Ah, maybe you are looking for something that is right now in your grasp."

Pepe felt the muscles in his face loosen, as if his face were sagging. A nausea ripped at his stomach, and he felt his throat tighten. "I don't feel well," he told Hector.

"Do you want me to have my wife bring some yerba buena?"

"Thank you, but I don't want to be a bother."

"Bother—what bother, you are familia now," said Hector, as he walked towards his small shack. It was good that Pepe was here, he thought; how nice to talk about things other than the cows.

The crickets echoed in unison. Pepe sat down on a pile of hay and tried to keep himself from vomiting. The sounds of the night rang loudly in his ears. He felt homesick and alone. If he died here, he thought, his family would never know. He would probably be buried somewhere in the desert, a wooden cross over an unmarked grave, like so many he'd seen along the countryside, no names, only a crude wooden cross reminding strangers that death was always near.

Pepe heard voices. They came closer. Then he heard footsteps. He thought that it was Hector bringing him the hot herbal tea.

"Look at him lying there like a goddamn king."

Pepe struggled to lift his head. He saw Juan Lara and Ignacio Montero standing a few feet away. Pepe said nothing.

"Eh, you work pretty good for a beggar," said Ignacio, grinning.

It was the first time either one had spoken to him. Pepe had often heard them mumbling behind his back as they worked in the fields.

"We heard that you are not feeling so well," said Juan. "Is there anything we can do?"

Pepe could tell they had been drinking.

"Eh, Juan," said Ignacio, "maybe he lost his tongue."

Juan, the taller of the two, crouched down and said to Pepe, "Why did you come here? There is hardly enough room for us. We don't want your kind."

Pepe spoke for the first time, "The boss decides if there is room or not."

"Look, you fuc ... "

Juan stopped Ignacio as he reached out to grab Pepe.

"Of course the patron decides. You're correct about that," said Juan. "Now since we all work together, we must learn to be friends."

After Juan spoke, he turned to Ignacio. Both of them lunged on top of Pepe. He knew they disliked him, but Pepe never imagined that they would go this far.

Ignacio jammed his fist into Pepe's stomach. Pepe rolled into a ball and strange sounds came from his throat. Juan stood and pulled Pepe to his feet. He dragged him from the corral and out behind a shed, where nobody could hear them.

"Andale, hard worker, let's hear you tell us to stop. Come on, beg a little, boy," yelled Ignacio.

Pepe was too sick to fight back. He laughed at them, and said,

"You two sissies can eat shit." Juan's fist smashed against the corner of Pepe's mouth. As Pepe fell back, Ignacio's right hand tore into his ribcage, just below the left arm. Pepe no longer felt the blows, even though the men continued striking him as he lay on the ground.

Gasping for breath, both men stood back and watched Pepe's wrecked body.

"Do you think we killed him?" asked Juan, frightened.

"No, he's a tough little bastard," answered the other.

"Come on, let's get out of here before someone sees us."

"No, let's finish him off. We can take his body out through the corrals and bury him in the desert. No one will know."

Juan stooped down and put his ear next to Pepe's mouth.

"He's still breathing. Let's leave him. What can they do to us for getting in a fight and roughing him up a little?" said Juan.

"You've seen how Perico keeps an eye on him, haven't you?" said Ignacio. "Perico will skin the both of us and toss our meat to the buzzards."

They heard Hector's voice calling out to Pepe. They ran off through the corrals behind the house, through the back gate and out into the desert. Hector found him, unconscious, a few minutes later.

The fever raged within each part of Pepe's body. He twisted and rolled, trying to find some relief from the penetrating heat. One minute he would pull a blanket up to his chin, clutching it tightly with both hands, and next he would push it away, feeling as if the fire were charring all of his organs.

The throbbing pain at the back of his head caused his eyes to nearly disappear under his lids. The animal taste in his mouth and the nausea in his stomach forced up any bit of water Hector tried to get into him.

Pepe was wasting away. He face grew gaunt and pale. Deep brown rings formed around his eyes. His cheekbones pushed against his skin. After a final round of convulsions wracked his body, Hector grew fearful that the boy might die.

Perico heard and went to see Pepe. Hector saw the anger spread across Perico's face.

"Is this why you come to us for more help? This is how workers end up?"

In the dim light of the little hut, Perico did not look too closely at first. He pulled aside a rag that was used as a curtain to allow some light into the room. The bruises on Pepe's face were dark blotches, and the cut at the corner of his mouth began to scab. Perico looked at Hector, his eyes the eyes of a madman. His lips barely moved when he asked, "What happened to him?"

Hector explained how he had left Pepe and how he had found him later, beaten and bruised. As he talked, Hector still could not figure out why Perico showed so much concern for Pepe.

"And no one knows anything else?" Perico asked, in a low but firm voice.

"No, Perico. As far as I know, I was the last to see him."

"Obviously you were not. And you know too damn much about this place—old man—so don't tell me you haven't heard anything."

Hector had heard how Juan Lara and Ignacio Montero spoke constantly behind Pepe's back. He had no doubts that they were involved. But he knew better than to let his mouth run loose.

"I have some ideas, yes, but I'm not positive, yet. Give me a few days. I will come to you when I know."

"Two days, viejo. I'll give you two days." Perico turned and walked out the door, ducking his head since the doorway was too low.

Pepe waivered between consciousness and sleep. He recognized no one and didn't know where he was. He moaned and sometimes screamed as if exorcising evil spirits. It was a sickness that neither Hector nor his wife, Gema, had ever seen.

At first they both thought the beating had done much damage. But there were few bruises or cuts on his body. Then Hector remembered how Pepe began to get sick right after they had talked that last evening. It was almost as if everything Pepe had suffered mentally these past months had taken on physical characteristics and were being released through this strange illness.

Perico sent the daughter of one of his soldiers to go and care for Pepe. She stayed with him while Hector and his family went to work each day in the fields. She placed alcohol on his neck and shoulders and cool, wet rags on his forehead. Sometimes she would sit for five hours straight. Beneath the sickness she saw the strong handsome face and body.

Isabel began talking to him because she knew he could not hear. "Who are you? Where are you from?" she would ask. "Are you nice enough to take my hand without hurting me."

Sometimes she pretended to be a princess and Pepe her injured prince. "Are you a mountain lion, waiting to eat the meat and leave the bones? They tell me that your name is Pepe Rios and that you have spent much time traveling. Were there nights you spent alone, afraid of the darkness? Were there nights you thought about holding a princess in your arms? I have been here waiting. I am a prisoner of the evil king. He has cast a spell on you, but just wait, you will get better." She placed a soft kiss on his lips. "Nothing can hurt you."

Isabel brushed the hair from Pepe's forehead. She ran her fingertips down the side of his face and then ran her fingers through his hair. If only he would rise and take her in his arms. She looked at him lovingly, not really at Pepe, but at what she wanted him to be. She leaned over again and kissed him, long and firm. It was nice, even if he did not respond. Embarrassed, she sat back up. The kiss sent chills through her.

CHAPTER THIRTY-ONE

Pepe regained consciousness four days later. Isabel felt uncomfortable when she noticed that he stared at her for moments at a time. She had been in command the past several days, controlling the situation as he turned and twisted in the turmoil of his delirium. Now, she became shy in his presence.

"Who are you?" Pepe asked, a sharp pain knocking at his jaw.

"My name is Isabel. My father told me to come and watch over you."

"What happened to me?" After saying the last word, Pepe remembered the beating he'd suffered by Juan and Ignacio. Isabel only shook her head, indicating she did not know.

Pepe forgot his pain for a while and concentrated on Isabel. Her hair parted in the middle and fell in two long braids. She had dark, neatly shaped eyebrows that gave a mysterious quality to her light green eyes.

"You're much better today," she said, "we were not sure whether you would live."

"Was I that sick?"

She nodded, "You look much better. Yesterday you looked like a drunken ghost. When I first saw you, you scared me, qué bárbaro!"

Isabel, despite her shy and humble appearance, was never at a loss for words. And she could be very direct when she wanted. This made Pepe laugh.

"Who is your father," Pepe asked.

"His name is Emilio Mendoza. He works for don Anastacio."

"What does he do?"

"He protects the ranch from thieves and bandits. And he also does other things around the ranch. Some people call him a soldier, but he's really not."

"Why did he send you to help me."

"Oh, it wasn't my father, but Perico. He told my father to send me. I've helped treat the wounded before."

Pepe wondered if Isabel would leave now that she saw how much he had improved. He liked her very much.

"I still feel very weak and sore all over," he said.

"You should try to get some sleep. Although you've been in and out of sleep for many days, you haven't slept well. I'll be here," she assured him.

Pepe smiled. He wanted to take her hand but was shy, and the pain in his muscles seemed unbearable. He closed his eyes and fell into a quiet, comfortable sleep.

Pepe grew healthier each day. Not only did he feel a new strength in his body, but he felt a clearness in his mind. The depression that had overcome him before his illness was gone. He felt happy, something he had not experienced in many weeks.

When Perico and Hector asked who beat him, Pepe refused to name anyone. This irritated Perico. He wanted to punish the man. Perico's irritation didn't last long. He understood and respected the idea that Pepe wanted to handle his own problem. A man who resolved his own problems was usually the stronger for it.

Pepe asked Perico and Hector to forget the incident.

"Just tell people that I was ill and fell against the corrals as I tried to find my way back to my hut."

So that was the version told to the other workers. But they all knew better. They all suspected Juan and Ignacio from the beginning. The two had never been well liked because of their laziness and disrespect for others. But Hector, because he knew that their families would suffer if he had them fired, refused to tell Perico or Anastacio about them.

The wall that separated the workers from the rest of the hacienda was like a border between two countries. The campesinos and the men and women who cooked and cleaned in the main house all lived in small shacks near the animals and corrals on one side of the wall. On the other side lived the cowboys, or soldiers as some called them, along with the family of don Anastacio and his chosen leaders, like Perico. The most important events and news that affected the lives of those on one side were usually unknown to those on the other, except for the personal and spicy gossip that traveled through the lips of the men and women who worked in the house. So it was rare that Isabel, a soldier's daughter, would go to the worker's side of the wall to nurse a campesino. And it was normal that the soldiers, and don Anastacio's elite, knew or cared nothing about Pepe's incident or about anything that happened on the campesinos' side of the wall. But strangely enough, even with this separation of status, nearly everyone on both sides knew each other.

In the eyes of all the field workers, monkeys as they were called by the soldiers on the ranch, Pepe had become a hero. A man who could hold his tongue earned respect. Pepe remained quiet and went about his work.

He started slowly, but eventually worked his body back into shape. He had become soft during his sickness. As he toiled he perspired heavily, releasing the last remnants of poison from his body. By the end of the first week, his muscles felt harder, and he didn't tire so easily.

One day while Pepe was swinging the pick, breaking hard clumps of dirt into tiny pieces, Juan Lara moved alongside him,

"You are a smart boy," Juan told Pepe. "You know what would have happened to you if you had told?" he said threateningly.

Pepe said nothing. He raised the heavy pick and let it fall into a clump of dried dirt. He lifted up on the handle. The metal point broke the dirt into many pieces. Pepe drove the pick into the dirt again. He felt the blood rushing through his arms and hands.

"Smart boy," Juan said, with an ugly giggle, "behave yourself and maybe Ignacio and I won't be so hard on you, eh."

Confident and cocky, Juan reached down to pick up a hoe he had dropped on the ground. Pepe lifted the pick high over his head and brought the heavy tool down with a bull's force. Juan did not see the pick but felt the air rush past his ear as the implement crashed into the earth, missing his hand by inches. The bravery fled from Juan. He jumped back, his knees shaking. He was about to scream at Pepe but instead looked around nervously at the other workers. He decided to hold his tongue. Pepe sneered at him. Juan backed slowly away, turned and quickly walked back to where Ignacio worked.

Pepe did not want to harm either Juan or Ignacio. All he wanted was to put a little fear into them. He spent some time thinking about it but did not put too much energy into the matter. There were many more important things to consider.

Perico had his own plans for Pepe. One of the soldiers, an old friend of Perico's, had been drinking too much, visiting the prostitutes and neglecting his duties. He had been warned many times, but the vice got the best of him. Perico would not stand for sloppiness among his people. If Pepe could handle a rifle and ride a horse, Perico would make a soldier of him. He was always looking for good men.

Perico asked Hector for reports regarding Pepe's work. He was pleased to find that Pepe was not only a hard worker, but he was also strong and smart, and he minded his own business.

But Perico had doubts. He knew little about Pepe's background, and he wanted to know as much as he could about the men he chose as his soldiers. He knew that soon there would be battles with the rebels, and he wanted complete loyalty from his soldiers.

Anastacio and Perico had spoken about the condition of the country. The rebels had gained ground and support the past few months. The regular army was filled with incompetent officers and green recruits. If the hacendados, the owners of the large haciendas of Mexico, were to keep their lands from the hands of the peasants, then each hacendado would have to recruit his own army to protect his interests.

After the evening meal on a hot, dry day, Perico sent for Pepe. Perico was not yet ready to offer Pepe a position as a soldier. He still wanted to find out more about Pepe.

When Pepe arrived, Perico was waiting with two horses. Perico told Pepe to mount up and follow him. Perico watched every move Pepe made. He studied the manner in which Pepe mounted, how he held the reins, how he treated the horse and the rhythm with which he moved as the horse raced along.

They rode away from the hard dirt of the ranch to an area where the land turned to desert. The air was still and heavy. Perico took Pepe to a mountain which was carved of rock. On the opposite side a spring flowed from beneath the mountain and formed a pond where short shrubs grew along the banks.

"Bueno, let's go in for a bath," said Perico, as Pepe followed.

Both men undressed and walked into the cool water. Perico took his rifle and set it down within reach. Pepe wasn't too concerned. Hector had told him that Perico wanted to know more about him.

"Hector tells me that you have decided to stay with us a while longer," Perico said.

"Yes, if it's all right with you."

"Tell me about yourself."

Pepe thought for a moment, a bit nervous, then began to speak. He told Perico everything that seemed important up until the time he rode with Mariano and the others. Pepe had learned much about allegiances these past few months, and he knew that Anastacio Burales, as all hacendados, would side with the government.

"How do you feel about a man's loyalty to his country?" asked Perico.

"I think that a man has a loyalty to his family and friends first."

Perico leaned back against a smooth rock. The water rose to his chest. "Do you think that all men who call themselves revolutionaries and claim to liberate Mexico of all tyrants are patriots?" he asked.

"There are many things wrong with our country," Pepe began, carefully. "It's true that some people starve while others live in luxury. My father taught us to respect everyone, regardless of their riches. I think that something must be done to help those who have nothing, but I don't believe that killing each other will help."

"But it's too late," Perico said. "Some have taken up weapons and are killing already. You yourself have said that you saw what was happening during your travels."

Pepe didn't speak. He waited for Perico to continue. Perico looked for Pepe to say something. After a long pause Pepe finally broke the silence. "Some things are beyond me," he said.

"Do you consider yourself a peaceful man, like Hector and the others?"

"I don't consider myself anything. I own no land, so I've nothing to defend. I have no need for land, so I have nothing to fight for. I suppose you might say that I'm just traveling along until I find something I want; then I'll try to hang on to it, whatever it is."

"Well then, for just a minute, put yourself in the place of one who owns land and has placed many years of hard labor, suffering and blood into his land. What would you do if others came to try to take your land away?"

Pepe did not answer immediately but gave the situation a little thought. Perico liked this; it showed that the boy was neither rash nor emotional.

"I think I would find out why people want to take my land, first of all," Pepe said. "If it was a simple matter of them stealing from me, I would defend what was mine. But if there were other reasons involved, I would weigh these before I raised a weapon."

"Ah, but don't you realize that people have many ways of stealing," said Perico, "and some of these ways, especially when shrewd people participate, can be very sneaky."

Pepe immediately thought of Conejo. The thought angered him. "Are you for or against the revolutionaries?" Pepe asked.

The question sobered Perico. What it inferred was that Pepe possessed little political knowledge. It was the innocence that Perico had hoped for in Pepe. And Pepe saw in Perico's face that the question did exactly what he wanted it to do. Pepe saw how Perico struggled to keep a straight face as he answered.

"The revolutionaries are led by ex-bandits and wealthy land owners who could not hold onto their lands. They receive money from the United States because the gringos think that Diaz is becoming loyal to the English and French. Much of our oil is being fought over by the gringos and the Europeans, and the gringos want it all. And the peasants who have chosen to fight, well they are simply those who are too lazy to work," Perico said with a calm seriousness. "I consider all rebels thieves who want to steal our land," continued Perico. "Their motto is land and liberty. They want the liberty to steal the land from those who have worked to develop ranches and farms."

"Well then, do you think that those who are starving should never own lands?"

"Who is starving?" Perico quipped. "The only ones who starve are those who don't want to work. Look at Hector and his people. Do you see them starving?"

A quick vision of Hector's hut came into Pepe's mind: the dirt floor, the cracked adobe walls, the thatched roof that hid scorpions and other insects ...

"No, I suppose not," said Pepe.

"Of course not," replied Perico, "they have everything that they need."

That is where the bath and conversation ended. Each man did not seem quite satisfied with the other's answers. Perico felt that Pepe was very intelligent, but that the boy was ignorant of reality and survival. Pepe seemed to lack the animal instinct necessary to survive in the brutal world.

Pepe saw that Perico apparently had no idea of the poverty that surrounded him, both inside and outside the walls of the Burales' hacienda. Either that or Perico didn't give a damn about the poor. But that came as no shock, seeing whom he worked for.

That night as he lay in his small adobe room, Pepe became angry. Why was it, he thought, that he saw everything around him in terms of rich and poor? When he lived on his father's ranch, the idea of poverty and wealth never seemed to matter.

Pepe remembered working on the ranch and going about his daily duties. In the evenings and during the seasons when work slowed down, he rode to villages and read the Bible to the people. In many of the villages the people were poor, but Pepe could not remember ever feeling sorry or pitying them. Maybe Perico was partly right. People who were poor were that way because they did not want to do the things necessary to become rich. But as Pepe thought about that, he remembered people who worked during the harvest time ten to twelve hours a day, every day until the crop was brought in. He remembered seeing men work from early morning to late at night, yet the only person who gained any wealth was the one who owned the land. Didn't that prove that many people worked hard and still remained poor?

Pepe began thinking about himself. What was he going to do with his life? He had never really given much thought to his own future. Always, he had taken for granted that he would inherit part of his father's land, marry and run the ranch along with his brothers.

He never realized how the break from his family would change his plans. He tried to remember the thoughts that ran through his mind when he first ran from the family's ranch, but everything seemed so cloudy. His memories were vague. He recalled the old Indian he'd spoken to in Saltillo, just before he was captured by the revolutionaries. Had he been dreaming? It seemed like so long ago.

Pepe had talked about going to the United States, finding a job and starting a new life. But he knew nothing about the land on the other side of the northern border. He wondered if poverty also existed there. He'd heard stories about jobs that were as plentiful as leaves on a tree, but hadn't Perico told him otherwise?

Perico claimed to have worked and had his money stolen by his very own boss. Was that so different than the stories El Estudiante had told of factory workers in Mexico who were forced to buy food from a store owned by the factory. By the time most workers purchased their food, clothing and other necessities, they owed the factory owners more money than they were paid. Could the United States also treat its workers so badly?

Pepe walked from his shelter, out through the corrals and into the fields. He looked at the silhouettes of the tall, mature corn stalks. Pepe rubbed his hands together and felt hard callouses. Funny, he'd never really noticed them before. They were like hard little bubbles.

He sat in the field for over two hours, thinking. He knew that he could not continue working in the fields forever. It seemed to him that Hector and the others received crumbs for the amount of work they put in each day. But why then didn't Hector and the others leave? The answer came quickly. Where could they go? What else could they do? They were responsible for wives and children. Even Juan Lara and Ignacio Montero, ugly as they were, had also become trapped like slaves. Each had a family and considered himself lucky to have food. Something about the whole thing appeared terribly wrong to Pepe.

He couldn't recall where he had heard it, but he remembered hearing someone once say that man was meant to suffer. Could this be true? Does man have no other purpose on earth than to suffer? Does Perico suffer? How about Anastacio Burales? The man does as he pleases and he answers to no one. Perhaps it is the lot of the poor to suffer. Maybe even Burales suffers in his own miserable way.

CHAPTER THIRTY-TWO

It was a Sunday, and everyone had finished work by mid-day. Most of the men had gone into town. Pepe spent the afternoon at Hector's home. Hector's wife prepared a fine meal. After dinner, Pepe walked through the corrals, out to the gate and into the main courtyard where he saw Isabel standing by the fountain with a young girl.

Isabel didn't look at Pepe but knew that he was near. Neither had spoken since his illness. Hector had told Pepe that Isabel's father would never permit his daughter to visit with the monkeys. Isabel was raised knowing that she would never be allowed to marry out of her class.

Pepe wanted to show that he wasn't simply a field worker. He wanted to prove that he could ride and break wild horses and herd cattle. But he also knew that if he showed this, he could be forced to fight against the revolutionaries when the time came. Pepe smiled, trying not to show too much emotion, just in case someone was watching. Pepe wouldn't think of trying to speak to Isabel, not yet anyway. He knew that she would be punished for such an act. He was content to stare and dream about her, about holding her in his arms, close and warm.

Pepe knew very little about women and even less about love. He had never slept with a woman before. His body rejected the prostitute that Chispas had tried to force on him. He was not sure if what he felt was love, but he knew that he wanted to be close to Isabel. If he could only talk to her, listen to the softness of her voice, that would be enough, he thought. He would talk to Hector and get the old man's advice on the matter. After all, Hector understood everything that went on in this ranch.

From the other end of the courtyard came the sound of a guitar.

Jorge Navarete, a dark Indian with a furious temper, strummed a soft folk tune and he sang in a low melancholy voice, which at times turned into a hum. The music echoed through the dry air of the hot afternoon. Isabel felt the pain of love tug at her heart. She turned again and looked at Pepe, as if trying to touch him with a glance. The music picked up tempo and the two string harmony hummed the tragic melody of the bullring, the tragedy of life.

A man, Rogalio Muñoz, walked through the gate next to Pepe, sat down against the adobe wall and listened. Another pacífico, a certain Pedro Villarreal, came out after Rogalio, and following him came Hector, his wife and all five children.

From inside the main house, the cook Eusebia Melendez and Patricia Samaniego, the wife of Elisio Samaniego, one of Burales' soldiers, sat on the long porch and also listened to the music pouring from Jorge's guitar. Veronica Escalera moved close to Jorge and sang along with him. Their voices carried through the courtyard and out into the dusty fields.

The sadness of Jorge's music touched each person like the tender fingers of an old woman. His hands moved slowly over the neck of the guitar, and his fingers slid expertly from one fret to another.

Within minutes, the courtyard was filled with monkeys and their families and the women and children of the soldiers and vaqueros. Jorge wrote his own songs, and with Veronica's harmonies, the music twilled and soared as if wings carried each note. Other than the music, silence penetrated the air. The atmosphere was one of deep respect for an accomplished musician. Pepe had never witnessed anything like it before.

Jorge played for over an hour. He numbed the audience. Emotions ran high. Pedro Villarreal was carried back to a time in his youth when his stepfather forced his mother to abandon him at the doorstep of a priest. He remembered pleading for his mother not to leave him.

The music made a man named Candido Burgess think of his wife Matilde, and how he felt when he heard that she had been sleeping with one of the hacienda soldiers. There was nothing he could do.

Hector looked at his children and wondered what life held for each of them. Would they live forever as monkeys on the hacienda of a wealthy landowner?

Pepe only thought of Isabel and how he would love to touch her, look into her eyes once again and talk about nothing important.

At the end of the last song Jorge sat in silence and looked out across the courtyard at nothing in particular. After a minute or so, he got to his feet and walked back to his hut, which was located in the stables. No one else moved or spoke for quite some time.

CHAPTER THIRTY-THREE

As night fell, a blanket of clouds covered the sky. A steady drizzle came down over the desert. There was a heavy silence within the walls of the hacienda. The children slept. What sounded like a coyote could be heard in the distance.

Pepe and Hector sat in Jorge's hut, as his wife poured each of them a cup of coffee.

"You are a very good guitar player," Pepe told Jorge.

"Gracias," replied Jorge.

There was a moment of silence before Hector spoke. "The coffee is excellent, thank you, Juanita."

Jorge's wife smiled and began washing the younger children, preparing them for bed.

"How did you learn to play the guitar?" Pepe asked.

"My father ... he played like nobody else. Each night after working in the fields, he would teach my brother and me a new chord. He taught my sisters to sing and dance."

"Was it hard to learn to play?"

Jorge thought for a moment, and answered, "I guess it is as hard as learning anything else for the first time. If you enjoy learning something, it doesn't seem so hard." He laughed, "And if you dislike learning something, it can be terrible."

"Ah sí, that's very true, very true," said Hector, after taking a sip of his coffee and placing the cup on the square piece of wood that was used as a table.

"I remember," Hector went on, "when my father tried to teach me to play the harmonica; Dios mio, it felt that my lips were as awkward as my feet. After a week he gave up on me."

"Hector, I thought you told me that you didn't know your father?" Pepe said.

174

"Bueno, sí, I didn't have a real father. The man I'm speaking of was more of a stepfather. He came around usually during the harvest."

"Listen," Pepe said, "I didn't mean to say anything I shouldn't have."

"Nada, muchacho. Everyone here knows that my real father was a priest. One of my cousins overheard his mother, my aunt, talking about it when we were children."

Pepe wanted to find out more but thought better than to ask.

"It bothered me for many years, when I was a child. I never had anything to do with the church after I found out ... no, I would never bother my mother with such a question. She had enough worries raising me and my four brothers. Ah, my mother, what a beautiful woman."

Hector's eyes gleamed as he spoke about his mother. But he grew sad when he told of how she walked along the streets of a small town outside of Chihuahua, a pail of soapy water and a brush in her hand, asking people if she could wash the streets and sidewalks in front of their homes for a few centavos.

"There were times when we went for days without food. Since I was the oldest, I walked into the mountains and cut fresh leaves from the nopales. In those days, bueno, just like these days for some, many poor people went into the mountains in search of tender nopalitos. Usually the freshest had already been cut."

"Do you think you are better off now than you were then?" asked Pepe.

Both Hector and Jorge looked at Pepe as if they had misunderstood his question.

"Hombre," responded Jorge, "we don't live in castles, and we don't own any land, but our children never have need of anything to eat. Always we have fresh beans and enough corn for tortillas."

"Then, that is enough for you?" asked Pepe.

"Things could be much worse, no?" answered Hector.

"And you are satisfied for your children to live and work here until they grow old?"

Hector scratched his head, thought and answered, "Muchacho, why are you constantly worried about the future? It seems as though every time we talk, something eats away at you, confusing your mind. The future comes tomorrow. Let's worry about it when it comes. We have enough to think about now."

Jorge spoke, "A man must find his place in life. No one can tell him how to find it or where to look for it."

Jorge got up from the wooden crate on which he sat. He walked over to where his wife kept the metal plates. He reached down and came up with a tall bottle of tequila and returned to the table and placed down the bottle and three glasses. Just then Pedro Villareal pushed open the front door and stuck his head in.

"Jorge, buenas tardes."

The three men turned towards Pedro.

"Hola, Pedro. Pasa, hombre, pasa," Jorge said, inviting him in.

Pedro walked in, removed his straw hat and sat down. Jorge returned to the kitchen and brought out another glass. Pepe noticed the awkwardness of Pedro's walk, as if one leg were shorter than the other. Jorge poured the liquor. All raised their glasses and drank to each other's health. Jorge refilled all of the glasses.

"Listen, Pepe, you said that you read the Bible to the villagers where you lived in Zacatecas, isn't that so?" said Hector.

Pepe nodded.

"Well then, tell me, do you think that Judas was guilty, you know, when he turned Jesus over to the Romans."

"Of course," answered Pepe, "the Romans gave him silver to betray Jesus."

"Yes, yes, yes, but that's not what I'm getting at. I know he was guilty of the act ... Let's see, how can I say it?" Hector, sipped his tequila, trying to think of the right words. "Bueno," he finally said, "but Jesus knew all along that Judas would be the one, the traitor, right?"

Again, Pepe only nodded. Jorged finished his drink and refilled his glass. Pedro scratched the stubby, white hairs on his wrinkled face and listened carefully.

"What I always tell myself is," again Hector stopped to get his words straight, "is, if Jesus knew that Judas was going to betray him even before the act was done, then Judas had no chance, right. I mean, he didn't have a choice. By doing what Jesus already knew he was going to do, there was no other way out for the man but to do it. Am I right or wrong?"

Pepe thought about it. The tequila made anything seem possible.

"I never looked at it that way before," Pepe said.

Pedro spoke only when conversations interested him, and he found that many words that people spoke were better off kept behind the tongue. But every once in a while a conversation would come up that made Pedro want to speak. "But Judas didn't know that he didn't have a chance, so in his mind he really did make a choice. Remember, Judas thought the Romans meant Jesus no harm."

"Yes, that's right," said Pepe, his head feeling a little light.

"No-no-no-no, it makes no difference what Judas thought," said Hector. "If everything he did, Jesus already knew, then everything he thought, Jesus also knew, so even his thoughts he had no control over."

"Ah huh," answered Pedro, "that isn't only true with Judas but with the entire Bible. Isn't the Bible full of prophesies. Didn't Jesus himself come down to earth to fulfill what the prophets foretold."

"Sí, sí, sí, that's exactly the point here, my point," said Hector, excited and drunk, "as with Judas, everyone of us is the same. We can't make a choice; bueno, better than that, there are no choices to make because our every thought, our every action," Hector burped, "excuse me—has already been proph-ph-e-sied, no?"

"So what is it that you are trying to say?" asked Jorge.

"Mmm, quién sabe? But I'm sure it must mean something."

"What you are saying, Hector, señor," said Pepe, slurring his words, "is that we have no more flexi—i—bility than a train moving down the tracks. If—I say—if there is a heaven—and—if, there is—is—a hell, it is already determined who is going to go where."

"Huh! and that's to say that no man is guilty for his actions. Those who go to hell only follow God's plan. If they are murderers, then it's because God made them that way. If they are adulterers, ay qué adulterers, qué bueno, it's also planned. And those who go to heaven haven't done anything good of their own." Pedro laughed, "It's just that they are skinny enough to fit through the eye of a needle."

"I don't know. It sure don't seem right to me. You all make it sound too simple. It's like saying I can go out and do anything I want to do. Besides, you're all drunk anyway," Jorge said, and refilled the glasses.

"No, no, no. Don't you see, that is just what you cannot do. You can't go out and do what you want. You're actually doing what you must do."

"Qué bárbaro!" cried Jorge. "This is all caca. Thinking like this will make us all crazy."

Pepe took a long sip from his glass. "Then, if what you say is true, just suppose it is," said Pepe, "then all of us right now here in this room are talking and drinking for some reason. This very moment was planned and all of us are following the plan."

"Pues sí," said Hector, "it's a little scary, no?"

"I don't think it's scary at all," said Jorge, taking a drink of tequila, "in fact, I think it's all horseshit. What difference does it make if Judas knew this or Judas did not know that. What difference does it make in our lives. Tomorrow we wake at dawn and go to work. What's so special about it, if I have a choice or not. Either way I know I'm going to go out in those fields and hoe dirt." Jorge seemed upset.

Hector looked at Jorge, disappointed that Jorge took the game so lightly.

"Yes, maybe you're right, Jorge," Hector said, "but I wasn't really trying to say that somehow what we were talking about would make any difference in any one of our lives. For me, the enjoyment of the argument makes the conversation worthwhile."

"Yes, I agree," said Pedro, "so often we are trapped discussing the same things women discuss when they wash clothes at the river. Hardly ever do we talk about things other than hard dirt, pulling weeds and harvesting corn."

"Just the same," answered Jorge, "I think that kind of discussion is a waste of time."

"I thought that you, more than any of us, would be moved to talk about such things," said Pepe.

"Why do you say that?" asked Jorge in surprise.

"Well, you are the artist. Somewhere inside you must ask certain questions that no one really has answers to."

"Pendejadas! I play my guitar, do my work and take care of my family. Anything else is nothing but a waste of time."

Pepe could see that Jorge was getting very drunk. He had heard stories of men killing each other over small disagreements. "Yes, I guess, perhaps you have something there, Jorge," Pepe said to him.

"Mmm, why do you agree with me so easily, boy? Don't you treat me like a baby. I'm warning you. I'm a man not a baby. Do you understand?" said Jorge, as he stood up from his chair facing Pepe.

"Jorge, please, sit down," whispered his wife. "You will wake the children."

Jorge looked at his wife, who lay with the children on straw mats in one corner of the room.

"You shut your mouth!" Jorge screamed, pointing his finger threateningly.

"I think we've had enough. We must be leaving now," said Hector, in a calm voice.

Jorge respected Hector. Hector was a good boss and did as much as he could for the monkeys, considering he himself was also a monkey.

"Bueno, Hector. But you know I don't like anybody humoring me, eh?"

Jorge looked ugly, and Pepe didn't like him at that moment. Pepe could see a look of terror in the eyes of Jorge's wife. She seemed to be pleading to Pepe and the others not to leave.

"I'm sorry if I've said anything to offend you, Jorge," Pepe told him, and then asked, "would you like to go outside for a short walk?"

Pepe hoped that Jorge would accept. The walk might help sober him up, take the bugs out of his head. But as Pepe expected, Jorge refused.

The men said their good-nights and left. As they walked past Jorge's little shack, they could hear arguing coming from the inside. They heard a loud slap, the short scream of a woman's voice and then silence.

"He changes very much when he drinks," said Hector.

CHAPTER THIRTY-FOUR

It was still dark when Hector went from shack to shack the next morning to wake up the workers. Pepe lifted his head for a few seconds, but he plopped back down on the straw petate, unable to rise. His sleep had been too good.

He opened one eye as wide as it would go. When that eye seemed fully awake, he opened the other. He placed his elbows under himself and lifted himself up into a half-sitting position. He was ready to get on his feet when the urge of going back to sleep came to him. Two minutes more, he thought, what could that hurt. The serape felt warm, and he slid himself back into the cocoon. His heavy lids fell shut, and just as he was about to sleep, he shook his head wildly and jumped to his feet. It would be no easier to wake in two minutes than two hours.

Pepe walked quickly around the low shelter, slapping his face gently and then rubbing his hands briskly through his hair. He hated getting out of bed. To Pepe sleep was a precious gift. He jumped up and down on his tiptoes. It helped get the blood moving again. He swore, as he did almost every morning, that some day he would fix his life so that he could sleep as long as he wanted. He threw his serape over himself, put on his hat and walked over to Hector's hut.

Already Hector's wife had started a fire outside the hut. Jorge and Pedro stood around warming their hands over the fire as Hector's ten-year-old daughter made the coffee.

"Buenos días, Pepe. How do you feel?" asked Jorge.

"Fine. My head aches a little, but it's nothing," answered Pepe.

"And you, Pedro, did you sleep well?" Pepe asked.

Pedro did not want to tell them that he had spent most of the night thinking about Judas and trying to figure out if the man was really guilty or not, so he simply answered that he slept fine.

"Dios, what a beautiful morning. Look at all those stars," said Jorge.

"Mmm, when you get to be my age," said Pedro, "every morning is a beautiful morning."

Jorge's voice became silent as he told Pepe, "About last night, I'm sorry. My wife told me I did not behave well with you."

"It's nothing, just a misunderstanding," said Pepe.

Hector walked up and placed his hands over the fire.

"Andale hija," he said to his daughter, "get us some coffee."

The little girl gave a cup to Hector, Pedro and Pepe. She poured the coffee. The steam felt good as it slipped alongside Pepe's face. Hector took a long sip and then spoke as if he'd forgotten to tell them something. "Oiga, did any of you hear the horses come in last night?"

"I didn't hear anything," said Pepe.

"Neither did I," answered Jorge.

Pedro just shook his head.

"Well, I don't know what was happening, but I heard horses come into the patio like they were rushing to a fire."

"Why's that so strange?" asked Pepe.

"Don Anastacio hates any unnecessary disturbances in the late hours. No one rides in like that unless something important has happened," said Hector.

"Have you noticed anything different around here, Hector?" asked Jorge.

"Mmm," Hector murmured, as he drank his coffee.

"What does that mean?" responded Pepe.

"I'm not sure. I can't figure it out exactly," answered Jorge.

"Ever since Perico had those boys killed out front, a mysterious mood has come upon the hacienda," said Hector.

"What do you mean?" asked Pepe.

"Quién sabe," answered Hector, "it's like an evil spirit is covering the ranch."

"Yes, that's it," said Jorge. "It's like something very evil is covering the ranch. I felt it as I sang."

"Death?" said Pedro.

"Not so much death," Hector told him, "more like murder."

Pepe's knees began to move. He gripped his coffee cup tightly. He remembered the look on the faces of the rurales that El Estudiante had killed the night of the cockfight. Then he remembered the executions of the soldiers after the battle, when Miranda had been captured. And at last he remembered the bullet striking Miranda. He saw his own gun blowing Chispas to the ground. It seemed that it had all happened so long ago.

"Do any of you ever leave the hacienda?" asked Pepe.

The men all shook their heads negatively.

"We have no need to go anyplace," said Hector. "Besides, don Anastacio prefers that we stay nearby."

"Many people are dying outside those walls," Pepe said, seriously.

"Perhaps it's better that we don't talk about it," said Jorge.

"That won't stop the killing," said Pepe, sharply, then added, "You feel it. You've already said that. Hector, you even touched it; murder you said, there is a feeling of murder all around us. It's as if the ground is covered with blood."

"We aren't soldiers, Pepe. We farm the land and go about our duties," said Hector.

"You have seen much evil out there, no?" asked Pedro.

"Sí. It surrounds us. Even as we stand here talking."

"We cannot discuss it now. There are too many ears around here," Hector whispered.

"You aren't as safe as you think," said Pepe.

"You have been to the war?" Pedro asked, his white hair glimmering in the rising sun.

"Be quiet!" Hector whispered, harshly.

"Tell us about it later. What do you say?" Pedro asked.

Hector became anxious. If the word got out that the monkeys were talking about the revolution, Burales would throw all of them into the streets, except for those he decided to kill.

"Come, it's time!" screamed Hector, "to work, let's go!"

Pedro leaned his bony arm on Pepe's shoulder and whispered exitedly, "Later, eh, later you tell me more."

CHAPTER THIRTY-FIVE

The fields were just a short walk from the hacienda. Since most of the land had been desert at one time, the man who owned the land before Burales had made hundreds of Yaqui Indians cart in tons of dirt from the nearby mountains. It took the Indians a year and a half to complete the job. The Indians had been supplied by the government. When they finished the job, they were shipped off to Vera Cruz to work the oil fields that were owned by the British and the Americans.

The field work began to bore Pepe. The hoe became his enemy. He disliked the smell of dry dirt. The penetrating sun, bearing down on his back, made him listless. He looked around at the others.

They worked slowly, yet steadily, for hours at a time. The sounds of the hoes slapping the hard dirt took on a dreary beat. No one spoke. They simply lifted the hoes and put them back down, cracking dirt clods after dirt clods, preparing new lands for the next planting.

Pepe wondered if these men and women ever dreamed of another life. Were they so imprisoned that their imaginations had died? Did they dream at all? What sort of power did the bosses possess that they could keep men working for years by offering them little more than a couple of bowls of beans a day and a straw roof over their heads?

As he worked, Pepe began to think about his own childhood. There was field work to be done, but the cattle also needed tending, and a man could ride his horse from one end of the ranch to the other the entire day. There were always many things to do, never the same things that could shrivel all hope. As Pepe thought, a very unsettling notion came over him. He suddenly realized that he was no longer an heir to a ranch. He had no horse to ride to the tops of mountains, where he could stare down into canyons. He wasn't free to ride from village to village and talk to the different people. He too, just like the others, pounded away at the dirt, chipping off little pieces of his life with each stroke.

Maybe it was time to move on, he thought. He could get a little food and make his way to Juarez; he'd heard that it was no more than a three day's ride. He felt better and saw himself riding away from the hacienda proudly, independent and heading north to a new life, a good life.

And just as quickly as one vision vanished another arrived. He remembered being alone in the vast ocean of sand. He remembered riding with the revolutionaries and how sometimes there was no rest, no peace of mind, but instead always the anxiety of a federal bullet. A terrible sickness rushed into his stomach as he thought about the battle in the mountains and how he had seen pieces of flesh hanging from men's bodies. Suddenly the hoeing did not seem so bad. The silence of the afternoon placed a certain lull over the fields. The clicking sounds of the hoes sent a calming chill through Pepe. The pain in his mid-section was gone.

As the sun beat down at its hottest point, Hector announced that it was time to rest.

All of the men and women walked back to their homes to eat the mid-day meal, usually beans, eggs and coffee. There they rested, the children sleeping, the women cleaning and the men smoking and talking until the sun had lost much of its strength. At that time, when the air had cooled, they would walk back to the fields to finish the day's work, which was normally when the red glare of the dying sun extinguished itself on the tips of the mountains to the west.

Waiting for the sun to cool, Pepe saw Isabel as he made his way to Hector's. She stood alone in the courtyard, filling a red earthen jug with water from the well. Pepe quickly ran to his little shed and picked up his water jug. He spilled the water from the jug to the ground and hurried over to the well. As he neared the well, he walked slowly. Isabel saw him approach.

Pepe kept his distance as if waiting his turn. He stood about five feet from Isabel. Excitement raced madly through him. He could feel himself being pulled towards her and wondered if she could hear his heart pound.

He looked around the courtyard to see if anybody was watching. A few people milled about, but no one seemed to pay attention to them. Pepe tried to speak but instead swallowed the words.

Moving a little closer, he saw that her jug was nearly full. One more pail from the well and she would be finished. He desperately tried to think of something to say, even though he knew conversation in the open would not be wise. He moved closer to her. He could feel the pull of her body. Three steps more and he would be next to her. If only he could wrap his arms around her. But the three steps might have been three kilometers.

Isabel took the water pail and poured the water into her jug. Pepe saw that he would lose her in a minute. She replaced the pail, looked at Pepe and smiled, a pained look in her eyes. She picked up her jug. Please don't leave, he wanted to scream. How could he stop her?

"Adios," she whispered as she walked towards the long, white building.

"Adios," Pepe said, not sure whether she heard.

He felt sad and alone as he filled his jug and walked back to his shack. Such a longing he had never felt. He wanted Isabel with him. As he sat down on his straw mat and leaned against a wall in the shadows of his little shelter, he thought of nothing except Isabel. Pepe lost himself in a daydream.

He pictured Isabel leaning her head on his shoulder and telling him how much she cared for him. And he saw himself telling her private things he had never told anyone. Sometimes a joke came out of their talk and both laughed. Sometimes she would tell him about the sadness in her life, and she would cry gently as he wiped away the tears and comforted her with kind words. She would cook and both of them would eat together. At night they would watch the stars and see how many they could count before losing track. Pepe dreamed and dreamed until Hector's voice shook him back to reality.

"A trabajar! Ya es tiempo señores y señoras. A trabajar!" he cried as he walked along the outside of the huts.

Pepe's dreams had been so real that he had lost all track of time. When he realized he had only been dreaming, his heart again grew heavy for Isabel and the enjoyment and peace he had felt in his dream once again turned to pain.

The monkeys walked back to the fields and continued working, carefully nurturing the growth of new corn and beans. A small amount of rainfall had been enough to pop the seeds and sprout the plants. But if more rain did not arrive soon, the plants would wither and die. The year before, there had been little rain and al-

ready there was a short supply of corn and beans. The monkeys of
Burales' hacienda did not worry too much about this since Burales
always supplied them with enough food to survive.

Pepe lifted his hoe weakly and let it fall without any strength
behind it. He could think of nothing but Isabel. He wondered if
she felt anything for him. The way she said adios, and the pain in
her eyes, he thought, maybe she was trying to tell him that she did
care.

What kind of life was this, he continued thinking, that such
a thing as a man's station in life could keep him from talking to
another human being. It wasn't right. He couldn't go on this way.
Pepe took his hoe and walked over to where Hector worked.

"How can I talk to Isabel?" Pepe demanded.

Hector stopped working, and he turned to Pepe. Then he went
back to his work. "You have no business with her, Pepe. You are
better off staying away," was Hector's answer.

"Hector, you don't understand. I think about nothing else."

"That's where you are wrong, my son. I know exactly how you
feel. You think that a man can live fifty-three years and not feel
the pains of love."

"You've felt the same? What did you do? Did you follow your
feelings?"

"Yes, Pepe, I followed my feelings," said Hector, stopping and
looking into Pepe's eyes. He continued, "Consuelo's father owned
the market in the town where I was raised. She told me she loved
me but could never marry me. I stole her from her father. He sent
men after me to kill me. But by the time they finally found me,
she had already lived under my roof for three nights. At that point
she was mine. But she lost everything her father would have given
her."

"And it worked out all right?" asked Pepe, like an ignorant
child.

"I have regretted it every day of my life."

"But why? You and Consuelo are perfect. You both seem so
happy. And the most important thing is that you are married to
the woman you love."

Hector shook his head and began working his hoe. He thought
for a minute and said to Pepe, "Look at my wife, Pepe. Take a
good look."

Pepe found Consuelo and watched her. She carried a straw
basket by a rope handle and filled it with rocks from the field.
When the basket was full, she walked a hundred yards to the end

of the field and dumped the rocks into a pile. Then she walked back to the field and continued the same process.

"Love," said Hector, "you see what love has done for Consuelo."

"But she still loves you," insisted Pepe. "You can't blame yourself because you are forced to work hard, that your lives are hard."

"Pepe, don't you think that Consuelo stays awake at night wondering what kind of life she could have had marrying someone in her class?"

"She told you this?"

"Consuelo never complains."

"Then you don't know how she feels. Maybe it's you who stays awake at night and wonders what could have been."

"Maybe," said Hector with a sigh.

"Then maybe I'm talking with the wrong person. Maybe I should be talking to Consuelo."

Hector shook his shoulders and continued working.

Pepe also went back to work. He began to put some strength into his movements. He worked up a sweat and found that it helped mask the pain. The blood rushed through his body. He could feel his heart pump faster. He dug harder at the thick, dry dirt clods. The veins in his forearms bulged with blood. Isabel was on his mind, but not with the longing and pain he'd felt earlier. Now she was there with a renewed energy. He didn't know how, but he would let her know his feelings.

The sky turned orange and the air stood still. The sharp edge of the day's heat had vanished, but the heavy warm air remained. The sound of the metal hoes striking the ground sailed through the fields. Everyone worked at a much slower pace.

The sound of thunder rumbled beneath the earth and a cloud of dust covered the hacienda. A dozen riders approached with Perico, his sombrero bouncing on his head, in the lead. The riders nudged their horses to the edge of the field and waved for Hector and the other workers to come over. Within minutes the men, women and children had assembled in front of Perico.

From atop his horse Perico looked over the throng. "Listen well," he called to them, pushing the front of his sombrero high on his head so that his face was clear for all to see. "All of your food rations will be cut in half starting today."

A low growl came from the dark faces of the people standing in the field.

"In case you have not heard, bandits are terrorizing the country-side. Consider yourselves lucky. Others in the towns and ranches around here are without food altogether."

"But we can hardly feed our families on what we now receive," Jorge cried out.

"That's no concern of ours. You are men, find ways to feed your families."

"All our time is spent working in these fields. We have no time to get any more food," said Jorge.

Perico shot him an angry glance. "There are others who would be glad to take your places," countered Perico.

It seemed that there remained little else to say. Perico had delivered his message and the workers were forced to accept the terms. The riders and the workers stared at each other. No other words passed for some time. Then Perico finally said, "We need more men willing to fight. If we don't protect what's ours, it will be taken from us."

No one answered.

"Think it over well. For those who decide to fight, there will be more food on your tables."

"What good is food to a dead man?" came a voice from the crowd.

"If you are cowards, it makes no difference one way or the other," responded Perico. He looked out over the crowd of peas-ants, shook his head to display his disdain for them, and rode off with his men.

As they walked back to the huts, a few of the workers spoke among themselves. Hector walked in the lead, Consuelo and the children right behind him. A feeling of dejection permeated the air. Once they thought about his words, what Perico was saying was that either they fight or starve. They must decide soon.

For the moment, Pepe forgot about Isabel. He looked into the tired faces of the people around him. A woman nursed her child. An old man coughed a continuous gurgle of mucous, but still he made it each day to the fields. A boy of about ten carried a pick and hoe over his shoulder. He moved slowly.

The people needed a dream, Pepe thought, a hope to pull them above the daily drudgery. A strange thought came into his head as he looked at the defeated mass: could death be a better alternative to this?

Pepe could not rest as he lay in his hut. He wondered whether he should tell the people what he knew about the revolution and that the rebels were not bandits but people like themselves. But if he told them about his own involvement, he would be labeled a rebel. Burales would surely kill him.

The people were angry. They felt used and rejected. Maybe it would be better for Pepe to listen, let the others do the talking. It did seem that some of the men, ignorant about the politics of their own country, would go and fight for Burales. Pepe could not let them know that he had already fought on the side of Anastacio Burales' enemy.

The men did not eat dinner that night. Whatever food remained had to be saved for the children. Secretly, a meeting was called at the home of one, Refugio Hernandez. Refugio sent his wife and children to Hector's house. The monkeys crowded into the one room hut that was built onto the pens where the pigs were kept. The men sat on the floor and against the walls, everyone talking at once until Jorge raised his voice above the others.

"Bueno!" he called out, raising his hands so he wouldn't have to talk too loudly. The men quieted down.

"So what do we do?"

A low mumbling sound spread through the room.

"What choice do we have?" someone said.

"Fight or starve, you heard the man," said Ignacio Montero, one of the men who had beaten Pepe.

Pepe snickered at that comment. Ignacio heard him, but pretended not to notice.

"But why should we fight? What reason do we have. And who is it that we are fighting against?" said Hector.

A louder utterance rose from the crowd. Jorge raised his arms again. "Listen, all of you, we must keep the talking low. If don Anastacio's men find us here, they'll butcher all of us."

"We fight to keep from starving," Juan Lara responded to Hector's questions.

"That's a good reason to fight, no?" said old Pedro, apparently enjoying the spectacle.

"We will be killed. None of us knows about guns or killing," demanded Ignacio Montero.

"Hector's right. What in the devil is all this fighting about anyway?" someone cried out.

Pedro looked at Pepe and waited for him to say something, but Pepe did not react.

"I've heard don Anastacio's soldiers talk about the fighting," offered a tall, thin man at the back.

"Well, what did they say?"

"One soldier said that it seemed like the whole world was joining the side of the rebels. Their armies grow bigger each day. And the other soldier said that everyone fighting on the side of the rebels is out to steal and rape, that the leaders are all outlaws."

"There, you see," said Juan Lara, "if we choose to fight for don Anastacio, we fight on the side of the law. It's our duty to kill thieves and other animals."

"Caray! That's the craziest thing I've ever heard," said Pedro.

"What's so crazy about that, old man?" screamed Lara back at him.

"Sí, Mexico has many robbers and thieves and other locos, but hombre, don't be so stupid; there are not so many that they would make armies to fight the government," screamed the old man, bravely.

"You can argue with me all that you want, viejo, apestoso; but don't ever call me crazy," Lara said, like an angry child.

"Ah, forgive me, Juan, I didn't realize you were so sensitive," laughed Pedro.

"Now you make a fool of me. I don't have to take this." Juan's anger overcame him. Some of the others in the room laughed at him.

Jorge was on his feet, again raising his hands to quiet everyone down. "Juan, you are getting too emotional."

"But you heard what he said," insisted Juan.

Pepe was enjoying himself for the first time in many months. He could hardly believe what he was seeing.

"Siéntate, Pelón, cabrón," somebody cursed at Juan.

Juan grew furious. He looked around the room to see who had called him a bald stud. Everyone laughed so hard that Juan rushed from the room.

"Now you see, Pedro, you have made him mad," somebody said.

"The pendejo thinks he knows everything. I get tired of always listening to him try to make fools of the rest of us. It's about time he learns how it feels," said Pedro.

"Ignacio, go out and bring him back. Tell him we need him here. The whole thing was a joke," said Hector. The truth was that nobody trusted Juan Lara, or Ignacio Montero.

"Fine, we've had our fun for the night," said Jorge. "Now we must decide what we our going to do. In a few days, we won't have enough food to feed our children."

"I'm against fighting. I'll stay and make the best of what they give us," said Hector.

"I agree with Hector," said another man. "Besides, we are both too old to fight."

"I still want to know what the fighting is about," said Jorge.

"You heard Perico. We fight to protect what is ours," answered Refugio.

"Ours! But nothing is ours. Everything belongs to Burales. If we fight, we fight to protect what belongs to him," said Rosalio Muñoz, who had worked for Burales for six years. Rosalio had been sent as a gift from another hacendado. Burales had helped smother a strike at the mines owned by the other hacendado. Along with five thousand acres, the man gave Burales his best monkey.

"I have worked in the fields since I was a child. My father worked in the fields and my brothers and sisters worked in the fields. I'm ready to fight! I can barely feed my children on the food we receive now. With a cut in rations, it will be impossible." The men knew that what they heard was true. Some did not want him to continue.

"Yes, I have decided that I will fight," said Rosalio, "but I won't fight for those who would take a handful of beans from the mouths of children."

"What are you saying, Rosalio?" asked Jorge.

"You know exactly what I'm saying. Burales and his men leave us no choice but to steal and rape. For a little beans they force us to our knees. No more! I say no more."

Rosalio's words drove deeply into Pepe and the others who listened. He said what the others had feared to think about.

Pedro turned to Pepe. The old man's eyes pleaded with Pepe to stand and tell all that he knew. There was no question that one way or another what was said here tonight would get back to Burales. It was too late. Pepe could hide no longer. He stood. The others looked at him. He spoke. His words came slowly, and he chose them carefully.

"It's true. Those who fight the government forces, those who fight men like Anastacio Burales and Perico are made up of thieves and rapists. They are the leaders of gente, of people no different than you and me. Men become thieves when there is nothing else left for them. They become desperate. And yes, it is as Rosalio says, they are made thieves and rapists by those like Burales who would hunt them down for stealing a sack of beans to feed their children."

"How do you know this?" came a voice from the back of the room, a voice that sounded angry.

"I rode with the rebels. I fought alongside them. I ate their food and shared their mountains. They are strong and determined to rid Mexico of all the Buraleses in the land."

Pepe told them of his travels from his home up until the time he found himself setting foot into Burales' hacienda. He passed over many of the details and focused only on those stories that might give them a better understanding of what the fighting was about. They let him finish without an interruption. As he spoke, Pepe kept one thing in mind. He knew that by morning he would have to leave the hacienda.

"I don't see that we have learned anything new," said Jorge, coldly and looking directly at Pepe.

"Hombre!" shouted Pedro, removing his hat in frustration, "didn't you hear. There is a war taking place. The people are tired of being driven over the land like burros. Why can't we own some land? We do all the work, don't we? We deserve more than beans for all our years of labor."

"I agree," said Rosalio, "better to die as men than live like slaves."

"And what about your wife, your children? What becomes of them once you go off to fight, or still yet, once you die?" questioned Jorge.

"Don't kill me before my eyes have closed," said Rosalio. "How much worse off can my family be without me. They sleep on a straw mat thrown on the dirt floor. They eat only beans and tortillas. Straw mats aren't too difficult to carry around. But as for dirt in which to set the mat down, well, I don't think any of us will argue that Mexico has no shortage of dirt, only a shortage of those who own it. My family will go with me."

"Well spoken, compañero. Muy bien dicho," said Pedro, rising from the wooden crate where he sat.

Just then Ignacio Montero and Juan Lara entered the room.

"Just don't try to make a fool of me, eh. I don't like anyone making a fool of me," said Juan. Both men sat down against the adobe wall.

Hector, always the mediator, the level head, stood up and looked around the room. "Well, my friends," he began, "I think it better that we speak no more." He paused, swallowed hard and continued, "It is time to make decisions. Too much talk is no good. We may say things that turn good friends into enemies. Words are like that. Tomorrow I expect all decisions to be made. Those of you who remain to work here, I will see in the morning, as usual. The others, God be with you wherever you go." And with those last words Hector turned and walked away from Refugio's home.

No one spoke, A heavy air of concentration filled the room.

"What the fuck was that all about?" said Juan.

Jorge rose next, excused himself and left the shack.

"All right, what's going on here?" Juan insisted.

Pepe got up and walked towards the doorway. As he stepped into the night, he felt the cool air on his neck. He heard Juan's voice address those who were left, "Hijos de la chingada, somebody better tell me what is happening around here. Eh, how about you? Tell me, please."

CHAPTER THIRTY-SIX

Pepe packed a sack with an old shirt, a blanket and a Bible that Hector had given him. A heaviness settled on him. The sadness of picking up the few tiny roots he had planted caused him deep commotion. And the thought of leaving Isabel suddenly threw him into a panic.

He had not even gotten the chance to talk to her again. A flood of questions entered his mind. Did she love him? Did she want to talk to him? Was her smile at the well simply an expression of friendship, or did it mean more? Could she ever be happy with him? Would she run away with him, now, tonight? God, where did that idea come from? he asked himself. Could such a thing be possible? He knew of men who actually kidnapped the women they loved, stole them from their fathers and mothers, just as Hector had done. Was it out of the question?

Pepe sat down on a sack filled with small rocks that he used as a chair. He leaned back against the wall of the shack and focused his eyes on the light reflecting on the adobe wall. The flame from the candle jumping and diving, burned inside a glass jar. The air had become cooler and he covered himself with his poncho. His mind moved from idea to idea. He had difficulty focusing on any one point since everything seemed critical.

There was little time to plan. The fear of leaving the comforts and security of the hacienda was all too real within him. He could feel a tightening in his chest and a rock in his stomach. The thought of traveling alone again into the desert, not sure of his destination, worried him. He still wanted to get to the northern border, but he was now unsure of himself; his sense of survival had been weakened by the complacency of the hacienda. The child in him was awakened, and he knew fear. There was no one to turn to.

He didn't have his father's strength to guide him nor his mother's warmth to comfort him. He pulled his knees to his chest, wrapped his arms around his legs and squeezed tightly.

And again, Isabel entered his mind. This time stronger than before. The fear in his heart turned into a painful ache. If only he could talk to her, touch her, even that might be enough. He could not leave without letting her know how he felt. But how? How could he get word to her?

Pepe rose from his seat, nestled the poncho around him and walked into the night. He listened to the voices of children playing. They were stretching out the night to its last minutes.

"Lucio," Pepe called to a twelve year old boy who ran past. Lucio stopped and walked back towards Pepe.

"Where is Margarita?" Pepe asked.

The boy wore a shirt made of coarse cloth that was used to make sacks that held the corn meal. He wore no shoes.

"She is talking with Amelia and some of the other girls, over by Hector's house," the boy answered.

"Do me a big favor. I need to talk to her. It's very important," instructed Pepe.

The boy lifted his shoulders, "Sure, I'll go get her."

"Lucio," Pepe called, "don't let any of the others know."

Pepe paced about in front of his shelter. He found the pacing unnerving, since it was not the kind of habit he usually gave into. He stopped pacing and sat down on a big boulder. He didn't know exactly what it was he wanted to tell Margarita. He tried to get his thoughts straight. When she arrived, his thoughts were as jumbled as when he had sent for her.

"Hola, Pepe. You wanted to see me?" said Margarita.

Margarita was Hector's daughter, a very beautiful ten year old with green eyes who reminded him of his own sister. Hector had once told Pepe that it saddened him to see his daughter grow so lovely each day. Beauty to the daughter of a monkey was a curse. She would be used by the men of the hacienda and tossed to one side when they no longer had any use for her. Hector had seen it happen to others.

"Margarita, you know everyone around this ranch, no?"

"Yes, I think so," she said.

"I need you to do me a big favor, little one," Pepe whispered.

"What is it? And I'm not so little as I look."

Pepe smiled at her. "Sí, I'm sorry, little queen. You grow more beautiful each day," Pepe said, wishing he could speak to women as freely as he could speak to girls.

"Promise you will tell nobody."

"I promise," she said, anxiously.

Lucio tried to stand as close as possible to hear what the two were saying. He caught a few words but not enough to understand. It made him crazy not to be able to hear.

"Can you get a message to Isabel for me?" Pepe asked in a serious tone.

Margarita looked at him as if she had just found out that he had broken one of the ten commandments.

"I know what you're thinking, little one," Pepe assured her, "but I don't have much time. If I don't see her tonight, I may never see her again. Do you understand?"

Margarita nodded.

Pepe continued, "Tell her that I will meet her in about thirty minutes at the side of the big house, on the side where Manuel ties his horse during the day. It's dark there and we'll be safe. Can you do that for me?"

"Sí. I can do it."

"Bueno, repeat the message to me," Pepe commanded.

"That Isabel is to meet you in thirty minutes at the side of the big house where Manuel ties his horse during the day."

"Good. Good, now go," Pepe said excitedly. "Don't forget, no one must hear you tell her. If anyone else is around, it's better she doesn't receive the message."

Margarita nodded her head. "I'll go tell her now. If my father sees me, he'll send me to bed," she said.

"Thirty minutes," he reminded her.

"Thirty minutes," she whispered and dashed off.

Pepe walked back into his hut. There was nothing to do now but wait. He scratched at an itch on the back of his hand. He paid little attention to his scratching. his fingernails gouged into the dry skin. Pepe could not think straight. He tried to formulate words, ideas to impress Isabel, but his mind leaped from thought to thought, many which were in no way linked together or made much sense. He took deep breaths of air and exhaled slowly, it helped slow down his pounding heart. He looked down at his hand and kept scratching. In the dim light he could barely see the long trails of dry skin that nearly reached his elbow.

Pepe wanted to relax but didn't know how, and he could not control the thoughts that came to him, it seemed, from all directions. His nerves caused little twitches in his right arm. Without

planning it or knowing why, Pepe slowly went down to his knees.
The sounds of voices outside his room vanished. The wild reflection on the walls disappeared, and he closed his eyes, clasped his
hands together and began to pray silently.

He didn't think about the words; it seemed that they came from
some vast storehouse of knowledge within him. He listened to the
words penetrate the silence of his mind. He not only heard the
words but acutally saw them as if they'd been written, patterned
and carved into his eyes.

A peacefulness came over him, a calming energy that seeped
into his pores. Somehow Pepe no longer existed. Something inside
him, something he knew but hardly recognized emerged as the
source of new strength. It was almost as if the body melted away
and made room for the spirit to act as an emissary into a strange
unknown power. When he opened his eyes, he was lying on his
back and staring into the straw ceiling of the hut.

He got up from the ground and dusted himself off. He blew out
the lantern and stepped outside to wait for Margarita. It surprised
him to see no children playing. He heard men's voices creeping
through the torn silence. Could he have fallen asleep, he thought.
Maybe an hour had passed, maybe even two or three. Should he
go to Hector's and speak to Margarita? Panic rushed at him but
did not last long. It wasn't his nature. He walked past Hector's
house, through the gate and out into the hacienda patio. Many
horses stood at the far end of the courtyard. Two men stood close
to the horses.

Other men talked outside the main entrance to the hacienda.
Perico had already posted guards. Pepe turned to look as the two
men near the horses continued talking. He noticed that the horses
were saddled and ready to ride. Quietly and keeping close to the
shadows, Pepe walked along the wall that divided the courtyard
from the stables.

As he walked, his left shoulder touched the adobe wall. In case
someone was to see him, he did not want it to appear that he was
sneaking around. He released a deep sigh when he reached the side
of the house where Isabel was to meet him. He peered carefully
through the darkness but did not see her.

Had he arrived too late? Again, his stomach began to tighten.
Squatting like an Indian, he reached down and grabbed a handful
of dirt. Pepe squeezed the sandy powder and let it fall between his
fingers slowly back to the earth. Looking at the sky, he watched
the stars sparkle as he located familiar formations. He had seen

them as a child, and they helped remind him that he was never completely alone. No matter how isolated he felt, or how confusing life seemed, the stars told him there were still relations in everything.

"I almost didn't see you."

Pepe jumped to his feet. Isabel stood near the front of the house. She stepped down from the porch and walked towards him.

"Why were you squatting down like that? Were you hiding?" she joked.

"I thought I had missed you," he said, nervously.

"Well, you did say thirty minutes."

"I know, but I fell asleep and didn't know the time."

"How pretty. You ask to see someone and then you fall asleep," she said, teasing him.

"Are you cold?" he asked, unable to think of anything else to say.

"A little," she answered, pulling a lace shawl over her shoulders. A long silence followed.

"Did you want to see me about something?" she finally asked.

"Isabel, I'm not good at this kind of thing," he said, as if suddenly remembering why he had come. She looked so beautiful. If only he could touch her. "But I want to tell you that ... that, I like you," he swallowed hard because he really wanted to say that he loved her, "I like you very much."

"Thank you," Isabel said to him, a little embarrassed.

Pepe became serious, and all the nervousness in his voice vanished.

"Something happened tonight, and tomorrow I must leave," he said, and unable to control himself, added, "I want you to come with me."

Isabel looked at him for a long time. She understood his words but didn't know why he had said them.

"Where do you want me to go?" she asked, calmly.

"I'm not sure, but I think I will go to Juarez and then to the north. I can find a job. There's much work on the northern railroads."

"I don't understand. Why are you asking me to go? What makes you think that I would leave?" she asked in a confused tone.

"I haven't been able to think of anything else except you," he told her. "Each night I lay awake and touch you. I see your face everywhere. If only I could touch your hand, I tell myself, I would be happy. Just to have you next to me would wash away all the badness in my life. And I know you feel something for me. Our eyes don't lie," Pepe said in a whisper.

No one had ever spoken to Isabel with such words, such sincerity. She looked into his eyes. She didn't notice the ragged clothes. She didn't care that he was a field worker.

"Do you remember the day we stood by the well?" he said, peering into her eyes, "I wanted so much to reach out and hold you in my arms. Just to touch you ... your smile carried me through the rest of the day."

He could not stop. Pepe placed his arms around her and slowly brought her close to him. Her body was golden. They remained locked for one sweet moment and separated holding hands. Her heart pounded crazily.

"I don't know what to say." Tears came to her eyes.

"Go with me," he said.

"My family is here. My mother and father, my brothers and sisters."

"I love you, Isabel."

She spoke quietly, "I'm not so sure that I love you, Pepe Rios," and quickly added, "Yes, it's true, I do feel for you, but I hardly know you. I've heard a few things, that your father owned a large ranch. But how can I go away with you."

"I can give you a good life," he said, pressing her hands softly.

Isabel's eyes fell to his dirty clothes, torn huaraches and long hair.

"I have been living free, with no one to worry about except myself," he said, guessing what she would be thinking of his poor appearance. "I stopped here only for food and rest. I work for whatever I receive. When a man owns little, he needs little to survive."

"You are a monkey, Pepe. You will always be a monkey, wherever you go."

He laughed and said, "I am a monkey because that's what I want to be, for now. I've not always worked in the field. I have done many things. But even if I were a monkey, what I feel for you is above everything else."

"I don't know," she said, anxiously, dropping her head, "I must have time to think."

"Time, Isabel, is one thing I cannot give you. By the time the sun rises tomorrow, I will have gone."

"But I can't just leave," she cried, sharply.

"I did. And I had everything that you have, probably even more."

She looked at him, curiously, not understanding. "Maybe you and I are very different people," she said, regaining her tranquility.

"Maybe, maybe not."

Pepe's confidence grew as he spoke, not so much confidence that she would leave with him but confidence about a future of which he knew nothing.

Isabel, as strong and assertive as her family and friends knew her to be, felt weak and vulnerable, and at the same time, she felt safe in Pepe's presence. She had only felt this way with one other man.

"I don't know if I truly love you, Pepe Rios."

"Maybe it's something we can both find together," he said, conscious of her hands in his.

The sound of men's voices screaming out orders and a horse's hooves tearing at the silence woke them to the immediate danger surrounding them.

"I must go back inside," Isabel said.

"I'll be gone one hour before daylight, when the rooster first begins to crow. If you decide to come with me, I will meet you at the place where the rocks are piled against the palm trees. You know where it is, towards the west."

He could see the nervous look on her face. Pepe knew what would happen if they were caught together. Isabel pulled her hands free. She turned to leave, stopped and returned to Pepe's arms. Their eyes met in the darkness. He leaned down and touched her cheek lightly with his lips. The kiss froze both of them. Pepe stepped back, kissed her hands and said, "Quickly, go inside before somebody sees you."

Isabel stared at him a moment, turned and disappeared around the front of the house.

Pepe waited some time before he walked back to the stables. He wanted no one to see him or Isabel walking away from the same area.

When he reached his shack, he couldn't help but smile. It was a great smile that lifted the corners of his mouth and sent happiness into his heart. The impossible now seemed possible. In the darkness, lying on his straw mat, he tried to relive the entire scene, the words, the kiss, the hands touching, she in his arms. Pepe was captured by love. As he dozed into a light sleep, a thought pecked at his mind, would she be there waiting for him in the morning?

CHAPTER THIRTY-SEVEN

A rooster's cry woke Pepe. He jumped from the mat and walked over to where he kept the water. He poured the water from the jug and into a small container. The water felt cold as he washed his face and moistened his hair. He put on his poncho and quickly grabbed the bag in which he had already packed his few belongings. One last time, Pepe looked around the little room. He hadn't realized how small it looked. The morning air chilled his face as he stepped outside.

The sky was still dark. Many stars still shone but with less brilliance as the night before. Pepe searched the small pathway in front of the huts. Everything was silent and still. He wished he could say goodbye to his friends, especially Hector, but he knew that they would understand.

He moved close to the shacks as he made his way through the corrals and out the backway of the hacienda. He knew that guards would be posted at all entrances. But he also knew that they seldom stayed awake past midnight.

Once free of the hacienda, Pepe ran across the open fields, hunched over so no one could see him. After a short time passed, the palm trees came into view. His vision was hazy and filled with shadows. As he moved closer, he could see the rocks piled at the base of the palm trees. There, next to the trunk of one of the trees, Isabel sat waiting for him. A large brown horse came from around the rocks.

"Where did you get him?" Pepe asked, walking up to the animal and running his hand over the neck.

"Don Anastacio gave him to me as a gift when I was elected queen of the fiesta two years ago."

Pepe looked the horse over carefully. The saddle was mounted correctly. A rifle was holstered along the side.

"And this?" asked Pepe, touching the smooth wooden stock.

"My father is a soldier. He has a lot of them; he won't miss one."

Pepe placed his foot in the stirrup and lifted himself into the saddle. The horse moved about nervously. Reaching out, he took Isabel's hand and helped her onto the horse. He was glad that she knew horses. He kicked the horse on the sides, and they rode off towards the north.

They rode for many hours before either of them said a word. The sun painted red streaks across the tips of the eastern mountains. Large shadows of cactus and brush covered the desert. Isabel held fast to Pepe's waist.

"There's a town, a small village called La Milpita about two leagues from here," she said, placing her lips close to his ear.

"Maybe we can get something to eat there," he said.

"Pepe, I told my mother I was leaving with you," Isabel said in a calm voice.

"They will follow us," he said.

"My mother said that she will give us time. They won't know which way we're going."

"But your father, he will ... "

"Isabel knew what Pepe was going to say. "My mother isn't a weak farm woman," she said, proudly. "My father will scream, and maybe hit her, but she doesn't fear him and he knows it."

Pepe tried to understand. He thought his own mother very strong, but she was always obedient to her husband, even though he would never hit her.

"You mean your mother let you leave. She didn't try to stop you."

"Hmph," Isabel pouted, "my mother wants none of her children to become ranch people. I'm fifteen. In another year, she would have helped me get away."

"You surprise me," Pepe told her, letting the reins fall loosely onto the horse's neck.

"Why?"

"I'm not sure. Maybe it's your directness. I'm used to people who talk in ... in riddles, you know?"

"Riddles?" she said, puzzled.

"Well, maybe not riddles exactly, more like using many words to disguise the true meaning of their ideas."

"I've never heard anything so stupid. I hope you aren't such a person, Pepe Rios."

"Oh, I can be. I can build words as high as pyramids, but I only do that when those I'm speaking to do the same."

"Then it's good for you to know," Isabel said, pushing loose strands of hair from her face, "that I say exactly what's on my mind. I don't like this thing of hiding behind words," she said, sternly.

Pepe had never met a girl with such fire about her. He thought all women were timid and meek, unless a tragedy had forced them to meanness.

"Do you understand me?" she added.

"Yeah, I understand. But there's also something that you must understand."

"And what is that?"

"As long as you are my woman, you will do as I say. Agreed?"

Isabel thought about that for some time. Finally she responded, "Agreed."

"Good," he said, satisfied.

"But if I find that you are an idiot who makes stupid demands and terrible decisions, then I will make the decisions. Agreed?" she said, giggling.

"Agreed," Pepe said, smiling.

As they rode closer to the town, they saw groups of people traveling along the main road. At first they saw small groups, but as the town drew near, the groups swelled. There must have been hundreds, maybe thousands, whole families with grandparents and children. Many of the men carried rifles, old fashioned muskets with splintered stocks. Others carried machetes, picks and crude clubs. The women carried sacks over their backs, and others carried bandoliers of ammunition.

Everyone seemed to talk about the war. Pepe heard the name of Pancho Villa uttered over and over again. Some spoke of victorious battles against the government. Others spoke of dances and parties which followed the victories. The people wore a strange conglomeration of clothing. Some wore white peasant tops with dark suit trousers and military boots. One man wore a top hat, a white silk shirt, a bow tie, unproperly fixed, dirty khaki pants and old huaraches. Some wore red arm bands, some green.

"Pardon me, but where are all these people going?"

The man, walking with a rifle over his shoulder, looked suspicously at Pepe and tipped his hat to Isabel. He smiled and said,

"Juarez, my friend. Señor Madero and the grand capitán Villa are preparing to attack the city. It will be the greatest victory of the revolution."

"Ayyyiii!" cried another man on horseback, overhearing the words.

"The federales think that Ciudad Juarez is where they will break our backs. But look! Look, amigo, at all the people who have come to fight: farmers, ranchers, laundrymen and shopowners. They are tired of the corrupt governments. Dictators for presidents, secret elections. Land for everyone!" the man screamed. "And you, compañero. Where are you going," the man asked Pepe.

Pepe turned to look at all of the people trekking along the road. "We too are going to Juarez," Pepe answered, hollering above the noise of the voices and horses.

"Oiga, where is your home?" the man asked.

"We come from a hacienda some leagues away from here," Pepe said, removing his sombrero and wiping his brow.

"A hacienda, huh? Why did you leave?"

Pepe was in no mood to answer questions, but he knew better than to refuse.

"We are tired of being treated like animals," was all that he said.

"Muy bien. Most of the gente here are also tired of being treated like animals. Now they fight to be treated like people."

"Are there leaders among you?"

"Bueno, sí. There are many leaders here." The man pointed towards a bearded rider who wore a white Texas-style cowboy hat.

"Over there, see. He is Aurelio Haro de Castilla. Together we have fought in many battles. He is a good leader, you see." The man pointed his finger to his head, as if the movement gave him more energy to think.

"I'm told that he owned a grocery store in Durango."

Isabel jumped from the horse. "I want to walk a while," she said, tying a bandana around her head. Pepe followed her as they moved smoothly with the flow of people.

The heat fell like fire. The sky was clear. Dust filled the air around the excited crusaders. Children, who thought the adventure a fantastic game, ran through the crowd laughing and screaming.

Twenty or so adobe houses, a chapel and one store made up the town of Milpitas. Since the revolution had stormed the countryside, the store owner no longer sold food. Each afternoon a shipment of sugar, coffee and beans, if he was lucky, always arrived. The supplies were sent immediately to Pancho Villa, who always sent back enough money to cover the expenses.

"If I hear that you make even one centavo from this food," Villa told him, "I will come back and kill you myself." The store owner believed him.

Pepe estimated that there were about a thousand people camped near the railroad tracks that ran alongside Milpitas. For many it would be their first train ride.

Smoke rose from what appeared to be hundreds of small fires. Women were preparing meals, while the men stood around in groups talking. The children continued their never ending games. Two women gave birth, and an old man died before the end of the afternoon.

"What chances do we have of taking Ciudad Juarez?" asked a young man, his voice a little shaky.

"They say that General Navarro has 3000 federales, good soldiers, defending the city," said the man who had been speaking to Pepe.

"Hombre, we are strong," shouted a man of about thirty years old, balding and missing a front tooth. "All of northern Mexico is practically ours. Orozco has seen victory in every battle, and the federales run everytime Villa comes near them."

"It's true," added an old man puffing on a corn leaf cigarette. "There seem to be no federales or rurales on the roads anymore."

"If we can take Juarez, the revolution will be ours. Each day we get stronger. No government forces will challenge our power," said the man with the missing tooth.

"We are in for an ugly fight, señores." The men turned to see the speaker. He was a tall, handsome man, probably in his late thirties. He carried two pistols at his sides. He wore a tight, custom made, brown charro suit, dirty from the war.

"They know we're coming," he warned. "They have blocked off all of the main streets, fortified their bunkers, and they have set up gringo machine guns to cover all fields of attack. They've been storing up food and ammunition for weeks. Right now they sit and wait."

"Many men will die?" asked a young rebel of about fourteen.

"There will be many widows and orphans after the smoke is gone from Ciudad Juarez. But remember, it's our testing ground. It's the first time we are attacking a major city. We must fight bravely, and we must be smart."

A woman arrived carrying a tin plate filled with beans. She gave the plate to the man Pepe had met on the road. His name was Simon. Other women came and one by one all the men started eating.

Pepe could feel his stomach growl as he smelled the beans. Isabel arrived and gave him a plate and a cup of coffee. She left and returned to eat with the other women.

Pepe didn't know where the food had come from. The men left those things up to the women. Somehow the women always saw to it that the men were fed.

Some of the men had brought along their own women, if not wives, then women who traveled with them like wives. Other men took whichever women happened to be free. After a battle, there were always women who would be alone. The families ate in groups as though they were still at home.

"You boy," the man with the missing tooth called to Pepe, "I haven't seen you before."

Pepe smiled as all the men stared at him. A familiar feeling came over him. He felt as if he had been in this same situation before. In seconds, the feeling vanished.

"I'm from Zacatecas. I have been working on the hacienda of Anastacio Burales."

Two men turned and stared at each other. Pepe saw their expressions.

"Is something wrong?" Pepe asked. "Do you know him?"

"Do you have familia there?" one of the men asked.

Pepe shook his head,

"No. Why?" he asked.

"Three hundred men, gente of Orozco, wiped the place out this morning."

Pepe felt the blood rush to his face. He stuttered, gained control and asked, "How do you know?"

"Five who were with Orozco came in this afternoon. The battle lasted only a few hours. The man, Burales, you say ... he was not prepared."

"How many people did they kill?"

"I'm not sure. Probably everyone, except the women and children, of course, and the men who chose to join the revolution. Usually, that's the way it works. There are, I'm sure, many assassinations taking place right now."

A blank expression crossed Pepe's face. His mind whirled in an eddy of confusion.

"Eh, how do we know that you are not one of the hacienda cowboys?" said the man without a front tooth. Pepe stared at him. It seemed that the blank space between his teeth left a gaping hole.

"I worked among the monkeys. The burros were treated better than I. Why do you think I left?" Pepe answered, confidently.

"How long did you work there?" asked, Simon.

"A month and a half, maybe two. I'm not certain."

"That's a fine horse you're riding," said another man.

"I stole him," Pepe answered, and after a second added, "I imagine now I don't have to worry about the owner coming after me." He laughed, a pain burning deep inside his belly. The men also laughed.

"Muy bien, so now you go with us to Juarez, eh boy. You will see history being made."

"Of course." Pepe wiped at his sweaty forehead and thought about Isabel. She looked very pretty, but a little tired as he saw her sitting among the women eating their food.

CHAPTER THIRTY-EIGHT

As the night moved in, the small fires became a circus of little lights that dimly illuminated the darkness. People in the distance became shadows and half-bodies as the fires lighted portions of their faces, necks, arms and legs.

A guitar and harmonica quietly echoed above the camp and murmuring voices. This army, the gente of Villa and Orozco and of leaders whose names were not so famous, found a certain peace in the desert. Many had been herded around haciendas all their lives. A large number had been forced to work the fields, mines and newly constructed factories. They were to pay a high price for their freedom, but even if that freedom were to last only one night, it would be a night where they were to see themselves as people, not animals. In the solitude of the desert, among rattlesnakes and scorpions, Villa offered his people a reason to exist. He gave them a sense of value, a chance to be a part of something much greater than themselves. Many were new and had not before seen battle. Many came because death was a preferable alternative to bondage.

Isabel spread the blankets over the sand. In their haste to leave the hacienda, neither had thought to take along a petate on which to sleep.

Isabel moved with the gentleness of a deer. She patted the blankets to remove the lumps and fixed their excess clothing to serve as pillows. Their new home was rugged, but she would make her man as comfortable as possible.

Pepe felt nervous and wracked with a deep sense of guilt. He was afraid to tell Isabel about the hacienda and even more afraid to sleep with her. Both things swelled within his mind. His legs felt weak and his chest heaved. He put on a brave face. His only comfort was that he had found some water with which to wash

208

himself, a small pleasure in such terrible circumstances.

She saw him as he appeared out of the darkness. The reflection from a neighboring fire gave light for each of them to see. Isabel's face shone. Her hair was loose and fell over her shoulders. She smiled as he neared.

The moon, not quite full, shone beneath the multitude of stars. Pepe stood with his hands in his pockets and stared up at the sky. Isabel stood and walked over to him. They searched the galaxies as if for an answer to their future.

"It's as beautiful as last night," Isabel said.

"Yes, and last night seems so long ago," he answered.

"Would you like to reach up and touch one of those stars?"

"I already have," he said, looking at her and slipping his hand into hers.

Isabel knew a little more about Pepe than she had let on. She had heard Perico talking about him. Perico had wanted to make him a soldier. Some of the others complained that Pepe was a stranger, and that he needed more time to prove his loyalty. Isabel always listened but knew that she could never ask questions about him. She had watched him as he worked and knew that he was different from the others. He acted and moved with a certain confidence. In talking, he never stammered or appeared too humble. She had not shown it, but she was delighted when he asked her to run off with him, even if she was scared.

She held his hand tightly. He turned and led her to the blankets. Most of the fires were low or already extinguished. She slid inside the blankets. There was a chill in the air. He moved in close to her and within minutes the coldness disappeared and a soothing warmth surrounded them.

"Pepe, I have something I must tell you," she said.

She was scared. She had sworn she would never tell, but being here with Pepe, alone, and feeling so close to him, she knew that he had to know.

"What is it?" he asked, in a low, gentle voice.

She remained silent for a moment, afraid she might pick the wrong words.

"This isn't new for me. I have slept with a man before."

Isabel felt his arms stiffen about her waist.

"Have you been married?"

"No, but I loved him as if we were."

Pepe couldn't seem to control his thoughts. Confusion raced through his mind. He felt deceived. He raised himself to one elbow and looked down at her. She was more beautiful than ever.

"Tell me about it."

"Are you sure you want to hear?"

"Yes, tell me."

"Last year. I was fourteen. The federales garrison from Las Nieves stopped at the hacienda. One of the leaders had come to talk to don Anastacio. Perico had us prepare food for all of them. That's when I met him. He was twenty-two and a lieutenant.

"I fell in love. He came back many times to visit. Finally, he told me we would marry, and I gave myself to him."

Isabel could feel the coolness come over Pepe. He was sitting. He didn't look at her.

"Should I continue?" she whispered.

Pepe had been taught that a woman must come to a man pure, untouched by the body of another man. As a friend had once told him, "There is nothing worse than a horse who has had other owners."

"I'm sorry," she said, when Pepe didn't answer. "Maybe I should have told you last night."

"Why didn't you marry him?" Pepe asked, hoping to get an answer that would satisfy him.

"He was already married and had a family in Ciudad Hidalgo."

"He never told you?" Pepe screamed, in a hoarse cry.

Isabel swallowed hard, "I knew."

"And you still slept with him?" Pepe said, hardly able to believe her words.

"I loved him," she pleaded.

"Don't use love as an excuse," he said, cruelly, throwing the blankets off himself.

Isabel's eyes filled with tears. She sat up. "I don't need to explain anything to you or to anybody else," she said.

"You don't even know what the word means, unless you used it as a reason to fuck him," Pepe said, angrily, turning his face towards her. She slapped him twice, hard.

"Is that why you decided to come with me, because no one else would have you?" Ugly thoughts came into his mind. He wanted to strike back. The meaner the words the better, he felt. Something or someone had taken over. He became vicious. His words shattered her.

Isabel's tough exterior crumbled beneath his cold dissection. She dropped her head and cried openly. Her body trembled. It was the first time she had completely broken down in front of anyone, except her mother.

Pepe stood up. He knew that many people around the camp could hear, but he didn't care. The devil within him made him swell with hatred. He looked down on her like a Roman gladiator standing over a fallen victim. She looked like a child, lost and helpless. His vile words came back at him. He could not believe he had said them. It was as if a sword had pierced him. He felt weak and began to cry silently. Who was he to judge her?

Bewildered, he did not know what to do. One part of him wanted to run off and disappear. The other part needed and wanted to hold her close. But his pride kept both parts perplexed. The pride dissolved and Pepe fell to his knees.

Her small body shook as he continued weeping. Pepe wrapped his arms around her tightly. He apologized many times. She had known that one day she would face the words Pepe had spoken. She had known the male mind could react only one way, but she hoped that Pepe would be different. She had trusted Pepe and wanted him to know the truth, and now with each tear, the guilt she had been carrying was suddenly released.

"Isabel. I'm sorry. Forgive me. Forgive," he repeated. "I don't care. I don't care. I love you, and that means everything. You have nothing to feel bad about. It's me. I'm the one who should feel bad."

As he held her, he realized that she had trusted him with the truth, the deepest secret in her heart. She could have proved her love in no other way. And he possessed neither the love nor the understanding to realize her sacrifice.

He lay her back down and pulled her close to him, covering them with the blankets.

CHAPTER THIRTY-NINE

Slowly the locomotive pulled into town. Behind it came a coal car with the large white letters N de M painted on the side, and following that, two flat cars, three cattle cars and a caboose. Clouds of dust from the rails covered the revolutionaries who stood at the side of the tracks. After a short time, the dust settled and the men in charge started ordering people to board.

A mass of people moved close to the train. They began throwing their belongings on board and rushing to find places to sit. Many of the younger rebels crowded onto the roofs of the cars, waving captured flags and screaming, "Viva México! Viva Madero! Viva Villa!" In no time at all, the cars were filled. It appeared as if everyone was heading for a giant celebration. Pepe, Isabel and the hundreds of others who could not board, watched as the engine moved lethargically down the tracks and disappeared into the horizon.

Loaded down with ammunition and moving down the lines of people, a soldier announced that more trains would arrive soon. Pepe watched as the man passed, then he returned to where Isabel waited some yards from the tracks. She dropped her eyes as he neared. They hadn't spoken since the night before.

He considered telling her about the massacre of the hacienda. For reasons he didn't understand, he decided to say nothing. As he walked to her, he realized the possibility that she had no remaining family. Battles between federales and rebels often wiped out complete towns and haciendas, which included the deaths of many innocent people.

"We'll wait for the next train." The suddeness of his words jarred her from her thoughts.

"Where will we go?" she asked.

"A place called Bauche station, some ten leagues from Ciudad Juarez. People from all over the north are gathering there."

Isabel felt suddenly as if she were in the company of a stranger. A firm expression was on Pepe's face. She started believing that Pepe actually enjoyed the excitement that was before them.

When she turned her head, Pepe sneaked a glance at her. The beauty of her face, perfectly lined, wide-eyed, still excited him.

They both sat in silence, pretending to observe the scene about them. Neither wanted the other to suspect that they were really thinking about each other. The intensity of their relationship seemed to suffocate them. Pepe wanted to talk about last night; he truly wanted to understand. Isabel wanted to tell him everything. She also wanted to understand.

"It's very hot and dusty today." His words sounded like a distant echo.

"Yes, it is," she replied.

"Are you hungry?"

"Not very." She lied. She had eaten very little the night before.

"Nor I." He also lied.

He looked down at Isabel's hand. If only he could hold it. But if he tried, she might pull away, and rejection was something he couldn't handle, not now. Better to sit quietly, he thought.

"What will we do when we arrive in Ciudad Juarez?" she asked.

"I must fight. Once the battle is finished, we can cross the border."

"Oh," she muttered, wishing she were home.

"Do you think you will like El Paso?" he asked.

"I don't know. I've never heard much about it."

"Well, do you think you might like it?" he persisted.

The strain between them began to ease with the words.

"I might like it. I might not."

"Oh," he uttered, glad that he had brought her.

They looked at eached other and began laughing.

"Yes. I think I'll like El Paso very much," she said.

"Good. I think I will too," and he quickly added, "Isabel, I want to apologize for last night. I don't know where all of that came from. That isn't the kind of person I am. You need to know that."

She took his hands and placed them between hers, squeezing, kneading and rubbing him softly.

"You know how I feel about you. That hasn't changed," he said, moving close to her. He should have felt embarrassed showing such emotion in daylight, but he didn't care who saw. Isabel, knowing about men, their pride and their ways, knew then that Pepe was different.

"Pepe. Why must you fight?"

He knew that she didn't know much about the war, and he wanted to help her understand.

"In my travels, I have seen many things, Isabel. There are good and bad men on both sides. But as for those who rule Mexico, there are only bad. They allow hunger and illness to kill the poor. They allow foreigners to make slaves of us. Don't forget, it takes money to fight wars. The French, British, Germans and Americans are all sending money and weapons."

"But why do they care about what happens in this country; we have no wealth?"

"Look, there is an American family, the Guggen ... Guggenuha ... heims, something like that, but they are rich, so rich that they couldn't spend all of their money in a lifetime. They are sending millions of pesos to the government so that the people, those who you see right here, will lose."

The intrigue fascinated Isabel. Pepe's words were like the novels she had read. She wasn't aware that so much was going on in Mexico.

"But why? Why do they care who wins or who loses?" she insisted.

"Because they own many banks, and they own most of the copper in the United States. The Maderos are bankers also, and they too own copper, here in Mexico. The Guggenheimers, they want to own all of the copper in Mexico. If Diaz defeats Madero, those who helped support Diaz will control whatever they want."

"And is it the same with the other countries. They will also win something?" she asked.

"Exactly. Diaz has given many oil rights to the British. This angers the American oil men who want all of Mexico's oil for themselves. So the American oil men give money to Madero to help him defeat Diaz, and the American copper men give money to Diaz to help him defeat Madero. The way I understand it is that in the United States, the government is given money by both copper and oil men, so the government has a difficult time deciding whether to support Madero or Diaz."

"How did you learn about all of this?" she asked, astounded by Pepe's knowledge.

"A man I once rode with. He was a student in Mexico City,

and he wrote articles for the rebel newspaper. We would stay up late into the night talking about these things. It seemed that he knew everything.

"But what you must remember is that Diaz has caused much suffering in Mexico. The people will accept suffering, it is their life. But they can endure only so much. There comes a time when they can endure no longer, and there is nothing left but to take up arms. And that is what we are seeing now."

As if remembering the beginning of the conversation, and thinking she'd somehow been led astray, Isabel sighed deeply. "But Pepe, you might be killed," she told him.

"Yes, I know it's possible. But I have a feeling it won't happen."

"But doesn't the possibility scare you?"

"Not now, although I'm sure later on it might."

"Have you fought before, Pepe?"

"Yes. I fought bandits who tried to rob our ranch. And I also fought the federales when I rode with the rebels from Saltillo to, I think it was, somewhere near Torreon."

"Your family really did own a ranch?" she asked, excitedly.

"You don't think I learned to ride by being a monkey do you? We owned about five thousand acres. It was called Las Amapolas."

"What a lovely name."

Pepe pulled a thick dry weed from the sand and placed it into his mouth.

"We raised cattle, and we owned many horses. The ranch was high in the mountains. From our home you could see the most beautiful canyons in all of Mexico."

"Were you a cowboy?"

"You promise not to laugh?" he said, sternly.

She smiled mischievously, like a little girl playing a game. "I promise."

"We were all cowboys, my brothers and I. Our father taught us how to ride, shoot and herd cattle. We planted and harvested our own corn and beans. We slaughtered our own animals for meat."

"Why should I laugh about that?" she said, squeezing his hands.

"Well, you see, I also learned to read and write. It was something I liked very much. My mother made me read the Bible, so every night I would read to my brothers and sisters, and after, we would talk about the stories."

Pepe described how he read the Bible to the villagers in the mountains and how the priests had accused him of stealing their parishioners. Isabel was irritated that Pepe would think that she could laugh at such a nice thing.

He continued telling her about his family and about how his father had always talked to all of the children, encouraging discovery through conversation. His father had even liked the idea of Pepe traveling to the other ranches and reading the Bible to those who would see no priest for long periods of time. Then somehow Pepe returned to the original topic about the fighting and the men and women who joined the revolution.

Together, holding hands like two children, they observed the people around them. Most seemed to wear old clothing, probably discarded rags. Many wore huaraches, some shoes, a few were barefoot. The people squatted or sat on the dirt. They appeared dark and huddled together like packs of rabbits.

Isabel pointed towards a family who sat about ten meters from them. The mother, dressed in a long, black dress, dirty and torn, was breast feeding a small infant. By her side lay a rifle and an ammunition belt. Isabel did not doubt that the woman could use it. The woman raised her voice, scolding her son who was fighting with another child.

"They are just like us," Pepe said. "If they steal and lie, it's because they have been robbed and lied to. If they are brutal, it's because they have been brutalized. They fight like savages because they have been treated that way."

"It's good that you speak to me, Pepe. I watched the women back home, and they spend the entire day gossiping among themselves because their husbands don't confide in them. Sometimes my mother and father would go nights without a single word. Are men and women so different that they have nothing to share?" she said, as she continued looking about the crowds.

A man who was carrying a large rifle over his shoulder walked up to them. He was rough looking and wore army trousers, leggings and boots, a short charro jacket and an American cowboy hat. Pepe stood as the man approached.

"I'm told that you're new around here?" the man said.

Pepe nodded but said nothing.

"Can you use that horse and rifle?"

"I can use them," Pepe answered.

"Have you fought in any battles?"

"Some."

"Good. Send your woman on the next train with your belongings. You can meet her at Bauche Station in a day or two."

"I don't understand," Pepe told him.

"We need men with horses, men who have been in battle. I can tell you nothing more than that. After the next train leaves, we'll assemble over by the water tank."

The man turned and vanished into the crowd.

Pepe walked over to the horse. He pulled the rifle from the holster and inspected it carefully.

"You're not really going to stay behind, are you?" Isabel said, moving close to Pepe.

"I must. I don't have a choice. They need help."

"But what about me. What will I do while you're off fighting." Isabel spoke in an irritated voice.

Pepe smiled at her childishness. "You will go on with the others. As long as your man is a revolutionary, the other women will take care of you. You can help out in the camp."

"And what about the other men?" she said, in a somewhat threatening tone.

"What about them?"

"Who will protect me if I'm traveling alone?"

Pepe stepped close to her and placed his hands on her shoulders. "Listen well," he started, "I have traveled before with the rebels. They are tough, and some are even swine, but if they know that your man is fighting, you will be fine. If you give any hint that you are without a man and that you are available, they will swarm you."

The smoke from the train formed a small cloud in the distance. The people alongside the tracks rose to their feet. They started grabbing their belongings in preparation to board the train. Pepe placed their sack in Isabel's hands.

"Pepe Rios," she screamed at him, "you better take care of my horse."

"I'll treat him like my own."

"Humph," she snarled. "If you treat him like you treat your woman, he will leave you in a day."

The train grew larger as it approached the waiting crowd. Pepe took Isabel in his arms. "I won't be gone long."

"Ay Pepe, take care of yourself," she whined.

Pepe lifted her face to his. He bent down and kissed her lightly on the lips. "I still love you very much," he told her.

She looked at him, and her eyes moistened. He was all she had.

"I don't know if I love you," she pouted like an angry little girl. "Surely even less now than before." She leaped at him, throwing her arms around his neck,

"If anything happens to you, I'll never forgive you." The train hissed and huffed as smoke flew from its steel wheels. The engineer did not stop the engines. People began filling up the cars. Pepe lifted Isabel onto one of the cattle cars and helped her inside. She pushed against the others who also fought to get on board.

The voices of crying children and screaming mothers could barely be heard over the fuming, loud breaths of the locomotive. Isabel saw Pepe's lips moving, but she couldn't hear what he was saying. She waved at him as if she understood.

Soon all of the passengers were on board. As the train began to raise the pitch of its engines to start its departure, Isabel looked out at Pepe one final time. She thought how handsome he looked, young and strong, standing among the other revolutionaries. His large sombrero was draped over his back. His light, brown hair shone blond in the sunlight. He appeared taller than the other men. She threw him a kiss. He waved back to her. The train moved. Someone closed the door and Pepe was gone.

CHAPTER FORTY

Isabel crouched into one corner of the car. The smell of coal, cattle, sulfur, cigarettes and human perspiration made her want to vomit. She belched, put her hand to her mouth and kept the sickness from coming up. She wiped at the moisture in her eyes.

There was no more laughter among the people. Isabel placed her head in the palms of her hand as she listened to the cries of children rising above the sound of metal wheels striking the rails. She could not believe that she had left her home for this. She started to cry. Fear gripped her and she felt faint.

After a little time passed and she'd shed her tears silently, she studied the people around her. Mothers tried keeping their children still, screaming at them and pulling their hair to make them sit down and behave.

The men were all ages. Isabel saw boys as young as ten years bearing bandoliers of ammunition. She felt guilty at the sight but saw that some men who were well into their years might not even make it to the end of the train ride. Why, she wondered, would these people leave the comfort of their homes for this? Could the worst injustices compare to traveling through the desert on a dilapidated train that was possibly delivering them to a violent death? She tried to remember how Pepe had explained the causes of the war to her, but at this moment she could understand none of it.

Isabel was shaken from her thoughts by a young woman's scream. The voice frightened everyone inside the car. A child, a boy of no more than five years old, placed his arms about the woman's neck, and he began to cry. An old woman made her way through the crowded car. When she reached the woman, she ordered those nearest to her to find other places to sit. Isabel sat a few feet from the woman.

"What is it?" asked the old woman.

"I think it's time," cried the younger woman.

The old woman placed a shawl under the other's head and lay her down on the dirty wooden floor. She placed her hand on the woman's stomach. It was big and hard. The woman breathed heavily. Isabel guessed that the woman was about twenty years old or so.

"I need a blanket," the old woman called out to everyone in the car.

A man rose to his feet, unfolded his blanket, shook it over the heads of those nearest him and passed it to the old woman. She took the blanket and gave it to Isabel, who was the first person she noticed.

"Spread the blanket and place it under her legs," Isabel was commanded.

Isabel looked at the blanket and froze. Her eyes grew enormous. She could not move.

"Did you hear me? Do as you're told, girl," screamed the old woman.

Isabel stood up, folded the blanket in half and place it beneath the young woman's outstretched legs.

A cold shiver shot through Isabel as the young woman let out a tremendous scream. She breathed hard and very fast. The old woman positioned herself between the woman's legs. She pulled the dress up on the girl's stomach, exposing the palpitating vagina. Blood covered the hair between the legs. The old woman saw the tip of the head break the opening. The young woman tossed and turned, screaming uncontrollably.

"Take her arms and hold her still, quickly," the orders came to Isabel. Isabel placed the woman's head in her lap and took hold of her hands. Another woman folded a small cloth and placed it in the pregnant woman's mouth and told her to bite hard. The woman did as she was told, and the screams came out muffled.

"Breathe hard. Breathe hard. Breathe hard," the old woman ordered.

The young woman did as she was told.

"Deeper! Deeper!" came the command from the old woman.

The girl breathed as deeply as she could.

"Now push, push hard!" screamed the old lady.

The woman pushed. Strange sounds came from her nostrils and from her mouth. She spit out the rag. Five other women formed a small circle around her. The men smoked cigarettes and continued talking.

Again, the old woman saw the head come out.

"Come on, m'ija, push. Just a little more. PUSH!"

The woman's body tensed as she heaved with every muscle. Her body quivered like a bowstring. The head came out a little farther. The woman could push no more. She released the tension with a loud cry. The head retreated.

Again the old woman gave the same commands and again the woman followed. The opening had appeared to have dilated enough, but the head would not come through. Isabel wiped perspiration from the young woman's forehead and face. Large beads ran down her chin and onto her neck.

One hour passed and then another. The train moved slowly along the tracks. The young woman screamed and squirmed like a tormented creature.

"Help her up! Help her up," screamed the old woman to the others.

They helped the girl into a squatting position. The old woman placed her hand under the bleeding vagina.

"Push on her stomach. Yes, you!" the old one screamed at Isabel.

Placing her hands high above the bulge on the woman's stomach, Isabel pushed down with all her might. There was a loud scream and the young woman nearly collapsed. The head popped completely out. The old woman carefully placed her hands close to the baby's head.

"PUSH! PUSH! Just a little more. Just a little more, niña."

The young woman breathed deeply, two, three, four, five times, then came the final push. The baby's shoulders plopped out. The old lady grasped the baby by the neck and shoulders and guided it as it fell into her hand. With one quick movement the old lady slipped the unbilical cord away from the baby's neck. Another woman handed the old woman a knife. She took the knife and cut the cord. A jet of blood shot out. The old woman tied the knot. Another girl, about thirteen, wrapped the baby in the cleanest blanket they could find.

Blood gushed forth and the afterbirth fell into the blanket. The young woman was lying down again, her head on Isabel's knees. Isabel looked into her eyes. She could tell the woman's eyes were not focusing on anything.

The old woman knew that there was too much blood. She

folded the blanket over again, but it was soaked. The young woman moaned in a low voice. No one knew what to do at this point. She seemed to be getting weaker. A man came over and brought another blanket. They placed it over her. It was dark when the train reached the halfway mark to Ciudad Juarez, and it was then that the young woman stopped breathing.

Isabel tried not to stare at the body which lay covered in a blanket at one corner of the car. Death wasn't new to Isabel. She had seen many dead people before. But on the hacienda even the poorest died with a shred of dignity. The young woman had died in the most miserable of circumstances. No one knew who she was. Who would care for her two children? Isabel again looked at the body and cried quietly.

The infant was passed through the car until it reached a woman who placed a shawl over her shoulder, pulled down the top of her dress and tried to breast feed the child. Two other women finished cleaning up the mess. They threw the dirty blanket out the door. A man offered the old woman a little water to wash her hands. She washed, went back to her place on the train and sat down. The dead woman's five-year-old child cried continuously. He could not understand why they wouldn't let him go to his mother. A young girl, about fourteen, moved close to Isabel.

"Are you all right?" the girl asked.

"I'm fine," Isabel replied, obviously shaken.

"My God, how sad it is. And nothing can be done about it."

Isabel said nothing.

"The poor woman was in such pain."

"Please," Isabel said, irritated, "I don't want to talk about it."

"I'm sorry, I didn't mean to make you feel bad."

"What's your name?" Isabel asked the girl, trying to change the subject.

"Elena. What is your name?"

"You can call me Isabel."

The girl, Elena, could see how hurt Isabel was. "I'm sorry, I know you don't want to talk," said Elena. "Do you mind if I just sit here next to you?"

Isabel looked at the girl. She appeared very homely. Her forehead was full of tiny pimples. A small scar crossed her eyebrow just above her left eye. Her top front teeth pushed against her upper lip.

"Yes," Isabel said, kindly, "you can sit here." She felt much older than the girl.

Isabel heard the girl's voice like a song in the distance. The clatter of the train pulsated gently. A strong, pungent odor permeated the car. Isabel closed her eyes and slept.

CHAPTER FORTY-ONE

When Isabel woke up, the people around her were rising to their feet. The train stopped and someone threw the door open. A man with a lantern jumped on board and lifted the light high.

"Bueno, this is it," he called, "Bauche Station. Everybody off."

Isabel reached down and picked up her bag. She moved past the others and ran down a steep wooden plank. She breathed deeply, trying to take in all of the fresh air her lungs could hold. Still, she felt drowsy from her sleep. It was dark, and all she could think about was finding a place to go back to sleep.

"Ay, you move so fast. You must be in a hurry."

Isabel looked behind her to see who spoke.

"Did you forget about me?" Elena asked.

"No," Isabel explained. "I had to get off of that train."

Elena looked at Isabel strangely, "All this is new for you, isn't it?" the girl said.

"Yes it is. How about for you?"

Elena let out a laugh, then answered, "I've been living this way for two years. I mean, we just started using trains. Most of the time we traveled through the mountains in small groups."

"But you're just a kid."

"I know," Elena said, smiling.

"Are you alone?" Isabel asked.

"For now. I'll find myself a man tomorrow."

Isabel stared at Elena, surprised at the girl's confidence. Elena just laughed.

"Ay, sí, you must be new at this," Elena said. "But don't worry, I'll show you."

"No," Isabel said, quickly, "I have a man."

"You mean the blondish boy who stayed behind to fight."

224

"Yes, he is my man," Isabel said.

"Ah bueno, that's fine. But don't expect him to come back."

"Why did you say that?" Isabel asked, as she followed the girl away from the tracks and into the desert where others were already making camp. A number of campfires lit up the early morning darkness.

"Why would you say such a thing?" Isabel said again.

In a child-like voice, but with the words of an adult, Elena said, "You learn to depend on no one out here, but yourself. I followed my father and brothers. One of my brothers ran off with a woman. He now fights for Orozco's people. My other two brothers and my father ... " Elena hesitated, her voice cracked, but continued, "They all died in different battles."

Isabel didn't say anything.

"I waited for each of them. They said the same thing. 'We will be back soon, hijita; keep the frijoles warm.' But they didn't come back. It's ugly to see the other soldiers return wounded on stretchers or sagging in their saddles as they come out of battle. And you don't see your man. You look and look. After a while all of the faces seem the same. But still, you don't see your man. Oh, you ask about him, but most of the other soldiers don't even know who you're talking about."

Elena found a spot close to a campfire. "Is it all right to share the warmth of your fire?" Elena asked the man who sat watch over the flames. Isabel saw that many children slept near the fire.

"Sure, daughter, find yourself a place."

The cold seemed to pass right through them. Isabel pulled tighter at the blanket hanging over her shoulders. Elena spread her things out on the sand. She motioned for Isabel to do the same. After a few minutes, the heat from the fire began to seep into their pores. Both girls remained sitting, blankets wrapped about them.

Isabel looked at the man who sat on the other side of the fire. He looked like her grandfather, maybe a little older. White hair like jagged splinters stuck out beneath his soiled, straw sombrero. He had many wrinkles on his face. A beard like a goat's dangled from his chin, and his eyes peered into the flames.

"Thank you very much," Elena called out to him.

The man looked up, smiled at them and turned his gaze back to the leaping flames.

"What did you do after you lost your father?" Isabel asked.

"Two men, sons of the devil himself, learned that I was alone. They came to me and asked that I choose between them. I was so scared all I could do was cry. One pushed the other away and claimed me for himself. The other picked up a handful of dirt and tossed it into the man's face. They began fighting. One pulled a knife. Another man, he was in charge, came up and ordered them to stop fighting. They stopped immediately."

Elena dropped her head. Her hair fell like two blinds covering her face. Isabel could tell that she was crying.

"I'm sorry," Isabel said, putting her arm around Elena's shoulder, "I didn't mean to be nosy."

"No, it's all right," Elena said, raising her head, "it's just that I haven't told the whole thing before. Let me go on. I need to."

The old man lit a cigarette. He removed his sombrero and held it to an angle so that the light from the fire allowed him to see inside. He searched carefully. There was little to see.

"The men told him what had happened," Elena continued. "I imagine, because they did not want to be punished, they told him I had started the fight by playing them both along." Elena let out a wry laugh. "I didn't even know what that meant. Anyway, the officer told them both to wait there. He would decide who I would go with."

Elena began to speak very slowly, every word precise and clear.

"He took me to his quarters, the home of a defeated hacendado. We walked from one room to another until we stood in front of a bed. On the name of Jesus, I didn't realize what he had in mind until that moment. He grabbed me roughly by the shoulders and pulled me towards him. I had never in my life even been kissed."

"Elena, you don't need to say anymore. I know what happened. I don't want to hear it," Isabel told her.

"You must hear it, all of it. You've chosen this life, so you might as well find out what it's all about."

Elena lowered her voice to make sure the old man did not hear. "I was stiff in his arms. I didn't know whether to scream or die. He was a big man and very handsome. 'You are afraid,' he said to me. I could only nod. 'This is your first time?' he asked. I asked him to let me go, but instead, he asked again, 'this is your first time?' I told him it was. Tears ran down my face."

Both girls were now warm. The old man placed more dung on the fire and went back to sit in his place. A peaceful look came over Elena's face.

"He kissed me very softly. His lips barely touched mine. I was scared and cold and could feel little. He told me to relax. He said to just let my hands fall to my sides and to lean completely against him. I did. He started at my neck and very softly massaged me along the neck, behind my ears, and all over my shoulders and back. I'll always remember his gentle hands. I didn't feel so scared anymore. I felt almost comforted. As he kept going, my body began to tingle. The cold left. He kissed me again, this time I kissed him back, or at least I pushed my lips against his. The wetness of his mouth made me feel like, like," Elena searched for the words.

"Like a melting candle." It was Isabel who said the words. Elena looked at her and smiled.

"Yes, that's it, just like a melting candle," she said, and looked at Isabel, with a smile.

"It was so beautiful. He lifted me like a feather and placed me on the bed. He covered me with a blanket and began to take off my dress. With each button he undid, he placed a kiss in its place. My body began to burn. I was naked and he sat next to me with all his clothes on. He placed his fingertips on my eyes and softly pushed them closed. I felt things I had never felt before and haven't felt since. He kissed the bottom of my feet. I felt his lips and his tongue take in every one of my toes. He did not leave an inch of my body without his kisses. I trembled a thousand times. Finally, he took off his clothes. Everything he did to me, he had me do to him."

"Elena, I don't think I want to hear any more of this."

"But you must listen."

Isabel nodded.

"I was very small, but he prepared me so well. There was a great deal of pain. I don't know how but automatically we moved together. I could have flown. He took me so high. And he finished.

"He stayed on the bed for a little while, got up and he dressed. He picked up my dress and threw it at me."

"Was he angry with you?" Isabel asked.

"He said, 'I have decided. I will give you to Araña.' Araña was the ugliest and meanest of the two men who had fought over me. I told him that I wanted to stay with him. I reached out to him, thinking that maybe he would hold me again. His fist hit me above the left eye. Everything went black for a moment. He grabbed my hair and pulled me up. He told me that if he ever saw his men fighting over me again that he would tie me to two horses and have me torn apart. He told me to go and be a good woman to Araña."

Elena covered her eyes. Isabel placed both of her arms around her to comfort her. The old man on the other side pretended not to notice. He took a long stick and moved the chips around the fire.

A hard look came over Elena's face as she threw back her hair and wiped her eyes.

"The man Araña treated me worse than an animal. It was my place to see that he always had enough food and a comfortable place to sleep whenever he returned from battles. In return he beat me, insulted me in front of others and had sex with me in an ugly way. He was an ugly scarfaced man who always smelled like a goat. His sex was nothing more than pulling my legs apart, no matter how I felt, entering me like a rock scraping rock, driving himself into me until he finished, which usually lasted three or four minutes. I died a hundred deaths with that man."

"Elena, how old are you?" interrupted Isabel.

"Fourteen."

"And when did all of this happen?"

"I went with Araña shortly after my thirteenth birthday."

"Ay Dios." Isabel could only shake her head.

"I was so happy when I found that Araña had been killed. Some of the women who had been around much longer than I told me to go out and find a man for myself before they came looking for me. And that's what I do. I talk to other women, they know who are the good men and the mean men. If we ask around, and we are careful, we will both find good men."

Isabel kept shaking her head, unable to believe the young girl's words. "Why have you stayed? Why didn't you get out the minute you could, when that evil man died?"

"And go where?" Elena answered, a little annoyed. "I have no family. Single women in the towns are at the mercy of both federales and revolutionaries. I am just learning to survive. Since Araña, there have been others. They weren't so bad. I treated them good, and they treated me as good as I could have liked.

"And that's the only choice a woman has out in this revolution?"

"Unless you have a man and a family, you are fair game, just like the deer in the mountains. That's what the men say."

Isabel clenched her fist in defiance. "Then this isn't a women's revolution. We've nothing to gain. It's all a man's game. What happened to you will never happen to me, even if it kills me."

"How can you escape it?" Elena asked.

"I don't know. There's still much I need to learn about this life. If I must, I will go back home."

Isabel's mind went into a brief panic. The realization came to her. Once a woman had left home to live with a man, especially if she ran off with him, she would never be allowed to return to her home. Isabel knew her father, and she also knew that he had probably already vowed to disown her.

Elena saw the look on Isabel's face and quickly understood. "You can't go home, ever, can you?" Elena asked.

Isabel shook her head. She tried to catch the flurry of thoughts that raced through her head but none took hold. Her panic turned to depression. "Before I become a slave to any man who says I have no choice but to serve him, I will take a gun, and if I don't kill myself first, I will kill him."

Isabel spread her blanket on the sand. She lay down and moved around until she felt comfortable. As she closed her eyes she heard Elena say, "Good night and good luck."

"Good night," Isabel said.

Isabel slept only two hours before the sun showed its first purple rays in the east.

CHAPTER FORTY-TWO

Isabel opened her eyes. Her head felt like it was filled with lead. She wiped her face and pushed back her hair. The bright sun took some of the sting out of the morning chill. She reached over and shook Elena. The sleeping girl moaned, opened her eyes and slowly rose to one elbow.

People were already moving around them. Women were brewing coffee and calling after their children. For many, breakfast was hard, dry tortillas, nothing else. The smell of burning wood and strong coffee filled the air.

"We must go quickly," Elena cautioned.

"Where?" said Isabel.

"To find out about the men."

"I won't go. I have a man who's away at battle. I'll wait until he returns."

"All right. But me, I'm going."

"Listen, Elena, why don't you just tell people that you're married and your husband is away fighting."

"It's too late for me, Isabel. I must have a man. I don't know any other way."

"But you're wrong. There are other ways. Even taking up a rifle and fighting alongside the men is better than being a servant."

"No, I don't know anything about guns. I need a man."

Elena gathered her things and placed them in a bag. Slowly Isabel rose to her feet. Elena moved close and embraced her tightly."

"We'll see each other again. The camps all look big, but they aren't so big," Elena said.

"Goodbye, and take care of yourself," Isabel responded.

"Always," said Elena and walked through the crowd of people towards a row of old wooden buildings.

Isabel collected her things. She stood and watched the action taking place around her. The people numbered in the thousands, she guessed. What man, or reason, she wondered, could have the power to bring all of these people together. She had never seen so many people.

"What is it? What do you want?" asked a woman, who appeared to be about forty, as Isabel approached.

"I ... I only wanted to thank the man who allowed us to sleep here last night," Isabel told her.

The woman squinted one eye and looked Isabel over with the other eye. She noticed that Isabel's dress was made of good, thick cotton, and although it was dirty, the woman observed that the garment was high quality, and it was still in good condition. The woman stared down at Isabel's boots. Not many women wore boots. Isabel became nervous the more the woman stared.

"He's not here, and besides, he doesn't need your thanks. He doesn't own the land, anyway," the woman barked.

"Well I suppose he doesn't own the land, but he was kind enough to us last night."

"So all right, you've said your thanks."

"Listen, I haven't done anything to you. Why are you so rude?" Isabel demanded.

"Don't raise your voice to me, girl. I didn't ask you to come over here."

"I need help. I haven't had anything to eat. I'll be glad to work."

"Does it look like I'm handing out jobs. Look around you. Hunger and filth, it's every place you look, hunger and filth," the woman repeated, stirring a pot of boiling coffee.

"I can see that life hasn't treated you kindly," Isabel said, picking up her bag, blankets and turning to walk away.

"What do you know about it! What do you know about anything!" the woman cried out, dropping the spoon into the coffee pot and walking towards Isabel.

Isabel peered into the woman's eyes, and in a calm but firm voice told her, "I know just as much about it as you."

The woman stood in front of Isabel. She was fuming. Her arms quivered. Then surprisingly, she said, "Ah, come and have a cup of coffee," and the redness drained from her face.

The woman poured herself a cup and sat down on the sand. Isabel watched her. "Well. Don't think I'm going to serve you. You can get your own," the woman said.

Isabel saw an empty cup. She picked it up and poured some coffee.

"Dolores!" The woman called. A girl of about ten came running up. "Pour the children some coffee. Make them drink as much as they can hold. It doesn't look like we'll have much food today, either."

The girl gave the three younger children cups and poured them coffee. Isabel was about to speak, but the woman quickly said, "No, they aren't mine."

Isabel said, "My name is Isabel."

"Well, did I ask ... " the woman stopped talking. She sipped at her coffee, and in a friendlier tone said, "My name is Sara."

Sara sipped her coffee. A long silence passed before Sara spoke. "What are you doing out here alone?"

"My ... my man," Isabel stumbled at the word, "left yesterday to fight in a battle. He told me to come on the train , and he would join me here."

"Your man, a rebel?"

"Yes. But we will cross the border into the north the first chance we get. He promised."

"Pray that he returns. Unless you can handle a horse and a rifle, this is no place for a woman alone."

"Are you alone?" Isabel asked. "Where did you come from?"

"There was a battle in my town. My husband owned three clothing stores. They took him prisoner. The rest of the men in our town were killed or captured. From what this weasel, Demetrio, tells me, he saved a rebel captain's life in the battle. The captain told Demetrio that he could have anything he wanted. He chose me."

Isabel saw that Sara was attractive, but because of the living conditions, unless one looked closely, she appeared no different than many of the other women in the camp.

"I had everything," Sara continued, her voice filled with disgust. "Two maids took care of the house and children. My grandchildren wore the best clothes in town, and they attended private tutoring classes. Look at them now."

Sara watched her grandchildren. They looked like the rest of the children who ran through the camp, dirty and dressed in ragged clothes. Only the oldest girl, Dolores, wore shoes, the rest wore huaraches.

"My grandchildren never owned a pair of huaraches in their lives."

"And your daughter, what happened to her?"

"She escaped just before the battle started. I don't even know how she got away. I curse her every day for leaving me with the children.

"And you? How is it that you are here," the woman asked.

Isabel told her about Pepe and how he had asked her to run away with him.

Sara began laughing. "Ha! She burst out, fooled by the cabrón devil himself."

Isabel became angry.

"Don't mind me, girl. Every time I find a woman who has fallen in love, I say her lover is none other than Lucifer himself."

"But Pepe isn't like that," Isabel defended.

"Don't be stupid, woman. They are all like that. Look at me! Out here with four grandchildren in the middle of the damn desert. Brought by a man. And for what? For what, I ask you?"

Sara took the cup from Isabel's fingers. She walked to the pot and poured more coffee. She returned and gave the cup to Isabel.

"Look at all of these idiots," Sara said, standing straight and looking over the huge throng of people,

"Most of them don't even know why they're here. No, I take that back, they do know. They know that they are here to scrounge a blanket or a pair of pants from the losing army."

The man Demetrio came walking up from behind Sara. He tipped his hat to Isabel and asked Sara for a cup of coffee. He sat down on a rock and took a long drink from the cup. When he finished, he raised his head and said to the two women, "It is all over."

Sara's face took on a distorted shape. She tried to understand what he meant. "What do you mean it's all over? What's all over?" she asked, in her usual harsh tone.

"The war, the revolution. The fighting is finished."

Two men who had been standing some yards away overheard Demetrio's last words. They came over and joined him.

"Oiga, where did that come from?" one of the men asked.

"Like everything else around here, the word just came down from mouth to mouth. All those who came from Sonora, the gente of Samaniego, should return to their homes. There will be no more fighting."

And it was true. All around them, people grouped together to discuss the strange message. No one screamed victory. There were

no cries of triumph rising from the camp of campesino revolutionaries.

"Well, who the hell won?" a man asked Demetrio.

"Who knows? I was standing over there," said Demetrio, pointing to the station building. He scratched the back of his neck. "Two
soldiers came in an automobile with a man who said he was sent
by don Francisco Madero. They said that there will be no more
fighting."

The two men grew angry and started cursing the universe. They
walked off to see if they could get more news.

Sara motioned Isabel to come closer. "We must go get food or
we will never make it back to Sonora. See how sick the little one
is."

Isabel saw the small girl who lay on a straw mat. The girl's eyes
were closed and only her head protruded from under the blankets.

"Yes, I'll help," said Isabel.

"Dolores!" Sara called.

Dolores came running. She had been talking to another girl, a
girl who had become a friend.

"Watch the children. I'll be back in a while. I must find some
food."

"Sí, abuela, I'll take care of them," the girl answered, automatically.

"And keep a close watch over the little one. She has no fever,
but she doesn't look well."

Sara said nothing to the old man. She always knew that he had
overheard everything. From the time he forced her to go with him
a month before, they had not spoken more that a few times. She
swore that she would make his life miserable.

CHAPTER FORTY-THREE

Never in her life had Sara thought that she would find herself begging. She walked up to the many families and asked for leftovers or extra crumbs of bread, as if she had been doing it all her life. A few women gave her pieces of dried tortillas. Food was scarce.

Isabel watched the men. They grew angry and began to fight among themselves. It was then she realized that this revolution had been lost. These people who had come to take part in the battle of Ciudad Juarez, a victory that could have proved the rebels were an organized army, instead found themselves as part of a retreating force.

Sara paid no attention to the packing or the bickering between the rebels. She didn't listen to the conversations. She had no time for retreats or withdrawls or whatever it was the people were talking about. A woman whose arm was braced between two wooden splints gave Sara a half bar of bread. Sara grabbed the bread and threw it into her knitted sack.

"No! No!" cried one man who claimed he had ridden with Villa, "It's a trick, a trick, I say. Pancho Villa will die before he allows such a disgraceful thing to happen. Retreat does not exist in the mind of Pancho Villa."

"It is over," said another. "The pelones have somehow outsmarted our leaders. We've been sold out."

Anger flowed through the crowd. Many in the gathering had never taken part in a battle. They came because they heard the legends of Pancho Villa and his famed dragoons. Some of the people actually believed Villa to be the reincarnated Christ. Rumors had it that Villa had given a blind man sight. Others told the story that he had brought a revolutionary killed in battle back

to life. Most didn't believe the tales. But none denied that Villa
had forced the bakers in a defeated town to work all night baking
bread. The next day he distributed the bread to the multitude of
followers. He apologized because he could not multiply the fish,
for there were few to be found in the deserts of Chihuahua.

The more experienced and disciplined soldiers refused to leave.
They made it clear they would not move until their leader, Miguel
Samaniego, himself, gave the order. Most of these soldiers had
recently come from fresh victories over the federales. Retreat was
a word quite distant from their present states of mind.

After two hours of searching for food, Sara and Isabel returned
to their camp. A large number of the people who had been camped
about them had already picked up their things and moved down
the road back to their homes, those who still had homes.

Sara toasted the bread and tortillas. The meal wasn't so deli-
cious, but the children didn't complain. Sara cursed the bread and
thought of better times.

"Can you believe it," she said to Isabel, "only a month ago
my grandchildren were dressed in the finest clothes. Private tutors
came to our home to give them lessons. They ate from the best
china. They associated with only children of high standing. Umph,
look at them now."

Isabel said nothing. She didn't want to tell Sara to stop re-
peating herself. Isabel was satisfied to chew on the small piece of
tortilla she'd been given. Demetrio stood nearby. Isabel could tell
that Sara was castrating him with her words.

"God, how could life have treated me so horribly? I had everything and now I have nothing," Sara continued.

Demetrio started laughing. First only little giggles came out
and then a steady cry of laughter. He laughed so hard that even
the children began laughing. Sara's face burned with anger. Isabel
bit her lip to keep from laughing.

"Animal!" Sara screamed. "Beast! Uncircumcised heathen."

That one flew right past him because he didn't understand the
word uncircumcised, and he laughed even harder.

"Barbarian! Pagan!" Sara desperately searched for more words
but was beginning to stutter, "You are a ... a ... a son of a whore."

Demetrio no longer laughed. A hard expression crossed his
face. He calmly walked over to Sara. She looked up at him dis-
dainfully. His open hand caught her full on the right side of her
face. She let out a small whimper. No man had ever struck her.
Stunned, she realized what had happened. Regaining her senses,

she leaped at him with outstretched arms, trying to scratch out his eyes. But she'd forgotten that her fingernails were down to her fingertips. Demetrio grabbed her arms and pulled them down to her sides. He held them there as she struggled to fight him. Her face strained and flushed as she fought to break free of his powerful grip. He stared into her eyes. She returned the look. She continued to struggle but he held fast. The struggle turned into a brutal challenge of strength and wills.

She was a powerful woman. Demetrio was tiring, but gave no sign of weakness. Like two rams locked in deathly combat, Sara and Demetrio held their ground. Sara relaxed a little, then let out one last surge of power. Her arms pushed against Demetrio's hold, but she could not break him. Drained of all energy, Sara dropped to the sand panting like a dog. Demetrio turned and comforted the children who had been frightened that he might hurt their grandmother.

CHAPTER FORTY-FOUR

The sun had just burned itself out. The movement of people breaking camp, men and horses going from one group to another and the general commotion left a film of dust hanging in the air.

The people had prepared for action. They wanted to fight. They needed to let out the frustrations that they held inside them. To strike down just one federal, would mean that they had succeeded in lashing out at the government, at the rich, at the foreigners who kept the poor just a strain higher than the dogs.

The men were angry that they didn't get a chance to butcher the enemy. But more than that, they were angry that they would not get the chance to win, to win new suits for themselves or dresses for their women, clothes and shoes for their children; some had heard stories of other revolutionaries carrying off sewing machines, plows and even automobiles after victorious battles. It seemed to them that the only chance they had to feel like real human beings was being taken from them.

But still, most of the people remained, the veterans of other battles and those who had no place to go. Perhaps someone had lied and the war was not yet finished. There had been much confusion the past few days, maybe the leaders had misunderstood. The rumors had it that the revolutionaries outnumbered the defenders of Ciudad Juarez by four thousand men. Who in his right mind would retreat at such odds?

And Villa? Villa would cut off both arms before surrendering. He would attack Juarez alone if he had to. The people would go wherever he ordered. If he commanded them to attack Juarez with fists and machetes, they would obey because Villa's strength and spirit stood grander than the whole federal army. The people needed to see Villa, hear his words. They had heard stories about

his army, the invincible revolutionaries who would attack federal
forces twice their size, defeat them and somehow disappear into the
landscape. The crowd of peasant soldiers who had seen and ridden
with Villa continued telling the stories, the legends. They would
not believe that Villa could surrender. Madero, maybe; Orozco,
possible; but Villa, never.

Isabel heard a train nearing the camp. It was the first train that
had arrived all day. Excitement rushed through her. It seemed like
a week since Pepe had left.

She asked Sara if Dolores could accompany her to the train.
Sara saw the excited desperation in Isabel's eyes. She nodded and
both girls walked off.

Isabel and Dolores made their way through the crowd and into
the thick clouds of smoke and dust. The train's brakes screeched
and wailed as the mass of metal came to a halt. Isabel's stomach
churned as she saw the hundreds of men and women leaping from
the cars.

"His name is Pepe Rios," Isabel screamed at Dolores, trying to
make herself heard above the noise. "It's getting too dark to see,
so walk near me and we will both call his name."

The two girls walked hand in hand calling the name Pepe Rios,
loudly, like two children looking for lost sheep. The noise and
chaos along the tracks was tremendous. The girls called louder.
They moved from one car to another, sometimes watching as all
the passengers unloaded.

"Pepe Rios! Pepe Rios!" they cried as each body filed past.

"We'll never cover all of the cars this way," said Dolores, "Let's
each take a different car and we'll meet at the end of the train."

Isabel didn't like the idea. She felt responsible for Dolores, but
the girl was right. They would reach more cars faster that way.

"You be careful," said Isabel.

"I'll be fine."

"Bueno, go then, and I'll meet you at the last car."

Isabel watched as Dolores pushed through the crowd. When she
could no longer see the girl, she turned and continued calling Pepe's
name, moving slowly from car to car. By the time she reached the
end of the train Isabel could hardly talk. She coughed, trying to get
the raspy feeling out of her throat. She started to look for Dolores,
disappointed that she hadn't seen Pepe, but still there was hope,
maybe Dolores had.

Numerous campfires began flickering throughout the desert.
Angry voices filled the air. Men and women continued walking

alongside the train, searching the empty cars for missing husbands, friends and relatives. One woman fell to her knees and began crying. After one week of searching the arriving trains, she finally realized that her husband would never return. But as long as the trains continued arriving, she would search. Her three children placed their arms about her. The youngest, about four years old, said to her, "Mama, don't cry anymore, please."

Isabel struggled to see in the dark. The moon had not yet risen. She could see silhouettes of people but little else.

"Dolores! Dolores! Where are you?"

Isabel heard the young girl's voice call out her name.

"Over here. Look what I have found," Dolores called, proudly.

Isabel saw her waving. She walked towards her and tried to recognize the two men who stood beside her. As she neared, she saw that neither was Pepe.

"What, what have you found?" Isabel asked, looking suspiciously at the two men.

"These men say they might know Pepe. They too have a friend named Pepe Rios."

Isabel saw that the man who spoke first only had one leg. The man went on to describe Pepe and tell Isabel a little about him.

"Yes, Pepe is a good friend of ours," said Mariano. "Isn't that right, Estudiante?"

Isabel could not see clearly the eyes of El Estudiante in the dark, but they grew large and very cold.

"Yes, of course," said El Estudiante in a casual voice,

"Pepe Rios is a very good friend of ours. We owe him a debt that we must repay."

Isabel did not trust them. The tone in El Estudiante's voice was hard. She lied when they asked her about Pepe. She told them that they were supposed to meet in Chihuahua but because of the battle, their plans had been changed. She said she wasn't sure if the word would get to Pepe that she was waiting here instead. Her search was simply chance. She also told them that she and Pepe had been married and that they had to run away, since Isabel's father was against the marriage.

Isabel took Dolores' arm. "Come on, we have to go," she said.

"We will be camping here, near the trains," said El Estudiante. "If another train comes in and we see Pepe, where should we say his wife is waiting?"

"We are camped just down the tracks here, you can't miss us," Isabel said, as she and Dolores walked away.

Mariano smiled, "Well, what do you think. Is it him?"

"I'm sure of it," said El Estudiante. "What should we do?"

"We'll wait. If we find him, we'll teach him what one must pay for treason," said Mariano.

"And the girl?"

"One thing at a time, my friend. One thing at a time."

CHAPTER FORTY-FIVE

Twelve soldiers rode into the camp the next afternoon. They rode strong, sturdy stallions. Each man wore a tan uniform, boots, leather leggings and sombreros made of cloth. They were big men, and they carried ammunition belts strapped across their chests. Each had a rifle and sword, and they all held the horses' reins in their right hands as they rode neatly in two columns.

The crowd of people moved to let them pass. One rider broke from the troop. He rode his horse next to an old flatcar that rested on the sand. He jumped up on the top of the car and motioned everyone to gather around him.

"Captain Villa," he called, in a strong, loud voice, "sent me here to tell you that there will be no retreat."

A loud cheer rose from the people. Some men began to fire shots into the air.

"Lieutenant Mendoza," he said to one of the riders, "send some men to bring back those who have taken to the road. And the rest of you, spread the word, we will need everyone for the attack on Ciudad Juarez."

Again the people cheered. "Viva Pancho Villa!" "Viva México!"

When the voices quieted, the officer spoke again,

"Our army is gathering around Ciudad Juarez. All of you will march to your positions this afternoon. Get your things, but bring only what is necessary to kill federales. Be patient and wait for your leaders to give the orders."

The man leaped off the flatcar and mounted his horse. He and the other men began locating the leaders and issuing instructions.

The excitement spread through the assembly. Men began strapping on pistols, knives and machetes. Others started cleaning their weapons, rifles of various sizes and makes. Ten wagon loads of

242

canned beans and tortillas were distributed among the people. The name of Pancho Villa traveled throughout the camp. The morale of this people's army reached a peak. Soon they would all have the opportunity to own a little land. Each would be a hero, taking part in the first major battle of the young revolution.

Within two hours large groups of men and their families began marching under the leadership of the designated leaders. The leaders were usually men who were experienced in battle and were raised in the same state as the people they led. Many women walked with rifles strapped to their backs, and they too, were ready to enter battle. Older women looked after the children and they walked behind the men and women carrying weapons. A guitar player, strumming away and singing freshly composed songs of the revolution, followed each troop of warriors.

Dolores had just finished making two long braids on Isabel's hair when the next train pulled into the station. Isabel told Dolores to stay with the family. She would go to search for Pepe alone.

Again Isabel moved from car to car, searching the faces of the passengers. The train was not as crowded as the night before. The minute people disembarked they were herded into military groups. Magnetically, Isabel's and Pepe's eyes met.

The shock stunned her. She stood still, unable to move. And a wave of excitement raced through her. She pushed people aside as they fought to reach each other. Dust filled the air and the noise from the train and screaming voices made hearing difficult. Finally when they met, they simply stood in front of each other and stared, embarrassed to touch.

Isabel took Pepe's hand and led him away from the train. She wasn't sure what to say. After a long moment, she yelled, "And my horse, what did you do with him?"

Pepe smiled. He put his arms around her and pulled her close to him. Although there was much commotion beside the tracks, few people stopped to look. Men and women hugging in public was not such a common sight, especially among the lower classes. Isabel could feel the eyes of strangers upon them. She snuggled close to Pepe. She wanted him to know how much he was missed. Then she pulled away and stepped back into a more accepted role. The strangers lost interest.

A young boy, barefoot and wearing old clothes, a new federal hat on his head, led the horses down the plank of a boxcar. Pepe walked towards him, got his horse and brought it to Isabel. She patted the horse on the snout, then walked around checking the rear and flanks.

"Well, at least you take good care of your animals, if not your women," she said, teasing him.

"Are you always so lively?" Pepe asked, taking the horse's reins.

"Yes, most of the time," Isabel laughed.

Pepe felt a lightness inside his stomach, and he was very happy that she had missed him. Her joy radiated. He had wondered how she would manage being left alone on the train with strangers and heading to a part of the country that was unfamiliar to her. He had even thought that maybe she would have become frustrated enough to make her way back home. Although he was hungry and tired, he felt very good to be back with her.

"I need some food. I'm starving. Also, a little rest would be very nice," he said.

"I'll fix you some food, but rest ... " Isabel became serious, "everyone in this camp is moving on to Ciudad Juarez. Some soldiers came riding in a little while ago. They said that all of you should be at your positions by tonight."

Pepe's face dropped. Isabel studied him. Little red veins crossed the whites of his eyes, and wrinkles tugged at the corners of his mouth. Bunches of hair stood up on his head.

"I don't look too good, eh?" he said, as she stared.

"You look tired but a hundred times stronger than the others around here," she said, trying to give him a little encouragement.

"I'm fine, honest. With some food, I'll be as strong as ever. And what else have the people around here been saying about the war?" he asked.

"Only what I've told you. Most of the other things I don't understand, so I don't listen."

"Well, have you learned anything?"

"Like what?"

"I don't know, just anything, I guess."

"Ay Pepe," she said, "how can you ask such a dumb thing?" They sounded like two children.

"I don't see anything so dumb about asking if you have learned anything."

"But anything about what? About the desert? About horses? About idiots? About the moon?"

He smiled, "Yes, about any one of those things or about any one of the millions of other things that need to be learned."

"You know, " she said, "I think you do need some rest." She patted the horse again. "Listen Cielo," she said to the horse, "you haven't kicked this boy in the head have you?"

Pepe laughed, stopped and called Isabel over to him. "Isabel, give me a kiss," he said shyly, looking down at the ground.

"Pepe, right here, in front of all these people?" she teased.

She saw softness and sincerity in Pepe's eyes. The joking mood left her. He stood close to Cielo's side so that the vision from one side was completely blocked and few people could see. She moved in close to him and lifted her face. Pepe leaned down and their lips met, softly. They heard no sounds. They elevated themselves above the chaos and pain which surrounded them. Isabel put her arms over Pepe's shoulders and pulled her body closer to his. He placed his arms behind her waist and pressed her tightly to him. Their breathing, heartbeats and bodies became one. It was the kiss and the moment that Pepe would carry with him forever.

CHAPTER FORTY-SIX

Mariano was ordered second in command. His people consisted of about twenty soldiers. Had it not been for his one leg, the command would have been his. The choice did not bother him, he was anxious to fight, nothing more, that is, except to bring Pepe Rios to justice.

All of the men who made up his group were experienced guerrilla fighters. They ranged from seventeen to forty-three. Nearly all had been raised with horses and guns, either as cattlemen or bandits. Like many other rebels, they did not wear matching uniforms, but instead wore an assortment of clothing from the white cotton of the campesinos to the ruffle-breasted tuxedo shirt of a fallen mayor. The men already received word that they would play a very important role in the battle of Ciudad Juarez.

Every man was asked to give up his rifle. In the place of some of the old, outdated weapons, they were issued new Winchesters, all the same make and model. This way they could carry much more ammunition of the same kind. Their older and different weapons were distributed among the peasant rebels who had no weapons. For these men it was difficult to find ammunition. They were instructed to use their rifles like clubs once the ammunition was gone.

The men of Mariano's troop were beaming over their new weapons when two men came into the camp leading Pepe and Isabel. Earlier in the day the men had been given orders to follow Isabel, watch and see whether she was joined by a young man arriving on the train. Once they saw her and the man together, they were to escort them to either Mariano or El Estudiante. Mariano didn't smile, nor did he give any indication of emotion when Pepe stood before him.

Mariano immediately saw the frightened, sick expression on Pepe's face. Isabel became nervous when she saw him turn pale. El Estudiante walked up and stood next to Mariano. Both had forgotten how young Pepe was.

Mariano had sworn that the minute he saw Pepe again, he would shoot him. But now that Pepe stood before him, for some reason, unknown to Mariano, he could not hate him.

El Estudiante, the logical, educated, cold-hearted philosopher, could not control his anger. He threw a punch at Pepe. Unable to dodge the blow, Pepe braced himself. El Estudiante's fist caught Pepe on the cheekbone, snapping his head back, but it did not knock him down. El Estudiante was neither big nor strong. Pepe knew that he had to show strength because that was what these men understood.

Pepe leaped at El Estudiante, trying to get his hands around the man's neck, but the two men who had brought Pepe in grabbed his arms. Isabel screamed and burst into tears as a stream of blood fell down Pepe's face.

"Enough!" Mariano ordered.

Other men came over to see the commotion. Mariano quickly waved everyone away. He shot El Estudiante an angry look. Isabel walked up to El Estudiante, and with the same warning that he had given Pepe, she slapped him hard across the face. El Estudiante drew his arm back to strike her, but Mariano commanded him to stop. Pepe struggled to get loose from the grasp of the men who held him.

"Take her and place her with the other women," Mariano ordered.

One of the men who had been holding Pepe grabbed Isabel. She screamed and fought him. She called out to Pepe.

"Isabel," Pepe said to her, "don't worry, I'll be all right. Go with them, I'll see you later."

"Let him go," Mariano said. The men released their grip on Pepe's arms. Mariano motioned with his head, and the men walked away. El Estudiante stood close to Mariano.

"You know, after you left," continued Mariano, "the federales attacked us. El Estudiante and I were the only ones to escape. We hid in the bushes and watched as they executed Buddha and Guero. They hanged them from a tree and then threw knives at their bodies for play. They raped Lilia, every one of them, and then they forced her to go with them. If not for your stupidity and cowardice, they would still be alive."

Pepe dropped his head. The news shattered him. A moment
later, he raised his eyes and looked at both of the men before him.
El Estudiante's face had aged, and his eyes radiated pure hate.
Mariano looked tired.

"Don't you have anything to say, you fucking squirrel," El Estudiante said, in a tension filled whisper that swelled the veins in
his neck.

Pepe turned to Mariano and peered into his eyes not knowing
what he expected to see, "I couldn't let you kill my brother," was
all he said.

"But he's dead, you fool. If the situation had been reversed, he
would have let the federales kill you," cried El Estudiante.

"He was my brother. I couldn't let him die."

"He was a federal!" screamed El Estudiante.

"Would you have allowed your brother to die?" Pepe asked.

"I would have taken a knife and slit his throat with my own
hand," said El Estudiante, coldly.

"Can't you understand, Pepe? Your brother sided with those
who torture the poor and make victims of the innocent," said Mariano. "But I can forgive that. I can forgive you for trying to save
your brother. What I can't forgive is Chispas' death. He was worth
ten men."

Mariano paused, picked up his rifle and placed it in his lap.
"Yesterday, after talking with your woman, El Estudiante and I decided to kill you. We planned on tying you to a horse and dragging
you through the desert until the meat was torn from your bones.
"But I have thought the thing through carefully in my mind. You're
still fighting for the revolution, no?"

Pepe nodded, indicating that he was.

"We will leave the affair in the hands of fate."

"What are you saying!" screamed El Estudiante.

Mariano held his hand out to him, commanding silence. "Soon
we will attack Juarez," Mariano said. "We need every man, even
traitors, if they can ride and shoot. Whatever orders we are given
for the attack, you will lead the way. The rest will follow behind
you. As for myself, I hope the first bullet fired at us pierces your
skull. But if it doesn't, and if you live, then neither Estudiante nor
I will lift a hand against you."

"No!" cried El Estudiante. "He's a traitor. Hang him like
Buddha and Guero were hanged. He can never be trusted again.
Kill him." El Estudiante's body shook and his face contorted in
anger.

"We haven't time to explain executions to those who would watch, besides, we need every man who can fight. It's the revolution that is important now, not our feelings," Mariano countered.

"I don't want to ride with a traitor!"

"Enough," Mariano barked at El Estudiante. "As long as I'm jefe, you'll do as I say."

El Estudiante's razor glance pierced through Pepe, then he turned to Mariano.

"Agreed?" Mariano said to him.

Reluctantly and quietly El Estudiante said the word, "Agreed."

CHAPTER FORTY-SEVEN

Within the hour, the men were mounted and riding towards Ciudad Juarez, which was a short distance away. The landscape was filled with what seemed like thousands of people. They were marching off towards a great battle. Up until this time, the rebels had been forced to use guerrilla tactics, with only a few attempts at liberating larger towns. But now they would attack Juarez, the large city that sat side by side with the United States. Some would have laughed at the notion that an army made up of peasants, both men and women, would even consider attacking a federal stronghold like Ciudad Juarez. For weeks, the troops under the command of General Navarro had been preparing for a possible attack.

The revolutionaries gathered in large camps to the west, south and east of the city. To the north was El Paso. For fifteen days, the citizenry of this North American city had come down to the international line, setting up chairs on top of buildings, lining the river with carts on which to sit, finding spots in the higher mountains to get a good view of the ensuing battle. Vendors walked among the spectators selling refreshments and souvenirs, federal hats, rebel huaraches and such, in anticipation of the event. And at the end of each day when no battle had taken place, irritated, they went back to their homes. But in the mornings they came back, waiting, hoping that someone would fire the shot that would begin the battle.

Many restless Americans had taken up arms and rushed across the border to join the revolutionary forces of Francisco Madero. All wanted to see and fight alongside the legendary Pancho Villa. The small cannon which had decorated the front of the El Paso City Hall had mysteriously disappeared. Rumors had it that the weapon had been carted away by Americans sympathetic to the rebels and was now in rebel hands.

Some mercenaries had come from as far away as France and Italy. They brought experience and military credentials as vast and wide as the ocean they crossed. Newspapers reported that Madero himself was receiving intelligence reports and instructions from Benjamin Viljoen, the hero of the famous South African Boer wars. But none of these things made any difference to the peasant soldiers who were the heart of this army and who had begun to surround the city of Juarez.

A number of revolutionaries had been positioned for over a week. Madero could not decide whether to attack or not. The rebels had become tired of waiting. Among the officers, rumors circulated that negotiations were taking place somewhere in New York between Madero's diplomats and those of President Diaz. Still other rumors had it that the American President, Wilson, threatened to intervene by sending in American troops if harm came to any American citizens. And some rebel leaders heard that Madero would not give the order to attack because his grandfather, who was an extremely wealthy man in Mexico, wanted the war to end immediately.

The latest reports stated that the federales' estimated strength was one thousand trained soldiers and a thousand new recruits. The federales had constructed barriers, machine gun nests and morter pits. Powerful cannons protected the perimeter of the city. Every entrance had been sealed off. A rumor spread among the men that Madero's European advisor strongly recommended against attacking the city. He argued that the federales had fortified the city against any possible enemy penetration. One captain who had visited Madero's headquarters reported that Madero was utterly confused, and he would not listen to the advice of his most loyal leaders, Villa and Orozco.

Mariano and his men rode into Villa's camp in the hills to the west of the city. It appeared to Pepe that there were thousands of revolutionaries ready to descend on Ciudad Juarez. But the men and women, since they were not preparing for the immediate battle, instead sat around in groups talking, playing cards and getting a much needed rest.

Pepe's mind was not on the battle but on El Estudiante who rode directly behind him. Pepe carried no weapon. Escape was impossible. Isabel was forced to walk with the women who were about two hours behind the men.

Mariano gave orders for the men to dismount and make camp.

Pepe walked his horse to a tree and tied the reins to a limb. The other men also found places to tie their horses. El Estudiante walked over and stood next to Pepe.

"I hope you try to escape, you son of a whore," El Estudiante told him. "Nothing would make me happier than blowing your fucking head off."

Pepe remained silent. He was exhausted, but his mind moved at great speeds. He tried to figure a way to get to Isabel and escape. Over and over he visualized both of them hand in hand running across and open field, across an imaginary line and into the city of El Paso.

The night came on quickly. The heat of the day turned to a biting chill. A hard wind blew through the Texas desert, crossed the border and made the night miserable. El Estudiante tied Pepe's hands and legs. He allowed Pepe a sip of water but gave him no food or bedding.

Mariano had made it clear to El Estudiante that he didn't want any of the other men to see that Pepe was a prisioner. That's why El Estudiante waited until after dark to tie him up.

"Well, you seem comfortable," El Estudiante said to Pepe, sarcastically.

"Why don't you untie me," Pepe told him, "I'm not going anywhere."

"No you're not, but I am," El Estudiante said in a voice filled with suspicion.

"So what does that mean?" Pepe asked.

"Bueno, you see, I have taken, shall I say, a liking to that little woman of yours. And since it's such a cold night, wouldn't you want someone to keep her warm?" Although the voice was calm, El Estudiante had the look of a madman.

Pepe reacted as El Estudiante had wanted. An expression of terror shot across Pepe's face.

"She hasn't done anything. It's me that you want. Leave her out of it," Pepe pleaded.

"Rios, you heard the jefe's orders. You are to be protected. I will obey. But he said nothing about your lady. Now, just sit back and imagine how she will enjoy my body on top of hers."

"No! no," Pepe screamed at him. But his words were useless.

Pepe twisted his hands against the coarse ropes. He grunted and groaned and the ropes burned deeper into his skin. He gritted his teeth and pulled hard, the ropes would not break, but he knew they wouldn't. There was nothing else he could do, so he continued to struggle, to fight himself and his tears.

El Estudiante walked down the hill and into the crowd of women huddled around a small fire. His eyes moved from face to face until he spotted Isabel.

"You, come with me," he said to her.

The others pretended not to hear. They stopped talking, but no one looked at him.

"What do you want?" she asked, coldly.

"Women don't ask questions. Just do as you're told," he said, irritated.

"This woman doesn't go any place unless she knows where she's going," Isabel said, refusing to be intimidated.

El Estudiante masked his anger. He wanted to cause no trouble among the women; there were too many of them. He knew that after all these weeks in the field, they had not only toughened, but they also reached their limits.

"Your man is up on the hill. He wants to see you."

Isabel reacted excitedly, but her excitement quickly vanished; she didn't trust this man.

"How do I know you're telling the truth?"

He was becoming very impatient with her. The other women began to look up at him—question him with their eyes. He had to think quickly. "If you don't come now, you might never see him again. It's possible that the battle will begin tomorrow. He's been assigned a position to lead the charge. Personally, I could care less whether you come or not. I told him I'd do this one thing for him. If you don't want to, then fine," and he began to walk away.

"Wait," she called. Isabel moved through the group of women. She wrapped a blanket tightly around herself and followed him.

El Estudiante walked up a small hill where others sat around campfires. He walked down the opposite side of the hill where the night became very dark, except for the light of the young moon. Isabel continued behind him for a short distance then, stopped, realizing he was leading her away from the people and into the chapparral.

"I'm not going any farther," she said to him, turned her back and started to return to the other side of the hill, but he ran to her, grabbed her by the arm and forced her down the hill.

"It's just a little way," he said.

She started to scream. El Estudiante placed a hand over her mouth. Only muffled cries came from her throat. She tried to bite and kick but could not loosen his grasp on her.

When he reached the bottom of the hill, he threw her down on the ground. No one could hear her if she screamed. His heart was pounding from a revengeful, animalistic passion and hers from fear.

"Make this easy on yourself. It's up to you," he said.

Isabel didn't know what to do. She watched as he carefully spread his poncho on the ground, keeping his eyes on her. She jumped to her feet and ran. The hill was too steep. Easily he overcame her. He slapped her hard, two, three times, grabbed her by the shoulders and pushed her on top of his poncho. He unbuttoned his pants, and as she lay panting, he placed himself on top of her. She kicked and pulled, pushed at him. He hit her across the face, took his gun so she could see it and set it near him, trying to scare her.

"If you fight me, I'll see that he dies," was all he said to her.

Isabel stopped fighting. She lay there like a corpse. She made no sound, kept her head turned to one side and stared at the silhouette of a large bush. She wondered if the bush had been planted by someone or if maybe it had grown by itself. It was a very tall bush, maybe it was over fifty years old. The long branches made intricate designs against the night. Isabel wondered if she were a painter could she capture the sight on canvas. What a strange sound the animal on top of her made. It sounded much like the snorting of a corralled pig. She felt a hard slap across the face, but the slap caused no pain, there was no emotion or feeling. It seemed as if the slap had struck someone else's face. The trunk of the bush was very thick. Could she build a house out of such wood. She heard the words, "Move, do something, bitch!" but it seemed that the voice came from far away. The voice and the piggish snorting had nothing to do with her. The only thing that mattered to her was this bush. She wondered if Pepe would come back and help her dig it up. How pretty it would look in front of a little house. Isabel gazed at the stars and the dark sky. As she turned to see the moon, she heard a vague sound, a blast that filled the night, and then everything went black and silent.

Pepe didn't want to think about El Estudiante and Isabel. But the images in his mind were too powerful. He saw El Estudiante making love to her. Pepe tried to shake his head free of the thought, but it wouldn't go away. He saw Isabel struggle to get away, but she was no match for her enemy. The ropes cut deeply into Pepe's wrists. He could not feel the physical pain of his torn skin and the exposed flesh. His torture was now purely mental. But something strange happened. The thought of El Estudiante and Isabel coupled together disappeared as a bubble pops in mid air. Pepe saw El Estudiante crawling around on the ground by himself, naked and caressing a stone. Isabel sat on top of a mountain far away from him and safe. She was dressed in a beautiful white gown. Her face was vivid, clear. She looked at Pepe and smiled. He watched as she tried to speak, but he couldn't understand. The thought vanished.

CHAPTER FORTY-EIGHT

The morning air was like a sheet of frost. Mariano ordered El Estudiante to untie Pepe, get him close to a fire and give him some hot coffee. Pepe could not keep the cup in his hands still. He shook uncontrollably. Each time he placed the cup to his lips he spilled coffee over his mouth. A medic came over and bandaged his wrists. But the only thing Pepe could think of was Isabel.

Finally when Pepe was warm enough and some strength entered his body, he pulled at El Estudiante's poncho and asked, "What did you do? Where is she?"

"What are you talking about?" El Estudiante answered, sipping at his coffee.

"Isabel, where is she? What did you do with her last night?" Pepe's voice quivered. He sounded like a small, frightened child.

Then he saw it, like a panic-stare, instantaneously numbing El Estudiante's eyes; then it was gone.

"Hombre, I didn't do anything with her. I've got women enough without having to go for little girls."

"But last night ... you said ... "

El Estudiante laughed, "I just wanted to make you sweat a little. It worked, eh?"

Pepe's mind was an eddy of confusion. He didn't believe El Estudiante. When El Estudiante went to talk to another man, Pepe followed.

"Where is she then?" Pepe said, "I want to talk to her."

El Estudiante turned on him angrily. "You can't talk to anyone. Remember where you are and what you've done. If I were you, I'd sit back down and keep my mouth shut. The bitch is someplace with the other women—and if you keep on about her, then something just might happen."

Pepe did as El Estudiante told him. He went back to the tree and sat down, and he waited. He waited for the precise moment to slip away, but it didn't come. El Estudiante's eyes were always on him.

Pepe felt it, he tasted it, he knew that something was wrong. He could think of nothing but Isabel. He watched as the men passed the ammunition around, filling their cartridge belts and rifles. Others cleaned their weapons, some even shined their machetes.

When the afternoon arrived and Pepe still hadn't heard anything about Isabel, he panicked. She would have tried to reach him by now. Pepe waited for the moment. He leaped to his feet and ran down the hill. When he saw the multitudes before him, he stopped. It looked to him as though the world had congregated around Ciudad Juarez. Where would he begin to look for Isabel?

The rifle butt struck him just under the left ear. Pepe fell to the ground, his face striking the dry dust. He didn't lose consciousness. As he lay on the dirt, he could feel the warm blood spreading over his neck. The pain exploded in his head.

"Get up!" he recognized El Estudiante's voice. He rose to his hands and knees when the point of the boot tore into his stomach. Again Pepe dropped to the ground. He couldn't breathe and curled up like a baby. El Estudiante reached down and grabbed Pepe by the neck.

"Listen and hear me good," El Estudiante whispered harshly into his ear, "if you ever try that again, you're dead."

Pepe got to his feet, coughing and fighting to take in a full breath of air. His skull felt as if it were crushed. The pain shot from his temples to his eyes. He struggled to make the walk back up the hill. El Estudiante pushed him against the trees and tied his wrists. Although many of the other men saw, no one said anything.

El Estudiante stooped down and leaned close to Pepe's ear. "She's dead. I fucked her and put a bullet through her head. No one will ever find her. Let's just call it even and say that she's the sacrifice you had to make for my friends." El Estudiante sneered at him and walked away.

Pepe was too weak to scream. The waves rolled from his stomach and turned into silent sobs. His body shook and his head bobbed. He knew that El Estudiante had told him the truth. The tears poured out. He made small, choking noises. The vision of Isabel's body entered his mind. He saw her lying next to his father, Ramon and Miranda. They were lined up as the executed federales had been lined up after El Estudiante had executed them on the road what seemed like centuries ago. The vision was a grizzly image filled with tattered clothing, disfigured faces, bullet holes, eyes bulging loose from their sockets and everything covered in blood.

He lost his sense of time. Turbid thoughts polluted his mind until finally Isabel came to him as if in a dream. Pepe closed his eyes. The dried tears left trails over the dust on his cheeks. She appeared more beautiful than he had ever seen her. Her hair was pulled back tightly and braided like an Indian's. She looked down at him and there were no words, but her large brown eyes told him not to blame himself. He wanted to touch her, kiss her one last time, but she was gone and only the sky remained.

Through his murky glare, the sight of El Estudiante standing in the distance came clear. The hate permeated every nerve. Pepe knew, at that instant, that he would not leave Mexico until he had killed this adversary, this monster.

Mariano gave the order for his men to assemble. As the men gathered around, they heard a low rumble, like an earthquake. Five hundred riders approached from the south. The peasant revolutionaries stood to see the long, perfectly spaced columns of Pancho Villa's cavalry.

The men rode fine, strong horses. All were heavily armed with cartridge belts strapped to their chests and around their waists. They wore their sombreros low over their foreheads so that their eyes were barely visible. All were clean shaven and many had grown thick, dark mustaches. They carried the newest rifles which Villa had received from friends across the border. The men appeared large and strong. They rode with a confident arrogance reserved only for Villa's elite. The sight filled the peasant revolutionaries with a new bravery. The spirit of Pancho Villa radiated throughout the camp. The people anxiously waited for the word to attack.

"God, they are the most beautiful sight upon this earth," said one of the rebels who stood next to Mariano.

"Each one handles a rifle and horse like a torero handles a cape and sword," said another.

The entire camp watched, mesmerized, as the last soldiers in the column passed. Even Mariano, with all of his experience in battle, could only shake his head in silent disbelief as he witnessed the discipline and execution of Villa's troops.

"Someone had better pray for the federales," a man called out.

Just then, Rafael Herrera, first in command, walked up to the Mariano and his men. "I've been in meetings all day with our leaders Villa and Orozco. They have informed me and other captains, Miguel Samaniego and Jose Orozco among others, that señor Madero does not want to go against the advice of his top advisor Viljoen. The European coward has advised that we don't attack Juarez. He says that too many men will be lost, and he wants us to break camp and move on to Chihuahua."

A murmur rose through the small group of men. Captain Herrera allowed them to let their anger and frustration take the form of whispered words. When the men were silent again, he resumed talking.

"We have been given the honor of instigating the battle of Ciudad Juarez."

Another low rumble of words arose from the troop of men who were assigned to both Rafael Herrera and Mariano. El Estudiante smiled happily at the idea of finally going into battle. Pepe heard the words, but they didn't penetrate.

"After I tell you what I have to say, no one will be allowed to leave our group. Mariano, I will leave it in your hands to see that the secret goes no further than our men here."

Mariano nodded to Captain Herrera.

"In about two hours, at approximately four pm, two men will be sent to start a small skirmish with the federales. Since señor Madero opposes our attacking Juarez, he will surely send some men down with the message to stop the fighting. Pancho Villa has already given orders to another group of men. This group will go down pretending to deliver Madero's order, but instead they too will engage the federales."

Some of the men began laughing as they listened to the neatly crafted plot. Another man whistled and all began to laugh.

"We will enter the Rio Bravo sometime after dark. We'll make our way up river and attack the city from the west. Other forces are already moving out. Once the sound of battle is heard, they will attack from the south and east of the city. The message that will be sent back to Madero will inform him that it's too late to pull back. An all out invasion must take place, and the rest of the army must attack."

"How will we know when to attack?" asked a young man of about nineteen.

"I'll be with you. I will give the command."

"But how is it that we'll instigate the fighting?" someone else asked.

Herrera smiled, "We too will take up our positions under the pretense that we are going down river to stop those who are firing their weapons. Instead, when we arrive, we'll be the last pieces of wood added to the fire. Once we begin firing, no one will be able to stop the battle."

The men were content. They waited on a small hill just to the west of the city. They listened carefully. After a short time, the first shots cracked the air. They could see nothing, but they could hear the sounds of battle escalate slowly. The sound to them was beautiful.

Upon hearing the first shots, señor Madero went into a rage. He sent for Pancho Villa. Both Villa and Orozco, so they could not be blamed for the battle, had crossed the border and were in El Paso having dinner. They waited patiently until Madero's messenger arrived.

Feigning surprise, both men rushed back across the border to Madero's headquarters. As planned, Rafael Herrera, with two men to accompany him, El Estudiante and Pepe, also rode the short distance to Madero's headquarters. El Estudiante kept Pepe to his front. Still in shock, Pepe didn't refuse Mariano's order to go with Herrera and El Estudiante.

Pepe noted a great deal of chaos where a group of important looking men shouted at each other. Pepe saw that some men wore expensive looking suits. Pepe didn't know that he was watching Madero, Villa, Orozco and Viljoen and a number of other generals and colonels discussing the complicated strategies of war.

Villa turned from Madero and walked to a man who stood close by. Pepe saw, but he couldn't understand what was being said. The man saluted Villa and ran down the hill. Pepe watched the bow-legged one who looked like a bricklayer, and never realized that it was Villa. Villa moved close to Herrera. He looked at Pepe. Pepe saw a wild, excited sparkle in the man's eyes. Villa stared at El Estudiante and finally turned to Herrera.

"It's going great," Villa told Herrera. "I've just sent word for Jose Orozco to send fifteen men to continue the fighting."

"And señor Madero?" Herrera asked.

Villa laughed, "Just as I suspected, he asked me to send some men to go and stop the fighting immediately. Ah, my presidente Madero is no military man, but that doesn't matter, I'll make a hero of him anyway."

For the moment, Pepe had forgotten about Isabel and El Estudiante. He succumbed to the charisma and the aura that surrounded this man with whom Herrera was talking. A strange energy and power seemed to radiate from him. All of the strength that Pepe had lost in the past days somehow was regained.

"This fucking general Viljoen thinks that because we're Mexicans we have no chance to win this battle. I'll show him," said Villa, looking directly into Herrera's eyes.

"When you hear a steady stream of gunfire," Villa continued, "make your move. Press hard, just as we discussed earlier. But once the battle begins, allow your men time for rest and for sleep. Make them fight as long as they remain strong. We're in no hurry."

"We'll do exactly as you say, Colonel," Herrera answered, because although Villa had not officially been promoted, that's how the people addressed him.

"Bueno, on your way," said Villa, slapping Herrera's horse on the snout. Again Villa looked at Pepe. Through the gaze, Villa somehow transmitted courage. Pepe could feel his muscles pumping. An electrical surge was upon him. He thought about the battle, but the thought didn't last. He began to think about how he would kill El Estudiante.

CHAPTER FORTY-NINE

The last rays of sunset had burned out in the west. The cold lifted from the desert floor, but the men of Rafael Herrera could not feel the crisp air as they moved quietly through the night. The water of the Rio Bravo reached the men at the waist. No one spoke. Only the sound of swooshing water could be heard as the men made their way towards the city. The echo of sporadic gunfire broke the night's silence. Since Mariano could not walk through the soft sand with the stump on his leg, he entered the battle with Felix Terrazas' men. El Estudiante replaced Mariano as second in command. He order Pepe to walk ahead of everyone else. If the first bullets fired did not kill Pepe, El Estudiante would. He walked directly behind Pepe.

Pepe gripped his rifle tightly. He eased his hands over the wooden stock and the area just below the barrel. The smooth wood felt soft in his hands. But Pepe didn't think about that. He thought about El Estudiante who was behind him, and he wondered when the bullet from the student's rifle would pierce his back.

The pain over Isabel's death had temporarily departed. He thought only about his present situation and how he would survive. Pepe strained his eyes to see through the night, but the blending of the dark water with the night air formed a black curtain. He could see the little lights glimmering on the hill and along the banks of the river on the United States side of the border. He saw the illumination from the muzzle blasts of rifles coming from the city. The sand beneath his feet felt soft, and he slipped occasionally on rocks that had been polished slick from the ancient river waters.

As the men moved closer to the outskirts of the city, they heard steady rifle fire. Pepe lifted his weapon and held it close to his chest ready to fire. He could hear the men behind him clicking their bolts and preparing for action. They walked hunched over, trying to make themselves smaller targets. The first barrage came without warning. Pepe heard a cry. The tiny chips of water splashed all around him.

Pepe screamed, as if he'd been shot. He stumbled towards the river bank and collapsed to the earth. The rifle flew out of his hands and struck another man on the side of the head. One man was shot through the neck. The body of the dead rebel splashed into the water and floated downstream. The others rushed to get out of the water. El Estudiante led the crawl up the bank. Once the men reached the top of the embankment, they began firing at the federal outpost. The night turned into a blizzard of screaming rifles and loud explosions.

When Pepe felt it was safe, he lifted his head and reached for the rifle that he made sure had fallen close to him. He listened and heard El Estudiante barking out orders and firing his rifle from one knee. The deafening noise of combat echoed in Pepe's ears. Slowly, he pulled the rifle close toward him. He waited. After a time, he nudged the butt of the rifle against his shoulder. Because it was dark, he could not sight down the barrel. Instead he leaned his head over the stock and aimed using both eyes. He pointed the muzzle into El Estudiante's back. Pepe squeezed the trigger slowly. His finger picked up the tension. He felt that the thing would never go off when the exploding rifle sent vibrations quivering through his body. El Estudiante screamed in disbelief that a bullet could enter through the back. He rolled down the embankment. The madness of the battle created so much chaos that no one realized what had happened.

The instant he fired, Pepe dropped his head again and played dead. He didn't know how much time had passed, a half hour, one or two hours? A few men began to charge the outpost. Cautiously, Pepe crawled about twenty feet to where El Estudiante lay. He was still breathing. Blood dripped from his mouth, and he made deathly moans. Pepe whispered in his ear and El Estudiante opened his eyes. Pepe made sure that El Estudiante saw his face. Both men lay frozen in the moment. Finally, Pepe smiled. He grabbed El Estudiante by the hair and collar and dragged him to the edge of the water. Pepe placed his arms on top of El Estudiante's head and pushed down with all his strength. He felt the face sink into the mud, and he held it there until the twitching and jerking stopped.

Pepe looked at the strange, disfigured shape of the body. Where there had been life a moment ago now lay only the stillness of death. Pepe slipped into the water. He floated along with the current, keeping only his head above water. When he was too exhausted to continue, he eased himself onto the Texas side of the river. In the darkness, he made his way up the embankment, slipping in the soft dirt. He sat down and looked towards Juarez. The sky was engulfed in flashes of lightning. He could hear the echoes of the voices that charged in the night.

As he had done many times before, he picked up a handful of dirt and let the ground fall through his fingers. It didn't seem any different than the dirt he'd held in Mexico. He started to laugh, easy at first but then harder. He laughed out loud and into the night. He laughed at the whole thing, and he realized that he didn't care who won the revolution. He didn't care about the United States or about Mexico. All that mattered now was the survival of Pepe Rios.